About the Authors

Annie West has devoted her life to an intensive study of charismatic heroes who cause the best kind of trouble in the lives of their heroines. As a sideline she researches locations for romance, from vibrant cities to desert encampments and fairytale castles. Annie lives in eastern Australia with her hero husband, between sandy beaches and gorgeous wine country. She finds writing the perfect excuse to postpone housework. To contact her or join her newsletter, visit annie-west.com

Kandy Shepherd swapped a fast-paced career as a magazine editor for a life writing romance. She lives on a small farm in the Blue Mountains near Sydney, Australia, with her husband, daughter, and a menagerie of animal friends. Kandy believes in love at first sight and real-life romance – they worked for her! Kandy loves to hear from her readers. Visit her website at: kandyshepherd.com

Jackie Braun is the author of more than thirty romance novels. She is a three-time *RITA*® finalist and a four-time National Readers' Choice Award finalist. She lives in Michigan with her husband and two sons.

Royal Weddings

Royal Weddings
The Secret Princess

ANNIE WEST

KANDY SHEPHERD

JACKIE BRAUN

MILLS & BOON

First Published in Great Britain 2022
by Mills & Boon, an imprint of HarperCollins*Publishers* Ltd,
1 London Bridge Street, London, SE1 9GF

www.harpercollins.co.uk

HarperCollins*Publishers*
1st Floor, Watermarque Building,
Ringsend Road, Dublin 4, Ireland

ISBN: 978-0-263-30486-2

MIX
Paper from
responsible sources
FSC C007454

REVELATIONS OF A
SECRET PRINCESS

ANNIE WEST

This story is dedicated to Agnès Caubert, Fabiola Chenet and all the other special women who make up Les Romantiques.

Thank you for your friendship!

Thank you too for your work in hosting the wonderful Festival du Roman Féminin and for always making this visiting Australian feel welcome.

CHAPTER ONE

CARO EMERGED FROM the café, huddling into her coat as the wind swirled around her ankles and bit her face. Funny that her skin could feel numb with cold while inside she was all churning heat. Nothing could extinguish that fire inside.

Except the possibility she might fail.

She faltered to a stop, grasping a lamp post with one gloved hand, fighting nausea.

Her head told her success was unlikely.

Her heart urged her on. Not with logic, but with desperate hope.

She'd never been courageous or adventurous. From infancy she'd been trained to do as she was told, never make waves or put herself forward. Her one attempt to break free and make her own decisions had been disastrous.

But that was years ago. She'd changed, reinventing herself in the aftermath of tragedy and pain. Caro might not be naturally intrepid but she was determined. She breathed deep, swallowing sharp, sustaining Alpine air. She'd do whatever it took now to succeed.

Caro looked up the street of the famous Swiss ski resort, ultra-exclusive with its astronomically high prices. Tourists gaped at the elegant shop windows, but they'd be gone by evening, driven away by the chic resort's unaffordability.

Up a nearby valley was one of the world's most iconic mountains. In the other direction lay her destination. Setting her jaw, she crunched over a dusting of late snow and got into her small rental car.

Twenty minutes later Caro nosed the car around a bend and emerged in a cleared space that hung partway up a mountain. The view was spectacular but she barely noticed.

She'd assumed she was driving to a ski lodge or an architect-designed home positioned for a multimillion-dollar vista. Instead she looked up at a wall of pale stone, a fairytale profusion of towers with steep, angular roofs. There was even a portcullis, raised to reveal a cobbled courtyard.

Caro stared at the centuries-old castle. This was no romantic ruin. It looked solid and meticulously maintained.

She'd known Jake Maynard was rich but he must have money to burn to live here. Her research told her he hadn't inherited it. His permanent home was in Australia.

She set her jaw. Caro had seen behind the scenes of the rich and famous and knew human frailties lurked there as they did everywhere. Wealth and overt luxury didn't awe her.

That was the one tiny advantage she had. Caro clung to it, feeling the nervous lurch of her stomach, tasting desperation on her tongue. Slowly she drove under the portcullis with its security camera, feeling each bump of the old cobblestones. Then she parked in the corner of the courtyard, next to a sleek, black vehicle.

It was only when she switched off the ignition and heard the silence thicken around her that she realised her hands shook.

Firming her lips, she reached for her purse, flicked a look in the mirror and pushed the door open.

She could do this.

She *would* do it.

Two lives depended on it.

'Ms Rivage is here.'

At the sound of his secretary's voice, Jake reluctantly looked up from behind his desk. Neil stood in the doorway, his expression bland.

Logic had urged Jake to excise this woman from the shortlist. She didn't have the experience of the front-running applicants. Yet one small detail in her application had caught Neil's eye, and Jake's. Small but vitally important. He raked a hand through his hair and told himself he'd give her fifteen minutes.

Neil stood aside and she walked in.

Jake felt his eyebrows channel down in a frown, his senses humming like the rigging on a yacht when a sudden wind rose. The nape of his neck prickled and his nostrils flared as if sensing...something.

She looked like a nanny straight from central casting. Yet at the same time not. He surveyed her plain skirt suit, scraped-back hair and apparent lack of make-up.

What was it about her that didn't fit? He'd learned to rely on his instincts and right now they sensed...something.

He got to his feet and walked around the desk, hand outstretched.

'Ms Rivage.'

His hand engulfed slim, soft fingers, yet her grip was firm as she returned his gesture. Most of the other applicants had non-existent handshakes. Either they'd simpered up at him, or were content to let him take the lead. This one looked him square in the eye.

But only for a moment. Then her brown gaze slewed from his and he knew she stifled anxiety.

Of course she's anxious. She's applying for a job. She must know her qualifications aren't impressive.

Yet his sixth sense tickled, telling him this was more than interview nerves.

'Please, Ms Rivage, take a seat.'

She nodded. 'Thank you, Mr Maynard.'

Her voice was deeper than he'd expected, with a husky resonance that teased an altogether earthier part of his consciousness. Perhaps it was the hint of an accent colouring her perfect English. But Jake had never been swayed by a sexy accent. Not unless it was accompanied by an equally sexy body.

Caro Rivage's body was hard to define behind the boxy jacket and skirt. She was tall in those heels, just half a head shorter than he, and her long legs were slender. She subsided into the chair with a grace that seemed at odds with the sombre suit. Brown clothes, brown eyes, dark, dull brown hair. She should look forgettable yet Jake found it hard to drag his gaze away.

Maybe it was the neat way she angled her ankles beneath her, accentuating an innate femininity that plain suit belied. Or the creamy skin that contrasted so startlingly with the dark suit.

Not completely pale. His gaze traversed her small, lush mouth and high cheekbones, both tinted the palest pink. Not, he'd swear, from make-up. This looked like the genuine article, a peaches and cream complexion, unblemished by the years of sun exposure he was used to seeing in his fellow Australians.

She shifted, her eyes lifting almost to his, then away, making Jake aware he was staring. The knowledge disturbed him. He wasn't interested in Ms Rivage's skin. Even if it looked as soft as a petal.

He pulled out his chair and sank into it, sprawling comfortably. Again that swift almost-stare from his guest before she looked down and smoothed her skirt.

Was she afraid of men?

But then she lifted her chin and their gazes collided. He felt the impact as a wave of heat.

Jake stared back, intrigued. What was this sensation? Attraction? Surely not for such a sparrow, even if she did have nice legs and an intriguing face. Suspicion?

Something about her made him cautious.

'Tell me about yourself, Ms Rivage.' He leaned back, elbows on the chair arms, and steepled his fingers under his chin.

* * *

Jake Maynard's voice was a delicious rumble that she felt like a burr of pleasure in her veins. Caro blinked, ordering herself not to be fanciful. She was immune to male charm—once bitten, twice shy. Yet even as the thought surfaced, she knew this man wasn't trying to charm. Despite the gesture of welcome and the barest hint of a welcoming smile, she sensed an intensity of purpose that made her pulse quicken.

Or maybe it was the laser-sharp keenness of his grey eyes beneath coal-black eyebrows. It made his eyes seem diamond bright and knowing, as if he saw beyond her carefully constructed appearance to those secrets she hoarded close.

It took everything she had not to shift in her seat or betray any other sign of weakness. Or break away from that glittering stare.

She drew a deep breath, conscious of the unfamiliar new suit, the pantyhose and heeled shoes that felt so different from the comfortable jeans, skirts and flat shoes she'd worn for the past few years.

The very act of putting on these clothes made her simultaneously grateful for the camouflage and unsettled by the reminder of her other life.

One black eyebrow climbed his broad forehead towards thick, ebony hair, reminding her he was waiting. With that hard but handsome face, powerful physique and enormous fortune Jake Maynard probably wasn't used to women making him wait.

The thought dampened the worst of Caro's nerves, helping her focus. She'd been distracted by the aura of strength emanating from him, courtesy of broad shoulders. By even features and that slash of a dimple in one cheek when he offered his half-smile. By his air of strength and dependability.

As if any man could be relied on!

She folded her hands and began. 'My application speaks for itself. I love working with children and I'm very good at it. As you'll see from my references.'

Her chin lifted as if anticipating an argument. Even now her father's habit of squashing her self-confidence had its effect. She expected Jake Maynard to disagree with her claim, though it was true.

For too long those cool eyes held hers, then his gaze fell to the papers before him. Caro's breath rushed out in relief. She'd have to do better than this if she were to convince him and win the job.

The possibility of being rejected was unthinkable. She bit her lip as he looked up, brows contracting as he read her features.

'You don't have formal qualifications.'

'A degree in early childhood education?' She shook her head. 'My experience is all hands on. But you'll see I've done a number of short courses on specific early learning issues.'

He didn't bother to check her application again, letting it fall to the desk. Caro's heart plunged with it. Surely that wasn't it? He wouldn't write her off so easily, not when he'd decided to interview her!

'I have to tell you the other short-listed applicants have both practical experience, years of it, plus excellent formal qualifications.'

There it was, the brush-off she'd feared. Nausea churned at the idea of being given her marching orders.

'Have you read my references? I believe you'll find them persuasive.'

He sat back further in his chair, as if getting comfortable while he watched her squirm. He didn't bother glancing at her application.

Maybe the contrast between his bronzed skin and the

dark jacket he wore teased her imagination, or perhaps it was his almost insulting air of indolence, but for a second Caro fancied something demonic in the knowing slant of those dark brows. Something fierce and compelling and totally at odds with this comfortable room full of old, leather-bound books.

'I'm supposed to be awed because one of your referees is a countess?' Had he memorised her application? Caro was surprised he recalled that level of detail. 'Unfortunately for you, Ms Rivage, I'm not swayed by an aristocratic title.'

His sneer rankled. Stephanie was a dear friend as well as a client. She'd given her reference in good faith. Caro sat taller, fixing her slouching interviewer with a stare.

'The key part of the reference is the description of my work, Mr Maynard, not my employer's title.'

Those straight eyebrows rose as if he was surprised at her response. Did he expect her to sit silently while he picked her application and her friends apart?

'Her son faced a range of difficulties when I began working with him. Together we made considerable progress.'

'You claim all his improvement was because of you?'

'No. It was a team effort that included some specialised programmes. But I was there with him every day, a major part of that.'

That might not sound as good as *I did it all myself*, but it was the truth.

No sign of approval on those stark features. Maybe that was how Jake Maynard looked while processing information—gaze sharp, brow frowning and mouth pursed. The expression emphasised the heavy planes of his jaw and the slant of his high cheekbones. He reminded Caro of a picture that had fascinated her as a child, of a medieval knight frowning in concentration as he pinioned a flailing dragon the size of small Shetland pony with his lance.

Her sympathies had always been with the little dragon.

'You think four or five years working as a nanny and preschool assistant make you the best person to look after my niece?'

She'd been wrong. The steely glint in his eyes was more condescending than the medieval knight who hung in a dark corner of the upstairs corridor. It reminded her of her father's chilly stare. The one that through her childhood had reduced her to apologetic silence.

That, as much as her desperation, stiffened Caro's spine.

Slowly she shifted position, sitting back in her seat and lifting one leg, crossing it over her other knee, feeling the slide of silky pantyhose. A flicker in that grey-eyed stare told her Jake Maynard noted the movement.

For some reason her chest constricted, as if the air turned thick and hard to breathe. She refused to let it show, instead adopting what she hoped was a relaxed pose.

'I can't speak about the other applicants, but if I'm given the opportunity I'll devote myself to your niece totally. You won't have any complaints.'

'That's a big claim.'

'But true. I know my capabilities, and my dedication.' In that at least she was absolutely the best person for the job.

Her stomach plunged. He didn't look impressed. Why should he? No doubt he had hordes of ultra-qualified specialists at his beck and call. The very real possibility of being ejected without a chance to prove herself seemed more likely by the moment. Then where would she be? What other opportunity would she have?

Caro re-crossed her legs. 'Clearly you were interested enough in my application to interview me.'

Her pulse thundered in her ears as she stifled fear at the prospect of failing. She'd known her chances were slim yet she'd obstinately clung to hope. This was her one opportunity to make things right. If Jake Maynard had any inkling of why she was really here she'd be out of the door before her feet touched the ground.

The thought flushed heat through her, eddying deep inside and burning her cheeks. Was his niece somewhere close even now?

'Perhaps I was interested in meeting a woman so confident despite her lack of solid credentials.'

Caro stiffened. His tone hadn't changed, hadn't even sharpened, but his words were like harpoons piercing soft flesh.

Fortunately it took more than words or dismissive stares to discomfit her these days.

'I'm sure, Mr Maynard, you wouldn't drag applicants out into the wilds of the Alps on a mere whim.'

At least she hoped so. Surely this interview meant she had a chance?

'Wilds?' He shook his head. 'You object to the location? The advertisement made it clear this is a live-in position.'

If he was looking for an excuse to reject her it wouldn't be that.

'No, I'm quite content to live in the country. In fact it's what I'm used to.'

Silvery eyes bored into hers and Caro looked back calmly. Her heart might be hammering an out-of-kilter tempo and her palms might be damp with nerves, but she wouldn't show it. Better to take the initiative.

'I understand your niece is from St Ancilla—'

'Who told you that?' He leaned forward abruptly, hands planted on the desk, as if ready to vault across the polished wood. Now she registered what his chilly expression had concealed. Protectiveness.

Maybe it was the innate caution of a wealthy, good-looking bachelor, a target for the paparazzi. Yet Caro sensed his protectiveness was for his niece. Caro warmed to him a little. She was glad the little girl had someone to stand up for her and keep her safe.

Out of nowhere emotion swept in, blindsiding Caro. It rose, a choking ball of heat in her throat, making her swallow convulsively. It roiled in her belly and prickled the backs of her eyes. If only she'd been stronger—

'Are you going to answer me?'

Caro blinked and met that searing stare, hating that moment of weakness. 'I did my research before applying for the position.'

For the first time since she'd walked into this room, Jake Maynard didn't look completely in control, despite his perfectly tailored clothes, his big desk and air of authority. 'That's not common knowledge.'

Fear rippled through her. Had she slipped up already? Her mind raced, thinking through what she'd said.

'It may not be common knowledge here, but in St Ancilla it's no secret.' She paused. 'The accident that killed her parents was reported by the local press.' When still he didn't say anything Caro continued. 'I'm very sorry for your loss. It must be a difficult time for you and your niece.'

Caro's heart squeezed. If her information was right, and she knew it was, little Ariane had been orphaned twice. Once as a newborn and then again a month ago when her adoptive parents died in a severe storm. The poor mite had had a rough start to life.

Caro was determined that the child's future would be brighter. In so many ways.

'And you somehow linked that small news item to my advertisement? I don't recall the St Ancillan press mentioning me.'

He sounded sceptical and she couldn't blame him. In fact he sounded downright suspicious.

That was the last thing Caro needed.

Jake Maynard was a self-made multibillionaire. You

didn't become a world-class financier without being clever and insightful, or by taking people at face value. Why had she ever thought this might be straightforward?

The answer was simple. Because she needed it to be.

She smoothed her hands over her skirt, buying time to conquer her emotions.

'A friend lives in that part of St Ancilla and happened to mention that you were now Ariane's guardian.' Caro paused, hearing the slight wobble in her voice as she said the little girl's name. Stupid to let emotion affect her now. She couldn't afford any sign of weakness. This man would pounce on it mercilessly. She looked straight at Jake Maynard and spread her hands in an open gesture. 'Later, when I saw your advertisement I put two and two together.'

'I see.' He leaned back again and she tried not to let her gaze drift to those imposing shoulders or that strong jaw. 'You do get around, don't you? First in St Ancilla, now in Switzerland.'

Why couldn't Jake Maynard be easy-going and friendly? Eager to employ a nanny from Ariane's island homeland in the Mediterranean?

Caro met his gaze with the polite smile she'd perfected as a child. The one her father had approved when she needed to look happy for the press.

She had no intention of admitting she only knew of Jake Maynard's search for a nanny because she'd been seeking a chance to meet Ariane. Let him think she was in Switzerland for some other reason.

'Fortunately both air travel and the Internet are available to many of us now, Mr Maynard.'

A hint of a smile turned up the corner of his mouth and for a second Caro saw a glimmer of appreciation in that hard gaze, making it look almost warm. The effect was startling.

She sucked in a slow breath, to her consternation feeling her bra scratch flesh that suddenly felt oversensitive. Deep inside flared a kernel of heat that had nothing to do with nerves. It felt like feminine awareness.

Caro told herself she was imagining things. She was immune to men.

'You think I should give you the job because you come from the same country as my niece?'

She brushed her sleeve, giving herself a moment's respite from that searching gaze.

'I think it's useful that I speak the language and understand the culture. Such things are comforting, especially at a time of loss.' She paused. 'Even if she's not going to live there, there's a strong argument for her keeping her native language.'

Slowly he inclined his head, as if reluctant to agree. 'Frankly that's the only reason you're here, Ms Rivage. Because Ariane needs someone who can speak Ancillan as well as English. She's lost her parents but I don't want her to lose her heritage too.'

His voice hit a gravel note and something shifted inside her. For the first time since Caro entered this imposing library she felt real sympathy for the man before her. His expression hadn't altered yet that tiny crack in his voice hinted at deep-buried grief.

He might remind her of a sexy fallen angel with that blatantly raw masculinity and a simmering impatience that bordered on arrogance, but he'd recently lost his sister and brother-in-law. Plus inherited responsibility for his niece.

He probably wasn't at his best.

'I have some experience of dealing with loss, Mr Maynard. If you give me the chance I'll do everything I can to support your niece and help her thrive.'

His eyes held hers and for the first time she sensed he wasn't quite so negative. Was it wishful thinking?

She didn't have a chance to find out for there was a tap on the door and it swung open.

'Sorry to interrupt, Jake, Ms Rivage.' It was the secretary, Neil Tompkins, who'd escorted her upstairs. 'There's a call I really think you need to take. The Geneva consortium.'

Jake Maynard pushed his chair back. 'My apologies, Ms Rivage. This is bad timing but it's crucial I take this.'

Even so, Caro gave him credit, he didn't simply march out, but waited for her response.

'Of course, Mr Maynard.'

'I won't keep you long.' Then the pair disappeared, the studded oak door closing behind them.

Caro shot to her feet as if from a catapult. Sitting under that icy scrutiny had taken its toll. Leaving her bag beside her chair, she paced the room, drawn to the incredible vista of snowy mountains, so different from her Mediterranean home.

Her mind raced through what he'd said and how she'd responded. What she could have said better. What she could say to sway him on his return.

If the other applicants were so much more experienced it was unlikely he'd entrust his precious niece to her. On the other hand, Ancillan wasn't a common language. Its origins were ancient, with roots in classical Greek and even, the linguists thought, Phoenician, but influenced over the centuries by trade and conquest so it had traces of Italian, Arabic and even Viking borrowings. If she was the only applicant who could speak it she had a chance.

The door banged open and Caro swung around. But it wasn't Jake Maynard who entered, nor was it the door to his secretary's office that stood open. It was a door on the other side of the room.

In front of it, poised as if in mid-flight, was a small, dishevelled figure. Her frilly dress was rumpled and her

plaits were half undone so her head was surrounded by a
bright bronze nimbus of curls.

Caro's heart stopped.

She breathed. She must have, for she didn't black out.
But she couldn't move.

Memory swamped her as the little girl turned a tear-
stained face and drowned violet eyes met hers.

Caro felt a trembling begin in the soles of her feet and
work its way up her legs to her hands and belly. She swallowed then swallowed again, unable to moisten her suddenly arid mouth.

She'd struggled, hoped and prayed for this moment. But
nothing had prepared her for the raw shock of reality.

Those eyes. That hair.

She was thrown back in time to her own childhood. To
the only person in the world who'd ever loved her. To gentle
hands, tender words and a thick mass of curls of the same
distinctive burnished bronze.

'Where's Uncle Jake?'

The little girl's words dragged Caro back to the present. She tried to smile but her mouth trembled too much.
Her knees gave way and she sank onto the padded window seat, her hand pressed to her middle as if to still the
tumult inside.

'He'll be back in a minute.' Her voice was barely audi-
ble, rough with emotion.

The girl's eyes widened. 'You speak like me!'

Caro hadn't realised she'd spoken Ancillan.

Then the girl she'd come all this way to find, the girl she
hadn't known about till a few weeks ago, slowly crossed
the room towards her.

Caro went hot then cold as relief, disbelief and wonder
hit. She was torn between the urge to grin and the need
to sob.

Or to gather Ariane close and never let her go.

CHAPTER TWO

OBLIVIOUS TO HER distress, Ariane stopped before her and held up a teddy bear that looked worn and well loved.

'Maxim's arm came off.' Her bottom lip trembled as she held up the separated limb. 'Can you fix him?'

It took Caro a moment to follow her words. She was so busy taking in the heart-shaped face, wide eyes and smattering of tiny freckles across that little nose.

Despite all the evidence Caro had told herself it was possible there'd been a mistake. Things like this—long-lost relatives and scandalous secrets—didn't happen in the real world.

But face to face with Ariane, doubt disintegrated. Those eyes, that hair, even the shy, questioning tilt of the head, were unmistakeable. Was it possible for a child to inherit a gesture, a way of holding themselves, if they'd never spent time with their birth family?

The impossible was real. Real and here before her.

Searing emotion smacked Caro in the chest. She gulped a noisy breath, unable to fill straining lungs. Her eyes filled—her first tears in years.

Instantly the little girl backed away.

That was possibly the only thing that could have helped Caro get a grip, the sight of Ariane retreating.

From somewhere Caro conjured a wobbly smile.

'I'm sorry. I didn't mean to scare you.' She lifted a hand to her eye, blinking back the unshed tears. 'I think I had something in my eye. Now, tell me about your bear. He's called Maxim?'

Ariane nodded but kept her distance.

'That's a fine name.' Caro resisted the urge to move

closer. She'd already upset the poor kid with her tears. It would do no good to rush this, though instinct urged her to wrap her arms around the child and hold her tight. 'Did you know there was once a king called Maxim? He was very brave. He fought off the pirates who tried to invade St Ancilla.'

Ariane took a step nearer. 'That's where I come from.' She tilted her head. 'Are you from there too?'

'I am.' Caro let her smile widen. She'd never allowed herself to imagine having this conversation, as if it might tempt fate into obliterating all her hopes.

This was a bittersweet moment. Sweet because after all the grief and years of emptiness, Caro had found the girl she hadn't known about. Bitter because of those wasted years.

But there was no time for dwelling on past wrongs. Suddenly Caro had never felt more alive, more brimming with excitement.

'What happened to Maxim? Was he in a battle with pirates too?'

Ariane smiled and Caro felt it like a dart of sunshine piercing her heart. 'No, silly. There aren't really pirates.'

'Aren't there?' Caro stared at the bright face with the dimpling cheeks and felt her insides melt.

Ariane shook her head. 'No. Uncle Jake said so.'

'Ah, I see.'

'So don't be scared if you dream about them. They're not real.'

'That's good to know. Thank you.'

Did that mean Ariane often had nightmares? Again Caro resisted the impulse to gather her close.

Ariane tilted her head, clearly curious. 'Who are you? You look...' her forehead scrunched in concentration '... like someone I know.'

Caro's heart thudded high in her throat. 'Do I? Who do I look like?'

She shook her head. 'I don't know.'

Caro drew in a slow breath, reminding herself Ariane was a little girl. She imagined Caro was familiar, possibly because they were from the same place. Maybe speaking Ancillan made her seem familiar. There was no more to it. Anything else was impossible, even if Caro felt the connection between them as a tangible bond.

'What happened to Maxim if he wasn't fighting pirates?'

Ariane pouted. 'I don't know. I woke up and he was like this.'

Caro eyed the bear, with its fur rubbed off on one side where he'd clearly been cuddled a lot. She'd guess Ariane usually held him by that arm and the stitching had given way after much use.

'That's easily fixed.'

'It is?'

'Of course. All we need is a needle and thread to sew him back together.'

Ariane stepped closer and held out the brown bear and his separated arm. 'Can you fix him now? Please?'

Those huge eyes in that grave little face would make any heart melt. As for Caro, it took everything she had to keep things light.

'I don't have any thread with me but we can patch him up till we get some.'

'Patch him?'

'Yes. If you get my bag from near the desk I'll see what I can do.' Because even now her knees felt too wobbly to take her weight.

She watched the girl dart across the room. Obviously Maxim was a much-loved bear. Who'd given it to her? Her parents? Her Uncle Jake?

Caro thought of the self-contained man who'd interrogated her across the desk and tried to imagine him with this precious little girl. She couldn't conjure the image, but that didn't mean he didn't care. He was protective of Ariane.

'Here.' She held out Caro's capacious bag.

'Thank you.' Caro barely stopped herself calling the child by her name. 'My name is Caro. Can you say that?'

'Caro. That's easy.'

'And what's your name?'

'Ariane.'

'What a pretty name.'

'My daddy said he and Mummy picked it because I was so pretty.' Those big eyes filled with tears and Ariane's chin wobbled.

Caro's excitement shattered, her insides curdling. Ariane had lost her parents. She was grieving.

'I can see that,' Caro said slowly as she reached for her bag and began to rummage in it. 'I know some girls in St Ancilla who are called Ariane. They're named for a famous lady. She was very pretty, but more importantly she was kind and brave too.'

'She was?' Ariane blinked up at her, diverted.

'Oh, yes. She lived a long time ago before there were good hospitals and medicines. When all the people were very sick from a bad illness the lords and ladies shut themselves away because they were afraid they would get sick too. But Ariane came out of her castle and visited the poor people. She made sure they had food and clean water and helped them get better.'

'I want to be like her. I want to help.'

'Well,' Caro said slowly, withdrawing a scarf from her bag, 'you can get some practice now, helping Maxim. Here. Can you hold his arm like this?'

Ariane nodded and stood by Caro's knee, head bent as she concentrated on holding the bear and his arm in just the right way. Caro felt the brush of her soft little hand. A flutter of sensation rippled up Caro's arm, arrowing to her heart. She tugged in a tremulous breath and focused on fashioning the scarf into a sling.

There'd be time for emotion later, when she was alone. She couldn't give in to it now. That would be self-indulgent, besides scaring a child who knew her only as a stranger.

But as Caro knotted the scarf, her attention wasn't on the bear but on Ariane, whose world had been ripped apart. Who needed stability, kindness and above all love.

Caro vowed that, whatever it took, she would be the one to provide that.

Jake stood in the doorway, watching the pair with their heads bent over the teddy bear.

There was nothing especially arresting about the sight. Yet there was something about the woman and the girl together that hit him like a fist to the ribs.

Because it should have been his sister Connie here with Ariane?

Jake released a slow breath from searing lungs.

That went without saying. He'd give everything he had to see Connie here, alive and well. But this skitter of preternatural awareness didn't spring from loss. Or not loss alone.

What was it about this pair that stopped him in his tracks?

They spoke Ancillan so he didn't understand their conversation. Yet he'd understood Ariane's sadness and the way Caro Rivage had directed the conversation, allaying the tears he'd seen brim in his niece's eyes.

His confidence in this woman as a potential nanny soared. Anyone who could make Ariane smile these days was good in his book. He liked Ms Rivage's sensitivity, the deft way she'd handled what looked like a fraught moment.

Not that he was ready to give her the job. Her qualifications were laughably light compared with some of the experts who'd worked in the field for decades.

Jake frowned, watching her wind something around the teddy's arm, murmuring to Ariane.

There was something there he couldn't put his finger on. Some…similarity between them. His nape prickled as instinct stirred.

It wasn't their colouring. Ariane's was vibrant whereas Caro Rivage had dull brown hair and dark brown eyes. Ariane's face was heart-shaped and Caro Rivage's was oval. Yet the slanting set of their eyes looked similar and maybe something around the shape of the nose.

He shook his head as his brain cleared. There *was* no link. It was merely the way they worked together, both intent, both speaking Ancillan. He imagined things.

For some reason his sixth sense had worked overtime ever since Caro Rivage arrived. So much that after the phone call he'd checked her application again at Neil's desk, looking for anomalies. But there was nothing that didn't fit. The references and qualifications of all the shortlisted applicants, including Ms Rivage, had already been checked.

His first assessment had been right. She was ordinary, not outstanding.

Jake always chose outstanding. He didn't have time for ordinary. That was how he'd built his business and his personal fortune, through excellence. Yet he couldn't stifle the idea that perhaps it wasn't outstanding Ariane needed but someone ordinary. Someone to help her grope her way back to normalcy after her trauma.

He frowned. That was crazy. He wanted the best for Ariane.

Jake ploughed his fingers through his hair. Maybe he was oversensitive when it came to choosing Ariane's nanny. This wasn't like his usual decisions. Then there was nothing at risk but money, albeit lots of it.

Where his niece was concerned, Jake refused to take risks. She'd been through enough. He thought of his sister and brother-in-law's car, crushed almost to nothing by a massive tree brought down in a storm. It was a miracle Ariane had survived when her parents died.

He owed it to her and Connie to keep her safe.

He stepped into the room. Instantly the woman in brown jerked her head up, those impenetrable eyes locking on his.

What was it about her that made his hackles rise?

Clearly, despite her apparent absorption in the child, she was attuned to his presence. Jake didn't know whether that was good or suspicious.

Or maybe, the idea surfaced again as their eyes held and his chest expanded on a deep breath, it wasn't suspicion tugging at him. Could it be attraction?

Jake dismissed the idea. Caro Rivage might have fine features and a certain understated elegance, and poise... definitely poise. But Jake preferred more in his women. Eye-catching beauty and scintillating personalities for starters. Jake didn't date dull sparrows.

Nor did he mix work and pleasure. No dating the staff.

He stopped before them, jaw firming. She wasn't staff. Not yet. Probably never.

'What happened to Maxim? Is he okay?'

Ariane looked up and he caught a fleeting smile. His niece was pleased to see him, even if not pleased enough to hug him. He stifled a pang of regret.

He couldn't blame her. He was still almost a stranger. His trips to St Ancilla hadn't been frequent and though he'd stayed with Connie and her family, he'd usually worked during the day when Ariane was awake.

'His arm came off. But Caro can fix him. We need...' She turned to the woman.

'Thread. Wool to sew his arm on.'

Ariane nodded. 'Wool. Do you have wool, Uncle Jake? Please? Then we can make him better.' Pleading eyes turned to him and Jake felt that familiar stab of discomfort.

It was crazy that he should be responsible for this needy child. What she required was someone who knew how to care for her. Someone who could fill the gaps he, with his lack of experience, couldn't.

'I'm sure we can rustle some up.' He hunkered near his niece, enjoying the way she smiled back, clearly delighted with his news.

What he hadn't counted on was discovering the surprisingly rich scent of the woman holding Ariane's teddy bear. Jake's nostrils flared as a hint of her warm, spicy fragrance reached him. It was the perfume of a sensual woman, not heavy but far more intriguing than the predictable floral scent he'd have expected of a prim sparrow. He inhaled deeply then wished he hadn't as his sense receptors shuddered into awareness.

Jake shot a look at her under lowered brows but she avoided his gaze.

Because she felt that jag of awareness too?

Grimly he yanked his brain back to order. There *was* no awareness.

'I'll call Lotte and we'll see if she has any wool, shall we?' The ever-efficient housekeeper would have some, or be able to acquire it.

'And a needle please, preferably a large one.'

Up close Caro Rivage's husky voice sounded surprisingly sensual. Was she trying to entice him into giving her the job? She was in for a rude awakening if she thought he'd be swayed by a sexy voice.

Yet once more when he looked she was all but ignoring him. Instead she smiled at Ariane as she put the teddy into the little girl's arms.

Jake stared, amazed at how that smile turned this passably pleasant-looking woman into someone almost…stunning. The joy in her expression could be bottled and sold as a tonic.

As if sensing his stare, she darted a glance at him then away, fussing over the sling she'd arranged.

'Please, Uncle Jake. Can you ask now?'

'Of course.' He got up and called Lotte on the house phone. The interview had been derailed by Ariane and her damaged bear. But perhaps that was a good thing. Despite requiring the best qualified person, he also had to find someone caring. Someone Ariane could relate to.

As he watched the two females together it seemed as if he'd found just that. Or, he amended, someone who could put on a good initial show but who might not have the depth of experience Ariane needed. The thought loosened the ribbon of tension tightening around his gut.

He didn't *want* to give Caro Rivage the job.

Yet there was no denying Ariane liked her. He owed it to his niece to give the woman a chance, despite his doubts. Without a solid reason to reject her she deserved that much.

Ariane spoke again.

'Can you speak English, Ariane?' that throaty voice asked. 'I don't think your uncle understands Ancillan and it's not nice to exclude him.'

Spoken like a true governess. As if he cared. He was just glad to hear Ariane sound so animated after weeks of being withdrawn and teary.

'Exclude?'

'It means to shut someone out so they feel all alone. It's not a friendly thing to do. You don't want to hurt your uncle's feelings, do you?'

Ariane shook her head yet she looked unhappy. 'But I like talking with you. It's like being home, talking with my…' Her mouth clamped shut and her little chin wobbled and Jake wanted to tell her he didn't give a damn what language she spoke. He hated it when she withdrew into that grief-stricken bubble where he had trouble reaching her.

He opened his mouth but Caro Rivage spoke first. 'Of course you want to speak Ancillan. I'm sure you'll soon be able to do that a lot.'

'With you?'

Jake's heart cramped as he looked into that woebegone little face.

'We'll have to see, won't we?' Full marks to Ms Rivage for not playing on Ariane's desperation to make promises she couldn't keep. She turned to the opening door. 'Now, is this Lotte?'

Jake crossed his arms and leaned against the desk to watch proceedings. As expected, Lotte had wool in several colours, plus needles and scissors. The housekeeper reached for Maxim, offering to sew him better, but she was forestalled by Ariane, who insisted Caro do it.

He saw the women's gazes meet, assessing and something more. Caro asked permission to use Lotte's supplies, then sought a second opinion on the choice of colour and needle size. By the time the two had discussed possible stitches and the need to reinforce Maxim's other arm, the women were firm allies.

Silently Jake applauded Caro Rivage. She knew she trod on the housekeeper's territory and had adroitly co-opted her as an ally rather than a rival. Lotte fretted over Ariane like a broody hen with a single chick yet now she smiled and nodded, praising the newcomer's stitching and telling Ariane that Maxim would be as good as new.

Caro Rivage was a smooth operator, able to read people's sensitivities.

Was that what she tried to do with him? Were those downcast eyes a ploy to make her seem the ideal nanny?

But she'd met his gaze steadily when she had to. He sensed she really was nervous, despite her show of calm. Clearly she wanted this job badly.

Was she broke? Her clothes looked new if unremarkable.

Maybe she wanted the kudos of working for him. A stint in his employ would open any door to her.

The idea eased his tension. Why shouldn't she want the job? This vague sense of something askew dissipated. The woman checked out. She had no criminal record and her references were good.

'Maxim looks as good as new,' he murmured when she cut the thread and handed the bear to a grinning Ariane.

'Thank you, Caro!'

Jake thought Ariane might even hug the newcomer, but instead she cuddled the toy while Lotte looked on, beaming from ear to ear.

Jake cleared his throat. 'Perhaps, Lotte, you could take Ariane for a snack while Ms Rivage and I conclude our business?'

It took some doing as Ariane didn't want to leave but finally they were alone. He watched Caro get to her feet. Her hands twisted together before she seemed to collect herself and let them fall to her sides. Her eyes met his and once more he felt the curious blankness of that dark-eyed stare. It struck him that when she was in control of herself she gave little away.

Jake was torn between annoyance and admiration.

'Shall I sit by the desk again?' She gestured to where she'd faced him across the expanse of glossy wood.

'No, Ms Rivage.' That deep voice rippled across her skin. 'The interview is over.'

Just like that dismay slammed into her. Her belly knotted with nausea. Caro flexed her fingers then linked them behind her back rather than press them to her roiling abdomen.

He couldn't dismiss her so quickly! They'd barely begun to talk when they'd been interrupted.

'I believe you should reconsider, Mr Maynard.' There.

Her voice was even, though a little hoarse. Amazing what desperation could do.

'Reconsider? You haven't heard what I have in mind.'

Amusement sparked in his cool, grey eyes as if delighting in her discomfort.

Outrage filled her. She'd been the butt of her family's amusement so often as a child that it grated. Because she was shy. Because she looked different. Because she didn't fit with the rest of them.

Okay, it was mainly her stepmother rather than her half-brothers who'd made her feel an outsider, but the wounds carved deep. Especially as her father had merely raised his eyebrows and told her not to be sensitive.

Caro planted her feet more firmly and met Jake Maynard's sparkling gaze with one of her own. 'Perhaps you'd like to inform me what you *do* have in mind?'

Her tone would have done her father proud. Cool, composed and superior. She saw Jake Maynard's eyes widen then narrow suspiciously but she refused to back down. This was too important. This meant everything.

'I had in mind to invite you to stay overnight. To give you a trial period with my niece.'

Caro felt the air whoosh from her lungs, leaving her gasping for breath. Only years of training at projecting the right image kept her on her feet, for her knees trembled like leaves in a gale. Her heart jammed up in her throat and there was a roaring in her ears, blocking out the rest of his words. She saw him speak, tried to focus and heard something about this not being a promise of employment.

'Well, Ms Rivage? You haven't said anything. Does that mean you're not prepared to stay?'

Caro shook her head, buying time while she found her voice. 'No, Mr Maynard, it doesn't mean that at all. I'll happily stay tonight and get to know Ariane.'

'Good.' He nodded but didn't smile. In fact he didn't look happy at all, though he was getting his own way.

Perhaps he was so used to everyone jumping to do his bidding he didn't consider how inconvenient it might be for a job applicant to make an unscheduled overnight stay. Fortunately Caro had the suitcase she'd brought to Switzerland in the car downstairs.

'Very well. I'll have my secretary draw up a simple agreement to cover us both in the event of any accident or liability during your stay.'

He really was a businessman through and through. Caro wouldn't have thought of that. But then she was in such a whirl she was barely capable of digesting what he'd said.

She watched him walk out of the door, heard the murmur of male voices in the outer room and reached out a hand to anchor herself. Her fingers clutched fabric and she blinked. She was grabbing the thick curtain as if it were all that kept her upright.

Caro sank onto the window seat, reeling. She felt hot and cold, anxious yet ecstatic.

She had a chance.

A chance to be with Ariane.

Her long-lost daughter.

CHAPTER THREE

'No, no, everything's under control, Mr Maynard. The young lady is excellent with her. It's good to see your niece smiling.' Jake heard the relief in Lotte's voice over the house phone.

Because, with a temporary nanny here, she had time to get on with her own work uninterrupted? No, that wasn't fair. Lotte had a soft spot for Ariane. He knew she was pleased to see the little girl happy.

As he was. Even if he wished Ariane responded as enthusiastically to him as she did to this stranger she'd only known a few hours.

Catching his thoughts, Jake scowled. He wasn't jealous. The idea was preposterous. He thanked Lotte and hung up.

'Dramas?' Neil looked up from his laptop.

'Apparently not.'

His secretary nodded. 'I thought so. I had a hunch about her—'

'So you said. But you'll forgive me if I refuse to rely on hunches where Ariane's concerned.'

Jake wanted solid evidence that the woman would be good for his niece. A couple of hours keeping her content wasn't enough to tip the scales in her favour. Not against the other applicants.

'You don't like her?'

Put that bluntly, Jake felt almost ashamed to realise he *wanted* Caro Rivage to fail. Because of some inexplicable hunch of his own.

He shook his head. He trusted his instinct. It had saved his life in his long-ago army days. Listening to it had proved invaluable since moving into finance too, where sometimes the truth behind a too attractive investment could have sunk him if he hadn't raised questions.

'I'm reserving judgement.'

He told himself it was true. He summed up people quickly, not having time to waste. But with this woman he found himself still guessing. Perhaps his inability to read her made him suspicious?

Usually women were easily read. They liked his money, his power, his body, or perhaps all three.

Jake's mouth twisted. How had he ever thought Fiona, his last lover, different? Because she'd lasted longer? It wasn't much of a recommendation. He didn't miss her and felt a judder of distaste when he thought of her. Her attitude to Ariane had sealed her fate. Now she was back in England with her privileged friends or perhaps cruising the Riviera, searching for his replacement.

Amazing that he'd considered even for a second being with her long term. Her double-barrelled surname and cutglass accent, her knack of knowing anyone who was anyone at society events, should have pressed every hot button. He despised trust fund hangers on, expecting life to give them what they wanted. But she'd seemed so natural, down to earth and appealing. He'd been blinded by her quick mind, sense of humour and great sex.

Maybe his sister had been right and he'd begun to hanker after more than casual affairs. Fiona had been on the same page with that. She'd had the nerve to talk about Ariane being an unnecessary encumbrance when he, they, started a family.

The Honourable Fiona Petrie-Mathieson was a snob. Instead of helping when he found himself responsible for a grieving child, his lover had focused on the fact Ariane was adopted. She'd called her an anonymous baby, saying she could have been anyone's. The Honourable Fiona didn't want to pollute herself with ties to a child who didn't come from class or money. She'd suggested Ariane would be better with others of *her sort*, at an orphanage school Fiona *happened* to hear about.

As if Ariane weren't his sister's child and his only living family.

'No need to look so fierce, boss.' Neil raised his hands in mock surrender.

'Have I been giving you a tough time?' Jake leaned back and raised one eyebrow.

His secretary grinned. 'On a scale of ten? Let me think…'

Jake grunted out a laugh. They'd worked together for years. Neil could take anything he dished out and was no pushover. He also had a quick, analytical brain.

'Do *you* like her?'

'I told you she'd be good for the job.'

'Not what I asked. Do you *like* her? Trust her?'

Neil's amusement faded. 'You really *are* concerned!' He paused. 'I've barely spoken to her. She seemed…nice. Trying not to show she was nervous while she waited for the interview. But I felt she was genuine, not ignoring me because I'm a lackey nor buttering me up for information about you. And she has a sweet smile.'

Jake shook his head. 'A sweet smile? Good thing I'm hiring the nanny, not you.'

Neil shrugged. 'You asked. I like her better than the one with two Masters Degrees. That one might know the theories of child development but I'm not sure she'd cope with a carsick kid.'

Jake thought of that eye-opening car trip through the Alps when he discovered Ariane didn't travel well.

'You have a point.' He shoved his chair back. 'I'll leave you to finish up. I'm going to check on this would-be nanny.'

Jake was at the door when Neil spoke. 'There was one

other thing I noticed about Ms Rivage.' He turned and caught the gleam in his secretary's eyes. 'She has spectacular legs.'

Those legs were on display when Jake reached Ariane's playroom. Rugs lined the floor and padded window seats held bright cushions and dolls. But it wasn't Ariane or her room that snared his attention. It was Caro Rivage standing on a small stool, arms raised above her head as she reached for something on a high shelf.

Neil was right. She had spectacular legs. Fabulous legs.

She'd taken off her shoes and stood on tiptoe, the stance accentuating the fine curve of her calf. She'd removed her jacket. Jake saw it draped over the back of a nearby chair. Her white blouse strained over her breasts.

Something dug into his belly, grabbing tight. His nostrils flared on a quick inhale. His gaze tracked down to her toes and up over the loosely fitted skirt to a lithe torso revealed by that taut blouse. Then up the long, feminine arch of her tilted neck to her bundled-up hair.

Jake's breath expelled in a rush that left him almost light-headed.

Stripped of her conservative shoes and unflattering jacket, Caro Rivage was slim, svelte, feminine and intriguing. A different sort of intriguing from the way he'd viewed her earlier.

Except Jake knew that was a lie. Despite her prim pose and drab clothes, he'd been aware from the first of this woman's magnetism. It was a sly thing. Not overt like Fiona's blonde beauty and overtly sexy curves.

Even as he'd catalogued and dismissed Caro Rivage's expertise, at another level, that of primitive male, he'd been aware of the attractive woman behind the pursed lips and downcast eyes.

Heat drilled down from his temples to his gut, boring straight to his groin.

Did this explain his resistance? Was it why he didn't want to employ her? Because he responded to her as a man to a woman, not a boss to a governess?

He sucked air into tight lungs. Business and pleasure didn't mix. He had no intention of beginning anything personal with a staff member.

After Fiona he'd found it easy to avoid the charms of the opposite sex. Except, to his horrified fascination, he realised sex was the operative word here.

Caro Rivage bit her lip, shifted her hips in a way that shouldn't be in the least provocative yet turned up his inner thermostat from hot to scorching. The tug of desire dragging at his groin told its own story. It wasn't one he wanted to hear.

But Jake prided himself on facing facts.

She wasn't gorgeous like the women he dated. She wasn't his type. He hadn't decided if he could trust her, yet he was attracted.

Urgently attracted.

Worse, he felt compelled to give her a chance despite his better judgement because his niece showed every sign of bonding with her. That rankled. Jake made a point of being the one to dictate terms. He didn't take kindly to being forced into decisions. But little Ariane had held herself aloof from everyone except her teddy since the accident that killed her parents. Seeing her shy excitement with Caro Rivage was a profound relief. It was the first time she'd smiled properly in a month.

What option did he have but to give this nanny a chance?

She expelled an exasperated breath that puffed up the strands of brown hair drifting free of her brutally neat bun. She looked ruffled and pink-cheeked and Jake knew a growing curiosity to see her flushed and rumpled for other reasons.

'Can I help with that, Ms Rivage?' His voice hit a resonant baritone note that betrayed the trend of his thoughts. He could only hope she wasn't as adept at reading men as she was little kids.

His deep voice came out of nowhere, lassoing her around the middle and drawing her off balance. Caro teetered on her toes, arms windmilling, then warmth enveloped her. Hard warmth that wound around her and held her steady.

She registered a broad palm and long fingers splayed across her hip bone. A solid body, all heat against hers, and near her breasts a head of tousled dark hair.

She hauled in a shocked breath and wished she hadn't. This close she could smell Jake Maynard's skin, warm and scented with bergamot and citrus. Her eyes sneaked shut for a self-indulgent moment, enjoying that fresh, masculine tang.

He was Ariane's uncle. A potential employer. An obstacle to be overcome. She couldn't think of him as a desirable man.

She hadn't considered any man in that way for years. Not since she'd been blindsided by Mike's smiling attentiveness, then gutted by his betrayal.

Reluctantly she looked down to Jake Maynard standing with his head a whisper away from her breasts. Dark brows contracted over brilliant grey eyes that no longer looked icy. Instead they reminded her of the heat haze she'd seen rising over boiling geothermal pools in Iceland. Heat drenched her skin and sank into her bones.

Still she shivered.

'You can let go. I'm not going to fall.'

She wondered if he heard her, though his gaze was anchored to her face.

'Even so. I'll get whatever you need. I'd rather you didn't take a tumble.'

His voice was brisk, his movements quick as he lifted her off the stool. Yet when he'd swung her to the floor he took his time releasing her. Caro was inordinately conscious of the weight and size of those hands. Of his tall frame, close enough to lean into. Of the tendril of beckoning male scent in her nostrils.

She stepped back smartly and he dropped his hold.

Belatedly she looked at Ariane, who'd turned back to the puzzle on the floor. Was it just Caro who felt the air thicken and clog when Jake Maynard was around? It must only have been seconds since he strode into the room yet it felt as if time had spun out far longer.

Panic whispered through her but she conquered it. She was stronger than this. No man would derail her plans.

'Thank you, Mr Maynard.' She pointed to the top shelf. 'There's a puzzle we wanted to try. If you could reach that one I'd be grateful.'

Of course he grabbed it easily, as she would have if he hadn't taken her by surprise.

'You like puzzles, Ariane?' Instead of handing it to Caro he crouched next to his niece. Caro registered the tautness in his folded frame as he waited for Ariane's response, and the ease of tension when she nodded and whispered that yes, she liked puzzles.

That was when Caro guessed some of his diamond-bright hardness might be down to something other than a demanding nature and a short temper.

Was he worried about Ariane? His movements as he settled himself beside the little girl were ostensibly easy, yet Caro saw how carefully he moved, as if not wanting to spook her. And though Ariane didn't move away, nor did she lean against his big frame. She didn't burrow close for reassurance as would be natural if she relished the comfort of a beloved uncle.

What was Jake Maynard's relationship with his niece?

As Caro put away the footstool and tidied a few toys, she observed them. Both were wary, treating each other with the politeness of strangers.

Caro huffed out a relieved breath. At least Ariane wasn't afraid of her uncle. If she had been... Well, she didn't know what she'd have done but she wouldn't have been able to watch without taking action.

The urge to declare herself and her relationship with Ariane was almost overwhelming.

Caro imagined announcing the truth, at which point little Ariane would fling herself into her waiting arms and it would be as if they'd never been apart.

Then what? Jake Maynard would simply relinquish his niece to her care?

She didn't even have to look at the obstinate angle of his jaw to know that wouldn't happen.

It was a nice fantasy but it would never be that easy. Announcing the truth would be complicated, especially since she had no intention of letting Ariane be taken from her again.

If she declared herself now she'd upset Ariane, who wouldn't understand why a strange woman claimed to be her mum. Plus she'd infuriate Jake Maynard who'd chuck her out of his castle before she could draw a second breath.

He'd think her mad.

Even if he didn't, if by some miracle she managed to convince him, he wouldn't let her stay. She'd seen his distrust and his protectiveness of his niece. If he had an inkling of the truth, she doubted she'd see Ariane again till they'd been through the mill of lawyers and courts. That could take years.

Caro pinched the bridge of her nose, tasting the rust tang of blood where she'd bitten her cheek.

She should have made a plan before coming here. A sensible plan with actions ready for every contingency. Instead, when she got this opportunity she'd sped here, needing to see Ariane.

Though it went against every instinct, Caro had to be patient. To wait, gain Ariane's trust and her uncle's. To work out how best to approach this.

Even if Jake Maynard didn't have a close relationship with Ariane, he cared for her. Caro guessed she was only here now because she and Ariane had connected. Not, she sternly told herself, because of their blood ties, but because they shared a common language.

It was ridiculous to think Ariane sensed their link though to Caro it was so blatant, so strong, she almost expected a fanfare and bright lights, as if a contestant on a TV show had won a fortune.

Abruptly the enormity of the situation hit her in slicing blows to her knees and stomach. She pressed her palm to her belly. There was a searing sensation inside, as if her baby had been ripped from her womb.

Caro's knees folded but she caught at a chair and collapsed on its cushioned seat. Ariane half lifted her head, looking for her, then, satisfied she was nearby, turned to Jake Maynard, pointing out something on the puzzle spread across the floor. Fortunately he was turned away from her. She hated to think of that intense scrutiny on her now.

Caro breathed through the pain, telling herself it wasn't real. There could be no physical pain now. It was well over four years since she'd gone through labour and an excruciatingly difficult childbirth.

But though her rampaging pulse slowed, the pain persisted.

It was the ache of loss, familiar because she'd endured

it so long. Strange to feel it now when for the first time she had hope for the future.

She breathed deep, absorbing the fact that she'd found her daughter.

It was a miracle.

Caro had never let herself believe it possible. The idea that her baby was alive somewhere without her had been the fraught stuff of nightmares, taunting her till she awoke tearful and distressed, to the real world where such things couldn't happen.

Except it had.

Her jaw clenched and pain spiked from her grinding molars. She knew who was to blame.

Her hands curled into fists that trembled with the force of her emotion. Slowly, each joint aching with effort, she smoothed her hands on her thighs, feeling the bunch of stressed muscles beneath the fabric.

One day there'd be time to think of confronting the person responsible. Not today.

Her gaze slewed to the bright head bent over the puzzle and her heart lurched.

All that mattered was that she'd found her baby. That she was with her. She'd do whatever it took to stay at her side. And she wouldn't let anything, including Jake Maynard, stand in her way.

Jake forked his fingers through his hair, leaning back in his chair and rolling his shoulders. He'd had enough for tonight.

Trying to make progress with this new scheme was like wading through treacle in cement boots. He'd thought it easier to do business in Switzerland where he could access the principals in person, and he'd been right, to some extent.

He swivelled his chair, surveying the tapestries on the thick castle walls. His lips twisted. A medieval castle was a far cry from his usual surroundings.

The exclusive location meant he'd been able to entice some of the key players to this ultra-private retreat after the international summit in the next valley. That had provided impetus to his plans, but not as much as he'd like. There was a lot of work to do.

He wanted to stay in Europe to see how Ariane went. He'd thought of taking her back to St Ancilla for a visit. He was torn between thinking it could ease her pain and fearing it might send her back into the blank state of shock she'd been in at the hospital.

She needed time and he needed expert advice. Meanwhile, they'd stay here. This castle, rented from an acquaintance, was as good a place as any to keep Ariane from the media limelight. If any more intruding journalists turned up he'd simply drop the portcullis.

Jake turned and noticed a scrap of wool on the floor. It must have fallen when Ariane's bear was mended.

His thoughts zipped from his niece to the woman he'd invited to stay overnight.

He couldn't quite believe he'd done that when he hadn't offered the better qualified applicants such a chance.

He got to his feet, shoving his hands into his pockets.

Caro Rivage had no criminal record and her references checked out. She was what she seemed, a woman who liked kids and had some experience with them. A woman well-regarded by her employers.

Yet something about Ms Rivage gave him pause. If only he could put his finger on it.

But how could he send her away after seeing Ariane's smile? The way she chattered with the woman, eager to be with her.

Jake stretched and looked at his watch. Almost midnight. He switched off the child monitor, knowing from the silence that Ariane was sound asleep. But he always checked on her before turning in.

Minutes later he reached Ariane's room. In the dim illumination from a nightlight he saw her curled up, thumb in mouth and her other hand hooked around her teddy. Jake's heart tugged.

She might not have been born Connie's daughter but Ariane was as much his niece as if his sister had carried her for nine months. Seeing the love in his sister's eyes for the tiny red-headed bundle, Jake had loved her from the first too.

He vowed he'd do better for her from now on. The first four and a half years of her life he'd been so focused on his projects that he hadn't spent enough time with his family, stopping by for quick visits and relying on long-distance calls to keep up to date.

Because he hadn't realised Connie would be ripped away.

That familiar pang filled Jake's chest as he thought of his older sister, moving across the world to be with the man she loved. After her early years of struggle it had been a relief to see her settled with a nice bloke.

Jake turned, ready for his own bed, and his gaze caught a figure sitting in the corner. A figure he hadn't noticed because it was as still as the massive, carved wardrobe behind it.

The hairs at his nape sprang to attention. His scalp prickled and even the hairs on his arms lifted.

Caro Rivage could have been a statue. Her absolute stillness was uncanny. As was the way her gaze fixed so intently on Ariane.

It wasn't surprising to see a nanny in a child's room but surely not like this? Suspicion stirred.

'What are you doing here?'

She jumped, her hand flying to her chest as if to hold in her heart. Her face swung wide-eyed towards him.

Instantly his urgent protectiveness of Ariane faded.

He'd never seen someone look so vulnerable. Her dark

eyes were…haunted. Her mouth gaped and her chest heaved as if she'd had the shock of her life.

This wasn't the expression of someone up to no good, but of someone utterly defenceless. Jake saw a terrible stark-ness in her face. Then her expression smoothed. She rose and crossed the room.

Did he imagine a pulsing charge of energy as she stopped before him? He frowned, thrown by the flight of fancy. Nevertheless, once more his senses stirred into over-drive in her presence. It was unlooked for and disturbing.

'I was checking Ariane.'

Jake darted a glance at his niece, still sleeping, then jerked his head towards the door. When they were in the hall he scrutinised the woman before him. The light was better here but it was impossible to interpret her expression. She looked self-contained, as if presenting an unreadable front came naturally.

Again his sixth sense twitched a warning.

'A glance would have told you she was settled. You looked as if you'd been there for some time. Why?'

Something stirred, a fleeting expression, and Jake re-alised how pale she was, how tightly she held her mouth. His gaze lowered, past a fast-flickering pulse at her throat to the enveloping jacket and skirt. She hadn't even been to bed?

She swallowed and something jerked in his belly as he watched her slender throat work, feeling the tension vibrate off her in waves.

Now, instead of suspicion, Jake felt concern. He was familiar with pain and he recognised its shadow in this woman's unnaturally still features.

'What is it, Caro? What's wrong?'

'Nothing's wrong.' Her lips curved in an unconvincing smile. 'I wanted to check Ariane before I went to bed. She's going through a difficult time and something she said made me think she was prone to nightmares.' She spread her hands in a wide, helpless gesture that told him more about her state of mind than her face did. 'Truly, I just wanted to make sure she was safe.'

Her words rang convincingly and for once instinct told him it was true. She *was* here out of concern for Ariane.

True but not simple. That awful vulnerability he'd glimpsed in her momentarily unguarded face, that wealth of emotion had bordered on anguish. It couldn't be about Ariane, whom she'd only known a few hours. So it had to be about another child. A child she'd cared for and lost? Cot death? Illness? Accident? The possibilities were endless.

Pity rose, a rush of sympathy that made him want to comfort her. He moved closer then stopped himself.

'Get some sleep. My room's next to Ariane's so I'll hear if she wakes.' Maybe if he gave her this job she'd sleep near Ariane too, but he hadn't yet made that decision.

She nodded. 'Goodnight, Mr Maynard.'

'Goodnight, Ms Rivage.'

When she'd disappeared from view he exhaled slowly, thrown by what had happened. He'd wanted to haul Caro Rivage into his arms and hold her close. To ease the grim shadows that rode her.

His nostrils flared and he stepped back into Ariane's doorway, glancing at the curled-up child.

Tonight had revealed several things.

Caro Rivage was serious about caring for his niece.

She carried some distressingly heavy burden.

And he, with no real knowledge of the woman, without even wanting her here, had been on the verge of easing her pain with his arms around her and his lips on that inviting pink mouth. He wanted to hear her sigh with delight instead of anguish. He wanted her to smile at him with the warmth she bestowed on his niece. He wanted…

No. She was *not* his type. He wasn't interested.

Yet he'd stood mesmerised by the gentle sway of her hips till she disappeared from view.

He'd been right. Caro Rivage spelled trouble. Yet for Ariane's sake he wouldn't turn her away.

Ariane's sake?

With a snort of self-disgust Jake turned and stalked into his bedroom.

CHAPTER FOUR

'I'M SORRY I don't have better news, Caro, but this situation is a minefield.' Despite the early hour, Zoe's voice was crisp. No doubt, as one of the finest lawyers in St Ancilla, she was used to cutting to the heart of complex issues. 'This is likely to become a protracted court battle unless the two parties come to agreement.'

Her words fell like sharpened blades, slicing the sinews at Caro's knees. She grabbed the carved post of her four-poster bed, letting it take her sagging weight.

She'd been excited when she saw who the caller was, hoping Zoe had rung because she'd found a simple way through what promised to be a legal nightmare.

Her lips twisted. Since when had anything in her life gone as she'd hoped?

Wishing for something wouldn't make it happen. A happy family, a man who'd love her for herself, a future with her precious child—she'd dreamed of them all but not one had become real. No matter how hard she'd tried.

Caro set her jaw. This time it *would* be real. No matter what it took.

Beyond the window was a magical vista of soaring mountains and sparkling, fresh snow. So clear and pristine. So different from the mess she found herself in.

'But surely the adoption wasn't legal? How could it have been when I didn't consent?'

She closed her eyes, her mind swimming with memories that had haunted her for years. The exhaustion, the blur of pain and fear, punctuated by moments of startling clarity when she realised something had gone badly wrong with the delivery. Her growing distress, and then…nothing, just blankness as the drugs took effect.

'That's something I'm trying to investigate. It's proving difficult.'

Caro dragged in a deep breath. She understood what Zoe wasn't saying. The impenetrable wall of denial and obfuscation that would meet her attempts to discover more.

Caro's father had pulled strings to arrange the adoption. He was a man adept at getting his way and as far as she knew no one had ever had the wealth, the will or the power to hold him to account.

Till now. In this he'd gone too far.

Sometimes, in her more desperate moments, she considered confronting him and calling him to account. Except she knew it would be like a gnat biting a bull. He'd swat her aside and immediately turn all his considerable power to making the problem go away. Then she'd be up against two powerful men, not one. Better to bide her time, for now.

'Difficult or not, there must be a way forward.' She bit her lip. 'I want to avoid a long court battle, for Ariane's sake especially.'

'It appears both sides can argue a legitimate claim to the child.'

She's not 'the child'. She's my daughter!

Caro clenched her teeth against the instinctive protest. Zoe was only doing her job, telling her the legal reality.

'My advice is to talk to her guardian. Negotiate. See if you can find common ground.'

Negotiate with Jake Maynard? The man was a world-class financier, regularly working with some of the largest and most successful corporations in the world. It was rumoured he was here for secret meetings with officials of unnamed governments. Caro couldn't imagine him negotiating with her. He'd be more likely to throw her out before she could do more than explain why she was here.

Then where would she be? Caro would fight with everything she had to win her daughter, but she wasn't fool enough to compare her power or negotiation skills with Jake Maynard's.

She couldn't quite stifle a choked sound of dismay.

'I don't mean straight away,' Zoe said quickly. 'Not till I've got to the bottom of the adoption process and checked some more precedents. Especially as Ariane's not in St Ancilla now. Different legal jurisdictions can complicate things.'

'As if they weren't already complicated.' Caro pushed her hair behind her ear, frowning.

'We knew that from the start,' Zoe's matter-of-fact voice cut through her troubled thoughts. She let a pause lengthen. 'Unless you don't want to proceed?'

'No!' Caro shook her head, her hair swirling again across her cheeks. She stalked to the window, pressing her palm to the cool glass. Along the horizon formidable peaks rose stark and seemingly unconquerable. Yet she knew that against the odds mountaineers had reached those impossible summits. 'I do want to proceed.' She drew a measured breath then said more evenly, 'I can't give up, Zoe. I can't.'

'Of course you can't.' Gone was the sharp voice of legal opinion, replaced by warm understanding. 'Who could, in your place?' The other woman sighed. 'Try to be patient. Time enough to talk to Ariane's guardian when I've done some more checking and we know exactly where we stand.'

As she ended the call Caro was torn between frustration and relief. Stupid to have thought there'd be any easy way through this, but after finding Ariane and spending time with her, it had felt as if anything was possible.

She'd gone to bed last night overcome by emotion at finally seeing her little girl. Being free to talk with her, watch over her as she slept. She'd assured herself it was a good

sign that Jake Maynard had invited her to stay. He wouldn't
do that unless she had a chance at the job.

Yet she didn't want to be a nanny. She was Ariane's
mother.

No wonder she hadn't slept. She'd tossed all night, imagining one scenario after another where Ariane's uncle
stopped her claiming her daughter.

Zoe was right. He was her uncle despite being no blood
relation. Before Caro met him she'd wondered if he might
be relieved to be rid of responsibility for his orphaned niece.
That hope had died as she'd seen his protectiveness for
Ariane.

Thinking about Jake Maynard disturbed her. He made
her…unsettled.

Caro told herself it was because he had a claim to her
daughter. His sharp eyes had softened when he watched
Ariane. Clearly he was determined to do his best for her.

He'd never tamely give her up, even to her rightful
mother.

That explained Caro's edginess. Because they were destined to be rivals, if not enemies.

It had nothing to do with the fact that he made her feel,
for the first time in ages, aware of her femininity.

She couldn't be so self-destructive as to be attracted to
the man who stood squarely between her and her daughter.

Caro stepped into the office, masking her nervously roiling stomach with a façade of calm. She was grateful for
her father's insistence that she learn to conceal her feelings
behind a show of well-bred calm. Being in the same building as her child for the first time in four and a half years
tested her to the limit.

'Take a seat, Ms Rivage.'

Instead she stopped beside the desk. How could she sit
while Jake Maynard paced the room?

He was even more intimidating than he'd been yesterday in his tailored business clothes. Those black jeans revealed muscled thighs and, when he moved away, a taut, rounded backside that turned her throat to sandpaper. His fine-knit pullover was a shade darker than his eyes and clung to broad shoulders and a flat belly. Even the way he'd pushed the sleeves up to reveal strong forearms dusted with dark hair did strange things to her insides.

He was potently masculine and far too disturbing.

And last night he'd called her Caro.

The knowledge beat in her bloodstream, slowing her pulse, making it ponderous with unexpected need.

For one crazy second she'd thought he might reach out to her as she grappled with yesterday's emotional onslaught. She'd been disappointed when he didn't.

When she'd thought of finding her daughter, she'd imagined Ariane's uncle as kind and ordinary. Not sucking up all the oxygen in the room. His presence shouldn't be electric, demanding, stifling the breath in her lungs.

How woefully underprepared she'd been.

He turned and surveyed her over his desk. No sympathy in his eyes now.

Not that it was sympathy she wanted.

She hurried into speech. 'I'd prefer to stand, thanks.'

One slashing eyebrow rose. 'You look like you're facing a firing squad.'

She inhaled roughly, her teeth digging into her bottom lip. How did he read her so easily?

He was right. After the way he'd quizzed her in Ariane's room last night, she knew he was suspicious of her. All through breakfast she'd been conscious of his piercing stare trained on her.

Did he hope to discomfit her? On the thought she pushed her shoulders back. He might be tough and used to taking charge but as an adversary he had nothing on her father.

Jake Maynard was a hard man but he seemed to play by honest rules, unlike her devious, despised dad.

'I'm expecting to hear your decision. And after sitting for the last hour with Ariane I'm comfortable standing.'

'As you wish.' He surveyed her in a leisurely way that made her skin itch. He might have all the time in the world but she needed an answer.

He must know she was on tenterhooks. Was this some extra test to pass? Despite her joy at being in the same building as Ariane, Caro felt as if she'd been scraped too thin by the emotional overload. She hadn't slept and her mind spun relentlessly like a mouse on a wheel, trying to work out the best way to deal with this fraught, complicated situation. She didn't have answers, just the certainty that whatever she did Jake Maynard wouldn't be happy.

'You still want to work for me?'

Caro's heartbeat accelerated, hope leaping. 'You're offering me the job?' She grabbed the back of the chair.

He raised his hand. 'Not quite.' Her heart plummeted. 'To be frank I still have reservations, but,' he forestalled her when she opened her mouth to respond, 'I've noticed Ariane has taken to you and how attuned you are to her.'

That was good, surely?

'But?' She leaned forward, willing him to put her out of her misery.

His eyebrows lifted as if he wasn't used to staff demanding answers.

'But my niece's well-being comes before everything else. I want to be sure I'm making the right decision, especially as on paper you're far from the best applicant.'

Caro choked back the impulse to say Ariane could have no better carer than her birth mother. But that would be disastrous. She couldn't reveal all too early and risk messing everything up. She had to choose her moment carefully, wait for news from Zoe. She guessed he'd resist her claim and he had far more resources at his disposal.

'So I'm offering you a job but with a six-month probationary period.' His crystalline gaze pinned her to the spot. 'If I'm satisfied with your work then we'll make it permanent.'

Permanent. That was precisely what Caro wanted.

But not permanent in the way he meant—with her as a paid carer.

Caro wanted her child. The right to love Ariane openly, to be acknowledged as her mother. Not because Jake Maynard employed her.

And, one day if she tried hard enough, maybe Ariane would love her back.

Caro's throat closed convulsively.

The situation was convoluted, with so much potential for failure. Caro met that questioning gaze. 'You accept?' One dark eyebrow slashed his brow as if he was surprised she hadn't eagerly accepted his proposal.

Caro hesitated on the brink of declaring herself. She abhorred lies yet she was deceiving this man, even if it was a lie of omission. Then she thought of Zoe's advice. And the very real possibility Jake Maynard would eject her when she revealed her identity.

So she curved her lips in the gracious smile she'd perfected almost before she could walk. 'That sounds ideal. I accept.'

'Good.'

He didn't smile. In fact, there was a crease between his eyebrows as if something bothered him. Caro silently vowed to do whatever it took to allay his doubts.

'Ariane already calls you Caro.' He paused, her name lingering in the silence. 'I'll do the same. And you can call me Jake. There's no need for formality in front of Ariane.'

A little shimmer of pleasure exploded deep inside as

Caro imagined the taste of his name on her tongue. Her pulse quickened.

A second later devastating self-knowledge slammed into her. To be thrilled at the prospect of saying his name? At hearing him say hers?

She blinked and concentrated on keeping her expression bland while inside anxiety coiled. Jake Maynard was a remarkably attractive man and she'd deliberately avoided such men for five years. Maybe that explained why he got under her skin. Whatever the reason, it wouldn't do. She had to keep her distance.

'Of course you may call me Caro.' She nodded briskly. 'However, I'd feel more comfortable calling you Mr Maynard.'

She watched his eyebrows lift, as if he were surprised to find someone who didn't instantly agree with him.

For a full ten seconds he said nothing. Finally he nodded. 'If that makes you feel better, Caro.'

Surely she imagined the way his voice dropped on her name and his intense scrutiny.

Abruptly Caro felt that, instead of blending into the background, she'd thrust herself into the limelight.

Exactly where she didn't want to be.

CHAPTER FIVE

A WEEK LATER Jake stood at his office window watching two figures track through a layer of white that was forecast to be the last, late snow of the season. They pulled a small toboggan.

When Caro had asked permission to take Ariane out he'd been sceptical. Since she'd left hospital in St Ancilla his niece hadn't shown interest in anything except staying inside with her teddy bear and toys.

He guessed her reluctance to go out stemmed from memories of the storm that left her parents dead and her trapped in their car, crushed beneath a massive tree.

Jake's belly clenched. At least Connie and Peter had died instantly.

He knew nothing about being a father, and not as much as he should about being a hands-on uncle, but he'd get there. He'd give Ariane the love and stability she needed.

Jake's mouth twisted. He wouldn't let her face what he and his sister had, a gaping hole where parental love should have been. It had been his determined older sister who'd given him the love, discipline and constancy their feckless mother hadn't.

He owed Connie everything and he was determined to give her daughter what his sister had given him. Once this deal was through he'd ease back, spending more time with Ariane. Which meant finding a permanent home. In Australia? St Ancilla? Renting a castle in Europe was useful for his current scheme but it was hardly the home his niece needed. Nor were his high-rise apartments in Sydney, New York and London. He'd get somewhere with a garden and plenty of sunshine.

He planted his hand on the glass, watching the pair skirt the castle. Ariane wasn't smiling but nor did she look nervous, as she had previously when he'd suggested an outing.

Caro had succeeded where he'd failed.

Jake stifled what felt suspiciously like jealousy. It didn't matter *who* helped Ariane come out of her shell of grief and shock. He should be pleased.

Plus, it reinforced the fact he'd made a wise choice offering Caro the position on probation.

Yet he reserved judgement on Caro Rivage.

Because he was drawn to her?

Jake forced the notion away.

Because of her patent wariness around him?

At first he'd assumed she suffered from interview nerves but it was more than that. He felt she watched each word, each nuance, always on guard. Did she have a problem with men in general or him in particular?

Yet she wasn't scared of him. She was…cautious. And he couldn't shake the idea that she wasn't all she seemed.

Jake frowned. Should he delve deeper? Get a comprehensive investigative report?

Or was he overreacting because she kept her distance despite the way she looked at him sometimes? As if she were fascinated, as inexplicably drawn to him as he was to her. Yet she avoided him when she could. It wasn't a response he was used to in women.

He huffed out a laugh. Was his ego so big he imagined a mystery because a woman didn't try to snare him? He should be glad. He didn't need that complication in his home.

He'd been cooped up inside too long, working on this deal. *That* was what made him stir crazy, not Caro Rivage. Maybe Ariane wasn't the only one needing fresh air.

Fifteen minutes later he approached a little valley on the far side of the castle. The air was so sharp he tasted it with every inhalation. Above was the wide blue bowl of sky and before him a cleared slope surrounded by trees.

It felt good to be outside. Especially when he heard childish giggles.

Jake's chest tightened. How long since he'd heard Ariane happy?

It unlocked memories of the last time he'd visited his sister on St Ancilla. They'd eaten outdoors under a vine-draped pergola. Connie and her husband had been the same as ever, the most content couple he knew, and little Ariane had been in high spirits, laughing at some nonsense game her father had invented with her. It had been idyllic and Jake had been glad to see Connie enjoying such happiness. She deserved it after those tough early years devoting herself to her difficult kid brother.

The sound of a husky voice interrupted his thoughts. It tickled its way through his belly then up his spine, drawing his shoulders tight.

Caro. Even if he didn't know the voice he recognised his response. The eddy of heat down low and the teasing prickle of awareness across his nape.

How was it a woman so prim and buttoned up had such a seductive voice? Last night he'd woken in a tangle of sweaty sheets, the echo of that throaty voice in his head. It had murmured an explicit invitation that made him feel as if it had been six months, not six weeks since he'd kicked Fiona out of his bed.

Scowling, he strode towards the sound.

To his surprise Ariane was on the lightweight toboggan alone, sliding down a gentle slope to where Caro waited on a broad flat area, arms wide in welcome.

It should have been his niece who captured his attention. Instead it was her nanny's amazing smile. Even from this distance it delivered a punch straight to his belly.

The sunlight on her hair picked out warm auburn highlights he hadn't noticed before. Suddenly she looked less staid and more vivacious.

She wasn't beautiful but still she was stunning. Jake frowned. It wasn't merely her hair and the colour whipped into her cheeks by the cold, but her look of sheer joy. Her smile was infectious. His mouth curled up at the corners.

Heat beat at his throat, his chest and lower. He wanted to see her smile at *him* that way instead of pretending his collar or the view past his ear was more fascinating. He wanted to see her flushed with pleasure and exertion, beaming up at *him*.

The realisation corkscrewed through him, jagging his libido and setting off alarms.

She was his *employee*. He still had reservations about her, nothing he could put his finger on but still...

'Well done,' he called out, heading towards them. 'You didn't tell me you were so good on the snow, Ariane.'

'Uncle Jake! Did you see? I slided all by myself.'

Her grin was the one he remembered from St Ancilla, from before the accident. It made his breath catch in his lungs. She'd always been a sunny child and he'd told himself she would be again. Yet seeing proof that with time and care she could recover from the recent trauma perversely reminded him again of how much they'd both lost, and how precious she was.

Nothing, he vowed, would upset her world again if he could help it.

'I saw. I'm very impressed. Was that your first time by yourself?'

She nodded so vigorously a bright coppery curl that had escaped her woolly hat danced around her face.

'Want to see me do it again?'

He nodded. 'I sure do. Then you could teach me.'

For answer she looked at Caro as if seeking permission. The nanny nodded. 'Remember, not too high, Ariane.'

Jake watched his niece climb off and head back up the slope, dragging the lightweight toboggan behind her. He was tempted to intervene and carry her burden, or offer to accompany her but he held back, seeing the determined thrust of her small chin.

He turned to find Caro watching him, an unreadable expression in her eyes. Instantly he felt that clenching awareness low in his belly, that hot swirl in his blood. Her arms were wrapped defensively around her middle. Did she too feel the tug between them, or was she just cold?

'I'll go and help her.' She made to turn and follow Ariane up the slight slope.

'No!' At his command she stopped, brows raised at his urgent tone. 'Let her do it herself.' Jake told himself he wasn't prompted by the need to keep the woman near him.

Caro looked over her shoulder at Ariane then nodded. 'You're right.' She slanted a look at him then away.

'What?'

She shrugged then met his stare. 'I might be wrong but I think, as well as the sheer fun of the slide, it's that sense of being in charge that she's enjoying.'

'Because everything in her life has upended?'

Caro nodded. 'All the things she could depend on have gone or changed. And though you've done what you can to establish a home and a routine, she probably feels the world is a scary place.'

The air Jake drew into his chest seemed thick and rough. She was right. Ariane had been through so much. She must feel powerless and adrift. Which was why it was important she have stability.

'You like working with her?' He hadn't consciously formed the question but suddenly he had to know. Providing the right carer for Ariane wasn't just a matter of him approving someone, but of that someone wanting to stay.

Given how Ariane responded to Caro Rivage it appeared that someone was standing before him.

Caro's eyes widened. 'Of course! Why? Aren't you satisfied with—?'

Jake raised a placating hand. 'I'm satisfied. So far,' he amended. 'I wanted to hear your perspective.'

Relief drifted across her face, making her expression unusually easy to read. It was another reminder of how rarely she let down her guard with him. So she really was invested in this job. 'I love caring for Ariane. I—'

She swung her head around at the sound of the toboggan approaching, then froze. A second later she was sprinting away from him across the flat little plateau towards the steeper slope at the edge of the clearing.

Jake looked up the hill, his gut curdling.

While they'd been talking Ariane had taken the toboggan high up the slope. Far higher than the track of her previous run. Now, with the added momentum, she was skidding downhill dangerously fast and at an angle that took her in a collision course with a stand of trees.

Jake's legs were already pumping, driving him through the snow towards the far side of the clearing, even though his brain told him he'd be too late. He was too far away.

His heart sank. So was Caro. She was stumbling, trying to make headway in the snow, but, as in a nightmare, seemed to be moving in slow motion.

His ears rang when Ariane's squeal of delight turned into a cry of fear as she torpedoed towards danger. He pushed himself faster, lungs burning, but knew it was impossible he'd make it in time.

The toboggan flew towards the trees and unspeakable visions filled his head. As a one-time soldier and peacekeeper he'd witnessed terrible injuries. But this was Ariane...

At the last moment, as impact with a tree seemed inevitable, there was a blur of blue as Caro threw herself at the toboggan. Snow sprayed as it spun, there was a resounding thump and a fall of white from the branches, obscuring his vision.

As he covered the last couple of metres Jake found himself praying.

Caro lay winded, her arms wrapped tight around the small, still body.

'Ariane! Talk to me.' The deep voice was raw with fear. A fear that matched her own. For the life of her she couldn't open her eyes and face what awaited her. Had she lost her daughter again? Permanently this time?

Anguish tore at her soul.

She thought she'd known fear before but it was nothing to the terrible yawning blackness that threatened to engulf her.

All she could do was hold on, *willing* her little girl to be all right. A tightness in her chest reminded her to breathe. She drew a ragged breath that sounded like a sob. Caro should never have taken her eyes off her, not for a second.

'Ariane!' The deep voice sliced the frigid air.

Large hands covered Caro's, pried them loose. She tried to resist, opened her mouth to cry out, when a little voice said, 'Uncle Jake?'

Caro's eyes snapped wide. Above her Jake Maynard filled her vision, surrounded by cerulean sky, like an angel in a painting. Except this dark angel's face was distorted with fear and, as she watched it transform, relief. Caro felt the same emotions unfurl within, so strong nausea punched her.

Her embrace weakened as her arms turned to water. Ariane moved out of her hold.

'Are you okay, Ariane? Where does it hurt?' That resonant voice was stark with emotion.

'I don't hurt anywhere.'

Caro could swear her heart dipped and lifted on the words. Ariane was okay, she was all right.

Her own eyelids flickered shut as emotion rose like a tide, filling her chest, closing her throat, forcing her to bite her lip against the sudden, appalling urge to cry.

'Caro?' That large hand was back again, this time lingering on the pulse at her throat then skimming up to her cheek and forehead. It was hard and surprisingly callused but incredibly gentle. Who'd have thought a man with such cold eyes could have such a tender touch?

'Is she…dead, Uncle Jake?'

The fear in Ariane's voice snapped Caro out of her reverie. After what had happened to Ariane's adoptive parents her fear of death wasn't surprising.

'I'm very much alive, sweetheart.' Even if Caro's voice didn't sound like her own, far too raspy and uneven.

When she opened her eyes this time two faces peered down at her. Dazed, she took in her daughter's hopeful expression and smiled. Her skin felt stiff, as if drawn too tight, but seeing Ariane smile tentatively back was worth the effort. Her heart thudded a double beat.

Then her gaze shifted to the broad-shouldered figure beside her daughter. Had she really thought Jake Maynard's eyes cold? They flared with a heat she felt all the way to her bones. For one suspended instant everything inside her stilled then burst into flame.

'Are you injured? Can you move?' His eyes belied his terse tone.

'Give me a minute.' She drew another quick breath, pressing the heel of her hand to her sternum, trying to force her lungs into action. 'I'm just winded.' Or too euphoric to feel pain. 'You're sure you're okay, Ariane? You didn't hit your head?'

Her daughter shook her head as tears filled her bright eyes. 'I'm sorry, Caro. I didn't mean to hit you.'

As if that wasn't exactly what Caro had aimed for. Better her than a tree.

'Why did you disobey Caro and climb right up the hill?' Jake's voice was low but steely and Ariane flinched. Caro told herself it was the voice of a man reacting to fear. They were lucky Ariane had escaped serious injury.

Seeing Ariane's tears spill, Caro found the energy to sit up, curling her legs under her and pulling Ariane to her. Her daughter burrowed close, her arms creeping around Caro's neck. Caro had never experienced anything like the burst of glorious happiness that exploded inside her.

This. This was what she'd missed all these years.

For so long Caro had been tempted to fantasise that her child hadn't been stillborn. But the fantasy was too dangerous and she'd forced herself to put it aside and face reality. Then, discovering Ariane *was* alive, Caro had been so focused on tracking her down that she hadn't allowed herself to imagine this moment. It had seemed like tempting fate into stealing away her daughter again.

She rocked Ariane, breathing in the scent of snow, pine trees and little girl. It was a perfume she'd remember for the rest of her days.

'Shh…it's okay, sweetie. No one's hurt.'

'Are you sure?' Jake Maynard frowned down at her, apparently still concerned about her. But Caro couldn't feel anything but the precious bundle in her arms.

'I'm fine.'

Ariane lifted her head. 'I won't do it again, Caro, I promise. I just wanted…' Her gaze flicked towards her uncle.

Suddenly Caro understood. 'You wanted to show Uncle Jake how well you could slide?'

Her ribs squeezed her heart. She'd seen Ariane's shy regard for the big man who was so concerned about her.

Ariane nodded. 'But I hurt you.'

'You must never do that again, Ariane,' Jake interjected, his voice gravelly. 'It's dangerous to go so high.'

Her little girl's head drooped lower and Caro rushed into speech.

'Ariane's promised never to do it again, haven't you, sweetie?' She watched her daughter's silent nod. 'And we're both okay.' Though Caro was beginning to feel an ache slide around her ribs and her shoulder throbbed. 'So why don't you show Uncle Jake how good you are at tobogganing? You could go together.'

Jake looked at her as if she'd sprouted another head and she hurried on. 'They say that if you come off a horse you should get on again straight away.' She met his stare, willing him to understand. There were enough scary things in Ariane's world without adding to them. 'I can vouch that it works.'

Caro had taken a toss off a pony as a kid and her father had insisted she get back on. It had stopped her developing a fear of horses, though they discovered later she'd fractured her wrist in the fall. She'd been more afraid of disappointing her disapproving father than of the pain.

But watching Ariane jump to her feet when Jake finally agreed there was time for *one* slide, Caro knew she was okay.

He pressed Caro again about injuries, but finally he was satisfied and she had time to gather herself, watching Jake and Ariane share the toboggan.

One slide turned into three, though at the end of each Jake strode across to check on her, his concern warming a part of her that had been frozen for a long time. Caro couldn't recall the last time any man had been genuinely concerned for her well-being. Not her father or brothers. Definitely not her ex-boyfriend who'd sold her out for personal gain.

By the time Jake announced it was time to go back, that he didn't want Caro waiting in the chill air any longer, Ariane was gleeful and her uncle's eyes had lost that stormy light.

Caro hoped that within a few days Ariane might forget how close to disaster they'd come. But her own spirits, after that initial burst of euphoria, plummeted.

It was clear Jake Maynard didn't merely feel obligated to look after his niece. He *cared* for her. And little Ariane beamed with pride and delight in his company.

What would happen when Caro claimed her daughter?

She had every right to do so. She'd been denied so much it hurt to think about the years of Ariane's life she'd missed. Even her name wasn't one Caro had chosen!

Once more she was tempted to come clean about her identity. Except Ariane was fragile and bewildered after losing her adoptive parents and Caro didn't want to add to her stress. She'd wait at least till she and Ariane had a good, strong relationship.

Plus there was another reason to delay. Jake Maynard was wealthy and powerful. If she went in assuming that because she had right on her side everything would be okay, things could go horribly wrong. Caro had been victim to the machinations of manipulative men. First Mike then her father. She'd be a fool to think Jake was any less dangerous.

He'd move heaven and earth to stop her claiming her daughter. Caro had little money of her own and her father would never support her in a court case. He'd do everything in his power to avoid scandal.

But that wasn't all. She drew a shuddering breath as she watched Jake, powerfully built and agile, utterly, fascinatingly masculine as he climbed the slope hand in hand with her daughter.

No, the worst of it was that Jake Maynard awoke something within her, a longing, that she'd never expected to experience again after years of numbness.

Desire. Not some vague sweet yearning but a piercing stab of need for his touch, his powerful body.

She sank her head in her hands. Was there any way out of this tangle?

CHAPTER SIX

JAKE COULDN'T STOP thinking about Caro Rivage. She was in his head every time he tried to read the report before him.

It wasn't figures he saw. It was Ariane's nanny, earlier today, throwing herself across the snow at risk of life and limb. Then later, limp and pale, making him curse himself for taking her word that she was uninjured.

He'd leaned down, about to lift her into his arms and carry her. For an instant he'd seen hunger in her expression. An answering beat of need had pulsed through his blood, but a second later her expression had morphed into something like fear.

Before he could prevent her she'd clambered to her feet, insisting on walking. But Jake wasn't fooled, he'd seen her stiff movements and insisted on a doctor.

Fortunately the doctor, checking out both nanny and child, had declared no harm done. Caro would suffer only bruising.

Yet Jake couldn't put her from his mind.

At least he knew he could trust her with Ariane. Caro might have been severely injured or killed with that desperate dive.

Jake's heart had been in his mouth. He wasn't used to being on the sidelines, watching others act. Guilt gouged him. He should have been the one to save Ariane but he hadn't been within reach.

The experience had changed him. Like varnish stripping away layers, there was nowhere now to hide the attraction he should *not* feel for his niece's nanny.

He tried telling himself it was because she was so good with Ariane. Even when his niece drew into herself or, very occasionally, acted up over something that to him seemed insignificant. There were times when he thought Caro too strict and others when her refusal to respond to a display of childish temper made him want to intervene. But he knew so little about child-rearing that he held back and each time he'd been glad, as Ariane became more like the engaging child he knew.

Frankly, those small displays of temper were a relief. When he'd first seen Ariane after the accident she'd been a shadow, withdrawn and wan.

Time, and Caro Rivage, were helping.

Yet hiring her hadn't been his best decision. Because no matter how he tried to distance himself, he couldn't ignore her. Or the awareness thickening his blood when she was near.

He didn't date staff.

He didn't pursue mousy women.

Yet, despite her penchant for wearing browns and dull navy, Caro Rivage wasn't mousy. The quiet manner couldn't conceal the lambent fire that blazed when she smiled at Ariane. Or when she forgot to be meek and treated him to a glimpse of that proud—and, he was sure, passionate— woman behind the mask.

That hidden woman made Jake's blood sizzle. He'd bet every million he'd made that hers sizzled too. Today her expression had made him want to forget every reason she was off limits. To break through the tension that hummed between them like electricity through a high-voltage cable.

He'd wanted to discover if she melted at his touch.

Even the way she dragged her hair into that tight bun, like a nanny a century ago, was perversely alluring. Instead of making her look frumpy, the style drew attention to the purity of her neck and jawline, and that small but exquisite mouth. Molten heat pooled in his groin at the memory of that mouth, as pink and delicate as a rosebud.

Rosebud? Delicate?

His last lover had been confident, sophisticated and gifted with a wide, mobile mouth that she used with sinful persuasiveness. *That* was the sort of woman he dated, clever, amusing and blatantly erotic.

Why did Caro Rivage tie him in knots? The other day he'd found himself pondering her neat collarbone, glimpsed beneath the V of another primly buttoned blouse, wondering if her skin was as soft as he imagined! He'd leaned in, drawn by the hint of sweet spice in the air as she moved, till he realised what he was doing.

Jake set his jaw, shoved his chair back and shut his laptop. It was midnight but he'd never settle to sleep. He'd work off this excess energy in the gym till he was too fatigued to think of rosebud mouths, creamy skin and that husky, feminine voice.

It was a good plan. The only trouble was, when he pushed the door open to the cellar fitness complex, there was Caro standing between the pool and the hot tub, head bent as she undid the belt of her robe.

Her hair, instead of being yanked back in a bun, fell in waves past her shoulders, making her look soft and young. The guarded, self-contained nanny was gone.

Jake's throat dried as she shrugged the robe off.

She was tall, slender but with a sweet, streamlined curve to her hips. She wore grey lace-edged knickers and matching singlet top. The outfit had none of the conscious seductiveness of a scanty bikini but she radiated an innocent eroticism that dragged his libido into raging life.

Every muscle tightened as blood hurtled to his groin. Every masculine response he'd fought to control roared into life.

Attraction.

Desire.

Downright hunger.

She must have heard the door or his sharp intake of breath because she turned and he saw her eyes widen before the swell of high, perfect breasts pressed against taut fabric caught his attention. She was braless and the little jiggle of her breasts as she sucked in air drove an arrow of carnal heat straight to his groin.

Through the thickening silence came a soft sound as the robe pooled around her bare feet.

Jake's brain told him not to move even as he covered the small distance and bent to pick it up. At the same time she did.

His fingers brushed hers and he stilled. The robe fell again and he drew in a breath scented with woman and warm spice. The perfume went to his head like a draught of fine cognac downed too fast.

She straightened and he grabbed the robe from the floor, discovering it still warm from her body. His fingers curled into the towelling, rather than reach for her.

She was Ariane's nanny. His employee.

Yet he couldn't move. His soles were cemented to the floor. He was so close he saw her shiver.

Watching the flush rise from her breasts to her throat and cheeks Jake knew she wasn't cold. He forced his gaze high and kept it there.

'You're having a swim?'

Congratulations, Maynard. Full points for observation.

His thought processes grew sluggish and it was the best he could do in lieu of marching back the way he'd come. That was what he should do but for the first time he could recall, his body refused to obey his brain.

She shuffled back a half step and he wondered in surprise if she found him intimidating. This last week she'd proved she was well able to stand up to him. He saw no fear in her face. Caro wore that guarded expression he'd come to hate, because his curiosity about her had grown insatiable.

He wanted to find out what went on behind that mask of calm as much as he wanted to taste her.

Neither, he told himself, was a good idea. He dropped the robe onto a lounger and managed his own half step away. The effort made him feel as if he'd run a half marathon.

'No. Not a swim.' The husky edge to her voice was pronounced, making it burr through his belly. 'I was going to try the hot tub, if that's okay.'

'Of course it's okay. Surely Neil made it clear you could use any of the facilities.' Jake wrestled with thoughts of Caro in the hot tub. Naked? The notion locked his knees so he hadn't a hope of walking away yet.

'I…thank you, he did.' She glanced down and away as if shy. Except that didn't ring true with the woman he'd got to know in the last week. Undaunted, courageous, fiercely determined, caring of Ariane and, when it came to herself, reserved to the point of blankness, that was Caro.

Besides, though he fought to keep his eyes on her face, he hadn't missed the way her nipples pebbled against her top. The area was well heated. He guessed it wasn't a reaction to cold, especially with that tell-tale blush.

Reaction to him?

The idea threatened his resolve.

He should go. He'd even managed to look past her to the door to the gym when she spoke in a rush as if needing to fill the throbbing silence.

'I thought the warm water might help.'

Jake's gaze wrenched back to her then down, skating over lithe curves to the expanse of pearly skin showing between her knickers and her top. A bruise marred her pale skin on one side, the sight reminding him of her bravery today and how he'd feared for her.

'Did the doctor give you something for pain?'

She tugged her top lower and she shook her head, hair

spilling around her shoulders. 'It's not that bad. I thought warm water might help me get to sleep. I feel…unsettled.'

Jake knew the feeling.

'I had a similar thought but I'm heading to the gym.'

Yet he didn't move.

Pale eyes blazed down at Caro. That silvery gaze was anything but cold. Wherever it touched her temperature soared.

Tonight, while she was suffering the after-effects of nearly losing her daughter on that snowy slope, the old, dark thoughts had circled again, waiting to swallow Caro whole. When she'd lost her baby the first time there'd been no one truly close to share her grief. Tonight she realised nothing had changed. Despite the friends she'd made in the intervening years, she was still essentially alone.

Except when she was with Jake Maynard.

The realisation slammed into her, fascinating and terrible.

With him she felt different. More alive. Less alone.

It had to be because they had a common purpose, caring for Ariane. Except as the atmosphere stretched taut around them she knew this wasn't about Ariane. It was about her as a woman and Jake as a man.

Did he feel this throb of awareness?

Caro couldn't afford to think so. Not with so much at stake. This masquerade. Ariane.

She *couldn't* risk her position here! She should run as far and fast as she could in the opposite direction.

But how could she leave when Jake looked at her that way? As if she were Venus herself, striking mortal men with yearning. A spark ignited deep inside that grew and grew as he ate her up with his eyes.

The old longing to be wanted rose again, her fatal weakness.

In childhood she'd hoped if she was good enough her

family would love her. When that never happened, she'd
fallen for Mike, convinced too easily of his affection. Now
here she was again, craving connection.

What would it be like to be truly wanted? And by Jake,
the man who occupied too many of her thoughts both waking and sleeping.

Today she'd faced the stark reality of life and death.
She'd almost lost her daughter. Was lucky to be alive herself. Recklessness rose. She wanted to live in the moment.

No. No. No! Think about Ariane. The reason you're here.

She set her jaw, summoning the will to move.

'Caro.' Jake's husky whisper carved a channel through
her good intentions. His hands closed around her arms,
gently enough that she could have broken his hold.

Caro told herself that was what she'd do. Soon.

His head swooped down, his lips brushing hers and she
lost her train of thought.

That hard mouth wasn't hard at all. It was soft, tender,
impossibly tempting. Long ribbons of fire unfurled within
her and she saw showers of sparks behind eyelids she hadn't
realised she'd closed.

Caro drew in a breath rich with citrus, bergamot and
something she'd almost forgotten, that tangy, inviting scent
of healthy male flesh.

The reality of Jake touching her, kissing her with infinite care sent need shuddering through her. She swayed
and reached up to steady herself. Her fingers found soft
cotton, taut over hot muscle. And more, his heart thundering as fast as hers. That undid her. The knowledge he was
vulnerable too.

Caro splayed her fingers over his sculpted chest and
felt him shiver.

She shivered too, the ripple starting at her nape and
running down her arms, her spine and right through her
middle.

One second. Just a second more, then I'll be sensible.

She'd firmed her hands on his chest, ready to push away when Jake let go of her arms. Dazed, Caro registered the grinding pain of rejection and told herself it was for the best.

Except it wasn't rejection.

Jake grasped her waist. Her top had ridden up and those hard fingers spanned bare flesh. Heat drenched her. She wanted those hands on her body. Everywhere. She no longer felt self-conscious that he'd found her in drab underwear since she didn't have a swimsuit here.

All that mattered was the intoxicating warmth of his touch. His deep hum of approval vibrated through her as her mouth opened to his and their tongues embarked on a dance of mutual seduction.

The taste of him. The tenderness. The languorous sensuality. There was heat, demand, a sense of bridled ferocity as he leaned in and she bowed backwards, losing her balance, reliant on Jake to keep her from falling.

Caro's hands slipped up over wide shoulders to the back of his head, fingertips slipping into thick hair that, like his mouth, was surprisingly soft.

Now there was no thought of leaving, of doing anything more than giving in to this compulsion.

Her breathing grew short and her pulse unsteady as the kiss became more than slow seduction. She needed Jake as surely as her oxygen-starved lungs needed air.

She gloried in it all. From the feel of his muscled thighs against hers to the possessive clasp of those powerful hands and the magic of his mouth moving with hers. She shuddered as Jake's tongue swept deep in a caress that detonated explosions right through her.

When he pulled back to nip at her lower lip, then press kisses to the corner of her mouth and down to her jawline,

Caro muffled a cry. He made her feel things she'd never felt before.

'Don't,' he murmured, nuzzling that sensitive spot at the base of her neck. 'I want to hear you.'

Her eyes snapped open. Eyes the colour of mercury, silvery bright, snagged hers.

'I want to know what you like.' His voice was different. Husky deep, like treacle over gravel, its rich abrasiveness turning everything inside her molten.

'Everything. I like everything.'

Caro didn't care that her voice betrayed her need. Not when he pressed close so his erection nudged her. She squirmed, planting her hands on his shoulders, trying to get closer.

'Everything?' One straight black eyebrow rose. His chest pushed her sensitised breasts as he drew a breath. Instantly her hard nipples ached and the ache drew down like an arrow, through her belly to the empty place between her legs.

She hesitated. A lifetime's practice in self-denial and caution closed her throat.

But not for long. Despite the alarm bells clanging in the back of her mind, and the hazy thought that for reasons she couldn't recall this was a bad idea, it felt so good. In Jake's arms Caro felt a wonder and a yearning that was totally new.

'Everything,' she gasped, cupping the back of his skull and tugging his mouth back to hers.

Now there was no languor, just fire and sizzling sensation. He looped an arm around her back while his other hand strayed over skin and fragile cotton, exploring, making her gasp. His fingers slid between her thighs, over her panties. She pushed up to meet his touch, eliciting a growl of approval from the mouth welded to hers.

The sound burred over her bare arms and slid like a liquid channel, down to the place where she burned for him.

Caro was aware of movement. The wide lounger behind her legs, then she was in Jake's arms, eyes popping open as he lowered her onto it and came down above her.

Fire was everywhere. Fire and longing. She plucked at his T shirt, drawing it up as she curled her ankles around his legs to stop him moving away. The press of his body set her alight.

'Wait.' It might have been an order except his voice was raw with a need that matched hers. Jake pulled back to straddle her hips, yanking his T shirt off.

Caro's mouth dried. She'd never seen a man with a body like his. Wide shoulders, a powerful, deep chest with a light fuzz of dark hair that accentuated the contours of muscles. Below that smoother skin, taut with more muscle that tapered to a narrow waist.

Caro reached for him but he caught her hands and shook his head. 'Soon.' He bent low, pushing up her old camisole top. Then he took her nipple in his mouth, drawing hard.

Caro didn't mean to cry out but the shocking delight was too exquisite. Need sang in her blood and she fought to free her wrists and reach for him.

'Patience, Caro.' He crooned her name, turning it into a caress as he moved to her other breast, using his free hand, his lips and tongue to work magic.

She felt almost overwrought at the sensations he evoked. After years of celibacy and emotional numbness, he brought her to life with a vengeance. Delight danced through her and the need for more, more, more.

When he moved lower, his tongue slicking her navel and beyond, Caro didn't know whether to weep or cheer. She loved what he was doing but she was teetering on an edge, where one nudge would make her fall off the precipice. She wanted to be with him when that happened.

Then his downward progress stopped. He traced a wide arc low across her belly. Then he looked up and the question in his eyes punctured the delirium of need.

'Caro?' For the first time since she'd known him, Jake looked hesitant. A line appeared between those dark eyebrows and his chest expanded as if on a sustaining breath. 'Are these what I think?'

Even then her bewitched brain couldn't make sense of his words. She levered herself up. He was looking at the pale striations across her abdomen.

Stretch marks.

Acquired during her eight and a quarter months of pregnancy.

Caro blinked, watching that tanned, capable hand stop on her belly. Jake's touch seemed more intimate than if he'd caressed her between the legs where she was wet for him. Sex was a finite thing, its pleasure fleeting. But carrying her child—that had changed her at the most fundamental level. It was the most precious thing yet also the source of an anguish that had haunted her for years.

She swallowed, her throat raspy and tight.

'You had a child?'

'Yes.' She didn't think of lying. She couldn't deny her daughter. Despite the masquerade she'd been forced to adopt to get close to Ariane, Caro would never do that.

It was madness to be upset now. The past was over. The future promised more than she'd dared hope for. Yet his question brought all today's emotions to the surface and pierced the armour she'd tried to build around her memories. Suddenly the past with all its terrible pain was upon her. Her guilt that she hadn't been able to keep her baby with her. She should have *known*, should have done something…

'Where is it now, Caro?'

'She.' The single word was automatic.

When the nuns had told her that her baby was dead they'd spoken of *it*, not *her*. There'd been no chance to see the child, no grave to visit, because her father had deemed it better.

Her father. He had so much to answer for. It had taken such effort even to prise out the information that she'd had a daughter.

Thinking of her lost baby as she, not it, had been a reminder that her child had been real, despite the determination of those around her to pretend she'd never existed.

Caro tried to swallow but her throat was completely clogged.

Maybe it was the gentle way Jake spoke, the concern in his eyes, now the colour of burnished pewter, dark with shadows. Maybe it was because she'd never had to answer that question before. Suddenly she felt as lost as she had years ago, both her body and her arms empty, her child taken from her.

She squeezed her eyes shut, willing the moment to pass. Trying to suppress the cold shivers.

'Where is she, Caro? Your daughter?'

It was his tenderness that undid her. She told herself it no longer mattered. She was over the grief, moving on to happier times. Yet it seemed that buried deep within was a residue of anguish that even recent events hadn't erased.

Frantically she gulped air and heard the terrible sawing sound of a woman on the edge. Past and present coalesced. Instead of seeing the little girl on the mountain who'd almost died today, it was the tiny, silent baby she'd barely glimpsed as they whipped it away. Adrenaline pulsed in Caro's bloodstream and her mouth crumpled.

'I lost her,' she whispered. 'I lost her.'

She gave up the battle and let the burning tears fall.

CHAPTER SEVEN

JAKE LAY BESIDE her and gathered Caro close, her head against his shoulder. Her tears tracking across him. His mouth set as she shook, her hiccupping breaths proof of her battle for control.

The contained, capable woman he'd begun to know disappeared. Wrapped against him she seemed fragile, slighter than when she stood up to him or when she'd kissed him. He tightened his hold.

'It's okay, Caro. Let it out.'

It didn't take an expert to know this pain had been eating away at her. Her tormented expression and the desolation in her eyes proved that. As did the fact she'd gone from the edge of rapture to blind grief in seconds. Her broken voice replayed in his ears and pity filled him.

How long had she carried this burden? Had today's drama dragged it to the surface?

Jake half rolled onto his back and pulled her across him while one hand went to the tumble of soft waves that had loosened as they kissed. He stroked her head, combing his fingers through her hair.

It was his fault she'd gone into meltdown. Why hadn't he smothered his curiosity?

But given Caro's age her baby would be young. He couldn't imagine her leaving her child in order to look after someone else's. It hadn't seemed to fit.

Now it did.

He swallowed regret, cursing his determination to uncover her secrets. Yet he was glad he knew.

Not because he was an expert in comforting distressed women. Though as a one-time peacekeeper in areas ravaged by natural disaster and violence he had some experience. But because his need to know about Caro was insatiable.

He was fascinated by her and not just because he'd doubted her suitability as Ariane's nanny.

His belly clenched as another shudder racked her. What would it be like to lose a child, one you'd carried in your body?

Jake remembered his sister Connie, her stiff upper lip as she'd told him via computer link about another miscarriage and their decision to adopt. He'd been on the other side of the world but he'd *felt* his sister's heartbreak. Jake had wanted to go to her but had been wary of interfering. The days of it being just the two of them against the world had gone. Connie had had her husband and Jake had feared intruding on their shared grief.

Who did Caro have?

There was no ring on her finger, no mention of a husband. Surely if she had a partner she wouldn't be so eager for a live-in position?

How long had she bottled up this pain?

Protectiveness engulfed him. Her abrupt transition from carnal excitement to anguish indicated she had a long way to go to come to terms with this.

Did you ever come to terms?

He hadn't given much thought to himself as a father, though over the last year he'd thought about creating a permanent base and finding a long-term partner. His experience of families and parents made him wary.

His father had abandoned them when Jake was born. As for his mother, she'd ignored her responsibilities, focusing on her own pleasure. With her stunning looks it hadn't been hard to find lovers who'd shower her with the trinkets, trips and the lifestyle she craved. That kept her away from home for weeks and months at a time till finally she found a rich aristocrat, holidaying in Australia, who wanted her long term. She'd abandoned her kids without a second thought.

Yet now he had Ariane, Jake discovered a strong streak of paternal protectiveness. It hadn't been simple, learning to accommodate a child in what had been a bachelor life. But he couldn't imagine life without her. Thinking of her rare smiles and growing trust made him glow.

If he were to lose her...

Jake rocked Caro in his arms, his lips moved against her hair as he murmured that it was all right. When, of course, it could never be all right.

Like a douche of iced water memory chilled him. The memory of Caro that first night, motionless and intent as she watched Ariane sleep. There'd been something so eerily focused about her that his sixth sense had prickled. He'd known something was wrong. Now he understood. Caro looked at Ariane but remembered her lost child.

Something plunged through his body, a weight descending to crash into his gut.

Caro's hiccups stopped and the shivers eased but she didn't move away. Instead it felt as if she was trying to burrow in his chest. Surprisingly Jake didn't mind one bit. She'd touched something inside. A chord of fellow feeling.

More. Something to do with Caro herself. He'd wondered what lay behind her façade of prim control. Now he knew at least one of her secrets. And she fascinated him more than ever.

Fascinated and attracted.

His mouth twisted. Whatever was between them, this wasn't simply sexual attraction. Sex was here—very much so, as his unsatisfied body reminded him—but so were compassion and something he didn't have a name for.

'Sorry.' Caro sniffed and rubbed her cheeks. 'I can't believe I melted down like that.' She moved her shoulders as if gathering herself to pull away. Jake's hold tightened.

'You needed to let it out.'

'Not like that. Not sobbing all over you like...' She paused and he felt the sear of her breath against his skin. It felt like a caress.

Despite everything, his body still equated Caro with sexual hunger. Jake shoved the knowledge aside, ashamed.

She lifted her head and red-rimmed eyes met his. 'I apologise. I don't know what came over me. I'm *never* emotional in public.'

Jake's eyebrows rose. 'It was hardly public.'

She shook her head and dark curls tickled him. 'It was weak and selfish to sob all over you.' She pulled back a little.

Normally the idea of a woman crying over him would make Jake avoid her. Even now he felt discomfited by the display of such visceral emotion. He'd learned to bury emotions deep. Yet when Caro voiced the same idea, as if her grief were shameful, he wanted to reassure her.

'It's been an eventful day. Emotionally charged. Seeing Ariane in danger triggered sad memories.'

Her gaze caught his and a zap like an electric current coursed through him. Then, in a flurry of movement, Caro scrambled off the lounger. By the time he stood she was shrugging into the towelling robe, wrapping it close as if for protection.

Jake's brow knotted. Surely she didn't think she needed protecting from *him*?

But seeing the hectic colour in her cheeks, he guessed she was embarrassed.

'Caro, I—'

'Please, Jake.' She paused, the picture of discomfort.

It was the first time she'd used his name. He wished it had been in the throes of passion instead of like this. His fingers curled hard and he shoved them into his pockets.

She opened her mouth to say something, something important by the look on her face, then she shook her head. 'I need to go.'

'Stay!' He made himself stand immobile rather than reach for her. 'Have that spa. I'll leave you in privacy.' Stupid to feel rejected because she needed time alone.

Her mouth hitched at one side but it wasn't a smile. Sadness was there and a tension he supposed came from embarrassment. 'That's kind of you but I'll go to my room. I need to think.'

She hurried away, leaving him staring.

Caro had plenty of time to think but it didn't help. Whenever she made up her mind to tell Jake the truth all the reasons it was a terrible idea crowded in.

Hair damp from the shower, wrapped in her fluffy robe, she curled in the deep window seat of her turret room, her back against tapestry cushions that softened the stone wall. She hugged her knees and watched the sun rise with relief.

She'd spent sleepless hours staring at the massive peaks glimmering pale against the starry night. The view had been peaceful, at odds with the churning in her stomach. She'd wrestled with her conscience. She couldn't let Jake think her child had died. Or that she was simply a nanny.

He wasn't the cold-hearted man she'd thought. Jake was caring, not just with Ariane but with her. He'd held her and showed no impatience when her tears interrupted their passion. Her limited experience of men told her his forbearance, putting her needs ahead of his, was rare.

The gentle way he'd embraced her, the way he'd rocked her, no one had ever done that. Maybe her mother when Caro was tiny, but no one since. When she hurt she was expected to suck it up and get on with things. Even after losing her baby—no, make that having her baby snatched—she'd got little support. The nuns in the convent had seemed kind but with a distant, impersonal charity. There'd been no hugs, no shoulder to cry on.

No one like Jake.

She'd known the man a week yet in his arms, with that deep voice murmuring reassurance, she'd felt such comfort. Such healing.

Caro drew a shuddery sigh. Her chest expanded with the first free breath she'd taken all night.

Watching dawn's rosy fingers spread across the mountains, turning indigo to peach, apricot and finally the dazzling white of snow, she made up her mind.

They all had to face the truth some time.

Today would be the day.

She'd do it one piece at a time. First the revelation that she was Ariane's mother. Then, after Jake had time to accept that, the rest. The full story would be a lot to absorb in one chunk.

Decision made, her tight shoulders dropped, the tension in her neck easing. Jake might react badly but the longer she delayed, the worse it would be.

Her relief lasted exactly fifty-five minutes. Till her phone rang while she was pinning up her hair, ready to find Jake. Few people had this number. Her lawyer, Zoe, and a couple of friends.

'Hello?'

'At last, she answers!' The terse voice splintered shards of ice down her spine. Caro froze, dropping the last hairpin. It seemed the only part of her still working was her heart, beating double quick.

'Father.'

'You remember who I am now, Carolina? That surprises me.' He thundered on. 'How dare you make me call you personally? I don't have time for this nonsense but my staff tell me you haven't answered their messages. You haven't said when you'll arrive for your brother's party. I'm forced to waste time doing the work of secretaries!'

His voice boomed so loud Caro lifted the phone from her ear. Remnants of old habits stirred. Habits of obedience and meekness. For years she'd let this man run her life and see where it had got her.

She wanted to scream that he'd stolen her child and let her spend years uselessly grieving. But she wouldn't scream, wouldn't respond to his bullying with emotion. Instead she'd be calm and in control, in contrast to his arrogant orders and malicious jibes.

When she *did* confront him it would be in person. She wanted to look him in those choleric blue eyes and let him see that he no longer had power over her. She wanted to see his reaction when the mouse of the family finally stood up to him.

'Are you there? Why aren't you answering?' Even at this distance that voice, like a thunderstorm crashing over mountains, made her skin twitch.

'I'm here, Father. And I did respond to the messages. I gave my apologies. I won't be able to attend—'

'Nonsense! Of course you'll be here.'

'Not this time.' Caro was proud of her even tone.

The silence that followed resonated with foreboding. No one, ever, said no to her father. Not her stepmother or half-brothers, not the prime minister, not anyone among St Ancilla's rich and powerful.

Caro almost wished she could see him, though the thought of being near him made her feel physically ill. Was there surprise as well as fury on that mottled face?

His voice when it came sent another polar freeze through her. 'Your brother's engagement is a major event. All the family will be there, you included.' He paused as if hearing her silent protest that she wasn't really part of the family. She hadn't been since he remarried and fathered the sons he'd so wanted.

'There'll be photos tomorrow evening before the first informal celebration. You'll be there and the rest of the week, doing your duty.'

Caro gathered her breath, storing it up in her lungs till she thought she'd burst. Her hands turned clammy and the butterflies in her stomach were the size of sea eagles.

'I'm afraid that's impossible. I—'

'I'll say this once, Carolina.' He said her name like an insult. 'It's vital we present a united front for this engagement. The wedding is important. Whatever you're doing in Switzerland you'll drop it immediately and come home.'

Shocked, her breath hissed in.

'Oh, yes, I know you're in Switzerland. My security staff keep me informed. I haven't asked them to dig deeper. I'm not interested. However…' he paused and the air turned heavy as if anticipating the next lightning strike '…if within the next hour my secretary doesn't receive details of your arrival time, I'll instruct security to find you and bring you home. By force if necessary. They're on standby. I'm told they can be with you within two hours.'

Caro opened her mouth to say kidnap was an offence when the line went dead.

The phone fell to her bed and she stared at it as if at a venomous snake.

Caro wrapped her arms around her ribcage where her heart thundered. She imagined the men in dark suits, driving vehicles with blacked-out windows. They gave her the creeps. They'd been the ones to spirit her back to St Ancilla when her father discovered her pregnancy, and to the isolated convent on the north of the island. They'd kept a discreet but not invisible watch on the convent and ensured she didn't run away before the baby was born.

She told herself they had no jurisdiction here. She could appeal to Jake for help. He'd protect her.

Then she imagined how that would play out. Swiss police, official reports, maybe press interest from those reporters who still kept an eye on this valley because of its connections to the rich and powerful.

Worse, she imagined Jake's reaction when he discovered not only that she was Ariane's mother, but who her family was, all in one terrible sweep. Fear pounded through her, drying her throat and churning her stomach.

She'd already decided she needed to handle this carefully. If he was bombarded with it all at once, especially with her father's henchmen battering at the door, he wouldn't take it well. He'd see her as the enemy, here to take Ariane from him any way she could. He was as likely to hand her to her father's goons as keep her from them.

Caro turned and paced, torn between distress and fury. There was something about all this she didn't understand. That final threat of her father's hadn't been simply because she'd annoyed him.

'It's vital we present a united front... The wedding is important.'

She knew enough about her father to understand he wasn't concerned about her brother's love life. It wasn't a love match but an arranged marriage. Why was her father so adamant they all be there, smiling and putting on a good show?

Caro shook her head. No time for that now. She had to figure out what to do. Unfortunately, she realised as she considered it from every angle, she didn't have a choice. Not if she wanted a chance to discuss Ariane's future calmly with Jake without her father interfering.

Jake strode the corridor towards his office. It was early but after a night of little sleep he might as well start work. The consortium he was trying to entice into this project was proving difficult to pin down. He needed to concentrate on that rather than Caro.

The woman perplexed him, intrigued and attracted him. He couldn't recall responding to any woman like this. Not even Fiona, his ex-lover, the woman he'd fleetingly considered as a possible spouse.

Every time he thought he had Caro pegged she surprised him. She awakened a host of unexpected feelings.

He turned a corner and slammed to a halt. There, silhouetted against the window, was Caro near the door to his office.

Jake recalled the feel of her slender body curving into his, the baffling intensity of the emotions she'd evoked and the less puzzling arousal. Then she'd worn next to nothing. Now she was in one of her drab skirt and jacket sets, in a colour that reminded him of mud. And still excitement throbbed in his blood.

She stared at a painting on the wall, the early sunlight limning her profile. Jake told himself she wasn't stunning the way some of his lovers had been, yet there was something about that pure profile, the angle of her chin, the neat curve of her ear and that long slender neck that drew his eye.

She moved and he caught a glint of russet in her brown hair. It reminded him of the fire that ignited in his belly last night. And of the volatile, passionate woman who'd turned to flame when he'd kissed and caressed her.

Heat punched low. All night he'd struggled against the need to go to her room.

To check if she was okay, he reasoned.

To take up where they'd left off, he knew.

Only the depth of her hurt had stopped him.

Caro swung around. Had she heard the sudden heft of his breath? Her eyes widened.

It was back, that pulsing heat. She bit her lip and he absorbed the fact she looked nervous, no, more than that. Scared. She swivelled back to the painting, fingers plaiting restlessly before her.

Her fear made him hesitate. She *couldn't* be scared of him.

'You like it?' Jake asked as he neared, forcing himself to look at the picture. He'd barely paid any attention to it. In the flood of morning light he discovered the face of a sombre man holding a globe and surrounded by maps and papers.

Caro shrugged and he noticed the movement was stiff, as if her shoulders were too tight.

Was she self-conscious after last night? He couldn't blame her, yet he wanted to make her turn and look at him.

'It's…interesting. At least four hundred years old.' She spoke quickly as if to fill the silence. As if nervous. 'I can't work out what it's doing here, in the direct sunlight. It should be in a protected position.'

'Maybe it's a copy.' Jake knew little about art and, though the castle's owner had provided an inventory, he hadn't looked at it. He was here to work, and build a relationship with Ariane, not stare at paintings.

Caro shook her head. 'Unlikely.' She bent closer. 'Highly unlikely.'

'You know old paintings?' If he'd been watching the portrait instead of her he would have missed her flinch.

'I studied art history.' She darted a sideways glance that didn't meet his eyes.

'I don't remember that on your résumé.'

She lifted one shoulder. 'I didn't finish and it didn't seem relevant.'

True, but Jake wanted to know more. Much more.

'It's my fault about the painting.' At his words she swung

to face him. Jake felt that familiar tug low in his belly when their eyes met. As if someone dragged a weight through his insides. 'It looked gloomy so I had it moved out of my study.'

'I see.' For a moment longer their eyes held, then her gaze slewed back to the painting and Jake found himself cursing her discomfort with him. He preferred her passionate and bold.

And eager for sex.

Heat spiralled like smoke up from his groin and he had to work at keeping his distance. Clearly she was nervous.

'I think you should move it.' Another darting glance. 'It shouldn't be here in the full sun.'

'I'll get Neil onto it.' He paused, watching the tic of her pulse at her throat and the way her hands refused to be still. 'Caro, we need to—'

'I have to—'

Both pulled up short. 'You first,' he invited.

Caro nodded but didn't look eager. 'In your office?'

'Sure.' He pushed open his study door and invited her to precede him. As she walked past he caught a hint of her warm, spicy scent and it went straight to his head. For a second he closed his eyes.

He'd be good. He wouldn't seduce the nanny in his office.

No matter how much he wanted to.

Caro's fingers twisted together, echoing the churning inside. This was more difficult than she'd thought.

She'd half hoped she could blame last night and the way she'd thrown herself at Jake on the high-octane mix of fear and elation resulting from Ariane's near accident. But it was still there, the desire for his touch, the yearning for his tenderness and passion.

Worse, she wanted to blurt out everything, ignoring the need to approach this carefully.

Hurriedly she looked down, veiling her eyes from that sharp scrutiny.

Her heart hammered and no matter how she tried she couldn't pull off the mask of composure she'd come to rely on. Because she wasn't just fighting her attraction to Ariane's uncle. Now her father had thrust his oar into these turbulent waters she felt in danger of being tugged under by forces too strong to withstand.

Now, instead of telling Jake the truth and trusting he was truly a decent man with Ariane's best interests at heart, she was forced to lie again. Because she couldn't afford to risk him withdrawing and taking her daughter away.

She felt sick.

'Caro?' A firm hand closed around her elbow. 'You look like you're going to keel over. Here.' He ushered her to a chair. 'Sit.'

She subsided thankfully, even as she castigated herself for weakness. This wasn't how she'd meant to face him. But when she'd seen him, all her hard-won resolve had disintegrated. She'd jabbered on about art instead of cutting to the point.

'Thank you. Sorry, I'm fine. I...' She shook her head. 'Something has come up. I need to go away for the rest of the week. I know it's not usual and I should give you notice but it's urgent.'

'Away?' His eyebrows tilted down. In curiosity or annoyance?

'To St Ancilla. I had a call from my…father this morning.' She couldn't suppress the shiver down her spine.

'Bad news?'

'A family matter. I'm needed there.' She paused and licked dry lips. 'Normally I'd never dream of asking for time off so soon but I don't have a choice.' Her father had seen to that. Caro straightened. 'I'd be back next week.'

Finally she looked him square in the face. What Jake saw there made everything inside him still. Not just tension but distress, and that fear he'd picked up on in the corridor. He'd read it as embarrassment after last night's intimacy. Clearly it was caused by something far deeper.

Not everything revolves around you, Maynard.

'Your family needs you.'

'I know it's inconvenient and I apologise but—'

He stopped her with a wave of his hand. Clearly this was important. From her expression he guessed serious illness or accident.

'Of course you can go.' What wouldn't he have given for the chance to spend even a few extra minutes with Connie, instead of being informed from the far side of the world that his sister was dead? 'Take what time you need. Lotte and I will manage.'

For a second her lip wobbled then she nodded briskly. 'I'll be back next week. You can count on me.'

CHAPTER EIGHT

'JAKE, DID YOU say it was St Ancilla Caro went to?'

Reluctantly Jake looked up from his emails. This project grew more complex by the hour and he wasn't devoting as much time to it as he should. He'd spent the morning with Ariane.

On the other hand, his niece's ease with him felt like victory. He owed her thawing, in part, to Caro, who'd done an amazing job in a short time. He'd been right to hire her.

Neil sank into the chair on the other side of his desk. His expression was unreadable, yet the fine hairs on the back of Jake's neck stood to attention.

'That's right. What's happened?'

Jake leaned back in his chair. A tough early life, a stint in the army then years devoted to wheeling and dealing in the turbulent field of international finance meant it took a lot to unnerve him.

'I tracked down another on our list of potential investors and discovered they were in St Ancilla for a big event.' Neil passed his tablet across the desk. It displayed a news article. If you could call it real news. Some royal event.

'So? Wait a few days then make contact.'

'Check out the photo. The second one.'

Jake looked again, scrolling past a photo of a young, formally dressed couple smiling at the camera with all the animation of marionettes. Prince Paul of St Ancilla and Princess Eva of Tarentia, just engaged.

Beneath was a group photo. An ornate balcony on an imposing building, crammed with elegant women and men in heavily decorated dress uniforms.

'And?' Jake had no interest in aristocracy. He did business with them but his personal experiences with them hadn't been happy. First had been the entitled foreigner who'd lured his mother away, on condition she abandon her kids. Then just months ago, his own girlfriend suggested he put Ariane in an orphanage rather than bother with her. Both had been uncaring of anyone else, expecting the world to revolve around them.

'Look closely. The one in blue.'

Jake frowned. Several of those uniforms were blue, plus a blonde in ice blue and…

He stared. It couldn't be.

Of course it couldn't. The woman in the deep blue dress was a vibrant redhead, not a brunette. Yet Jake felt adrenaline burst into his blood with a jolt.

He zoomed in on the woman, amazed at the likeness.

'Princess Carolina of St Ancilla. The King's eldest child.' Neil's voice was flat with suppressed excitement.

'*Princess* Carolina?' Carolina. Caro.

No. It was impossible. Mere coincidence.

Yet the buzz in Jake's bloodstream didn't abate.

'Yes, but she's not his heir. Her younger brother is. Carolina isn't in the limelight these days. She lives fairly quietly in the north of the island though she's very active in a number of charities, especially relating to children.'

Jake peered at the woman. She was a ringer for Caro, except for the clothes and hair. And the royal connections.

'Maybe our Caro is a distant relative.'

Our Caro? His choice of words made her sound—

'There's more.' Neil took the device and opened another page, handing it back. With his usual efficiency he'd collated a precis on the woman.

The Princess had a string of names, had been born almost twenty-five years ago and lost her mother early. Her father had remarried when she was two and she had three half-brothers. She'd studied in the US but didn't finish her degree. There'd been a scandal. He read headlines about wild parties and drug use. Jake wasn't surprised. Most of Fiona's privileged friends preferred parties to work. What did surprise him was that after returning to St Ancilla, Princess Carolina had all but dropped off the radar. She didn't live in the palace, merely appearing in the press at charity events or major royal celebrations like this, her half-brother's engagement.

He scrolled lower, studying the shots Neil had collected. Stiff and formal on the same balcony with her family when she was a little girl. Again in her teens, looking almost gawky despite her expensive clothes and with her flame-coloured hair now turning auburn, her head turned towards her father, her expression curiously closed. A shot of her with one of her brothers, both smiling for the camera but neither looking happy.

Jake began to feel almost sorry for her. Had the wild partying been rebellion after an unhappy childhood?

Then he scrolled lower and his breath caught.

This photo was different. Candid. He doubted she knew it had been taken. She wore casual clothes, her hair in a ponytail and she was in a crowd with other young people. At a party, by the look of it. She was half turned away, looking over her shoulder, but there was no mistaking the warmth in her expression as she smiled at someone beyond the camera. Her eyes, a remarkable deep violet, glowed. *She* glowed. Jake felt the impact of her joy judder through him.

He swallowed, mesmerised by those eyes. They were so like Ariane's that for a moment everything, his pulse and his breathing, seemed to stop. He'd always thought the colour rare. Maybe not so on St Ancilla.

He touched the screen, enlarged the photo and then his breath really did stop.

There, on the back of her shoulder next to the strap of her top, was a small birthmark shaped like a comma.

Jake had seen that mark three nights ago.

It had peeked out beneath the strap of a grey camisole when he'd held Caro in his arms.

By midnight the scowl on Jake's face threatened to take up permanent residence. His emotions veered between shock—he who'd believed nothing had the power to surprise him any more—fury and grim determination.

There was pain too, a sliver of hurt that he'd allowed her to play him as she had, but he buried that deep.

There was no time for such luxuries. With every hour came a new revelation. That was what happened when you could afford the best investigators.

No wonder the initial check of her application hadn't found any criminal record for Caro Rivage. She didn't exist, except technically, for Rivage was the family's name though royalty traditionally didn't use it.

Caro was royal. Daughter of a king. Her full name and titles took up four lines on the report filling his computer screen.

Jake stared at it and felt the blood jump in his arteries as if seeking a way out. His body was screwed so tight even an hour with a punching bag had done nothing to relieve it.

Once they knew which direction to pursue, the investigators hadn't taken long to prove Princess Carolina and Caro Rivage were the same person.

Some of what she'd said was even true. She had worked in a preschool. The references had checked out because she'd actually worked as a nanny for a couple of families. In between swanning off in couture clothes to charity events and royal parties. That in itself was curious. From socialite royal to nanny wasn't a normal progression. But she was definitely royal.

There was a photo of her taken six months ago at a ball, wearing a tiara and a complacent smile that made him grind his teeth. A tall guy with medals across his chest and a hungry expression was at her side, holding her as if he didn't want to let her out of his sight.

Jake swore and shoved his chair back, stalking the length of the room. He understood the feeling. The woman couldn't be trusted an inch.

Yet still he registered that hum of expectation deep inside. The expectation of what would happen when he held her in his arms again. Even her bald-faced deceit hadn't destroyed his desire for her.

He ploughed his fingers through his hair and spun on his heel, pacing again.

She'd lied from the first. Not only about her identity. About everything.

That scene by the spa? Had she waited for him, knowing he often worked out at night? She'd sucked him in with her passion and counterfeit distress. First reel him in by giving him a taste of what he wanted, a taste of mind-blowing sex, then play on his protective instincts to stop things going further. She'd teased and distracted him.

Ego told him she *had* been attracted to him. He'd seen the evidence almost from the first.

His brain said it was all a lie. Or if it wasn't, even if she had wanted him, she'd wanted something more, to lure him into feeling sorry for her. She'd wanted him in the palm of her soft little hands.

That sob story about needing to go to her family? The implication, unspoken but there in every throbbing silence, that some terrible tragedy had occurred? All lies.

She'd gone to a *party*!

Was the tall guy with the possessive look there with her? Or had she moved on to some other gullible bloke?

Jake frowned as pain radiated up his arm. He looked down and saw he'd pounded his fist against the stone wall beside the bookshelves. Gingerly he unfurled his fingers, feeling pain slice through his hand and seeing a graze of blood.

The woman had got under his skin in ways he could barely believe.

Even Fiona hadn't made him so furious. Because he'd begun to see her true colours despite her efforts to paper over the cracks of her innately selfish personality.

With Caro... Carolina, he'd been completely taken in. Except for that tingle of premonition that she wasn't what she'd seemed. He'd been distracted by his need to find a way to connect with his niece, and his attraction for a charlatan.

She hadn't just lied about her identity. If only that were the worst of it!

He shoved his hands in his pockets, peering out at moon-washed peaks, taking in the twinkle of lights further down the valley that made him feel, for the first time in years, as isolated as he'd been as a kid, shutting himself off in an attempt to lessen the pain of his mother's desertion.

He'd actually *felt* for Caro. Had wanted to care for her as much as he'd wanted her in his bed.

Whereas she didn't want him. She wanted Ariane.

Nausea swirled in his belly and he swallowed the rancid taste of disgust.

If the investigators were right, Ariane's birth mother was Princess Carolina of St Ancilla. Everything pointed to it. The way she'd been bundled home when news broke of her wild partying. Her seclusion at a convent on the northern end of the island for the better part of a year. The fact that Ariane's adoption took place in the same region and there appeared to be a link to the same convent.

As if that weren't enough, someone else had been investigating Ariane's adoption lately, requesting records and asking questions. A lawyer in St Ancilla. A lawyer related to the countess who'd supplied a reference for her friend, the masquerading Princess.

It was easy to see what was happening. A group of aristocratic friends colluding to help each other.

Why?

The answer made Jake's blood steam.

So the pampered Princess could get her hands on Ariane.

Jake shook his head, breathing deep and filling his lungs as far as they'd go. Even so it felt as if barbed wire wrapped around his chest, constricting his air, drawing tighter as his ire rose.

He didn't give a damn if some party-girl princess had a change of heart about the baby she'd abandoned. Ariane was better off without her. For what was to stop her changing her mind again?

What Ariane needed was love and stability. Family. That was where he came in. *He* was family.

Carolina of St Ancilla signed away her rights years ago. It was too late to change her mind. Ariane was his niece, his only link with his beloved sister.

He had no intention of giving her up to some spoiled, deceitful woman who used her body to get her own way.

A shudder stormed his frame as he thought of her giving herself to man after man, a commodity to get what she wanted. She was an expert cheat, given the way she'd fooled him. An expert at using sex and deception.

But she'd messed up this time.

He'd never release Ariane to such a woman.

He might have been born working class and only just avoided being made a ward of the state when his older sister stepped in to raise him. But he was a man to be reckoned with. Apart from his considerable wealth, he had powerful contacts.

More, forewarned was forearmed. He wouldn't wait till

the Princess tried to snatch Ariane, or filed a lawsuit to claim her.

Right now arrangements were being made to increase security on the castle and on Ariane in particular. No one would steal her away.

As for a lawsuit… His mouth curled disdainfully. He already had a team of the best legal experts onto it. Birth mother or not, Carolina wouldn't get custody. If he had his way she wouldn't get access to Ariane for years. By which time her whim to be a mother would no doubt have passed.

Jake's smile became a grin. He wanted to see her face when she discovered she'd been outmanoeuvred.

Caro's smile felt like a rictus and her fingers ached from shaking hands with the throng of people her father had invited to the ball. Yet a glance at the mirror on the other side of the palace foyer reassured her. Her smile appeared real and she looked as regal as jewels, haute couture and years of mind-numbing training in etiquette and deportment could make her.

Her father would have nothing to complain about tonight, at least as far as she was concerned. No doubt he'd find something else to take umbrage at. He was never happy unless unhappy with something.

What had possessed him to invite such a huge crowd? Not only royals and people from both St Ancilla and Tarentia, but a slew of others. There was an unusually high number of foreign bankers and financiers.

Surely the whisper she'd heard couldn't be true—that the royal finances were rocky.

Caro pushed the idea aside. Probably her father planned some new scheme and had decided to finance it with someone else's money.

She smiled at another guest, answering him in his native German, hiding a wince at his too hearty handshake.

Through the formal welcomes her mind kept straying to Ariane. Was she sleeping or was she beset by the nightmares?

Did she miss Caro?

Caro told herself it was too soon for that, though *she* missed her daughter with a permanent ache beneath her ribs. After years believing her child dead, the impatience to be with her grew stronger not less. She'd only just resisted calling again tonight to check on her. Lotte had been reassuring this morning when she phoned. That had to be enough.

Soon she'd be free to go back to the castle. To Ariane.

And Jake.

Sinuous heat swirled through Caro's middle at the thought of Jake.

Feminine desire battled with trepidation whenever she thought of him. The man she'd almost given herself to. The man she wanted. She, who'd believed no man could ever again tempt her into intimacy, much less trust.

The man who'd been considerate and caring in a way unmatched by any other man in her life.

The man who stood between her and her daughter.

Except surely the person she'd seen behind the forbidding exterior and rapier-sharp mind needn't be an enemy? He wanted the best for Ariane. Surely, once he knew the truth he'd understand. Cooperate.

Caro clung to that thought through the last of the welcomes. In a couple of days she could return to Switzerland, see Ariane and explain to Jake.

He'd be surprised at first but he was no ogre. They'd find a way to negotiate this situation and—

'Princess Carolina.' The deep voice, like trailing velvet dipped in arsenic, wrapped around her.

Her thoughts shattered. Slowly, using every effort to

turn a neck suddenly stiff with tension, she looked to the next guest.

She felt herself sway, wondered distantly whether she might black out. But she didn't have the luxury of escape.

Jake Maynard stood there, superb in formal clothes tailored lovingly to his tall, broad-shouldered form. He'd looked daunting in business clothes, vital and handsome in a knitted pullover and jeans, raffishly sexy in gym gear. It shouldn't surprise her that in a bow tie and dinner jacket he was devastating.

Yet he stole her words as well as her breath. Caro stared up at the man watching her with the hooded silvery gaze of a predator. So handsome, with such a palpable aura of danger and power she instantly thought of a fallen angel. Or maybe that was because of the hot mercury stare pinning her to the spot.

'Or do you prefer to be called Caro?'

Nearby someone snatched a shocked breath at his effrontery but Caro was too busy standing tall when that poison-drenched voice wound tight around her, stopping the air in her lungs.

Without waiting for an answer he captured her hand. Instead of shaking it, he lifted it slowly, ostentatiously. He didn't bend his head, instead raising her arm high so she could see her pale hand in his as he pressed his lips to her fingers.

Involuntarily her fingers curled around his as energy jagged from her hand up her arm and down to her breasts and lower, to that empty space deep inside. The blood racketed around her body so fast she felt light-headed.

Caro heard a hissed breath, hers, then felt the convulsive shiver of her body's response. To him. To the anger sizzling in that half-lidded stare. And, heaven help her, to his bold challenge.

'Mr... Maynard.' Her hesitation made it sound as if she

was trying to remember his name, which was better than revealing how undone she was as he stood there, arrogantly stopping the queue of guests and holding her hand so close she felt the warmth of his breath on her fingers. The flesh across the back of her shoulders drew tight and her skin prickled. 'How good of you to attend.'

'You were expecting me?' His eyebrows rose as if in polite enquiry but Caro was busy reading the rest of his face. The grooves carved down his cheeks by the tight set of his jaw, the pronounced tic of a pulse at his temple and the flare of his nostrils as if assailed by some unpleasant smell.

Caro wavered on the verge of panic. She couldn't do this. Not here, not now. She needed quiet, a place to explain away from curious ears. She needed his understanding and compassion, not his enmity.

But finally Caro steadied herself. She had no option.

'I hadn't realised you were on the guest list but I hope you enjoy the ball.'

'I'm sure it will be most entertaining.' Still he didn't release her hand. She was conscious of the increasing number of stares trained on them.

'Please go on through.' She nodded towards the double doors flung wide to the gilded ballroom. Footmen stood on either side of the entry with trays of champagne. Beyond them guests milled, quaffing drinks, showing off their finery, chattering in anticipation.

Slowly he lowered her hand. But instead of releasing it, Jake curled his fingers around hers. His hold tightened into an implacable grip that matched the forbidding angle of his jaw. 'Perhaps you'd like to show me around, Your Highness?'

The suggestion defied royal protocol and good manners. She was here with her family to greet their guests.

'I'm sorry.' She made to pull her hand free but found it trapped. 'But I—'

'An excellent idea,' the familiar voice boomed from nearby.

Caro's face jerked around to find her father, resplendent in a scarlet uniform almost a perfect match for his colouring, beaming at them. Beaming! Her father!

Caro had a powerful moment of disbelief. So strong she wondered for a second if she'd strayed into a dream. Even her stepmother beside him wore a slight smile.

'You two young people go ahead. Enjoy yourselves. We're almost finished here.'

Inadvertently Caro caught the eye of a long-term diplomat in the queue, waiting to be greeted. In his eyes she saw a reflection of her own astonishment. Her father was a stickler for the rules, especially those promoting formality at court.

'Thank you, Your Majesty.' Jake inclined his head then, before Caro had time to catch her breath, he led her smoothly towards the ballroom.

As they stepped into the glittering room with its ornate ceiling paintings, crystal chandeliers and scores of massive mirrors, his breath whispered across her cheek.

'I'm sure tonight will be memorable.'

He spoke softly but the look in his eyes, and the feel of those long fingers manacling her wrist, sent a chill of deep foreboding straight to her marrow.

CHAPTER NINE

JAKE WAS KNOWN for his self-control. For an early responder in disaster zones it had been a quality almost as important as his skills at organisation and saving lives.

Yet tonight sorely tested him.

She tested him. Waltzing by on the arm of the man who'd held her possessively in that photo.

The simmering heat in Jake's gut rose in a seething flood of impatience. His plans to confront her in a quiet anteroom had been foiled by the press of people, all wanting to speak to her or him. Then there was the sheer formality of the proceedings. Her first dance had already been allocated and, short of hauling her away in front of a fascinated audience, he'd had no choice but to relinquish her.

He gritted his teeth, berating himself for the spurt of fury that had propelled him to the palace. He should have waited and chosen his venue better but his blood was up and for the first time in years he'd acted rashly. Goaded by the smiling redhead in the dark violet dress.

Simply watching her did excruciating things to his self-control. Jake told himself it was wrath but there was an edge to his anger that felt like more.

Like want.

Worse, like disappointment, because he'd felt something for her.

Except the person he'd begun to know was a mirage, constructed by the duplicitous woman now swanning around the dance floor. Her long skirt belled around her legs, calling attention to that tiny waist and acres of creamy skin bared by a dress that hung off both shoulders.

Jake's blood pounded in counterpoint to the beat of the

waltz. Colours blurred and faces flashed by but still he had no difficulty keeping her in focus. Caro Rivage aka Princess Carolina. She moved with a grace that despite his anger evoked raw hunger in the pit of his belly. Or maybe it was the smile she gave her partner, bending to murmur in her ear.

They swept past and for a second violet eyes caught Jake's. Wide, impossibly beautiful and, if he didn't know better, scared.

No, this woman wasn't scared. Disconcerted perhaps but she'd brazened it out, introducing him to guests as if they really were simply acquaintances. Keeping up a flow of small talk that made him want to muffle her mouth with his till she was so breathless, speech was beyond her.

With difficulty Jake slowed his breathing, searching for calm. They needed to talk. He needed confirmation of what he'd learned. Needed her to admit it. Then he'd inform her she had no hope of getting Ariane.

Sanity resurfaced. He told himself to wait till tomorrow when he could see her alone.

Except that would give her time to regroup. He'd find her surrounded by lawyers and royal officials who'd try to deflect him. This was between the pair of them. He wasn't in the mood to wait.

The music ended and her skirts spilled onto the gleaming floor as she curtseyed to her bowing partner. He was Prince of Tarentia, Jake had learned. Brother to the woman whose betrothal they were celebrating. How cosy. No doubt the two royal families were close. Maybe there was a second wedding in the pipeline?

Jake grimaced as acid stirred in his gut. Caro inhabited a privileged world where old family connections mattered and worth was measured by inherited wealth and titles.

But her privileged past didn't give her the right to sail into Ariane's life and disrupt it. To make the little girl believe her birth mother cared, only to be crushed when she discovered the woman who'd borne her had no staying power.

Jake knew how that felt.

He wouldn't let it happen to Ariane.

Stalking forward, he cut through the milling crowd to Caro and her partner.

'My dance, I believe.'

He didn't wait for a response, ignored a protest from the Prince and slipped his arm around Caro's waist. As he claimed her he felt her jolt of response. Satisfaction stirred. A second later the music started and Jake propelled her into the centre of the dance floor.

He hadn't planned to dance, had decided merely to separate her from her partner, but this was the simplest way to do it.

It had nothing to do with the greedy way his fingers splayed over her narrow back. The surge of rampant triumph as he pulled her close. The way her eyes dilated and that glossy cupid's bow mouth opened as if she couldn't catch her breath. Or the sheer rightness of her slender form in his embrace.

She matched his steps as if they'd danced together before. As their bodies had aligned perfectly when they'd kissed and when he'd held her, sobbing in his arms.

Jake tasted disgust on his tongue. Those tears had been faked. *She* was fake.

He glanced at the fine golden wires studded with purple gems threading her auburn hair, the matching long earrings that swung with her every move. Heard the swish of her rich ball gown billowing around his legs. But the trappings of royalty meant nothing to him. Glamour couldn't make up for a good heart. The fact his body still responded to her only made him more determined to wrest himself and his niece free of her pernicious influence.

'So tell me, Princess Carolina. Since you're the eldest in the family, why aren't you married yet? No desire for a family and children of your own?'

Caro faltered and would have tripped but for Jake's iron-hard embrace. He didn't slow at her misstep, swinging her, if anything, faster into the next turn, so she had to clutch him to keep her balance. Hard muscle and warm fabric teased her palms.

The mention of children hit her like a blow to the solar plexus, the impact shooting through her body and turning her legs nerveless.

For a heartbeat, for two, she could do nothing but hang on and try to keep up.

She shouldn't be surprised he was such a superb dancer, he had the strength and agility of an athlete. Yet it was his words, not his moves that worried her.

How much did he know? Her double identity, certainly. Anger radiated from him in waves. But not, surely, the rest, about being Ariane's mother.

'No plans to settle down with your Prince Charming?' He didn't bother keeping his voice down and the glittering challenge in those icy eyes told her he relished the idea of her objecting and trying to quiet him. No doubt he'd say something more outrageous.

Was that why he was here? To embarrass her?

For several seconds her tongue stuck to the roof of her mouth. A lifetime's reserve, of doing as she was ordered and being the one to back down, urged her to murmur something placatory. She hated scenes.

The twisting distress in her belly urged her to flee.

Caro did neither. She looked him straight in the eye.

'No plans to marry, Jake.' She pronounced his name casually as if they were old friends. As if the taste of it on her tongue didn't evoke a clandestine thrill of self-destructive pleasure. 'And you? Are you looking for a wife? I could introduce you to some lovely women here.'

She let her gaze drift over the crowd as if searching for said women. As if she weren't avoiding his blistering contempt.

For years she'd caved at the first sign of her father's displeasure. Even now she was nervous about the prospect of facing the King when she finally got time alone with him. But for some reason, standing up to Jake, despite the knowledge he stood between her and Ariane, made her blood sing in her veins.

'I've no intention of marrying.' The words bit like glacial shards, grazing her skin. 'I have too much experience of lying, manipulative women to trust one that much.'

It was a direct body blow. Caro felt it smash through skin and bone, felt herself absorb it like soft flesh cushioning a knife thrust.

It didn't help that he was right. She *had* to lied to him. But how could she have done otherwise? She'd had her reasons, as he'd discover when she had a chance to explain.

'You need to be careful. You sound like a misogynist. You don't want to turn into a lonely old grouch.'

A flash of something that might have been astonishment lit his features then disappeared. His lips rucked up at one side in a derisory smile that perversely reminded her of how wonderful his mouth had felt on hers a few nights ago.

'No danger of that, Caro. There are always women chasing me. Some even smuggle themselves into my life undercover.' Her breath caught at the steely light in his eyes. 'But I can tell a woman on the make. They don't have a hope of getting what they want, no matter what inducements they offer.'

His gaze dropped slowly, insolently, to her mouth, then lower, to her throat, bare of jewels, then across her décolletage. Suddenly the beautiful dress she wore seemed totally inadequate to protect her from that scorching, lazy stare.

Indignation rose, fiery and glorious, eclipsing nerves and her innate dislike of scenes.

Abruptly, after months, no, years, of coping and carrying on despite the hurt, Caro reached breaking point.

She was tired of being wrong-footed. Of being assessed by men and found wanting. By her father, who'd ignored and belittled her because she wasn't a boy. By Mike, who'd read her gullibility then turned nasty when he discovered she wasn't the docile meal ticket he'd assumed. He'd taken cruel delight in telling her she was far below the standard of his usual lovers.

Now by Jake Maynard, who made her feel cheap. Because in a moment's madness she'd dared to act on the attraction shimmering between them.

It hurt. All her life those rejections had hurt.

She'd had enough.

With a strength that surprised her, Caro wrenched free of his hold and stepped back. She saw his eyes widen then she swung away through the swaying couples.

There'd be speculation and shocked looks but she didn't care. She marched on till she was out on the terrace, lit by flambeaux and still too full of people.

Behind her she heard something that might have been her name but it was drowned by the beat of blood in her ears. Turning, she headed inside again and down a corridor, the sound of her high heels clicking on inlaid marble matching the quick thud of her pulse.

Still she continued, past state rooms, dining rooms, libraries and offices, past startled footmen bringing supplies from the kitchens.

Her ball gown swung wide as she turned up a familiar staircase, skirts lifted for speed, her breath coming in raw gasps that betrayed her pain.

Along another corridor, right to the end of the palace furthest from the rest of the family's rooms. There, highlighted on a wall, was the victorious knight in armour, running a lance through a whimpering dragon. Caro didn't have to look to know the knight wore the same look of cold disdain Jake had as he'd stripped her soul bare.

Caro pressed a hand to her pounding heart and wrenched open the door to her rooms.

Sanctuary at last! At least for the ten minutes she'd give herself to regroup.

She swept in and turned to close the door but a dark figure loomed in the doorway. Before she could react Jake inserted himself into the closing gap, crossed the threshold then stood, looming over her.

'Perfect,' he purred in a deep rumble that danced along her bones. 'Just what we need, a quiet place to continue our discussion uninterrupted.'

Fingers welded to the doorknob, Caro struggled for breath. His effrontery left her speechless.

'No! I want you to leave.'

'Why? Are you scared to be alone with me? You'd rather have witnesses for this discussion?'

'It's not that.' Despite his anger she wasn't scared of Jake Maynard. More of her inability to deal with him until she had her emotions under control. With him she felt as if she walked a tightrope, one false move and she'd fall into…she wasn't sure what, but every sense screamed she couldn't go there. Especially with so much at stake.

Caro drew herself up, projecting the regal assurance the rest of her family did so well and for which she'd had to struggle.

'I didn't invite you here.' The sight of that big, brooding form in her private sanctuary sent a strange jolt through her. As if he trespassed on something more fundamental, more personal than a mere room.

'That's unfortunate, *Princess* Carolina.' He said her title as if it were tainted. 'We have so much to talk about.'

Caro hefted a breath that didn't fill her lungs and tried to get a grip. 'We do. But not here. Not now—'

Jake shook his head. '*Yes*, here and now. And as for you not inviting me, let me be absolutely clear.' He bent towards her, thrusting his starkly sculpted face into her space. 'I would never have invited you into my home if I'd known who you were. You owe me.'

Caro's eyes bulged at the venom in his voice. 'Look, I know my identity is a surprise and I regret not telling you in the beginning but I had excellent reasons—'

'To lie and cheat? Perhaps to steal too?' His eyebrows contracted in a mighty scowl and the atmosphere thickened as if a thunderstorm threatened.

'I don't cheat and I definitely don't steal!' Horror mixed with an anger she couldn't suppress, despite the voice inside telling her she needed to be calm and reasonable. That had always been her default position.

And look where it got you!

'So you say. But from where I stand you're a liar and a cheat.' He shook his head. 'To think I almost felt sorry for you with your sob story the other night.'

'I wasn't lying!' Her distress had been only too real.

'Except your baby didn't die, did it, Caro?' He stepped so close his breath wafted warm across her skin. 'Your child is alive and well.'

'You know?'

How did he know? It didn't seem possible. She'd never have believed it herself if she hadn't finally been told the truth by someone who'd been there. The knowledge staggered her. Her numb fingers slid from the doorknob and Jake shut the door with a solid thud, closing them together in the shadowy room.

'I know.' There was no satisfaction in his eyes, only a

burning emotion she felt like a brand on her skin. 'And I tell you now, you can't have her. You'll *never* have her. I'll do whatever is needed to make sure of it.'

'No!' She wasn't aware of launching herself at him but suddenly she was grabbing his lapels, leaning into him as if she could change his mind by the force of her desperation. 'Don't say that.'

His big body froze, all except for the rise of that wide chest and the quick flick of the pulse at his temple.

'Are you going to try using your body again to persuade me? It won't work this time.'

'I'd *never* do that!'

'No?' He looked so supercilious, staring down at her with hateful superiority. It dragged up memories of the many times she'd felt powerless, when others, principally her royal father, had twisted circumstances against her. 'You're saying you had no ulterior motives when you offered yourself to me? You weren't using your body to get what you want?'

Caro didn't want to think about what had happened that night by the spa, much less try to explain her actions. Not to this grim-faced stranger who bore only a superficial resemblance to the Jake Maynard she'd come to know.

That man was gone, if he'd ever existed outside her imagination.

Yet to Caro's dismay even his piercing disapproval didn't eradicate her profound response to him. Furious as she was, her body still registered the excitingly hard outline of his solid chest, the breadth of his shoulders that made her feel appallingly aware of her own feminine desires. A crazy part of her actually revelled in this flashpoint of physical intimacy though they were on opposing sides.

'Don't be insulting. I'd never do that.'

'No? Because you're a virtuous, responsible royal princess who never put a foot wrong?' Jake shook his head, his eyes not leaving hers, his tone censorious.

'Because you'd never make the headlines for drug use and drunkenness, would you? Or have an illegitimate child and abandon it and the father without a second glance?' Impossibly his expression hardened even more. 'Did you *once* think about where your child might end up? Leaving a vulnerable baby to the mercy of total strangers because you couldn't bother facing your responsibilities?'

Caro would have staggered back in horror except Jake wrapped a powerful arm around her waist, holding her against him.

'You don't deserve to be a mother.' His voice hit a low note that resonated through her bones. It reminded her of the terrible, insidious voice of despair that had hounded her darkest days after the loss of her baby. 'You might have been born with a silver spoon in your mouth but you're nothing but a selfish sl—'

The slap cut his words off, rocking his head to one side.

Pain burst across her palm and up her arm. Belatedly he captured her hand, pressing it against his shoulder. She saw his jaw work and the bloom of dull red across his cheek.

'You don't shut me up so easily, *Princess*. I'm not one of your lackeys, afraid to offend royalty. I tell it as I see it and as I see it you—'

Caro couldn't listen. Nerves stretched to breaking point, body shaking from the desperate surge of adrenaline filling her blood, she did the only thing she could think of to stem the flow of vitriol.

Rising on her toes, she smashed her mouth against his.

CHAPTER TEN

A THUNDERBOLT SHEARED through Jake, cementing his feet
to the floor. His body rocked, hands clasping her tight.

As if he feared she'd step back?

Impossible.

She was a liar, a cheat. He couldn't trust a word that
came out of that beautiful deceitful mouth.

Yet as Caro's lips sealed his and her soft breasts pushed
against him something shuddered through him that wasn't
abhorrence or repudiation.

Desire. Hunger.

Need.

A need so powerful it made a mockery of the diatribe
that he'd spewed out. Even her resemblance to his faithless
mother, abandoning her children because they didn't fit her
chosen lifestyle, faded into the background.

In his arms he held fire and feminine passion. A desperation that matched his. She tunnelled her free hand through
the hair at the back of his scalp, pulling his face down as
she kissed him with an urgency that sent every sense throbbing into overload.

Already clinging to the borderline of control, Jake
opened to her kiss, letting her tongue slip between his lips.
He reciprocated, devouring her mouth with a thoroughness
that spoke of this woman's seductive allure as much as his
own recent celibacy.

Somehow this physical attraction survived disillusion-
ment. Incredibly, it wasn't eclipsed by negative feelings.
Fury and desire coalesced into something headier, stronger, hotter than he'd ever experienced.

He wanted to despise himself, wanted to wrench away

from her pliant body and the addictive sweetness of her mouth. Yet he couldn't.

She gave a mew of satisfaction that coiled through his vitals. He realised he'd bent her back over his arm, kissing her the way he'd like to take her body, with a single-minded carnality that already had him fully erect.

Jake tried to gather the ragged remains of his self-control. This was the second time she'd kissed him, each time trying to play him for a sucker.

Yet even that knowledge couldn't quell his need. It was bone-deep, undeniable and, it seemed, unquenchable.

The only way out was to make her pull back.

He covered her breast, warm and thrusting towards him. His grasp tightened and he heard again that encouraging purr in the back of her throat.

Jake told himself he was spurred by the need to make Caro retreat. He hooked his fingers into the top of the strapless dress and yanked. Impossibly soft flesh pillowed the backs of his fingers. He yanked again and the purple dress came down just enough to reveal a creamy, raspberry-tipped breast, not large but an exact fit for his hand.

Jake's erection throbbed as he covered her with his hand. Instantly an electric current zapped up his arm, lifting the hairs on his nape before shooting down, straight to his groin.

Caro watched him beneath drowsy eyelids. But there was nothing passive about that purple-blue stare. Jake felt the air freeze in his lungs as their gazes meshed.

Deliberately, driven by a compulsion he couldn't resist, he bent, kissing her nipple then drawing it into his mouth.

The assault on his senses was instantaneous. The delicious taste of her. The flood of rich, feminine scent, delicate yet sensuous in his nostrils. The incredible surge of arousal.

Far from repudiating him, Caro arched higher, lifting

her pelvis to bring her lower body flush against him, cushioning his erection against soft flesh.

Fumbling, Jake hauled down more material, exposing her other breast. He worked it with his hand, the other with his mouth, and the sound of Caro's faltering cry of pleasure drove him to more lavish caresses.

His groin was iron hard, forged and furnace hot.

For an instant, no more, he retained enough sense to hesitate, then caution shattered and he gave up the fight.

He wanted Caro so desperately his hands shook. The taste of her drove him wild. The sound of her panting, the hitch of her breath when he suckled harder, were pure encouragement.

So aroused it hurt to move, he straightened, pulling her upright and ignoring her pout of disappointment. With kiss-swollen lips and bare breasts pushed up towards him by the dislodged bodice, she looked like some raunchy male fantasy come to life. The contrast of all that exquisite bare flesh with the prim tiara still nestled in her bright hair made him feel as if he were debauching Cinderella.

Except those eyes, that mouth, held erotic awareness.

For this moment it didn't matter what she'd done or planned to do.

Who knew that fury and physical desire could be such potent bedfellows? That hate sex could be so powerful?

'Sorry?' He'd seen her lips move but his tumultuous pulse drowned the words.

'I said, don't you dare stop.'

Satisfaction crested like a curling wave thundering down onto a beach. Finally he had the real Caro. Stripped of lies and subterfuge. As vulnerable as he to the stark force of mutual attraction.

Ridiculously Jake's heart lifted. They both wanted this, both needed it. And when it was done the niggling ache he'd felt ever since Caro Rivage stepped into his world would be gone.

He couldn't wait.

Sliding his hands down warm silk to that slender waist, he lifted her off the ground, intending to find the bedroom. But the movement brought her exquisite, jiggling breasts high. His mouth dried, his ability to plan more than a few steps ahead disintegrated and instead he deposited her on a nearby piece of furniture. He didn't know what it was, only that its height meant she now sat almost level with his groin.

Without hesitation he stepped closer, hands in her voluminous skirts. Caro didn't try to stop him. Her knees fell open, inviting him closer, and her own hands were busy tugging his bow tie undone, ripping at his shirt.

Finally his questing hands met sheer nylon. He closed his eyes in frustration. He should have guessed a princess would wear pantyhose for a ball. He'd have to—

His fingers touched bare flesh. Stockings, not pantyhose. Elation rose. He touched lace between her legs, then, sliding his fingers beneath it, damp curls.

A shudder of lust racked Jake. He set his jaw, searching for the willpower to exhibit some control.

Soft hands palmed his chest, nudging his shirt and jacket wide. They slid down from chest to navel, to the top of his trousers. A second later nimble fingers undid his trousers.

His eyes snapped open as his clothes fell away and her hands curled around his length.

Arousal quaked through him. His skin pulled taut as heat shot hard and heavy to his groin.

Jake pulled her against him, his lips on hers, driving into her welcoming mouth.

There was no thought involved as he bent his knees to bring his erection to that sweet spot between her thighs. Or tugged her lacy underwear aside. Only the same instinct that made him plant one hand on her hip, tilting her towards him.

Something stirred in his brain. Some thought he couldn't catch. Something…

She shifted and suddenly he was there, the head of his shaft testing slick velvety heat. Her tongue swirled against his, her hand tightened on his length and the fragment of thought disintegrated.

Pulling her hand away, he planted it on his backside before drawing her legs over his hips and plunging into her beckoning depths.

Someone groaned. Was it him?

Caro's fingers wrapped possessively around his neck while she laid waste to his senses with that eager mouth. Her other hand clawed at his glute as if to hold him exactly where he was.

But Jake couldn't stay still. With a deliberate slowness that took him right to the edge of sensory overload, he withdrew then thrust again, deep and sure. Instantly she quivered. Tiny ripples of movement that coalesced into a powerful, clenching shudder that drew tight around him and hurled him over the edge with her. It was too soon, far too soon, but he was powerless to resist the force of this rocketing climax.

He was no stranger to sexual gratification but this pleasure was so sharp, so intense he lost himself utterly.

Instead of darkness there was light and colour. The deep blue-purple of the sky at twilight surrounded him, drugged him, lulled him through the force of that potent climax until, a lifetime later, it resolved into Caro's wide eyes, holding his in dazed wonder.

Jake shivered as aftershocks powered through him and he spilled again and again in hot, urgent pulses.

Even when it was over he couldn't process anything like a clear thought. Only the need to stay where he was, lodged within her, eaten up by those big violet eyes, with her long legs wrapped tight around his hips and his soul in paradise.

Finally, tentatively, he shifted his weight, only to feel her hands clutch tighter as if she couldn't bear the separation.

He understood the feeling. They hovered in a cushioned cloud of ecstasy.

Yet as the thought rose, so did others. Jake remembered the sheer perfection of losing himself in her intimate heat, pulsing hard and unfettered.

Because he hadn't used a condom.

The realisation cramped his gut and foreboding feathered his spine.

Jake closed his eyes, silently cursing his loss of control. It had never happened before and he'd believed it never would. How had it happened? Because Caro Rivage was a sexy siren who drove men out of their minds?

He breathed deep, inhaling the smell of sex and woman. To his amazement, despite the shock of his dangerous behaviour, Jake found it arousing.

Was this how she'd got pregnant with Ariane? Driving some poor sod crazy with desire so he forgot to take basic precautions?

No. Jake wasn't such a poor excuse for a man. He'd acted of his own volition. It had been his responsibility as much as Caro's to think about safe sex. He'd failed. For the first time in his life he'd let his libido conquer common sense. He despised himself for that.

Drawing a deep breath, he withdrew, clenching his teeth and shutting his eyes at the tormenting friction against sensitive skin.

If he wasn't careful he'd be ready to go another round with her and make exactly the same mistake. Even now he was tempted to forget everything but the need to bury himself in Caro's lush body and take them both to heaven again.

Which was why his movements were quick as he yanked

up his underwear and trousers. He didn't trust his control when they were skin on skin.

Control? He grimaced. He had none around this woman.

The sooner he put a distance between them, the better. Sex with the enemy was a mistake. One she'd hope to exploit in her favour. Best he set her straight immediately. Jake opened his eyes and his mouth at the same time but what he saw stopped the scathing words he was trying to form.

Instead he cursed under his breath.

For Princess Carolina hadn't moved. She sat, tiara at a tipsy angle in that dark red hair, cheeks hectic with a blush that spilled all the way down her throat and covered her trembling breasts. Her hands were clamped, white knuckled, to the edge of the carved wood where she perched and her shoulders bowed forward as if in defeat.

Despite the temptation of those perfect breasts, it was her expression that compelled his attention. Lines of pain gathered around her mouth and furrowed her forehead. Worse, glittering tear tracks spilled down both cheeks.

He'd hurt her.

She'd conned him and led him on. But he'd hurt her, and the sight of her pain made him feel wrong inside.

Caro closed her eyes, just for a second. *Then* she'd be strong. Then she'd pick herself up and face what had to be faced as she'd always done. Because there was no alternative. She was alone, always had been, with no champion but herself. She didn't have the luxury of weakness.

But when she'd seen Jake grimace…

There'd been no mistaking his disgust, the shudder of distaste as he pulled away. Disgust at what he'd done. Disgust at *her*. Because she'd lied and because he'd given in to the raging need for sexual completion that had sprung up between them like a clawing beast.

There'd been nothing civilised about their coupling. It

had been raw and intense, fulfilling a primitive need that was beyond her limited experience. Sex with her ex-boyfriend had been pleasant but not compulsive. Caro didn't understand the desperate woman who'd invited, gloried in being shoved onto an antique chest and taken without finesse or preamble.

It didn't matter. What mattered was that Caro had loved it. Had exulted in being ravished with such urgent thoroughness, eager for Jake in that visceral way as if she'd waited for him her entire life.

It had been glorious. *He'd* been glorious and made her feel special, strong, *wonderful*.

Until he realised what he'd done and hated himself. As he hated her. He'd stuffed himself back into his trousers so fast she guessed he feared she might touch him again. As if her touch tainted.

She recalled the ugly words he'd shot at her like bullets from a gun.

A great shudder built behind Caro's ribs in the vicinity of her heart. It curled round to her spine then up to her skull and down to her pelvis. Finally, mastering herself, she swallowed, put her shoulders back and forced her eyes open.

To find a grey gaze surveying her with what looked like concern. Something skimmed her cheek. She jumped then realised it was Jake's hand.

Caro leaned back. She should pull up her bodice, she realised as she registered her unfettered breasts and the discomfort of the boned bodice pushing them high. But her hands were too unsteady. Besides, he wasn't looking at her bare breasts but her face.

'You're crying.'

'Rubbish.' She turned her head away and began to wrestle with her dress when gentle fingers brushed her cheek again and she felt the smear of wetness there.

Caro stilled. Blinked.

Horror slammed into her. Bad enough to see his distaste, but to have him witness her distress was mortifying. This was the second time she'd cried in front of him. She, who'd spent years burying her emotions!

'I was rough. I hurt you.' Jake's voice sounded different, not the familiar mellow rumble that tickled her insides but taut and scratchy.

'You didn't hurt me.' Caro looked down, focusing on the bodice she couldn't tug up. Probably because she was sitting on the dress, holding it down. Desperately she shifted her weight, trying to drag the skirt higher so the bodice would move.

'Then why are you crying?'

'I'm not!' The tears must have escaped earlier.

Instead of moving away, Jake confounded her by capturing her chin in his broad palm and lifting it so she had to look him in the face.

'You looked like you were in pain.'

Of course she did. No woman wanted to be abhorred. But Caro couldn't bring herself to say that. The pain was still there but she masked it as she'd learned to mask so much.

'You're wrong. I'm fine.'

Except for the anguish deep inside. And the other, disturbing sensation that urged her to lean into his touch and ask for more, as if she had no pride.

Those pale eyes were intent. 'If you weren't in pain, why did you cry?'

Caro shrugged. 'It was an intense experience. It surprised me.'

She waited for him to say something offhand or derogatory. Instead she thought she saw a glimmer of understanding in his face. Until his next words.

'Not because we had unsafe sex?'

It was like being smacked in the face. Her head reared

back in disbelief. She gave up struggling with her dress and wrapped her arms protectively around her chest, as if to ward off his words. But, pressing her thighs together, feeling the wetness, she realised it was true.

How could she not have given it a thought? With Mike she'd been the one to insist on safe sex, despite his protests. It had been like fate laughing at her to discover she was pregnant, given the precautions they'd taken.

Her eyes locked with Jake's and she read her surprise reflected back. And more. Something that again, fleetingly, looked like understanding.

'I'm safe,' he said. 'You won't get any health problems from me.'

Except a possible pregnancy.

Caro bit her lips rather than blurt the words. Her first accidental pregnancy showed she was, or had been, very fertile. Her mind boggled at the idea of another baby. Jake's.

His forehead creased as watched her. 'This is where you're supposed to say you're clean too.'

'I'm clean too.'

'You don't sound very convincing.'

Probably because she was still stuck on the possibility of pregnancy. If it could happen once…

'How many lovers have you had lately?'

Caro frowned, his terse tone penetrating the fog of shock. 'None.' Then, when he lifted his eyebrows in disbelief, 'Well, one, but years ago. When I got pregnant.'

For long moments nothing moved except her blood pumping and the unsteady rise of her chest with a new breath. Jake looked as if he'd been turned into a statue. A frowning, disbelieving statue.

'You're telling me you've only had one lover?' At least his voice wasn't starkly accusing, but his disbelief tore at her self-respect.

She hiked her chin higher, profoundly glad that her crossed arms covered her bare breasts.

'Is that a crime? I don't ask how many you've had. I take your word that you're…clean.' She was lucky she was too, given what she'd discovered about Mike's lifestyle.

'What about the wild parties that made the headlines? The drugs and sex that made your father bring you home?'

Cold shivered through Caro. 'You know about that? You really are super-efficient, aren't you?'

Jake's shoulders lifted. 'I employ Neil for his efficiency.'

Nausea curdled her insides. She thought she might actually be ill. Bad enough that Jake, who despised her, thought the worst. Somehow the idea of Neil, the quiet, funny man who had treated her with such kindness, believing the press reports made her feel like vomiting.

'It wasn't true,' she said finally, her strangled voice not her own.

'Sorry?'

Anger rose and she was glad. Anything was better than feeling defeated and miserable. Caro stiffened her spine and met his gaze proudly. 'The stories weren't true. My boyfriend, Mike, was the one who partied to excess and took drugs, though I didn't know about the drugs till later.'

'How very convenient.' His mouth curled and suddenly Caro had had enough.

Ignoring the need to cover herself she put both hands to his chest and pushed. He was physically stronger but eventually he stepped back, leaving her free to slide off the high chest onto her feet. Caro gritted her teeth, her clammy hands slippery on the silk as she tried to right her dress. But the bodice refused to rise.

'Let me.' A big hand covered her shoulder, turning her. Before she knew it he'd lowered the zip of her dress.

'Stop that! I don't want—'

'Try again now that the dress is loose.'

He was right. She hadn't been thinking clearly. Of course it was easier without the bodice tight around her middle. This time the material rose easily and she sighed in relief.

A second later the zip rose and with it the touch of Jake's fingers on her back. Fire sizzled from there, loosening her spine and her resolve. Did she imagine his touch lingered then slid into a caress?

Setting her jaw, Caro stepped away, almost crying out at the loss of his touch. It made no sense. His distaste should have cured her of any attraction yet to her shame she still longed for Jake Maynard.

'It's time we talked.' To her surprise his tone had lost that harsh, hurtful edge.

She glanced at the time, realising in horror that they'd been away from the ball longer than she'd imagined.

'I should go back.'

Then she caught their reflection in the mirror on the far wall. Jake looked stern but attractive, the only sign of their carnal interlude his sexily rumpled hair and missing bow tie. Already he'd done up his shirt.

She, on the other hand, looked utterly...wanton. Her lips were swollen, her hair a mess and her designer dress suggestively crushed.

'If you show up looking like that you'll create a scandal.' He might have read her mind.

'If I go back wearing something else it will be just as bad.' She lifted a hand to the tiara listing to one side. She wanted to take it off but it was secured with scores of pins and her fingers shook.

Caro was damned no matter what she did.

'Father will be livid.'

To her surprise the thought, instead of making her feel worse, lifted her spirits. She hadn't set out to cause a scandal at her brother's party. From Paul's expression since she'd returned to St Ancilla he had too much on his mind to worry about gossip. His would be an arranged marriage but Caro suspected it wasn't a happy arrangement. However, the idea of annoying her father, childish as it was, pleased her. She still hadn't had the opportunity to confront him alone about stealing her baby.

Caro swung around to Jake Maynard. The man who'd once been so warm and kind. The man who'd been so cruel that remembering his words slashed at her soul. The man who was her enemy. And her lover.

The man she wished would sweep her up in his arms and take her back to that rapturous place she'd known for such a short time. At least now he wasn't sniping at her. He was ready to listen.

'You're right.' She felt the weight slide from her shoulders. 'It's time I told you everything.'

CHAPTER ELEVEN

SHE SWITCHED ON a lamp and its mellow light turned her into a mediaeval illumination with her rich auburn hair, violet-blue eyes and deep purple gown.

Jake sat on an armchair opposite and reminded himself not to trust her. Just because she made his pulse hammer with longing, because her mix of defiance and melancholy twisted him inside out, didn't mean he could relax his guard.

Yet it was hard to reconcile the woman who'd clung to him as if he were her whole world with the scheming liar he knew her to be.

He ignored the treacherous urge to sit with her on the sofa. This time he'd think with his head, not another part of his body.

'How did you change your hair, your eyes?' It wasn't the most important question but he still wasn't accustomed to her flagrantly exquisite colouring.

She looked like a painting by an old master brought to life. Except the memory of her toned, surprisingly strong body was vivid. This woman was no delicate work of art. She was bold and so alive his skin tingled being close to her.

Because you still want her. Despite everything.

Their eyes locked. Jake's pulse thudded.

'Coloured contacts and a rinse. I visited a hairdresser in St Ancilla to get me back to my natural hair colour for this week. The rinse wouldn't have lasted anyway and that would have given me away. But I was impatient to see Ariane.' Her mouth crinkled in a moue of self-derision. 'When I finally discovered where she was I couldn't wait. I acted rashly, but I had to see her as soon as possible.'

She shrugged and Jake was surprised at how the simple movement of bare shoulders could so entice. He jerked his gaze back to her face but Caro wasn't looking at him. Her eyes were fixed in the distance.

'What was the plan? To snatch her?'

Now Caro looked at him, her face full of astonishment. An act?

'I'd never do anything like that. Apart from anything else, Ariane just lost the only parents she knew.' Did he imagine her voice wobbled on the word 'parents'? 'She's struggling to cope with the changes in her life. Kidnapping her…' Caro shook her head, staring as if *he* were the one at fault. 'She needs stability, not more trauma.'

Caro drew a deep breath. He watched as she sat straighter, chin up, hands loose in her lap. With the movement she became more regal, more untouchable. He fought the urge to go over there and reduce her to the desperate lover she'd been minutes ago. Sexual awareness still thickened the atmosphere and his body was taut and eager.

'I acted on impulse applying for the job. My lawyer advised me to wait before confronting you. And I thought if I told you the truth you wouldn't let me see her.'

Jake's hackles rose. There, she finally admitted it.

'You plan to claim Ariane.' Bitterness filled his mouth.

'She's my daughter.'

Caro spoke quietly but with a pride Jake couldn't mistake. Nor did he miss the sparkle in her eyes.

Just as well he'd taken the precaution of increasing his niece's security. He hadn't brought her to St Ancilla. He didn't trust this woman's royal relations not to twist the law in their own country and rip Ariane from him.

He shook his head. 'You gave up your rights to her when you abandoned her.'

Despite her wounded look he didn't hide his disdain. He abhorred mothers who deserted their children.

'Let's get one thing straight.' Jake leaned forward, his hands fisted on his knees. 'You're not Ariane's mother. My sister was. She and her husband were the ones who sat up with her through the night as a baby. Who suffered the sleepless nights. Who played with her and loved her and taught her everything she knows. *Not* you. It never *will* be you. Not while I've got breath in my body.'

Jake's words were arrows, piercing her heart. Reminders of all she'd missed. All she hadn't been able to give her daughter.

Would Ariane ever forgive her for that?

Caro swallowed convulsively, ignoring the blistering pain as the acid of his hatred penetrated. How could she have given herself to a man who despised her?

Yet even on opposing sides, Caro felt that trembling awareness that was always present around Jake. Shame engulfed her. Even now she couldn't conquer her yearning.

'It wasn't like that. I didn't abandon her.' Caro drew a shuddering breath. 'She was taken from me.'

Jake lifted his eyebrows in disbelief.

Finally he spoke. 'They still believe in fairy tales here? You'll have to do better than that, Princess Carolina.' She hated the sneering way he said her name. 'No one could take your child unless you wanted it gone. You were an adult, a mother. You had responsibilities. So did your lover. Yet you both gave her up.'

His words echoed the guilt that dogged her in the darkest hours. The shame, the belief that somehow she should have intuited the truth and stopped them taking her baby.

Caro blinked, feeling the hot glaze at the backs of her eyes but refusing to shed more tears.

'Ariane's father died before she was born.'

Jake stilled, a frown descending. Then he shook his head. 'You're after sympathy?'

'No!' She looked down at her hands, twisting in her lap. 'All I want is for you to hear me out.' She'd hoped to skate over some details but Jake already knew so much and had put the worst interpretation on those. She had to make him understand. 'Can you do that?'

For answer he crossed his ankles and leaned back in his seat, his silvery gaze fixed on her like a steely skewer.

For all his sprawling arrogance Caro had the crazy urge to get up and kiss him full on the lips till he lost that haughty attitude and scooped her close. Because, bizarre to admit it, she'd found not just carnal satisfaction with him but something more. Something that had, for a fleeting time, felt strong and real and good.

How many times could she fool herself into believing what she wanted to believe? Surely Mike had cured her of that.

Shifting her gaze to the small landscape painting on the wall beyond Jake, Caro cleared her throat. 'After school I was allowed to study in the USA. It was the first time I'd lived outside the palace.'

'And you kicked over the traces, of course.'

Her gaze slewed back to his. 'There's no of course about it. I was nervous but excited. To have the freedom to make my own friends, not the ones approved by my father…' Looking at Jake's stony face, she gave up trying to explain.

'I spent a lot of my time studying. Art history mainly. I'd hoped eventually to work in a gallery or museum.' That dream was long gone. She frowned, dragging herself back to the point. 'When I was there I met Mike, another student. He was everything I wasn't. Confident, outgoing, charming—'

'You do yourself a disservice.' Jake's drawl interrupted her. 'You were all those things at the ball tonight.'

Her eyes darted to his then away. 'Learned skills. In Mike it was innate. He was…' She shrugged. 'Actually, he wasn't the man I thought he was. But I fell for him. We became lovers and I was as happy as I'd ever been.' The change had been amazing after her dour family situation with her perpetually disapproving father and a stepmother who saw her as an encumbrance.

'We did go to parties and some of them got out of hand, but I usually left early. I wasn't into drugs.' Which was why she hadn't realised the signs that Mike was. She'd truly been naïve. 'Then I found out I was pregnant. I suspect Mike tampered with the condoms.'

'Another bit of embroidery, Caro? Young guys aren't generally eager for parenthood.'

'Mike wasn't like most guys. I discovered later that he saw me as a ticket to wealth and privilege. Getting me pregnant was his insurance policy.' She met Jake's narrowed eyes and hurried on. 'At first it was so romantic. He proposed and I accepted. I thought we were in love and we'd have a wonderful future. Until I came home early one day to find him in bed with another woman.'

Jake leaned closer, his disbelief replaced by anger. He muttered something savage that, though it couldn't change the past, made Caro feel better.

'I was devastated.' Looking back now, she'd had a lucky escape. Cold iced her bones as she imagined not discovering Mike's true colours till after the wedding. She rubbed her hands up her arms.

'I dumped him and when I refused to take him back he turned nasty. He wouldn't give up. His moods became erratic, possibly because of the drugs he was taking.' Caro shivered, remembering how he'd frightened her.

'He threatened you?' Jake's gaze darkened.

'It doesn't matter now. What matters is that he contacted the palace. He told my father I was pregnant, hoping my father would force me into marriage. He's very strict and

wouldn't abide me bringing up an illegitimate child.' Caro
grimaced, remembering.

'But you didn't marry.'

'No. My father paid him for his silence.'

So much for the undying love Mike had professed. Even
after all this time that had the power to wound. All her life
she'd longed for love. She had only the vaguest recollection of her mother's warmth. 'With Mike's help the press
got hold of stories of me partying wildly. My father used
that to explain my return to St Ancilla.'

'And your lover?'

Caro tilted her head, surveying Jake. Why the curiosity
when he knew Mike was dead?

'He used the money to indulge himself. He died of an
overdose months after I left.'

'I see.' Jake scowled and Caro wondered what it was he
saw. 'So you came back here, to your family.'

Her mouth twisted in a smile that held no humour. 'Not
to the palace. Nor to my *family*.' She drew a sustaining
breath, remembering how frightening it had been, hus-
tled from the airport by a team of anonymous men who
wouldn't even speak to her, much less tell her where she
was going. 'I was taken from a private airport to a convent
on the other end of the island. I was kept on the estate there
till after the birth. My only contact with my family was a
note from my father saying he'd see me after my little problem was resolved.'

'And you agreed.' Was Jake's anger directed at her or
her father? Suddenly tired, Caro didn't care.

'Of course not. I walked out several times. When that
didn't work I tried to sneak away. I didn't get far. His security team had the place under surveillance and they were
very…efficient.' Even now the sight of her father's minders
made her feel sick in the stomach. 'I had no phone or computer and my friends didn't know where I was. My father

said nothing but I discovered later that *"sources close to the royal family"* hinted I was recuperating from an unspecified health condition.'

Caro saw the flash of confirmation in Jake's expression and knew he'd read those rumours that she'd been in rehab or recovering from a breakdown.

Sitting, recounting those days was too much. She got to her feet and paced to the window, clutching the curtain as she looked across the royal gardens, lit with thousands of lights for tonight's party. Her father would be furious at the scandal she'd caused. Already gossip would be in full swing.

But now the prospect of his temper didn't make her cringe. She wouldn't give in to his bullying any longer now she had something to fight for. Ariane.

'I gave birth there.' It was easier speaking about it with her back to Jake. Despite her father's wishes, Caro had resolved to raise her baby, even if it meant leaving St Ancilla with nothing. But she'd underestimated her father and her weakness after the birth.

'It was long and difficult.' She'd lost a lot of blood and drifted in and out of consciousness. 'I never heard the baby cry. I didn't see her, just the midwife's back, taking her away. They told me she was stillborn.'

Caro swallowed and unlocked her stiff fingers from their death grip on the curtain. She pressed her hands to her stomach, remembering the terrible anguish of that night, fighting the urge to bow her shoulders and curl in on herself.

She focused on the garden illumination and the strains of music in the distance.

'It took a while to recover. Afterwards I refused to return here, except for official events. I made my home at the far end of the island, working with children.' Caro cleared her throat, striving for a lighter tone. No need to explain that after losing her baby, she'd been driven to connect with other children.

'Recently I was contacted by the younger of the two midwives who'd been at the birth. She'd just had her first child and...' Caro faltered then made herself continue. 'She said she'd always felt guilty about what happened that night. But it was only when her daughter was born that she knew she had to tell me the truth. She said my baby was alive. That it was taken away, she assumed for adoption.'

Caro forced down the tangle of distress choking her throat.

She'd have to do better than this when she confronted her father. The knowledge gave her the energy to turn and look at Jake.

To her surprise he was no longer sitting, but stood mere paces away, on the other side of the window. His expression was unreadable yet he radiated tension. It hummed from him, making the hairs on her arms stand up.

'You know the rest.'

His hooded gaze raked her. 'I have the resources to check your story.'

Because even now he didn't believe her? The knowledge sent adrenaline buzzing through her, as if she'd taken a shot of spirits. A laugh emerged from her dry mouth. 'Is that a warning? Go ahead. The more corroborating evidence, the stronger my claim to Ariane.'

It was the wrong thing to say. That half-lidded stare turned laser bright and, despite her resolve, trepidation scuttered down her backbone.

But Caro was done with giving in to bossy men. She wanted her daughter and no one was going to stop her. She met Jake's narrowed eyes with determination.

Jake gritted his teeth, refusing to argue. Time, and the best investigators and lawyers, would give him the ammunition he needed. No matter what had happened in the past, Ariane was his niece and she needed him. He'd protect her with his life.

Yet Caro Rivage muddied the waters with her story. He'd felt anger and sympathy stir. Dangerous undercurrents when this woman was his rival for Ariane.

She was challenging, dangerous. Around her his emotions became stronger, more unwieldy.

Through her story he'd felt horror, sympathy and outrage but even now he didn't know whether she'd manipulated him. Her story was far-fetched and he wanted to dismiss it as fantasy. Except no one was that good an actor. He'd not only seen but felt her distress and pain.

There was a chance her story was true.

When she'd talked of her lying scum boyfriend her expression had revealed bitter betrayal and Jake had felt the urge to smash the guy's face. His skin crawled at the idea of her father keeping her captive, cut off from friends.

As for stealing her baby... Surely no father would do that!

Yet Jake knew that simply having children didn't make someone a caring parent. His mother was a case in point.

Had Caro given him a sob story to win him over while she found a way to get Ariane? Watching that challenging stare, he was torn between doubt and the desire to believe.

And desire of a different kind, for carnal pleasure. Their quick coupling hadn't eradicated it. Instead it was as if one taste of her no-holds-barred passion left him addicted.

It was appallingly difficult to focus on the past.

Had she abandoned Ariane or had her daughter been stolen? That was the crux of the matter. If she was lying she was the best liar he'd ever met. His gut told him she spoke the truth. Yet he needed evidence.

'I'll reserve judgement till I have proof you didn't give her away.'

Instead of her being downcast at his words, her expression lightened. 'I'll arrange a meeting with the midwife.'

She looked almost excited. The contrast with her earlier vulnerability was almost painful to observe. Surely that meant he could trust her.

Except people could be bought, stories altered.

'You do that.'

Jake wouldn't easily be convinced. He clenched his jaw against the wild see-saw of emotions. He was used to assessing situations quickly, trusting his instinct and taking decisive action. This uncertainty, the conflict between his desire to believe and the knowledge he couldn't, yet, was maddening.

'Well...' for the first time since she'd stormed out of the gala she looked uncertain '... I suppose it's time you returned to the ball. Do you need me to show you the way?'

Jake frowned. 'I'm not interested in the ball. I only came here to see you.'

The words echoed with a profound resonance. It was truer than he'd thought. Even now, when he knew he'd get no further proof tonight, he was magnetised by her. He didn't want to leave.

Whether it was the sexily mussed look of her ripe lips, untidy hair and crumpled dress, or the deeper thread of sympathy stirred by her story, Jake didn't know. But he felt...connected, drawn to her. Though he couldn't allow himself to trust her.

His voice must have revealed his doubt. He saw her react, her pupils dilate and her body sway infinitesimally nearer, till she jerked back.

'It's late. There's no proof I can give you tonight.'

'You want me to go?'

Caro felt her eyes widen as Jake's low voice rumbled through her.

She opened her mouth to say of course she wanted him to leave. He'd been brutally insulting. He'd made her feel like dirt.

Right before he'd made her feel as if she'd found heaven.

A squiggle of arousal stirred deep inside and she rubbed her damp palms down her skirt. Jake's eyes tracked the movement. To her dismay her nipples budded against her silk bodice while between her legs that slow circling ache of want started up anew.

Caro swallowed. She tried to summon a convenient lie. *Yes, I want you to go.* But her tongue didn't cooperate.

'Caro?' That gravel-wrapped-in-velvet voice reminded her of the night she'd kissed him and he'd held her while she cried. It was rough yet tender and strangely reassuring. It shouldn't be. They were on opposing sides.

'I—'

'Because I don't want to leave.' His features took on a grim cast, the planes of his face stark and sheer.

'What *do* you want?' The words came this time, breathless and quick.

'You.' He didn't move closer but it felt as if he did. As if he'd reached out and trailed his hand over her flesh, awakening dangerous longing. 'Us. Together. Again.'

'You despise me.' She summoned her pride as a last defence against his appalling power to tempt her. He'd flayed her with his insults. She wouldn't forget that soon.

He shook his head. 'I did, before you told me what happened.'

'You're saying you believe me?' It couldn't be so easy.

She was right. 'I told you, I'll reserve judgement till I have proof.'

He drew a slow breath and for the first time she realised he was as tense as she. His big chest rose in a shudder and the muscles in his jaw worked as if he held himself back with difficulty. 'But I still want you. More than ever.'

The words, delivered not in challenge but with devastating honesty, loosened her knees. Caro snatched in air to her overworked lungs but couldn't fill them.

'I've wanted you from the moment you sashayed into my office looking ridiculously sexy in that brown outfit. You made me feel like some Victorian reprobate, lusting after the staff.'

Caro stepped back in shock, straight into the window embrasure.

'You were attracted then?'

The voice of self-preservation told her it didn't matter. Nothing mattered but Ariane. Yet it wasn't true. This— whatever it was between her and Jake—was so powerful she felt it at a visceral level. In his arms Caro felt renewed, happy, vibrantly alive.

It made her weak when she needed to be strong. But oh, what weakness!

Even angry, desperate sex with this man had felt profound.

Surely it was a catastrophic mistake to give in to it, yet it felt anything but wrong.

'You couldn't tell?' He stepped close and she felt hot all over from that silvery stare. 'I thought it was obvious.' Another deep breath. This time that broad chest came within a hair's breadth of her breasts and she had to fight not to lean into him.

Caro shook her head. 'Sex would complicate things between us.'

Jake's mouth rucked up at one side in a disarming smile that turned her insides molten. 'A bit late to worry about, don't you think?' He paused. 'Whatever the rights and wrongs, we find ourselves in a…fraught situation. Why not indulge in a little recreational pleasure to relieve the tension?'

He made it sound not only logical but laudable. This man was incredibly dangerous!

And yet... She wanted badly to put aside her hurt, even for a short time.

'And afterwards? We part as enemies?'

He lifted his hand, feathering one finger down her cheek, then across to her mouth where her lips promptly opened for him. Heat drilled deep inside and she shuddered as she inhaled the citrus and male scent of his skin.

'How about we call a truce?' he purred. 'Till the negotiations begin.'

It was absurd. Reckless and irresponsible.

Utterly tempting.

Caro shuddered, her senses on overdrive. She told herself to be sensible. She opened her mouth to spurn him and heard herself say, 'Perhaps just once.'

The words were barely out when he scooped her into his arms. He carried her as easily as if he did it every day, leaving her hyper-aware of his strength and a sense of wellbeing. It was crazy but nevertheless real.

Then they were in the bedroom and he put her on her feet, reaching to flick on a bedside lamp. Caro waited for the frenzy of need, the urgent hands, hard on her body, that had so excited her before.

Instead, to her surprise, Jake lifted his hands to her hair. Gently, with deft patience, he drew out the pins that secured her tiara and kept her hair up. He wore a lazy half-smile as his fingers moved in her hair in a series of caresses that made her shiver all over.

Finally he removed the delicate tiara but instead of stopping, those hard hands massaged her scalp, turning her boneless. The exquisite sensations, the unhurried intent in those glittering eyes and the stroke of his breath on her skin turned it into the most amazing foreplay.

Caro's head fell back, her hair cascading in waves

around her shoulders. She clutched his upper arms as he kissed her jaw, her throat and down, down, down to the low-sitting line of her bodice.

That was only the beginning. Caro had expected fast and hard. What she got was endless patience and a sure sensuality that made her realise how limited her experience was. Mike had never seduced her with such infinite patience, or with such devastating knowledge of how to excite her.

By the time they were on the bed, he in boxers and she in nothing at all, she was quivering with anticipation, her breath coming in broken snatches. Finally, unable to wait, she reached for him, hand closing around his fabric-covered erection.

'Wait.' Hard fingers encircled hers and she saw Jake grimace as he throbbed against her touch. 'We need a condom.' His ragged voice made her realise that in this passion they were equals.

She almost smiled till his words sank in.

'I don't have any.'

He frowned, head turning to the bedside table.

'Not there. Not anywhere.' She pulled her hand away, feeling almost embarrassed. As if it were a crime to be celibate! 'I don't have sex.'

Jake stared as if he'd never seen her before. Because he hadn't believed her when she'd said there'd been no one but Mike? But before she had time to take offence, his mouth curled up in a sexy grin that made her heart leap against her ribs and her throat jam.

'You do now, Princess.' He kissed her quickly but with a naked intent that had her writhing beneath him.

Then suddenly she was bereft as he rose and reached for his trousers. Moments later he was naked, rolling a condom onto his impressive erection.

Caro swallowed hard, overwhelmed by her need for this magnificent man. She told herself her emotions were more profound because of the intense circumstances, the roller coaster of hope and fear since she'd heard Ariane was alive. But as Jake met her eyes and that ponderous pulse of connection pounded between them, Caro feared it was more.

He came to her, held her, kissed her, then, despite his arousal, slowly explored her with his mouth and hands. By the time he reached her sex, his breath a caress, she couldn't take any more.

'No!' He lifted his head and Caro stared, overwhelmed, at the sight of him there between her legs. One more touch and… 'I want *you*.'

'I haven't finished—'

Raising herself on her elbow, she reached for him, her hand sliding through the dark silk of his hair. 'Please.'

The teasing light in his eyes faded, replaced by something that felt heavy in her chest. Something warm and almost reassuring. Jake prowled up her body and carnal excitement stifled everything else.

This time when they came together it was slow and sure and almost familiar as he held her gaze and she held him. This time the fizz of sparks didn't explode as fast but the way their bodies rocked together, the searing strands of fire threading through her at every movement, every breath, every touch, made the climax more compelling.

Caro's orgasm bore down upon her, first in tiny ripples that made Jake's eyes glint with approval. Then in great undulating waves that made her cling and bite her lip against the urge to cry out.

She hung suspended, held from oblivion only by that grey gaze. Then his wide shoulders quaked, he flung his head back and powered deep inside and ecstasy took her.

CHAPTER TWELVE

JAKE WOKE ALONE in her bed.

Daylight streamed in yet he couldn't bring himself to move. Caro's 'perhaps just once' had turned into a long, vigorous night. Good thing he'd had condoms in his wallet. The more he had her, the more he wanted, and Caro had been equally needy.

Now he was content to wait for her to emerge from the bathroom.

Last night's madness could have been a major error. The last thing he needed, if it did come to a court case, was a sexual relationship with Princess Carolina muddying the waters.

Yet he couldn't regret that amazing night.

His belly warmed at the memory of her coming apart in his arms, her generous passion and his exultation. Caro had been everything he desired, though more than once he'd observed surprise at some of his caresses, and his ability to bring her multiple climaxes. Ego suggested the quality of his lovemaking surprised her but he suspected she really had been pretty inexperienced.

Which put an intriguing slant on what she'd told him. Some of it was true, possibly most of it. But he couldn't accept it all without proof, despite what felt like the best sex of his life.

It was tempting to believe they'd shared something extraordinary. His sated body and the smile tugging his lips confirmed it. But Jake was cautious. He preferred to ascribe this feeling to a particularly compatible woman and recent celibacy.

Jake surveyed his surroundings, curious at the difference between this room and the rest of the palace. Despite its high ceilings, ornate plasterwork and spacious dimensions, it wasn't as opulent. The furnishings looked comfortable, the fabric on the armchair in a shaft of sunlight actually looked frayed.

Probably because Caro only stayed here occasionally. But the bookcase on one wall, stuffed full, proved it was more than a convenient bolthole. Intrigued, he investigated.

Children's books jostled with classics and tomes on art. On one shelf was a stack of sketch books. He plucked one, leafing through and discovering drawings of formal gardens, a servant in livery and a bird on a branch.

He turned, looking for information about the woman he'd spent the night with. Nearby was a single framed photo. The resemblance was so intense Jake's pulse jumped.

Picking it up, he saw a woman of about thirty with Caro's slim build. Her hair was red but not Caro's dark auburn. This woman's was lighter, matching Ariane's, and her eyes, deep violet with that familiar slanting angle that made them look mysterious and happy at the same time, looked like Ariane's eyes, and Caro's.

This must be Caro's mother. Ariane's grandmother. She held a baby with a fuzz of reddish hair, one tiny hand reaching towards her mother.

Abruptly Jake put the photo down, recalling Neil's report on Princess Carolina. She'd lost her mother when she was tiny. Her father remarried almost immediately. This photo seemed to indicate a bond with a mother she could barely have known, rather than with the woman who'd raised her.

He thought about Ariane losing her adoptive parents. And Caro's story of having Ariane stolen from her.

What if it were true?

What if the passionate woman he'd bedded wasn't a spoiled princess who hadn't wanted her child? What if she'd genuinely believed her child dead, the maternal bond broken, as with her own mother?

Something lodged in Jake's belly. A weight that, against the laws of physics, rose within him, crushing his lungs and stopping his breath.

He swung around, needing to find her. She'd been in the bathroom a long time. Too long.

Jake walked past a wooden-faced footman on the ground floor. Either the servants were used to guests ending the night in a royal bed, or too well trained to bat an eye. He didn't care. What he cared about was locating Caro.

His need to find her had grown from a niggle to a presentiment of trouble. No matter how unaccustomed she was to nights of passion, it was unlike the woman he knew not to face him this morning. His nape tightened.

Finally, when he was almost at the ballroom, he heard a loud voice. Pushing open a not quite closed door, he found himself in an empty sitting room. On the far side French windows stood open to the garden. Following the sound of voices, Jake stepped outside then realised the conversation was taking place in the next room. He moved to another set of French windows and looked inside. It was a study with gilded antiques and floor-to-ceiling books that looked, unlike the ones in Caro's room, as if they'd never been opened. The occupants didn't notice him on the threshold.

King Hugo of St Ancilla sat behind an oversized desk. Caro stood before him in a tailored skirt and jacket, spine straight and chin up. Jake silently applauded her, for the monarch wasn't holding back his tirade in mixed English and Ancillan. Jake's stomach curdled at his blistering vitriol.

He was about to make himself known when Caro spoke. 'I did what you insisted, came back and attended every event this week. As for leaving early last night…' She shrugged. 'I'm not here to discuss that.'

'How *dare* you speak to me like that?' The King's face darkened.

'Oh, I *dare*, Father.' Amazingly Caro's defiant tone made the King stop, eyes widening. 'I only came here because you threatened to send your goons to haul me back, and, in the process, wreck my plans.'

'Plans? You don't have plans. You spend your time playing at being a preschool teacher. It's time you toed the line and came home.' He sat back, an ugly smile on his face. 'I've a mind to organise your wedding next. There's a banker in the US I'm cultivating.' His tone turned sneering. 'I know your weakness for Americans.'

Any thought Jake had of revealing his presence died as Caro turned parchment-pale. She wouldn't thank him for witnessing this.

Besides, it could be his chance to discover whether she'd told him the truth.

'Or perhaps the Australian you spent the night with. We could turn your scandalous behaviour to advantage, put pressure on him to come up to scratch. His fortune is huge.'

Jake was absorbing that when Caro stepped up to the desk. She slapped her hands down and leaned forward.

'Make your plans for my brothers, not me. I wash my hands of you.' She drew a deep breath and Jake, seeing the light glinting on her bright hair, realised she was shaking. 'I know what you did. The lies you told, the laws you broke.'

For a moment the King said nothing. When he spoke his voice was venomous. 'Careful, Carolina. I've let you go your own way for years but I can bring you to heel like that.' He snapped his fingers.

Slowly she shook her head. 'Not this time. Not any more.' She straightened, her hands clenched. 'You stole my child. You had her illegally adopted without my consent.'

Jake's hand closed so hard on the door frame that pain shot from his palm up his arm.

It was true. Unbelievably it was true.

His mind boggled and his stomach dropped.

He'd got her so wrong.

The things he'd said last night!

Jake rocked back as guilt and horror filled him.

'There was never any question of you keeping it.'

'Her. I had a girl.'

'A bastard.' Her father shrugged. 'As if I'd allow that blot on the family name. I did what I did for the family. You should be grateful—'

'Grateful? Hardly. I know where she is and I'm going to get her. We're going to live together. I'm going to raise my daughter the way a child *should* be raised and—'

'You'll do no such thing. Put the idea from your head right now. Unless you'd like another year living under guard till you see sense?'

Jake couldn't take any more. He rapped on the window frame, feigning a smile as they whipped round towards him.

'Good morning, Your Majesty... Carolina. I hope I'm not interrupting.' He paused, looking from one to the other, willing Caro to follow his lead. She looked pale, her features drawn.

He'd heard enough to suspect that, with only a little more provocation, her father would have her clapped in a dungeon or a tower, guarded by sentries. Jake recalled her bleak expression when she'd spoken of being held against her will by the King's security men. Until he could get her out of St Ancilla, she wouldn't be safe.

Jake didn't question his determination to get her away. She'd told the truth. He owed her more than an apology for last night's scathing words.

'Not at all.' The King recovered first, stretching his mouth into a smile like a hungry shark's.

'I'm so glad.' Jake stepped into the room, standing beside Caro and planting his palm reassuringly at her back. She shivered and he had to bite back the words he longed to fling at her father. Instead he made himself smile. 'Carolina promised to show me something of the countryside today, didn't you, darling?'

She blinked, her brow furrowing at his words. Before she could speak Jake ploughed on.

'I must thank you, Your Highness, for the invitation to last night's event. It was spectacular. I'm honoured to have been invited.' He smiled as if his one aim in life were to hang out with pampered aristocrats, then added the bait. 'Especially as I understand there are some interesting investment opportunities in your country.'

Ignoring Caro's scowl, he watched the King and saw his ruse had worked. Perhaps Neil was right and the royal coffers weren't as plump as they used to be. He'd noticed a number of high-profile financiers attending last night, including a few involved in his latest project. It wouldn't hurt if the King thought he planned to stay and look at business options.

'It was our pleasure to have you here.' No sign of a scowl now on that crimson face. 'You must accept our hospitality for the rest of your visit.'

'You're most kind, Your Highness.' Jake slipped his hand from Caro's back to capture her hand. He squeezed it reassuringly. 'I'd hoped to make an early start on our sightseeing. Unless...'

He let his words trail off as he gave Caro a melting smile. Best if her father thought he was unaware of the dark undercurrents in the room.

'Of course. Carolina, see you take Mr Maynard to the business park on the way out of the city.'

Caro opened her mouth and Jake spoke first. 'That

sounds perfect. But maybe on the way back. There are other sights Carolina promised to show me first.'

'I'm sure there are.' The King's suggestive chuckle curdled Jake's belly but he kept his expression light.

Finally, to his relief, Caro spoke up. 'That's right. We'd better leave now if we're to fit everything in.'

'Come and see me when you return, Carolina.' It wasn't a suggestion but an order.

Jake wore a calm face as they traversed the palace. He was determined the servants wouldn't see anything amiss, though restraining his seething emotions took concentration. Caro's hand was cold in his and she moved stiffly, shoulders high and face blank.

He was torn between slashing guilt over the way he'd treated her, disbelief at the enormity of what he'd witnessed and the desire to do serious damage to the man they'd just left.

Jake had thought his own mother appalling. She had nothing on Caro's father.

They remained silent till they reached Caro's rooms. As the door shut, Jake wrapped his arms around her, breath expelling in a rush when she didn't push him away. He didn't deserve her trust.

His scorn last night proved he had no filter and precious little control where Caro was concerned. He'd told himself he was furious on Ariane's behalf but this was more, much more.

Caro leaned close, fracturing his thoughts and filling him with relief. He inhaled spice and woman, her hair tickling his cheek, her body warm and trembling.

His arms tightened. 'I'm getting you out of here. Now.'

Caro let Jake lead her from the helipad along the path to the castle. She'd been away less than a week yet spring had arrived in the Alps. The air was warm and the snow had begun melting. Further down the slope she saw the first traces of wildflowers. The air felt fresh with promise and the fragrance of growing things teased her nostrils.

While she felt chilled.

Everything had happened quickly. Maybe she was in shock. The confrontation with her father, then Jake spiriting her off St Ancilla in a private jet, followed by this short hop in a helicopter. She wasn't used to anyone, especially a man, coming to her rescue. That added to the air of unreality.

If ever she'd doubted Jake's ability to make things happen, today would have disabused her. He'd made one call while she gathered her most precious possessions in a large shoulder bag. Her mother's photo, her mother's jewellery that she'd worn last night and some illustrated books she'd had when she was young and had always wanted to give her own child. Then they were heading to the garages and from there to an airfield.

All the time fear tingled down her spine as she imagined her father's reaction when he found her gone.

She had no illusions that his threat to hold her by force was bluster. He was ruthless. While she was in St Ancilla he had all the power, despite what the law said.

'I have to thank you. Getting me off the island.' She stopped and turned to Jake as the helicopter lifted off and its throbbing thunder retreated.

He looked the same, dark-featured, broad-shouldered and with the air of calm competence that reassured.

Alarms tripped in her brain, warning that she couldn't relax her guard, couldn't rely on anyone but herself. Yet it was too late. She'd gone so far with him, in so many ways, she couldn't pretend none of it had happened.

It felt as if a lifetime had passed since they met.

'There's no need for thanks. I was glad to get away too.' There was so much to discuss but neither was eager to start. They'd barely spoken on the trip. Caro because she grappled with a barrage of emotions and Jake because he was busy working on his phone. Because his business couldn't wait or because he realised she needed some quiet time?

Pewter-grey eyes surveyed her. 'You're feeling better now you're off St Ancilla?'

Caro breathed deep and nodded, looking away to the magnificent vista of fields, forests and soaring mountains. On the other side of the valley towering waterfalls, fed by melting snow, plunged to the valley floor.

'I wouldn't have got away so easily without your help.' She faced the horrible truth today had revealed. 'I love my country but I can't stay there. Not with my father's threats hanging over me. If he sends his men after me…'

She shivered and hunched her shoulders despite the warm sunlight on her back. To be virtually exiled from her homeland was bad enough. To fear returning because it could only be on the King's terms was even worse.

'Don't worry. I've got people working on it.' Caro raised her eyebrows but before she could question Jake continued. 'Let's talk about it later. For now just know you're safe.' He gestured to the castle, golden in the sunlight, its machico-lated towers charming yet sturdy, its massive walls solid. 'I'll make sure no one, not even the King of St Ancilla, can harm you or Ariane here.'

'Thank you. That's…good of you.'

It meant everything to have breathing space to decide what to do next. To know her daughter, and she, were safe for now.

Caro felt stiff facial muscles twinge as she smiled. 'You're sure you're the same man who stalked into the palace last night with vengeance in his eyes?'

He'd looked like an avenging angel.

There was no answering humour in Jake's features. If anything he looked even grimmer.

Warmth enveloped her hand and she looked down to see he'd captured it in both of his. Heat radiated from his touch and the tension stringing her muscles began to ease.

'I owe you an apology.' Jake winced. 'I jumped to conclusions about you that were unfounded and hurtful. Can you forgive me? I cringe when I think of what I said. The way I treated you, in private and in front of others. You didn't deserve that. I lost control and I'm ashamed.'

Caro read his remorse. His words, his contempt, had hurt. Badly. With a lancing pain that drove right to her heart. But he hadn't known the truth.

'I can't blame you for doubting my word. I came here in disguise, lying to you.' She paused. 'I apologise for that. My only excuse is I was desperate, scared I'd lose the chance to see my daughter.' Caro tried to summon a smile but it felt like a grimace. 'I was afraid if I told you who I was you'd stop me seeing her when I'd just learned she was alive.'

'Caro, you don't—'

'I do have to explain. I hated lying. I knew soon enough that you loved her and wanted to protect her, but I knew you'd see me as an enemy, particularly when I told my story. It was so far-fetched. You were right, it does sound like something from an old story.' The sort that had evil stepmothers and awful curses.

Caro's stepmother wasn't evil. Just wrapped up in her own family with no warmth to share for another woman's child. As for her father, he was larger than life with his selfish, manipulative ways and towering temper.

Not for the first time she wondered what life would have been like if her mother had lived. Everyone said she was gentle yet fun-loving. Caro had a horrible feeling life with her royal husband would have been hellish.

'Nevertheless, I should have waited to be sure of the facts.' Jake's stern voice sliced her thoughts. 'Abandoning children is a hot button for me. I saw red and acted before thinking. Believe it or not, that's not my usual way.'

He looked down to where his thumb described a half circle again and again on the back of her hand. He seemed so abstracted she guessed he had no idea of the powerful, delicious sensations his caress evoked.

Here she was, fleeing her country, her father and her King, with her life in chaos. Yet she found it impossible to concentrate on her problems because of Jake Maynard and the feelings he evoked.

She tugged her hand free, ignoring that twitch of dark eyebrows.

She cradled her fingers, warm from his touch, in her other hand. 'Don't worry. I'm tougher than I look.' She'd had to be. 'I'm not about to collapse in tears or have a breakdown.'

Caro was acutely aware of the fact Jake had seen her at her lowest ebb, unable to stop the grief she'd carried for so long. She'd wept in his arms, finding a solace she'd never known before. But she wouldn't do that again. The humiliation of having him witness that scene with her father still cramped her insides. Even though it had convinced Jake she told the truth, she hated him thinking she was a helpless victim.

His smile when it came was crooked but totally disarming. It set light to her last defences like flame to paper. She could almost hear the whoosh of conflagration as her resistance crumbled to ashes.

'It seems those stories about your breakdown years ago were exaggerated.' His smile died and Caro read concern in his smoky gaze. 'You don't have to convince me you're strong, Caro. To get through what you did, to keep going, and deal with *him*…' He shook his head. 'That takes guts.'

Caro's heart swelled. It was the first time she'd received such a compliment. 'I've never held my own against him before. I let him—'

'Don't!' Jake raised a palm to stop her. 'Don't blame yourself. He was your father and your King and he held all the power.'

Jake's stare pinioned hers. Instead of her feeling cornered, her confidence rose, a warm glow that felt like happiness.

They stood, gazes locked. Caro didn't want to move. The quality of Jake's regard, how he made her feel about herself, were new and precious.

'I've got one question.' His voice made her blink.

'Yes?' Absurdly, now the worst was over, she was breathless.

'Do I have to call you Carolina now?'

She smiled and took a half step back, suddenly aware she'd canted towards him. 'I've come to loathe my full name. My father insists on it but as he's usually in a bad mood he makes it sound ugly. My friends call me Caro.'

Jake bent forward in a formal bow as if he were a master of court etiquette. 'May I call you Caro?'

Did that mean he saw her as his friend?

Caro wasn't sure whether to be pleased. She should be. It meant he trusted her. Yet given her deep-seated, confusing feelings for him, 'friend' was such a lukewarm word.

'Of course.' Looking into his eyes, she felt a zap of energy that warned she was vulnerable to this man. Hurriedly she gathered her wits. 'And now? What happens next?'

Caro would call her friends in St Ancilla and her lawyer, to warn them the King would be on a rampage when he discovered she'd left. She didn't think he'd take out his wrath on them but he could be unstable when crossed.

'Next?' Jake's smile was easy. 'We'll work it out one step at a time. There's no rush. For now concentrate on the fact you and Ariane are safe.'

Caro swallowed. He didn't want her thanks yet he gave her so much, refuge when she needed it most. They still had to work out Ariane's future. Ostensibly they were on opposing sides, yet Jake treated her as someone to be protected.

The knowledge stirred the most poignant feelings. Here was a man she could respect as well as…

'And us? Is there an us?' Instinctively she lifted her chin, ready to pretend it didn't matter if he said last night's passion had been a mistake.

Jake's face turned unreadable.

She'd give anything to know what he thought. Did he regret having sex? Was it gauche and embarrassing to mention it now they'd moved on from those moments of heightened emotion?

She wished she knew one-night-stand etiquette.

'Do you want there to be?'

Caro had imagined this morning that confronting her hectoring father would take all her courage. Yet, looking into that piercing gaze that gave nothing away, her heart thudding against her ribs, she discovered her courage could still be tested.

She craved more of what she'd experienced with Jake, that soul-searing passion that went beyond anything she'd known. Yet with everything so uncertain—

'It's okay. You don't need to answer now, Caro. Shall we take that one step at a time too?'

She slicked her dry lips, searching for the right words when a shout made her turn.

Rounding the corner of the castle were Jake's secretary Neil and Ariane, hopping beside him.

Abruptly it hit her, the fact that she was here, safe for

now from her father's machinations and with her daughter. Her incredible, lovely daughter. Caro's breath shuddered through her as relief and joy filled her.

'Come on, Caro.' She felt Jake's hand warm at the small of her back. 'It's time to see your little girl.'

CHAPTER THIRTEEN

JAKE SURVEYED THE pair sitting across from him and fought to hide his response to the picture they made.

Ariane had begun the trip down the mountain's steep cog railway on the seat beside Caro. But as Caro pointed through the carriage window, his niece had climbed onto her lap. Now Caro's arm rested around Ariane's middle as they chattered about the view and the quaint Alpine farm-houses.

His ribs tightened at their glow of happiness. His niece and her mother. Not that Ariane knew Caro was her mother. They'd agreed to keep that quiet till Ariane was better able to understand.

But she was still his niece and always would be.

His lawyers said there were legal arguments on both sides, for him as Ariane's permanent guardian, and for Caro as birth mother. Though they thought, despite the wrong done years ago, they could successfully argue that the continuity of living with him would be best for Ariane.

Jake felt no triumph at the news.

He didn't *want* a legal wrangle with Caro.

He watched their faces, alight with pleasure as Caro spotted hikers with a frolicking dog. Two shades of red hair, one coppery and the other a deep, ruby auburn, touched as they craned to look. Two sets of violet eyes and two smiles, each capable of twisting his heart.

He wanted Ariane with him. And he wanted Caro.

The twist of heat moved from his chest to his groin. He *had* Caro. She'd been his lover ever since St Ancilla.

That first night back he'd been surprised by the rap on his door. When he'd found Caro there, huddled in a robe

with her hair in waves around her shoulders, he'd pulled
her inside, expecting to hear her appalling father had managed, despite Jake's precautions, to contact her with threats.

It had taken all Jake's once considerable restraint to hold
back from her, invite her to sit, turn his brain to tactics to
stymie the King's machinations.

But instead of talking about her father or Ariane, Caro
had surprised him. Gone was the wan woman who'd left St
Ancilla beside him. Instead he'd been visited by the ardent
siren who'd given herself so generously the night before.

Had he held back? Worried about taking advantage when
he knew she'd been rocked by recent experiences?

Jake counted himself a decent guy, if hard-nosed in business. But he wasn't into self-abnegation. He'd hauled Caro
into his bed. For the last ten days he'd made sure she was
satisfied, more than satisfied, there.

He truly was selfish. He had Caro each night and still he
wanted more. He had no name for this craving. To possess
her physically. But more too. To bask in her smiles. Enjoy
her in ways that had little to do with sex.

'Uncle Jake…?'

He found two pairs of eyes on him.

'Sorry?' He yanked his thoughts to the present. Their
trip up the mountain. His sense of victory when he'd finally persuaded Caro it was safe to take Ariane out. That
her father's henchmen couldn't grab them. Even then she
hadn't relaxed till his own security staff boarded the next
carriage, keeping a discreet distance.

Jake hated the need for such a precaution but the deeper
the experts dug, the less he trusted the King to behave rea-
sonably. He'd do whatever it took to keep Ariane and Caro
from the monarch's reach.

'What are you thinking, Uncle Jake? You look funny.'

'Do I?' He met Ariane's bright eyes, so like her mother's, and felt his fluency desert him. His brain went com-

pletely blank. Because he'd been thinking about sex with
Caro and how his need for her kept growing, not dimin-
ishing with familiarity.

'This sort of funny?' he asked as he crossed his eyes.

Ariane giggled and the tight sensation in his chest eased.
He loved hearing her happy.

'Or this?' He stuck his tongue in his cheek and scrunched
his eyebrows down.

His gaze caught Caro's. She was smiling, the shadows
he sometimes saw in her eyes banished.

Elation hit. By rights it should be because he was finally
on the verge of closing the deal he'd come to Switzerland
to accomplish. Or because he might have found a way to
protect Caro and Ariane from the King long term. Instead
this burst of happiness came from the sight of Caro's eyes,
dancing with approval as he made a fool of himself in front
of a bunch of tourists.

The realisation shook him. Her smile and her approval
had such power.

What did that mean?

And what did he intend to do about it?

Caro lay on her back, heart pounding, legs weak as over-
cooked pasta and a smile of well-being curving her lips.
How often had she felt like this in Jake's bed, basking in
the afterglow of his loving?

The man had a knack for diverting her worries about
the future and her conniving father. And the sight of Ariane growing more confident and loving proved that good
things *could* happen.

They hadn't discussed Ariane's future. It had been
enough to know she was safe from the King. Despite furious messages from her father Jake had somehow managed
to convince him to keep his distance. But they'd have to

face their problems. Caro wasn't naïve enough to believe this state of glorious limbo could continue.

Zoe had rung today, warning again that winning custody of Ariane wouldn't be simple. She favoured a negotiated arrangement with Jake. Which suited Caro. She couldn't imagine them on opposing sides in court. Yet nor could she envisage Ariane living part time with her and part with Jake, possibly on the other side of the world.

She should be relieved Jake hadn't forced the issue. Yet they couldn't go on like this despite his insistence that for now Ariane needed calm and stability. But Caro had never found the right time to shatter this peaceful interlude.

Caro rolled onto her side and watched the early light gild the mountains. She'd found peace here, such happiness, she didn't want it to end. Not only for Ariane but for *her*.

The bathroom door opened and there Jake was, naked but for a towel around his hips, his hair damp and the muscles in that glorious torso shifting as he moved. Despite her satiation Caro felt the tug of attraction deep inside.

Longing for him filled her yet she knew their peaceful bubble must shatter. Was today the day?

'You're awake?' He approached, smiling, and she smiled back, almost accustomed to the fillip of joy gathering behind her breastbone. No one, ever, had made her feel the way Jake did. The thought lodged and Caro stilled as its implications penetrated.

'Something wrong?' He watched her as she struggled to stifle a sudden, disquieting idea.

'No, nothing.' She made a production of turning to plump up pillows behind her and sit up, drawing the sheet under her arms. By the time she faced him again she had her calm face on, the one she'd learned in the palace, forged under the lash of her father's contempt and her stepmother's disapproval.

Yet her heart pounded wildly and perspiration prickled

her hairline. Her powers of concealment weren't as good as she'd hoped for Jake sat beside her, frowning. He took her hand and she experienced that familiar jolt of delight.

'Are you worried about a possible pregnancy? Because of that first night?'

Heat blossomed in her cheeks. 'It's unlikely, given the timing.' That was what she'd told herself again and again. 'Time enough to worry about that if it happens.'

'You wouldn't be alone, Caro.' His thumb stroked the back of her hand. 'I'd look after you. I don't abandon my responsibilities.'

And that, Caro realised as her heart landed somewhere near the floor, was part of the problem. She didn't want to be a responsibility to Jake. Nor did she want to be a rival for Ariane. She wanted to be someone he—

'I was going to wait till later but now's as good a time as any. We need to talk, Caro.'

His gentle tone, the way he watched her, assessing her reaction, made her heart skip. Tension crawled along her shoulders to the back of her neck. Was he going to say he'd decided he couldn't give Ariane up?

It was stupid to jump to conclusions but a lifetime of disappointment, of things going against her, had conditioned Caro to expect the worst. She tugged her hand free and folded her arms over her chest.

'I agree. We can't continue this way indefinitely.'

Keen eyes surveyed her. What did he see? She had the unnerving notion he saw far more than she'd like.

'My time in Switzerland is almost over. The project I've been working on is complete.'

Caro's eyes widened. Despite telling herself this wasn't permanent, she hadn't thought about Jake leaving. Distress coated her tongue.

'It's not long term?'

He had investments globally. From the snippets she'd

heard between him and Neil she'd imagined his current work continuing.

He shrugged. 'It is, but now everything's in place I don't need to be here. My role was to cajole the other investors into participating.'

Caro frowned. 'Is that normal? Moving from place to place with each new investment?'

Jake shrugged. 'This wasn't business in the usual sense. It's a pet project. I had to chivvy reluctant investors.'

'Surely if you can prove they'll make a good return they'd agree.'

'You're assuming the investors would reap the financial rewards.'

Now Caro really was intrigued, despite the low-grade frisson of nerves, reminding her they had more personal things to discuss. Was that why she was eager to talk business? To put off the evil moment?

'You make it sound like a great mystery.'

He laughed. 'No, at least not now we've got agreement. I developed a self-perpetuating investment scheme. But instead of profits returning to investors they'll be channelled into programmes for child victims of war and natural disaster. I came here to lobby some powerful corporations and governments. Especially corporations that need to rehabilitate their reputations as global citizens.'

'Companies that could do with positive press?' Caro could name a few. 'You tapped into the high-level talks here to establish a charity?'

The region regularly hosted talks between governments and attracted lobbyists from some of the world's most powerful corporations.

'There's nothing like face to face meetings to drive a project, especially when you're asking for substantial sums they'll never see again.'

Caro sat back, taking in the satisfaction on Jake's face.

He glowed like a man who'd sealed a deal to make his fortune. Instead the deal was for others.

'Why children? Why in war zones?'

'Not just war. In areas hit by tsunamis, hurricanes, any large-scale disorder.' His eyes held hers. 'You don't think it a good cause?'

'I think it's wonderful. I'm just curious.'

She'd thought she knew Jake. Living with him and Ariane, seeing him with his staff, she'd discovered many sides to his character. This was something new. He loved Ariane but she'd thought that was because he was her uncle. Maybe there was more to his motivation.

His gaze slid to the window. 'I spent a few years in the army. We were deployed in the Asia Pacific region mopping up after natural disasters, and once after a civil war. Some of the children…'

He stopped and Caro realised he wasn't seeing the glorious Swiss scenery. Her heart squeezed as his features tightened.

'Children are the most vulnerable, especially if separated from family. It can take years to reunite kids with remaining family, if there *is* any. Most disaster support is for food and shelter. Only a few agencies address the longer term process of finding secure, loving homes for lost children.'

Caro heard emotion beneath his words. She recalled images of disaster-ravaged zones worldwide and shuddered, imagining Ariane alone and lost.

Jake must have seen her shiver. His hand covered hers. This time she didn't object.

'What you're doing is important. Clever too, to target the big companies to contribute.'

'It will be good PR for them.'

Caro guessed Jake wouldn't claim any of those kudos. She wanted to say she was proud of him but stopped herself. She had no right to sound proprietorial, even if she felt it.

After her earlier revelation she needed to be careful.

'I didn't know you'd been in the army,' she said, trying to distract herself.

'It wasn't a long career. I didn't have the temperament for being ordered about.' At her questioning look he said, 'I got into trouble as a kid and my sister convinced me it was a ticket out of the place we lived.'

No mistaking his bitterness. 'You weren't happy at home?'

Reading the tension in those broad shoulders, she wondered if he'd answer. But eventually his lips curved in a rueful smile. 'It probably wasn't too bad but I was trouble. A misfit. My sister told me if I didn't sort myself out I'd end up in gaol. I was starting to act out.'

'Your sister, not your parents?'

Gunmetal-grey eyes met hers. 'I never knew my father and my mother abandoned us on a regular basis. She only came home when her latest boyfriend dumped her. The last time she left I was barely fourteen but Connie looked after me, stopped me from going into foster care.'

The air whooshed from Caro's lungs. No wonder he had a thing about lost children. And women abandoning their kids. She remembered his lacerating words when he thought she'd abandoned Ariane. No wonder he'd been so savage.

'Yes.' He nodded, as if reading her thoughts. 'I've got baggage. Usually I keep it under wraps. But with you…' He shook his head. 'It was like a red rag to a bull. I'm sorry I—'

'Don't.' Caro put her hand up. 'It's in the past. So you went into the army. That's a far cry from finance.'

Jake spread his hands. 'The army taught me discipline and that there was a big world out there. It gave me the drive to work hard and improve. Then my sister and I had a windfall. There were plans for a giant shopping complex in our suburb but the planners forgot to acquire a small parcel of land.' He smiled reminiscently. 'Ours. We lived

in our grandparents' tiny house in a rundown neighbour-
hood but suddenly it was worth a fortune. Connie used her
share to travel. I invested mine and got a job in the city,
learning finance.'

'And never looked back.'

Caro marvelled. From troubled teen to billionaire took
a lot of doing.

'Oh, I had setbacks. But I found mentors and learned
from my mistakes.'

Jake made it sound something anyone could do. Caro
thought of herself, all those years giving in to her father,
not even able to look after her own baby—

'Hey.' He cupped her chin. 'What is it?'

Her heart turned over at his gentle touch.

'Nothing. Except that I'm incredibly impressed.' She
tugged in a sharp breath. She'd avoided the inevitable for
too long. Time to confront it. 'What did you want to talk
about? You said it was time to leave.' Caro was proud of
her even tone. 'Where will you go?'

'Somewhere to make a home for Ariane. I'd thought of
St Ancilla, till your father…' He lifted those bare shoulders and Caro followed the movement, remembering how
she'd clung to that broad expanse when they made love.
'Maybe Australia or—'

'Australia!' Caro's voice hit a shrill note. 'If you take
Ariane I'll never see her.'

He dropped his hand. Caro's heart dropped too.

'Unless you come with us.'

'Sorry? You want me to move to Australia?'

'Or somewhere else. I'm open to suggestions. Somewhere we can make a home for Ariane.'

We. Her heart thundered. He'd said *we.*

'What, exactly, are you suggesting, Jake?'

He hesitated and to her surprise, Caro saw uncertainty
on his face. It couldn't be. This was the man who'd stalked

through a royal ball like an avenging angel intent on retribution, uncaring of scandal. Who'd spirited her away from her father and kept her safe from his machinations. Jake didn't do uncertain.

'We could bring Ariane up together.'

She couldn't think of anything she'd like more. Her pulse tripped and she had to stifle a surge of elation. It didn't seem possible.

'Together, not taking turns looking after her?'

'I want her to have stability and a loving family.' He paused, his long fingers squeezing hers. 'We could be that family.'

Caro tried to speak but the words stopped in her chest. She told herself to breathe, think this through, not jump to conclusions. Yet her heart leapt.

Less than twenty minutes ago she'd had a revelation, discovering the reason Jake affected her so profoundly.

Because she loved him. She'd fallen completely, devastatingly in love with Jake Maynard.

Her feelings for Mike hadn't been love, more excitement at escaping her restrictive life, the thrill of being wanted. He'd been her first crush. And he'd cured her of crushes for life.

Till Jake. Honourable, protective, tender, funny. He was everything she hadn't dared hope for. And now he talked about them making a family.

Because he'd fallen in love too? Excitement scudded through her.

Jake leaned in, warmth in his eyes. 'We could make it work, Caro. A marriage of convenience for Ariane's sake. What do you say?'

CHAPTER FOURTEEN

JAKE SAW THE fire in Caro's bright eyes die. It didn't flicker or fade. It was snuffed out in an instant.

In the same instant cold engulfed him.

Her lips thinned as she pressed them together. Within his grasp her hands jerked then stilled. She blinked once, twice, the dark pupils widening, making her look wounded, as if he'd hurt her.

Yet it was Jake who felt the punch to his gut, like a hunting knife jabbing flesh, piercing a vital organ.

He forced himself to breathe slowly. She was surprised. She wasn't rejecting him.

'It's a perfect solution, don't you see?' He sounded more confident than he felt. Like a desperate salesman giving a final pitch. That made him pause. He didn't do desperate. There was no reason for the anxiety gripping his belly.

'I realise it's an unusual solution to our situation.' Actually it was perfect. 'But think about it. Ariane needs stability and a family to love her. We're that stability. We give her that love. Even after such a short time I see the difference since you came into her life. We can be all she needs. And we're good together, you know we are.'

Jake made himself stop. He wasn't a snake oil salesman, pushing her into a purchase she'd regret. He knew she'd enjoyed this time together since leaving St Ancilla. It wasn't only her relief at leaving her father's kingdom, or even, he suspected, being with her daughter. Caro revelled in his company and his lovemaking. She'd been gratifyingly eager for both.

Yet Caro looked anything but eager as she slipped her

hands from his and hitched the sheet high. She trembled so much Jake could see it.

The blade at his belly twisted, gouging deep.

Jake had never laid himself open to rejection by a woman. Not after being rejected time and again by his mother. He'd kept his relationships with women to simple sexual transactions. This was the first time he'd put himself on the line.

It was impossible she'd shun him.

Yet his pulse juddered as he looked for a sign of understanding and agreement.

'But…marriage?' She frowned as if marriage to him was some distasteful medicine.

'Why not?' He shrugged his bare shoulders, chilling now despite the warmth of the room, and wished he'd waited instead of rushing into this. Instead of getting the easy agreement he'd anticipated, he had the unnerving sensation her response wouldn't be an enthusiastic 'yes'.

Would he have done better dressed for business in his office, with Caro sitting on the other side of the desk? The idea was preposterous. Yet—

'Isn't it a bit extreme? Couldn't we share custody, six months with you and six with me?'

Something heavy shoved down through Jake's middle. Disappointment or something stronger? Because she didn't leap at his suggestion. He told himself they discussed a pragmatic arrangement, that she wasn't rejecting *him*.

'You said it yourself. If we live on opposite sides of the world one of us would miss seeing her when she's with the other. This way she gets both of us.'

And we get each other.

'Besides, if you're pregnant, wouldn't it be the best outcome?'

Any thought that argument would clinch the deal died as

Caro's face leached of colour. It was like watching flesh and blood turn to parchment and it curdled the hope within him.

'You're covering all bases, aren't you?' Instead of admiring his foresight, it sounded oddly as if Caro resented his pragmatism.

'We have to be practical.' He waited for her to agree. When she said nothing he went on. 'Neither of us want to fight for Ariane in court.'

Finally, to his relief, she nodded. At least there was one thing on which they agreed.

'We need a solution for Ariane that will work for us both. Why not stay together? Build on what we already have? I can see it working.'

He could see it so clearly he had to bite his tongue from insisting she must too. It was the best, the only solution.

'Can you?' Her gaze held his. It wasn't the look of a happy woman. A woman offered security and caring, plus wealth beyond most people's imaginings. Offered *him*.

Suddenly, instead of a billionaire with the world at his feet, Jake felt like someone else. Someone unwanted, never good enough even to hold his parents' attention.

The sensation lasted only a second but it rocked Jake to the core.

So when Caro thanked him politely and said she needed to think about it he merely nodded and stood, forcing himself to rise and walk away on stiff legs.

The sun was warm on Caro's face as she drank in the peaceful scene. White-topped mountains that now seemed like friendly guardians rather than sombre presences. The alpine meadow dotted with the season's first flowers was tranquil, the only sound her daughter's voice.

Caro inhaled the scent of meadow grass, listened to Ariane's chatter as she played with Maxim, and willed herself to feel happy.

She had so much to be thankful for. They were safe, they were together and they were far from her father's influence. He still sent irate messages but it seemed he had more on his mind than pursuing his errant daughter. Money troubles, said Jake, who'd made it his business to find out. Significant money troubles, which explained why her father hadn't done more than bluster about her absence.

Caro and Ariane were building a real bond, which grew stronger daily. It was more than she'd once dared hope for.

She owed Jake so much. He made this possible. He could have prevented her seeing Ariane till the legalities were sorted out but he wasn't that sort of man.

Unlike her domineering father, Jake didn't play with people and their emotions for his own ends. He was decent, honest, reliable, and he cared for Ariane so much it was impossible not to love him for that alone.

As if Caro didn't love him anyway.

Her chest tightened painfully. It shouldn't be possible after so short a time but her feelings were clear. She loved him as surely as she loved her daughter.

How much longer would he wait for her answer?

How much longer could she pretend she didn't know how to reply?

Last week he'd offered her a convenient marriage as a solution to their tangled situation. Ariane would acquire a family. Caro and Jake would get to be with her permanently.

It was simple and workable.

Except Caro wanted more. She wanted someone to love *her* for herself.

She reminded herself she'd have Ariane's love. But she'd grown greedy. Having spent this time with Jake, she wanted it all. The physical intimacy and more besides. She wanted Jake to care for her, not as a co-parent but because she was unique, someone he didn't want to live without.

Not because she might carry his child.

Caro looked at the tiny daisies in her hands, the flower chain she was making crushed.

When she'd asked for time to think Jake's expression had turned wooden. She'd seen the shutters come down before he strolled away to dress. Since then there'd been a barrier between them. Even in bed, at the height of passion, when Caro was on the verge of blurting out her feelings as he drove her to peak after peak of pleasure, she was aware of something different in Jake. As if he held something of himself back.

Jake gave her everything except love.

She'd lived without love all her life. She could live without it now, especially as she had Ariane. Her daughter would grow to love her, Caro felt it in her bones.

In time, if she wanted, there'd be more children, and she'd love them too. She should take what she was offered and be content.

'What's wrong, Caro? You look sad.'

She turned to find Ariane regarding her solemnly. Though her daughter was brighter and more relaxed now, she was sensitive to negativity, still easily worried.

'Nothing at all.' Caro smiled. 'I was thinking how peaceful it is here.'

'Maxim likes it. He's not sure he wants to live somewhere else.'

'Somewhere else?'

The solemn little face nodded. 'I heard Uncle Jake and Neil. We're moving.' The little girl swallowed. 'Will you come too, Caro?'

And that, of course, put her personal woes into perspective. What was more important than Ariane?

Caro leaned in and cuddled her daughter. 'That's the plan, sweetie.'

So it was decided.

All Caro had to do now was tell Jake she'd accept his marriage of convenience.

She'd marry the man she loved, yet it felt as if she gave up her soul. She'd have to spend her life pretending not to love him. Learning not to care when he wearied of their passion and sought pleasure with other women.

Caro set her jaw and pushed her personal feelings aside. They weren't as important as Ariane.

An hour later, as Caro headed to Jake's office to tell him her decision, her phone rang. She'd tired of her father's staff calling her old number to harangue her and had changed it last week. Was it Zoe? This would save Caro calling to tell her there was no need for legal action.

'Hello?' Caro tried to sound bright and happy. But the smile she forced felt like a grimace.

'At last.' Her father's voice struck like a blow. Caro stumbled to a halt, her stomach churning. Once more he'd managed to get her private number! Before she could gather her wits he went on, his voice serpentine with venom. 'Don't even think about hanging up, Carolina, or I'll make your lover pay.'

The sun was sinking when Caro forced herself up from the window seat where she'd slumped. Every joint felt stiff, as if she'd aged a lifetime in an hour. Not that her father had stayed on the phone that long. His call had been brief but it had changed everything.

Earlier this afternoon she'd felt sorry for herself, on the verge of marrying the man she loved to make a family with him and her daughter.

She hadn't known how lucky she was!

Now that choice was denied her. She had to give Jake up and Ariane too. Her father had made that clear. He was a man who didn't make empty threats.

It didn't matter that Jake had done nothing wrong, had

broken no law. If her father vowed to destroy him he would. Even if it took years, he'd manipulate the truth, plant evidence, bribe people, all that and more, to destroy Jake's reputation and his business. The King had the contacts and the lack of scruples to do it. He'd even threatened extradition to St Ancilla on trumped-up charges relating to the disbursement of Jake's sister's estate and alleged mismanagement of an investment scheme there. He'd ensure Jake didn't get a fair trial. Destroying his reputation would devastate his business.

Unless Caro gave up her daughter and returned, alone, to the palace.

He'd taken his time planning his revenge for the way she stood up to him. It was something he excelled in. How had she let herself forget that?

The threat had made her realise too that her father would continue to influence their lives, spreading poison that would eventually infect Ariane, unless she, Caro, gave her up. There'd be no escape and ultimately Ariane would suffer.

Caro's throat constricted but she refused to cry. Now, more than ever, she had to be strong.

She didn't know how she was going to walk away from Jake and Ariane but she had to believe her daughter would be fine without her, because she'd have Jake. It wasn't as if Ariane knew Caro was her mother. Now she never would. Caro would have to get Jake to promise that at least.

Yet, here in her room, the room she hadn't slept in since returning from St Ancilla, Caro wondered how she'd find the strength to do what she must.

But surely it was simply one step then another, like after Mike's betrayal. And when she'd believed her baby dead.

Drawing a deep breath, Caro took a step, then another, towards the wardrobe where her suitcase was stored.

* * *

Jake had waited long enough. The days had stretched out and still Caro hadn't given an answer. She drove him crazy.

She made love as ardently as before, yet their emotional connection had severed.

He'd given up being patient. It was time for answers.

Answers he got as he opened the bedroom door and saw Caro with her back to him, suitcase open on the bed.

For a second that seemed to last for ever his feet stuck to the floor. He couldn't move, could barely process what he saw. But only for a second. He crossed the room and she swung around.

There was a flash of something in her eyes. Relief? Pleasure? Something that made the bleakness inside ease and hope surge.

Then it disappeared. Those violet eyes turned dull and shadowed, dropping to his chin.

He knew why. She'd decided he wasn't good enough. Why marry a commoner when she had handsome aristocrats hanging off her every word? He'd seen them at the ball, panting after her.

The weight within his ribs crushed him. His lungs laboured. Jake had to force himself to stand still and not haul her to him and insist they could work this out.

'This is your answer?' Another time he'd have winced at the raw emotion in his voice. 'Were you going to tell me or just let me work it out when you vanished?'

She jumped at his lashing words and Jake was torn between wanting to soothe her and wanting to make her hurt as he did.

Had he ever felt such pulsing, writhing pain? He had a hazy recollection of something similar as a kid. The day he'd come home from school to discover his mother had cleared out again. Jake shoved the memory aside. He'd given up caring about his mother. But he cared about Caro. He'd thought…

She lifted her face slowly, as if reluctant to face him.

'I was going to tell you. I'm sorry, Jake. But I…' She shook her head and her glorious hair, loose around her shoulders, shifted like a living thing, attracting all the light in the room. It was burnished in shades of blood and rust, like the metallic tang of defeat filling his mouth. 'I've given your suggestion a lot of thought but it won't work.' She opened her mouth as if to say more then paused. 'It's time I left.'

She turned away and reached for a blouse, folding it methodically.

That was all the explanation he deserved?

His anger notched higher and so did his determination. He never quit. Never gave up on something worth fighting for.

Jake snagged a rough breath, then another. This wasn't the end. He refused to let her go like this.

'So you're going to fight me for custody of Ariane.'

Caro jumped and the blouse fell to the bed. For a long time she stood, utterly still, though tension emanated from her. He felt it like waves pummelling him.

'No… I've decided that won't work.' She picked up the blouse once more and began folding it with excruciatingly slow movements. 'Ariane is better off with you. You're her uncle. She knows you, loves you.' Caro's voice wobbled alarmingly and Jake felt its echo reverberate inside him as a shudder of astonishment.

He couldn't be hearing this. It was impossible. After all she'd been through Caro would *never* contemplate renouncing her child.

'You're giving up your *daughter*? The daughter you wanted so desperately? So desperately you came here under false pretences. So desperately you stood up to your father?' Jake stalked across to stand behind her shoulder. She hitched an uneven breath as the fabric in her hands became a mangled ball. Jake felt like mangling something himself. 'I don't believe it.'

What was going on? Did she find him so repulsive she'd give up Ariane rather than stay with him?

He couldn't believe it. He knew Caro. Even if things weren't as good between them now, she'd proved again and again that she was attracted to him. He'd cherished hopes it was something deeper than attraction.

Those narrow shoulders straightened. Her chin lifted and he caught a glimpse of Caro's proud profile.

'I've made my decision.' A pause, a long pause, so fraught Jake sensed she struggled. But if this was hard, why not accept his proposal? 'Ariane will be happy with you. I know you'll look after her. With me…' Her shoulders rose. 'It's better if she grows up without any connection to my family.'

Jake pounced on the mention of her family, a glimmer of hope easing the raw ache in his gut.

Because he couldn't believe she'd spurn him otherwise? Was he so desperate?

The answer was a resounding yes. For days he'd been on tenterhooks, giving Caro space to decide. In that time one thing had become abundantly clear.

That he had his own reasons for offering marriage and they weren't confined to Ariane.

Jake needed more from Caro. Not convenience. Not a mother for his orphaned niece.

He needed Caro for himself.

She spread the blouse on the bed a third time, smoothing then folding it. But her hands shook. Jake stood so close he felt the tremors, heard her uneven breathing.

This took more from her than she wanted to admit.

'What is it, Caro?' His voice was husky, rough with emotion he struggled to leash. 'What's wrong?'

'Nothing.' Her movements quickened, the fold lines on the shirt askew, but she didn't stop, almost throwing it into the suitcase and reaching for another.

Jake wanted to make her look at him but he didn't dare touch her. Not yet. He feared that if he did he wouldn't let her go.

'Why not marry me and give Ariane the life we both want for her?'

The life we both want for ourselves.

'I made a mistake. I'm not cut out for motherhood. I need to—'

'Caro.' Her name was a caress as he closed his arms around her, pulling her gently back against him, revelling in the feel of her there, where she belonged, even if she was rigid with tension. 'Tell me what's wrong. I know something is. You're a terrible liar.'

He felt the sob rack her though she stifled it. Still she didn't relax. Instead her movements grew quicker, her breathing too, as she leaned away from his restraining hold, grabbing fistfuls of clothes and tossing them into the suitcase.

'Please, don't make this more difficult, Jake. I don't want to marry you. We'd make each other unhappy and that wouldn't be good for Ariane.'

'And if you're pregnant?' He slid his palm to her abdomen. He'd told himself he'd support her if there was a baby. In fact he was thrilled Caro might carry his child. He'd begun to imagine what the baby would look like, how it would feel in his arms.

'I won't be. The odds are against it.'

She spoke so softly he had to crane to hear. Which brought him to the spice and warmth scent of her skin. Jake closed his eyes and inhaled. That undid him.

'Sweetheart, tell me what's wrong. I promise we'll find a way to deal with it.' Jake didn't care that his voice revealed his feelings. 'I want you with me. You and Ariane.'

If she'd been tense before it was nothing to her iron rigidity now. It felt as if she didn't even breathe.

'No! It's impossible. We can't.'

But Jake was listening now, really listening. He didn't hear rejection but desperation. A woman who didn't care for him or her child wouldn't sound as if she were being torn apart.

Her pain wrenched at his vitals. He'd do anything to take the hurt away.

He kissed the curve where her shoulder met her neck and felt her instant response as if her knees gave way. He gathered her closer. Caro's breath became a sigh and instead of fighting his hold she angled her head a fraction to allow unfettered access.

Triumph rose. Relief so profound it almost overwhelmed him.

Jake lifted one unsteady hand, pushing her hair aside, nuzzling that sensitive spot as she leant against him.

Even if she didn't feel the same way about him, he could work with that. He was determined, single-minded and patient when he needed to be. He'd *make* her love him if it took years.

'You want to be with me,' he murmured against her skin, feeling her shivers of response.

She tried to move away, but Jake was implacable. He needed to understand and it seemed the only way to learn the truth was when he weakened Caro's defences. Her words confirmed it.

'Let me go, Jake. Please. You're wrong, I don't want you.'

Her body told another story, as did her voice. She sounded desperate but not convincing. Scared rather than angry. Of what? Surely not of a future together?

'I don't believe you.'

She stilled.

'What happened, Caro? What are you frightened of?'

'I…' She shook her head as if she'd run out of lies to distract him.

Gently Jake turned her to face him. Her eyes were wide and her mouth a crooked line of pain but it wasn't rejection he saw in those purple-blue eyes. It was fear.

Surely not of him? Jake was processing the possibility when abruptly his mind clicked into action.

'It's your father, isn't it? He contacted you.'

The instant flare of her eyes told him he'd hit the truth.

Silently Jake cursed. He'd done everything he could to stymie the King's attempts to reach Caro and thought he'd succeeded. What he'd learned in that confrontation between father and daughter at the palace had horrified him. Now the man turned even more vicious and unstable. Not simply because Caro dared defy him but because the house of cards he'd built around himself was being swiftly and methodically exposed.

Jake hadn't hesitated to probe into the monarch's affairs. Between them, professional investigators and Jake's well-placed business associates had uncovered an unsavoury, not to mention illegal web of financial misappropriation and fraud. King Hugo regarded the public purse as his own, but the structures he'd used to hide his misdoings were crumbling under pressure.

'That doesn't matter.' Caro's face was drawn and tense. 'I can't live with you and Ariane—'

'I still don't believe you.' Her head jerked up and she looked him in the eye. 'You want to be with us but you're frightened.'

How he welcomed her spark of annoyance. Seeing her frightened made him desperate. 'Has anyone ever told you you're arrogant, Jake Maynard?'

As a diversion it might have worked, once, weeks ago before he'd got to know Caro. 'Yes. You have, and it's true. But I'm right. You can't lie to me, Caro, you're no good at it.'

It was true, despite her earlier masquerade. Deliberately, lifting his arms wide, he stepped back, giving her space, though it went against every instinct to release her rather than embrace her.

Jake needed her to trust him.

'Tell me what he said, Caro. Playing by his rules hurts all of us.'

Finally she nodded. 'He demanded I return. He wants me there, to marry someone he's chosen.'

'Or what?' Jake kept his voice even despite his building fury.

'Or he'll destroy you. He means it, too,' she said in a rush. 'He hates me for repudiating him and you for taking my side. He'll find a way to bring you down. He said he'd make it his mission, no matter how long it takes.' Caro reached for Jake, grabbing his hands as if to convince him by sheer force. 'He'll bring trumped-up charges against you, get someone to testify you broke the law in your financial dealings—'

'Is that all?' Jake threaded his fingers through Caro's, melding their hands.

'All? Don't you understand? He'll destroy your reputation and then your business! You don't know how devious he is, the lengths he'll go to.'

'Oh, I know.' He should have been prepared for this, but he'd thought there was no way the King could worry Caro here. 'What I don't know is whether you'd stay with me if it weren't for his threats.'

She shook her head, the picture of desperation. 'Jake, please, listen. He'll wreck everything you've worked for. I can't let him—'

'He won't, Caro. Because he's about to go under.' Jake willed her to focus on his words, not her father's threats. 'He's stolen funds and borrowed against assets that don't belong to him. He's dipped into the public purse on a huge scale.'

Finally she was taking it in. Her eyes grew huge.

'He got careless and some of us in the finance sector have been doing our own investigating.' Because he needed to protect Caro and Ariane. 'He's a spent force, Caro. Don't believe his bluster. This is a last-ditch effort to save himself through you. My guess is he thinks I'll call off the creditors if he has you in his clutches. Believe me, he can't touch you. I promise.'

His pulse thundered through the silence and he watched as, gradually, the fear eased from Caro's face. If Jake had had any doubts about her belief in him, the fact that she took his word now proved otherwise. It warmed him from the inside out in a way only Caro could.

'*You* did all that? But why?' She frowned. 'You didn't know he'd threatened you.'

Seeing her puzzlement, Jake realised how alone she must have felt all those years. Had there ever been anyone to stand beside her? He swallowed, his throat constricting painfully. Her stoicism and determination really were phenomenal.

'You don't know?' Jake's voice stretched. He'd hoped she'd understand. 'For the same reason I hope you really want to marry me.'

His breath grew shallow, his lungs working overtime. No longer was he a savvy investor, a world-class businessman, secure in his success. Jake hovered on a knife edge between hope and disaster.

'I fell in love with you, Caro. I want you, not for Ariane but for myself.' He lifted her hand to his lips and allowed himself a fleeting kiss to her hand, taking courage from the throbbing pulse at her wrist. 'I know it's been a short time but I've never been more certain of anything.'

Jake watched emotions chase across her face, so fast he hadn't a hope of deciphering them. Her fingers shook in his grip.

'Caro?' His confident words deserted him. It emerged as a croak.

'You love me?' She shook her head and he slipped his other hand up to cup her cheek, holding her steady so she could read the truth in his eyes. 'It's not possible.'

'It is. That's why I took it badly when you needed time to think about marriage.'

'You said it was a marriage of *convenience*!' Jake heard her outrage and hurt and understood how badly he'd blundered with that impulsive proposal. But he'd been so excited at the idea he'd been unable to wait.

Now he had to get it right.

'It's taken me a while to confront what I feel. I'm not used to loving.'

Or being loved. His heart rose in his chest as he waited for her response.

'Nor am I.' Suddenly Caro was laughing, though it sounded ragged. And beautiful. 'I can't believe it.'

'It's true, absolutely true.' He stroked his thumb across her velvety cheek, watching her pupils dilate. 'What I don't know is how you feel about me.'

Their eyes locked and he felt that slam of connection, as real as a fist to his heart.

'Even when I hated you that night of the ball, I was afraid I loved you too.' Her words were magic, her expression mesmerising. 'Since then…it's been so hard feeling the way I do about you and thinking you didn't reciprocate. I don't know how I came to love you, Jake, or when, but I do. Totally. You devastated me when you offered a convenient wedding. I thought you only cared about Ariane, not me.'

Jake was filled with mingled pain and ecstasy, torn between exultation and regret.

He was spellbound by her luminous joy that belied the hurt she described.

Caro loved him!

His face split with a grin and he felt like whooping. Or kissing her senseless, except he needed more of her beautiful, wonderful words.

He planted her hand on his chest where his heart danced to a rackety beat and looped his arm around her, drawing her close where she belonged.

'Caro, I'm sorry. I'm better with numbers than emotions.'

'You're wrong, Jake. I've seen you with Ariane. I know how deeply you feel about her.'

'Not just about Ariane.' He revelled in the feel of her right here against him. With her hand on his chest she could feel his heart thundering out the truth. 'Will you be mine, Caro, for ever? I need you.' To his surprise, Jake discovered the admission, far from weakening him, made him feel stronger than he'd ever been.

'But my father...'

'Trust me to deal with your father.' Jake would let nothing come between him and the woman he loved. 'He's going under, Caro. He won't be in a position to threaten any longer.'

'Of course I trust you.' Her free hand slid to his shoulder, her grip firm and possessive. He loved it.

'So you'll marry me,' he pressed. He wanted everything clear between them, despite the urgent need to taste and caress her.

Her smile turned from misty to mischievous and he loved that too. 'Do you always negotiate this hard?'

'Only when our happiness is at stake. I won't allow anyone to stand in the way of that, king or no king.' What Jake felt for Caro, and what he saw shining in her expression, were too precious to abandon.

Caro's smile died and she rose on tiptoe, cradling his face in her palms. 'I love you, Jake.' The words filled him with awe and gratitude. 'If you're really sure…the answer is yes, because I don't think I can live without you.'

Jake drew his first easy breath in days. Caro was his. She loved him and they had all their lives to be together.

With a groan of release he gave in and covered her lips with his. Caro was as eager as he, kissing him back with all the fervour, all the caring a man could want. Jake sank into her, losing himself and finding more, far more. Together they were magnificent, one entity forged of trust, respect and love. He'd never felt so strong, so blessed. Gratitude vied with desire.

When, finally, they pulled apart enough to haul air into starved lungs, Jake looked down into a face made even more beautiful because of the gift they shared.

'You make me the happiest man in the world, Caro.' Maybe other lovers said it too. All Jake knew was that no one meant it more than he. 'Let me make you just as happy.'

EPILOGUE

'THERE YOU ARE! I followed the giggles.'

Caro spun around in the shallow end of the infinity pool overlooking the blue Pacific Ocean. There he was. Jake. Her lover, her man, her husband. Just back from meetings in the city, he'd shed his jacket and tie and was rolling up his sleeves as he crossed the flagstones.

Their eyes met and, as ever, she felt that hard pump of blood as if their hearts realigned to beat in sync. He smiled the slow, sexy smile that undid her as easily as his deft hands undressed her each night.

'Uncle Jake!' Ariane squealed and splashed out of the pool to cling to his legs. 'We waited and waited for you.'

Jake lifted his niece onto his hip, regardless of her wetness. Ariane's heart gave a great thump as she saw them together, the big man and the adoring little girl, bonded by a love so strong sometimes Caro had trouble believing this was real. Their family was better than any fantasy.

'Sorry, sweetie. But I have to work sometimes.'

Jake had reduced his hours, but their home on Sydney's exclusive northern beaches allowed him to commute to the city occasionally. Very occasionally. Mainly he worked from home, or delegated.

'Did you have a good day?' He bent his head towards the little girl and Caro smiled as Ariane described her day in detail. The withdrawn child she'd met in Switzerland was gone. Now Ariane was confident, secure and adventurous, already making friends with other local children.

Caro got out of the pool and went to fetch a towel, but Jake got in the way.

'Haven't you forgotten something important, Caro?' Ebony eyebrows lifted over teasing eyes.

'Well, if you don't mind getting even more wet...' She leaned close, kissing him soundly. When she pulled back he was grinning. His eyes held a promise that sent anticipation sizzling all the way to her toes.

'You're not listening, Uncle Jake. We have a surprise.' Caro blinked at Ariane's words. When Jake looked at her that way...

'A surprise?'

Her daughter nodded importantly. 'A visitor.'

Jake's eyebrows rose and Caro clarified. 'A visitor tomorrow.'

Ariane nodded. 'But I want to look for a book to share with him. Can I go now? Please?'

Fifteen minutes later, leaving Ariane dry, dressed and sorting her picture books, Caro returned to the terrace with its ocean views. The view had never looked so good as now with Jake powering through the pool wearing only surf shorts.

'A visitor?' He waded to the edge of the pool and stood between her knees as she sat with her feet in the water. Jake pressed a luscious kiss to the base of her neck. Caro's nipples pebbled and her thoughts frayed.

'Mm hm.' She tilted her head so he could nip his way up her neck to that spot below her ear that drove her insane. 'Paul.'

'Paul?' His voice was a husky whisper.

Caro planted her hands on Jake's wet shoulders and leaned back. She couldn't kiss and think. 'King Paul of St Ancilla. We invited him, remember?'

The last couple of months had been dramatic with her father bowing to pressure and abdicating in favour of his eldest son. There'd been some scandal but the full depths of the old man's deceit and theft hadn't been made public.

The ex-King had quietly retired to a small estate on a distant island. The public didn't know he'd been banished. Meanwhile Jake helped Caro's brother work to restructure the royal debt with an ambitious plan of reinvestment and repayment. No one had the stomach for unseating a monarchy and destabilising a nation, so long as the man responsible was out of the equation.

'You're happy with that?' Jake's silvery eyes turned piercing.

'I said so before, didn't I? Paul could do with some time out, away from the court and the press.' And his mother and fiancée, though she didn't say that. Caro guessed neither of the women were particularly supportive but the way Paul had stepped up to his responsibilities, his honesty and genuine concern at their father's wrongdoing, had impressed her.

'The press will follow him here.'

Caro shrugged. 'I'll cope. I'm used to it, remember. Besides, if we accept his invitation and spend part of each year in St Ancilla we'll be in the spotlight even more.' She cupped Jake's harsh, handsome face in her palms. 'Are *you* sure you want to take that on? Associating with royals. Going to balls and such?'

'It's your home and your heritage, Caro, and Ariane's. I can cope if you can.' The glint in Jake's eyes grew wicked, turning her insides liquid. 'I enjoyed my first royal ball enormously.'

'It wasn't the ball but what came after.'

'I have a weakness for princesses.'

Caro huffed in mock dismay. 'Then you can't go to royal events. Who knows what princesses and duchesses there will be, even queens?'

Jake's expression made her pulse stutter. 'How could I notice them, Caro, when you've shown me what love is? You're Queen of my heart.'

That organ rolled over, beating frantically against her

ribs. 'Sometimes I think you're too good to be true, Jake Maynard.' Her words were husky with love.

'I *know* you are, Caro. Which is why I intend to do everything I can to make you happy. Now come here and kiss me.'

* * * * *

FALLING FOR THE
SECRET PRINCESS

KANDY SHEPHERD

To Elizabeth Lhuede, good friend and my first critique partner on my romance writing journey.

She's still there, with wise and informed feedback not only on writing but also on the quirks of human behaviour.

Thank you, Elizabeth!

CHAPTER ONE

NATALIA KNEW SHE should have eyes only for her friends, the bride and groom, as the deliriously happy couple exchanged vows in the grounds of a waterfront mansion on Sydney Harbour. The correct etiquette and protocol for every possible social occasion had been drummed into her since birth. *'You must always follow the rules, Natalia.'* She could almost hear the commanding tones of her parents. But, although she knew it was an impolite no-no, she could not help her gaze from straying to the tall, darkly handsome guest on the opposite side of the informal garden aisle. He was hot. Unbelievably hot.

What *was* it about Australia? Since she'd arrived in Sydney, five days previously, she'd never seen so many good-looking men. But none had triggered her interest like this one.

She'd noticed him as soon as the guests had started arriving—broad-shouldered and imposing, black hair, wearing an immaculately tailored charcoal tuxedo. Spanish? Middle Eastern? Greek? It was difficult to tell from this distance. She'd sneaked more than a few surreptitious glances since, each lingering longer than the last. This time he must have sensed her gaze on him because he turned to meet it.

Mortified, she froze. For a long second her eyes connected with his and he smiled, teeth dazzling white against olive skin, dark brows raised in acknowledgment. She flushed and quickly averted her gaze, looking down with feigned interest at the Order of Service card in her hand.

Despite her reputation in the gossip pages, Natalia wasn't a flirt, or a ruthless breaker of men's hearts. In fact she could be cursedly shy when she encountered an attractive man. But there was something about this fellow wedding guest that made her want to smile right back boldly. To flutter her eyelashes and let him know how drawn she was to him.

Instead she twisted the card between her fingers, determined not to look up again. Breach of protocol aside, she'd been warned to stay right under the radar so as not to take attention away from the bride and groom by her presence. That *didn't* mean conducting a public, across-the-aisle flirtation with a handsome stranger.

But then she remembered with a giddying rush of excitement that she was here incognito and in disguise. Those constricting rules need not apply to her alter ego. *She could do whatever she liked.*

No one but a select few were aware that she was Princess Natalia of Montovia, second in line to the throne of a small European kingdom, notorious for her six refusals of proposals of marriage from royal suitors and her seeming determination to stay single.

Her presence could draw unwanted media attention. The press intrusion was here, even in far-away Australia. Her brother Tristan, the Crown Prince, had married a Sydney girl, and every move they made was newsworthy. The condition of Natalia being allowed to accept the invitation to this wedding, where her brother was a groomsman and his wife a bridesmaid, was that she—Princess Heartbreaker—stayed out of the gossip pages.

So Natalia had chosen a full-on disguise for her stay in Sydney. Her shoulder-length dark brown hair had been straightened, lengthened with extensions and lightened to a honey-blonde that complemented her creamy skin. She'd tried coloured contact lenses to darken her blue eyes, but they'd hurt so she'd abandoned them. Her exclusive designer clothes had been replaced with a wardrobe purchased from a smart high street chain—she'd picked outfits that a regular, non-royal twenty-seven-year-old woman would wear—and her priceless jewellery was locked in a safe back home at the palace, save for a single pair of diamond ear studs.

So far, to her delight, no one had guessed her secret. And the more she knew she was getting away with her disguise, the bolder she'd become at testing it.

Not-Princess Natalia—at this moment not bound by her kingdom's rules—lifted her eyes and turned back to face the handsome guest, to find him still looking at her. She smiled, sure and confident, though she was racked with nerves inside. His answering grin made her flush grow warmer and awareness shimmer through her body.

Natalia had a sense that he was assessing her, in a subtle yet thorough way. Daringly, she did the same to him. On longer examination he was every bit as hot as he had appeared at first glance. Her smile danced at the corners of her mouth and she angled her shoulders towards him, scarcely aware that she was doing so. His grin widened and he nodded almost imperceptibly in acknowledgment of their silent exchange.

Her heart started beating in excitement. What next? Should she—?

At that moment the celebrant declared Eliza and Jake man and wife, and the newlyweds exchanged their first married kiss, to the accompaniment of happy sighs and cheers from their assembled family and friends. Natalia automatically turned towards the flowered arch where her friends were kissing, and watched as the couple started their march back down the grassy aisle. The bride was flaunting a neat baby bump, which was cause for great celebration.

'Don't you want to have children?'

Natalia's mother, the Queen, had asked that question—for what must have been the zillionth time since Natalia had turned eighteen—as she'd reluctantly said farewell to her only daughter.

Of course she did. And she wasn't averse to marriage. But she wasn't going to couple up with a man she didn't love just so she could have children and ensure further heirs to the throne. Besides, at twenty-seven she wasn't panicking. She simply hadn't met a man who thrilled her, either before or after the lifting of the edict that royals had to marry royals. In theory, she could now marry anyone she liked. That was if she ever fell in love.

Was it because of the men or herself that she'd never felt that giddying elation? Maybe she had to face up to the fact she wasn't a 'falling in love' person. Perhaps she didn't have it in her to trust someone enough to fall in love. Certainly there were very few examples of happy relationships in her family to inspire her.

She believed with all her heart that Tristan and Gemma's happy marriage would last the distance, but it was an exception. Her other brother's arranged marriage had been trumpeted as a 'love match', but his wife had turned out to be cold-hearted and greedy. Her selfishness had, in fact, contributed to her husband's death. And then there were the King and Queen… As a teenager she'd been devastated to discover her parents' marriage was a hypocritical sham.

But this wedding here in Sydney was the real deal, and it gave Natalia a skerrick of hope that true love could be found—among non-royals, anyway.

The bride shone her a special smile as she passed between the rows of white chairs set out on the lawn of the mansion. Eliza was one of the few here who knew her real identity. Eliza and Jake were friends of her brother Tristan. And Eliza and Tristan's wife, Gemma, along with their friend Andie, who was married to the best man, Dominic, ran Sydney's most successful party planning business, Party Queens.

Gemma now lived in Montovia and participated in the business from a distance. Her new sister-in-law had become a close friend, and Natalia had met the other two Party Queens on their visits to Montovia.

She had been thrilled to receive an invitation to Eliza and Jake's wedding. Not just because Eliza was a friend, but also because she'd wanted to see Sydney—the place where Tristan had met his wife Gemma, the place where he had spent a glorious few weeks as an anonymous tourist. She'd wanted a rare chance to be anonymous too. To be herself. Possibly even to find herself.

After the rest of the bridal party had passed by, she looked over to the handsome stranger with bated breath, only to see an empty chair.

Finn was caught up in a swell of well-wishers, all rushing past him to congratulate the bride and groom. As they thronged around him he lost sight of the beautiful woman across the aisle. By the time he'd elbowed past the other guests he could only see the back of her head as she hugged Eliza, her long blonde hair glinting golden in the afternoon sun. Then he himself got caught up in conversation with the best man, Dominic.

Weddings tended to bring out the grouch in Finn. He was what people delighted in calling 'an eligible bachelor'. He'd even, to his horror, been included in a well-publicised list of 'Bachelor Millionaires'—but he was a private person and loathed being in the spotlight. A wedding seemed to bring out matchmaking efforts in even the most unlikely of his friends and acquaintances, all keen to introduce him to potential spouses in whom he had no interest whatsoever. Marriage was not on the cards for him. Not in the foreseeable future.

Thankfully, property developer Dominic wanted to talk business, not potential brides, but real estate was the last thing on Finn's mind. He ground his teeth in frustration at the effort of being polite when all he ached to do was find an opportunity to see her again—the gorgeous sexy woman in the dark pink dress that hugged her curvaceous form. He had to see if she'd felt the same zing of attraction. That instant awareness that hadn't struck him for a long, long time.

After Dominic went on his way Finn politely but impatiently brushed off a stranger who wanted to gush about how romantic the wedding was and headed for the veranda of the beautiful old Kirribilli house where the reception was being held. He had one thing on his mind—to find that lovely woman before some other guy did.

Where was he? Natalia searched the throng of guests, the women wearing a rainbow of dresses, the men in shades of grey and black. No hot guy.

Eliza had ridden up the makeshift aisle on a pony, and a cluster of people had gathered to admire the little mare tethered under the shade cast by the late-afternoon shadow of a towering fig tree. Hot guy wasn't there either.

Natalia was five-foot-five in bare feet. Her stilettos gave her some height advantage over the crowd, but not enough to locate him.

She headed for the mansion where the meal was to be

served. Then climbed the short flight of wide, sandstone steps to a veranda that gave a view of the garden to the harbour beyond.

From her new vantage point she scanned the throng in the garden below. *Dignity, Natalia, dignity.* A princess did not chase after a man—no matter how devastatingly attractive she found him.

She rested her hands lightly on the veranda railing, so any onlooker would think she had paused to admire the view of the Opera House with its white sails on the opposite shore of the harbour. Then she tensed at the sudden awareness that tingled along her spine. All her senses seemed to scream an alert.

Him.

Slowly she turned around. The hot guy stood behind her, framed by the arched sandstone windows of the mansion. Just steps away he looked even more handsome than at first glance. Sculpted cheekbones, and his eyes... Not the dark brown she had expected but lighter—hazel, perhaps. A sensuous mouth that lifted in a half smile.

He held a flute of champagne in each hand, tiny bubbles floating rapidly upwards like the excitement rising in her. He stepped forward and offered her a glass. 'I snagged these from a waiter heading out to the garden.'

That voice! Deep, resonant, husky... The tone sent shivers through her. Her hands felt suddenly clammy with nerves. But it would be most un-princess-like behaviour to wipe them down the sides of her dress. She reached out for the flute, hoping it wouldn't slide out of her grip. The movement brought her closer to him, so close that she caught his scent—spicy, fresh, *male*—so potent it caused her pulse to quicken.

She wanted to close her eyes and breathe him in. Instead she took a breath to steady herself. 'Thank you,' she murmured.

'Most welcome. You're a friend of the groom?' he said.

How did he know that? Panic seized her voice, choking any possible reply.

'You were on the groom's side of the aisle,' he prompted.

'Yes. Yes, of course. Jake is a family friend.'

Tristan, Jake and Dominic had been friends for years, having met on the ski slopes of Montovia long before their Party Queens spouses had come along. Jake had been Tristan's best man at his wedding to Gemma.

But Natalia didn't want any questions about their connection. 'You, of course, were on the bride's side.'

'I went to university with Eliza. Since then I've done business with her party planning company.'

'I met her quite recently,' Natalia said.

Eliza had been one of Gemma's bridesmaids at her brother's spectacular wedding in the grand cathedral the previous year. Just the kind of wedding her parents intended for *her*. Dread squeezed her at the very thought. Marriage Montovian royal-style seemed more like a trap than a gateway to happy-ever-after.

'Eliza's lovely, and she seems so happy.'

'Yeah,' he said. 'And Jake's a good guy.'

Natalia had devised a cover story for her alter ego, but it didn't go very deep. Stalling, she gulped some champagne as she tried to keep the details straight in her mind.

Hot Guy seemed to have no such hesitation. He transferred his glass to his left hand and offered his right. 'Finn O'Neill,' he said, by way of introduction.

Natalie stared at him, spluttered over her champagne, and coughed. Then she quickly recovered herself. 'I'm sorry, I—'

'You were startled by my name? Don't worry. You're

not the first and I'd lay a hefty bet you won't be the last. Irish father; Chinese grandfather and Italian grandmother on my mother's side.'

So that was where those exotic good looks came from. 'No. I…er…' She started a polite fib, then thought better of it. To conceal her identity she was being forced to fib. No need to do so unnecessarily. 'Yes, I was surprised. Your name doesn't match your looks. Not like the Irish guys I've met, that is.'

'I'm a fine example of Australia's multicultural population,' he said lightly.

He was a fine example of a male.

Before she could dig herself in any further, she took his hand in a firm shake. 'Natalie Gerard,' she said. Natalie seemed a less memorable name than Natalia; Gerard was her father the King's name. She actually didn't *have* a surname—she was simply known as Natalia, Princess of Montovia.

'By the sound of your accent, you're English,' he said.

'Er…yes,' she said.

She didn't like to lie. But she'd promised her family not to blow her cover to anyone, in case of leaks to the media. Princess Heartbreaker in disguise at a wedding would be the kind of thing they liked to pounce on. So lie she must—though she'd rather think of it as tactical evasion.

Thank heaven for the English-born tutor married to a Montovian woman who had taught her perfectly accented English from the time she'd started to speak her first words. She also spoke impeccable German, French and Italian, with passable Spanish. So for today she would be English.

'Do you live here?' Finn asked.

She shook her head. 'Sadly I'm just visiting on vacation. I wish it were longer. Sydney is fabulous.'

'Spring is a good time to visit,' he said.

'Yes, it is,' she said. 'I'm loving it here.'

Just plain Natalie, a tourist, had spent the last three days riding the ferries, visiting the beaches, taking in a concert at the Opera House. She'd revelled in her freedom and anonymity—even though her two bodyguards were always at a discreet distance. As they were here now, masquerading as waiters.

Perhaps Finn had snagged the champagne from one of them. She was so used to the constant presence of household staff and bodyguards she scarcely noticed their presence.

'Where do you live in England?' Finn asked.

'London,' she said.

The royal family had a house in Mayfair, where she'd lived for a while when she was studying. Until the paparazzi had snapped her staggering out of a nightclub after one too many cocktails and she'd been recalled in disgrace to the palace before she'd been able to finish her degree in architecture.

'Whereabouts in London?' he said. 'I visit there quite often.'

No need to get too specific… Natalia chose to answer the second part of his question instead. 'What takes you to London?'

'My import/export business,' he said.

Which could, she thought, mean anything.

'What do *you* do?' he said.

Nothing she could share with him. Being Princess of Montovia was pretty much a full-time role. She wasn't allowed to be employed—rather had thrown herself into charity work.

Her main occupation was with the charity she'd started, which auctioned worn-once designer clothes and accessories donated by her and others in her circle to benefit her particular interest—the promotion of education for girls wherever they lived in the world.

Her online fashion parades and auctions had taken off way beyond anything she'd anticipated. Donations of fashion items now came from wealthy aristocrats and celebrities from all over Europe. Bids came from all around the world. The administration was undertaken by volunteers, so profits went straight to where they were needed. She was proud of what she had achieved through her own initiative. But that had nothing to do with Natalie Gerard.

The fact was, she'd been destined for a strategic marriage rather than a career. Especially after the tragic accident nearly three years ago that had robbed Montovia of her older brother Carl and his family, and pushed her up to second in line to the throne after Tristan, now Crown Prince.

Her life had changed radically after the tragedy, with her parents now obsessed with maintaining the succession to the throne. She'd had to work within their restrictions, not wanting to add to their intense grief in mourning their son and two-year-old grandson, still reeling from her own grief, not to mention the outpouring of grief throughout the country.

But she was beginning to weary of doing everything by the royal rules. She wanted her own life.

She couldn't share any of that with Finn. Instead she aimed for impartial chit-chat. 'I work in fashion,' she said.

That wasn't too much of a stretch of the truth. Organising her high-end fashion auctions *was* a job, if not a paid one.

'Retail or wholesale?'

'Retail.'

Her role often required several changes of formal clothing a day. That involved a lot of shopping in the fashion capitals of Europe. In fact, that had kicked off her idea for the auctions—she and other people in the public eye were expected by fashion-watchers to appear at functions in a different outfit each time. That meant expensive garments were often only worn once or twice.

'You fit the part.'

His eyes lit with admiration as he looked at her simple sheath dress in a deep rose-pink overlaid with lace. It wasn't silk, but it was a very good knock-off of a French designer whose couture originals took up considerable hanging space in her apartment-sized humidity-controlled closet back at the palace before they were moved on to auction.

'Thank you,' she said, inordinately pleased at the compliment. 'What do you import and export?' she asked, deflecting his attention from her.

'High-end foods and liquor,' he said. 'It takes me all around the world.'

She nodded. 'Hence your work with Party Queens?'

'Exactly,' he said.

She finished her champagne at the same time he did, then placed her glass on the wide veranda railing. Someone would be along to pick it up.

But Finn reached for it. 'I'll put that glass somewhere safer,' he said.

Mistake, she thought as he took the glasses and placed them on a table just inside the doorway. Regular girl Natalie would *not* be used to household staff picking up after her.

Finn was back within seconds. 'Tell me, Natalie, are you here with a partner?'

He glanced at the bare fingers of her left hand—without realising he did so, she thought. She did the same to him. No rings there either.

'No partner,' she said.

'Good,' he said, with a decisiveness that thrilled her. 'Either here at the wedding or in my life.'

'Me neither,' he said. 'Single. Never married.'

Her spine tingled at this less than subtle trumpeting of his single status. She was single and available too. For today.

Maybe for tonight.

'Likewise,' she said.

This handsome, handsome man must be thirtyish. How had such a catch evaded matrimony?

'D'you think they've put us at the singles table for the meal?' he asked.

'I have no idea,' she said. 'I…I hope so.'

'If they haven't I'll switch every place card in the room to make sure we're seated together.'

She laughed. 'Seriously?'

'Absolutely. Why wouldn't I want to sit with the most beautiful woman at the wedding?'

She laughed again. 'You flatter me.'

He was suddenly very serious. 'There's no flattery. I noticed you as soon as you walked across the grass to take your seat. I couldn't keep my eyes off you.'

She could act coy, not admit that she'd noticed him too, flirt a little, play hard to get… But she'd never met a man like him. Never felt that instant tug of attraction. And time was in very short supply.

'I noticed you too,' she said simply.

For a long moment she looked up into his eyes—up close a surprising sea-green—and he looked down into hers. His gaze was serious, intent, totally focused on her. The air between them shimmered with possibility. Her heart set up a furious beating. She felt giddy with the awareness that she could be on the edge of something momentous, something life-changing. He frowned as if puzzled. Did he feel it too?

'Natalie, I—'

But before he could say any more Gemma came up the steps, Tristan hovering solicitously behind her. Her sister-in-law smiled politely, as if Natalia were just another guest, although her eyes gleamed with the knowledge of their shared secret. Tristan's nod gave his sister a subtle warning. *Be careful.* As if she needed it. She was only too aware of her duty.

Duty. Duty. Duty. It had governed her life from the moment she was born. Duty to her family, to the Crown, to her country. What about her duty to *herself*? *Her* needs, *her* wants, *her* happiness? She was twenty-seven years old and she'd toed the line for too long. If she wanted to flirt with the most gorgeous man she had met in a long time—perhaps ever—she darn well would, and duty be damned.

She took a step closer to Finn. Smiled up at him as Tristan went past. The rigid set of her brother's shoulders was the only sign that he had noticed her provocative gesture. But Finn mistook her smile for amusement.

'I know,' he said. 'It isn't every day you go to a wedding where the groomsman is a prince and the bridesmaid a princess and everyone is pretending they're regular folk like you or me. That's despite the security detail both out on the road and down on the water to keep the media scrum at bay.'

'Bizarre, isn't it?' she said lightly.

In fact, it was rare that she went to a wedding where the bride and groom *weren't* royalty or high-ranking aristocracy. This wedding between people without rank was somewhat of a novelty.

'Bizarre, but kinda fun,' Finn said. 'When else would our paths cross so closely with royalty? Even if the Prince is from some obscure kingdom no one has ever heard of.'

Obscure? Natalia was about to huff in defence of her country. Montovia might be small, in both land mass and population, but it was wealthy, influential and punched above its weight on matters of state. But for today she was just plain Natalie—not Princess Natalia. And she wanted to enjoy the company of this very appealing Aussie guy without getting into any kind of debate that might give the game away.

'A prince is a prince, I guess, wherever he hails from,' she said.

'And a princess always adds a certain glamour to an occasion,' Finn said drily.

'Indeed,' she said.

A smile twitched at the corners of her mouth. *If only he knew.*

'Talking of fun…let's go inside and swap those place cards if we need to,' she said.

'Yes, ma'am,' he said.

Startled, she almost corrected him. *Ma'am* was a term of address reserved for her mother, the Queen, not her. But of course he was only using the word generically. She really had to stay on the alert if she were to successfully keep up the act.

She went to tuck her hand into his arm but decided against it. If she touched him—even the slightest touch—she wasn't sure how she'd react. She'd only known Finn O'Neill for a matter of minutes but she already knew she wanted him.

He could be the one.

CHAPTER TWO

FINN FOLLOWED NATALIE along the veranda towards the ballroom of the sandstone mansion where the formal part of the wedding reception would shortly take place. He couldn't take his eyes off her shapely swaying hips. How could she walk so surely and confidently in those sky-high heels? Maybe it was the sexy shoes that gave her bottom that enticing little wiggle. Maybe—

She stopped abruptly, so that they collided.

'Sorry,' he said automatically. Although he wasn't sorry at all to be suddenly in such close proximity to this enchanting woman.

'No need to apologise,' she said, not moving away from him.

Her blue eyes glinted with mischief and her lush mouth tilted on the edge of laughter. He was close enough to catch her perfume...sweet, enticing and heady. She didn't seem in the slightest bit disconcerted by the sudden intimacy. Whereas he was overwhelmed by a rush of sensual awareness. He ached to be closer to her. *To kiss her.*

He took a step back from temptation, cleared his throat. 'Why did you stop?'

'I believe this is the room where the meal is to be served,' she said in a conspiratorial tone, gesturing to where wide French doors had been flung open to the veranda. She glanced furtively around her in an exaggerated dramatic way.

'Coast is clear,' he said, amused by her playfulness.

Drinks were still being served in the garden. They

had time before the other guests would flood into the ballroom.

He followed her as she tiptoed with dramatic exaggeration to the threshold of the room. Over her shoulder he could see circular tables set up for a formal meal, with a rectangular bridal party table up top. All elegantly decorated with the Party Queens trademark flair.

'No one in there,' Natalie whispered.

'Okay. Commence Operation Place Card Swap. We'll make a dash for it. You—'

She put her finger up against her lips. 'Shh… We have to be covert here. No bride likes her arrangements to be tampered with. We can't be caught. You go in—I'll guard the door.'

Finn found Natalie's place card first and filched it from its silver card holder. Then he searched for the place that had been assigned to him. As anticipated, he had not been seated anywhere near Natalie—four tables away, on the other side of the room, in fact.

Predictably, Eliza had placed him near Prue, a friend of hers from university, who was an attractive enough girl but who didn't interest him in the slightest—in spite of Eliza's matchmaking efforts. There was also the fact that Prue often played fast and loose with the truth, and if there was one thing Finn loathed it was a liar. Yet Eliza persisted.

That was the trouble with weddings. There was some kind of myth—promulgated by women—that a wedding was the perfect place to meet a life partner. Love being in the air and presumably contagious. As a result, weddings brought out their worst matchmaking instincts. As if, at the age of thirty-two, the combined efforts of his Italian, Chinese and Irish families to try and get him to settle down weren't enough, without his friends getting in on the act.

Marriage didn't interest him. Not now. He'd lost the urge when his first serious love had broken both their engagement and his heart. No one he'd met since had made him want to change his mind. Besides, he was in the midst of such a rapid expansion of his business, opening to exciting new markets, and he did not want the distraction of a serious relationship. International trade could be tumultuous. He had to be on top of his game.

He removed Prue's place card and deftly replaced it with the one that spelled out *Natalie Gerard*. Things were definitely looking up. Now he'd be sitting next to the only woman at the wedding who held any appeal for him. The only woman who had sparked his interest in a long time.

'I'll put this place card where yours came from and no one will be any the wiser,' he explained to his accomplice, who had now stepped cautiously into the room.

'Except Eliza,' Natalie said.

'Who I doubt will even notice the swap,' he said.

Natalie, for all her bravado, seemed unexpectedly hesitant. A slight frown creased her forehead. 'Is it really the right thing to do?'

'To sit next to me? Without a doubt.'

'I mean to mess up the seating plan.'

'A minor infringement of the wedding planner's rulebook,' he said.

'An infringement all the same. I…I usually play by the rules.' She averted her gaze, looked down at the pointy toes of her shoes.

'Perhaps it's time to live dangerously?' he said.

Her frown deepened. 'I'm not sure I know how to do that.'

'Live dangerously?'

She looked back up to face him. 'Yes,' she said uncertainly. The mischievous glint in her blue eyes had dimmed to something distressingly subdued.

'Then let me be your tutor.'

'In the art of living dangerously?' she said.

'Exactly,' he said.

She sighed. 'You can't imagine how tempting that sounds.'

The edge to her voice surprised him. 'Don't you ever give in to temptation?' he challenged.

Her smile returned, slow and thoughtful, with a sensuous twist of her lips. 'It depends who's doing the tempting.'

She was so tempting. Finn held up his hand. 'Consider the position of your tutor in Living Dangerously for Beginners to be officially filled,' he said.

She laughed, low and throaty. 'I hope you find me an apt student.'

He hoped so too.

'We'll start by finishing the place card swap. Why don't you do it? Your first "living dangerously" challenge.'

It would be a step towards others infinitely more interesting.

'That's not so dangerous,' she said, with a dismissive sweep of her perfectly manicured hand.

There was a touch of arrogance to her gesture that surprised and intrigued him. 'You think so? The sun is setting and I think I can hear people coming up the steps to the veranda. You'll have to be quick if you don't want to be caught in the act and bring down the wrath of the bride on your head.'

Any hint of haughtiness gone, Natalie made a sound somewhere between a squeal and a giggle that he found delightful. Without another word he held out Prue's place card.

Natalie snatched it from him. 'Mission accepted,' she said.

He watched as she quickly click-clacked on her high heels—hips swaying—to the table where she'd originally been seated and slid the card into place. When she returned she gave him a triumphant high five.

'Mission accomplished.'

'Well done. Now I won't have to find excuses all evening to visit you at your table.'

'And I won't need to take any opportunity to seek you out at yours.'

She coloured, high on her cheekbones, in a blush that seemed at odds with her provocative words.

'Would you have done that?' he asked. 'Seriously?'

'Of course,' she said. 'You are by far the most attractive man here.'

She seemed such an accomplished flirt, and yet her blush deepened and her eyelashes fluttered as she voiced the compliment.

'Thank you,' he said.

Considering the men of the bridal party were all good-looking billionaires—one a prince—Finn could only be flattered. And gratified that the instant attraction wasn't only on his side. He wasn't a fanciful man, but insinuating itself into his mind was a thought, wispy and insubstantial but growing in vigour, that this—*she*—was somehow meant to be.

'You know I intend to monopolise you all evening?'

'Monopolise me all you want,' she said slowly.

She was looking up at him with what he could only read as invitation, although there was an endearing uncertainty there too.

'You won't be able to escape me.'

'Do you see me running?' she murmured.

Her gaze met his for a long moment, and he wasn't sure of the message in those extraordinary blue eyes.

Then she smiled. 'Talking of escape—thank you for rescuing me from the table of people I don't know at all but who I suspect are Eliza's elderly relatives.'

'Don't speak too soon. We don't know who we've got sitting at my table.'

'Yes, we do,' she said.

He frowned. 'How did you—?'

She spoke over him. 'Each other. And that's all that counts.'

The words hung between them, seemingly escalating their flirtation to a higher and more exciting level of connection. Finn felt a buzz of excitement and anticipation.

'Quite right. Your first exercise in living dangerously has paid off. I don't care who else is on the table so long as your place card is still next to mine.'

Attending this wedding solo was more duty than pleasure, fond as he was of Eliza, and keen as he was to keep up his contact with Party Queens. But he wasn't one for wasting time on social chit-chat with strangers he might never see again.

An evening spent in the enchanting Natalie's company was a different matter altogether. Enjoying the pleasure of her company was now at the forefront of his mind.

Finn was about to tell her so, but there was a sudden burst of chatter from outside on the veranda. 'The other guests are starting to arrive. We shouldn't be seen in here.'

Natalia's eyes widened in alarm. 'We've got time to get out through that connecting door.'

He reached out his hand and pulled her towards him. 'Let's go before they realise we've been up to no good.

Then we'll march back in with the other guests and take our places at the table.'

'Innocent of any crime of swapping seats,' she said.

Not so innocent were his thoughts of where he hoped the evening might lead.

Natalie couldn't have borne it if she had been forced to sit on the other side of the room from Finn. She didn't want to waste a minute of this wedding away from him.

Tristan had probably had a hand in where she had been placed in the seating arrangements and might not be pleased at the switch. Too bad. Princess Natalia might have to sit dutifully where she was directed—not so just plain Natalie. She was going to grab this chance to be with Finn, no matter if she got dressed down for it later.

Tristan took his role of Crown Prince seriously. That meant protecting her. Since the loss of their brother, she and Tristan had looked out for each other. But sometimes she had to remind him that she didn't take kindly to being bossed around by her brother.

With Finn holding her hand, she made it safely out of the room without detection. Just the casual touch of his hand clasping hers sent shivers of anticipation through her. Never, ever had she felt this kind of thrill.

She was pleased when he didn't drop the connection after they'd made it to safety. Then, together, they strolled casually back into the ballroom alongside a group of other guests.

Each time she looked up to catch his eye she had to suppress a laugh, and saw that he did too. She felt like a naughty schoolgirl. Although in the private all-girls school she had attended there hadn't been anyone as handsome as Finn to get into mischief with.

Their surreptitious work had paid off—the swapped

name cards were still in place. Finn was hers for the duration of the celebration. She was scarcely able to believe that this gorgeous man was real and seemed to want to be with her as much as she did with him.

'We did it,' he said in a low undertone after they'd taken their seats at the table. 'I caught Eliza glaring at me, but there's nothing she can do about where we're sitting from where she is, way up there on the bridal table.'

'Clever us,' Natalia said, holding his gaze and revelling in the warmth of his smile.

So this is what it's like to be really attracted to a man.

Her thoughts were filled with nothing but him. *Insta lust.* That was what her English-speaking friends called the sudden overwhelming desire to be close to a man. But it wasn't just a physical attraction. She liked Finn more than she could have imagined she could like someone in such a short space of time. Yes, she ached to touch him, to feel his smooth olive skin under her fingers, and wondered what it would be like to kiss him. But she also wanted to talk with him, listen to him, laugh with him, find out all she could about him.

She had never felt like this about a man before. Certainly never for any of the six men of noble birth she had rejected as potential husbands. Not even for the boy she'd had a crush on as a teenager in London.

It hadn't just been her being caught out at a nightclub that had seen her recalled home to Montovia. She'd also been seen kissing Danny—a fellow student definitely not on the palace-approved list. It had hurt when she hadn't heard from him again, and part of her heart had shut down, never to recover. It hadn't been until much later that she'd discovered he'd been paid off by the palace to disappear from her life.

Her family's betrayal had added a whole new level of hurt.

Back then, the law that forbade her and her brothers from marrying someone not of noble birth had still been in place. She'd discovered they'd done the same thing to Tristan—paying off the parents of an English girl he'd loved and moving her to another part of the country. Tristan had been understandably bitter at their interference. Especially considering what a sham their parents' marriage was—the King still had a long-time mistress.

The history of unhappy, loveless marriages in their family had made both her and Tristan deeply cynical about marriage. Fortunately Tristan had found Gemma. For Natalia there had been no one.

On a trip to Africa the previous year, to visit a girls' school that her charity had funded, she had travelled with an attractive photographer. Sparks had flown between them—not the kind of powerful attraction she'd felt instantly for Finn, but sparks just the same. But he had made it clear he would never get involved with her. Not when he knew his life would come under scrutiny and he would have to play second fiddle to a princess. Natalia had appreciated his honesty but had felt wounded because she hadn't even been given a chance.

That had been back then. Now Natalia wanted to shut the rest of the world out, so it shrank to just her and Finn. She resented the time spent chatting with the other six guests at their table. But politeness dictated that she distributed her time evenly. All that royal training in graciousness and good manners didn't go away just because she was in disguise.

The other guests were all pleasant people from Eliza's pre-Party Queens life. Natalia made it a point to chat with each of them. Finn joined in too, charming and thoughtful in his conversation. The others seemed to assume she and Finn were a couple, and neither of them did anything to make them think any differently.

One of the women was Chinese, and Finn surprised Natalia by exchanging a few words with her in her own language. 'You sound fluent in Chinese,' Natalia said when he turned his attention back to her.

'Thankfully, yes,' he said. 'One of my biggest new export markets is mainland China,' he explained. 'It's a great advantage to be able to speak Mandarin.'

'I can imagine,' she said.

'My grandfather spoke to me in Chinese when I was a child and my mother insisted I study the language formally when I was older. I studied Italian to please my grandmother—also useful for the business. And my sister Bella studied both languages too.'

Natalia wanted to tell him she was also multilingual, even chat to him in Italian, but it was too risky in case she tripped up over the details of a made-up background. The less she said about herself, the better. Pretending to be someone else, denying the truth about herself, wasn't as easy as she'd thought. Not when she really wanted to impress Finn.

'Sounds like your grandparents were very influential in your life,' she said.

Hers had been too. Her late paternal grandfather had been King when she was a child and had ruled his family like a tyrant, although he'd been seen as a benevolent ruler of the country. She'd been terrified of him. Thankfully her mother and father, despite their differences and the restrictions of their royal duties, had been united in being loving parents to her and her brothers.

'My wonderful grandparents are both still around, fortunately,' Finn said. 'I have them to thank for my start in the business.'

Natalia hadn't mourned the death of her grandfather, and her grandmother had remained a distant, disapproving figure. She'd never known her mother's parents.

'Really?' she said, fascinated to know every detail of his life in the short time she had with him. Through him she could view life through a very different lens. 'I'd love to hear about it.'

'My grandfather and grandmother met each other in high school. It was like *Romeo and Juliet* set in the western suburbs of Sydney. His family owned the local Chinese restaurant—her family the Italian. Neither family was happy for their child to marry out of their culture—the old migrant story.'

Natalia leaned closer, sensing a real-life romance very different from her own family history of loveless arranged marriages. She was better off being single than being pushed into that kind of marriage—although to be fair to her parents, they had not pressured her, even when she'd said no to each of the unsuitable and unlovable six.

Anyway, how could you be sure of love? Her late brother Carl's marriage to Sylvie, the daughter of a duke, had supposedly been a 'love match'. Carl had been head over heels with her, and she'd seemed the same with him. But once she'd had her lavish wedding in the cathedral she'd proved to be greedy and avaricious, more in love with the wealth and status of being Crown Princess than with her husband. And there was no divorce for Montovian royalty. Make a bad choice and you were stuck with it for life.

'It must have been difficult for them if they had to defy their families,' she said.

'They say it only made them all the more determined

to be together,' said Finn. 'Once they were twenty-one they could marry without their families' consent and they did. Fortunately they were both passionate about food, and my grandparents ended up running both restaurants. Their parents imported authentic ingredients from Asia and Europe, supplying other restaurants too. My *nonna* was a canny businesswoman and she soon grew the import side of the business so that it eclipsed the actual restaurants and they sold them.'

'So where did you come in?'

'I inherited their interest in food. However, my family also had a passion for education. I did a business degree at university, but worked all my vacations in the business. I went full-time when I graduated. I soon saw the opportunities for export as well as import. My grandparents handed the business over to me and I expanded it way beyond its original parameters. They still have a stake in it, but they're enjoying their retirement. I take all the risks.'

'Didn't your parents and your sister feel they'd been passed over?'

The rules for inheritance were very strict in Montovia—for everyone, not just royals.

'Not at all. My mother is a pharmacist. My father has his own construction company. My sister works with him. Seems we like keeping things in the family.'

'Sounds like your family is very close.'

'Yeah. It is. But that's enough about me. What about you?'

'My family story isn't as interesting as yours,' she said.

Of course it was—an unbroken line of rulers stretching back hundreds of years—but she couldn't share that.

'Just ordinary, really. I have a brother.' It was too painful to mention her other brother, whom she had adored; his loss still cut too deeply. 'My parents take rather too much interest in my life—which is annoying, considering I'm twenty-seven—but I guess that's okay.'

'It would be worse if they didn't take an interest, wouldn't it?' he said with a smile.

'True,' she said, returning his smile and gazing into his green eyes for rather longer than was polite on a shared table.

Their heads had been bowed closely together, their voices low for the duration of the conversation. Reluctantly she broke her gaze away and returned her attention to the other people at the table, as good manners dictated.

A pleasant middle-aged couple sat opposite them— Eliza's neighbours. Natalia and Finn chatted with them about how much they were enjoying the meal.

Once the plates for the main course had been cleared, the woman—Kerry—sat back in her chair. Her narrow-eyed gaze went from Natalia to Finn and back again. 'So, is all the romance of this lovely wedding giving you two ideas?' she said.

'I beg your pardon?' said Natalia, completely taken aback.

'You and Finn. Any plans for a wedding of your own?'

Natalia wasn't often lost for a diplomatic reply to an unexpected question. But the Australian woman's blunt questioning had her floundering. She looked up to Finn for help, only to see him struggling too.

'No plans yet,' he finally choked out.

'You haven't popped the question?'

'No!' he said.

'How long have you been together?'

'We…er…we only just met,' Natalia said, flushing hot with embarrassment.

The woman frowned. 'Really? Forgive me. It's just that…'

'Just that what?' Natalia prompted, suddenly curious.

'I've been around a while, and I can usually tell a perfectly matched couple. You two look so right together.'

Natalia gasped. She didn't dare look at Finn, and was at a complete loss as to what to say. But Finn diplomatically came to the rescue.

'I think we're right together too,' he said smoothly. 'But it's very early days.'

Natalia wished she could sink through the floor.

The woman smiled. 'I see a wedding and I'm never wrong,' she said, before turning her attention to her husband, who'd been trying to shush her.

Mortified, Natalia kept her eyes on her plate.

'Don't worry about her,' Finn murmured in her ear. 'She seems harmless. Unfortunately I seem to attract matchmakers. Weddings bring out the worst in them.'

If he only knew the level of matchmaking that had gone on—and continued to go on—when it came to Princess Natalia of Montovia. Finn O'Neill from Sydney, Australia—a merchant—would seem, in the eyes of her parents and the royal court, like a very unsuitable match indeed.

She was glad when the speeches started and she was able to turn away from the odd woman and any talk of matchmaking and marriage to face the top table.

CHAPTER THREE

THE SPEECHES WERE over and the bride and groom were dancing their first dance together. All the guests had been invited on to the dance floor to share the bridal waltz. At last Finn had Natalie in his arms—if only as a dance partner.

There was something intimate about an old-fashioned waltz. With her hand on his shoulder, his arms around her waist, she was kissing-distance close, her flowery perfume already familiar but no less alluring. Her body so near to his was warm, soft, sensual, and her innate rhythm kept them perfectly in step.

'You dance very well,' she said.

'I tried to get out of lessons at school but there was no escape.'

'You learned to waltz at *school*?'

'Private boys' school. Ballroom dancing was seen as a social skill. But I only waltz at weddings.' He twirled her around the room until she was breathless and laughing. 'You're a good dancer yourself.'

'I also had lessons,' she said.

Finn noticed she didn't elaborate in any of her answers. Perhaps her life really had been ordinary, even dull, although he wondered how someone as poised and vivacious as Natalie could come from dullness. Maybe she hadn't had the same opportunities in life he had been fortunate enough to have. Or the truth might be that her life hadn't been very happy and she was reticent about reliving an unhappy past even in social conversation.

Sometimes he was guilty of taking for granted the happy

and supportive family life he enjoyed. This wedding—the happiness Eliza had found with Jake—had got him thinking. He wasn't as immune to wedding fever as he'd thought. Now, at the age of thirty-two, perhaps he did need to shake himself up, settle down and start a family of his own.

His *nonna* certainly thought that was the case. His broken engagement was ten years behind him—he could not in all reason continue to blame it for his aversion to marriage. He had to name it for what it was: an excuse—one he used to convince himself as well as others. The truth was that he hadn't met the right woman. Not one he could contemplate sharing his life with. When he did, he would willingly make that walk down the aisle. But he wouldn't compromise. And it wouldn't be any time soon—not when the business took up all his energy and time.

Perhaps...

He couldn't let himself think there was any chance of Natalie being that woman. No matter what that crazy Kerry had said. No matter how he'd found himself agreeing with her that he and Natalie did feel right together. Not when Natalie was English. A tourist. Her home a twenty-two-hour plane ride away.

Long-distance dating had been a disaster with his former fiancée Chiara, the girl he'd met in Italy ten years back. Her level of treachery had left him bitter and broken.

The frequency of their phone calls had decreased. He'd been preoccupied with exams. But the day exams finished, on impulse he'd decided to make a surprise visit to Italy and booked a flight for the next day.

Chiara had been surprised, all right. Not only had she found herself another guy, she was pregnant. But she'd still hung on to Finn's engagement ring. He had vowed never, ever to try long-distance again. This—Natalie—was purely for the short term. He had to keep telling himself that.

'Those lessons paid off,' he said to Natalie now. 'You're very graceful.'

It felt as if they were dancing together in their own bubble of awareness. But the reality was that they were dancing alongside other guests. When would he be able to get her alone?

She looked up at him. 'That woman… Kerry. It was kind of weird, what she said.'

'Yes. But I wasn't lying when I agreed with her that something seems right about us being together.' He could hardly believe he was saying this to a woman he had only known for a matter of hours.

Her blue eyes widened. 'You meant that?'

'About the rightness? I feel it. Do you?'

Her forehead pleated in a frown. 'Yes. I…I think I do. But I don't understand—'

Finn felt a tap on his shoulder and turned to find a beaming Eliza and Jake cutting in on him and Natalie for their obligatory dances. He had no choice but to relinquish his intimate hold on the most gorgeous of women. He cursed under his breath that he hadn't got a chance to hear what Natalie had been about to say.

Reluctantly he let her go and watched Natalie waltz away with Jake, smiling up at him. A spasm of jealousy shuddered through him at the sight of his beautiful dance partner in the arms of another man—even though Jake was a newlywed husband who adored his new wife.

What was happening here?

He'd only just met Natalie. He hardly knew her. But he'd never felt such a connection with a woman—if that was what you called something so compelling. He'd dated. He'd had steady girlfriends. He'd been engaged. But none of those relationships had started with a lightning bolt from nowhere.

'Surely you can take your eyes off her for long enough to speak to me?' said Eliza drily as he danced with his friend the bride.

'What do you mean?' he blustered.

'You're mesmerised by Natalie. She's beautiful. Charming. I get it. But you need to back off from her, Finn. She's not for you.'

'This is about Prue, isn't it?' He gritted his teeth. 'How many times do I have to tell you I'm not interested?'

'Even so, it was rude of you to change those place cards. What on earth got into you to do such a thing?'

Eliza had always been an outspoken kind of friend.

He shrugged. 'Sorry.'

But he wasn't sorry at all, and Eliza's sigh told him she knew it.

'This can't end well. That's all I can say.'

In spite of himself, he felt a chill of foreboding. 'Are you telling me that Natalie has a criminal record or—?'

Eliza looked aghast. 'Of course not. Don't be ridiculous.'

'Is she after my money?' he joked.

Ever since that Sunday newspaper had included him in a list of the most eligible young millionaires he'd been plagued by women whose interest in him was purely mercenary. Which had made him even more cynical about relationships.

'I very much doubt it,' Eliza said. 'She's just not for you. You'll have to trust me on this.'

He snorted his disbelief. 'You're warning me off? In the meantime, your neighbour Kerry is suggesting I propose to Natalie because we seem so perfect together.'

'What?'

'Yeah. In fact she asked if we'd made wedding plans.'

'Really?' Eliza frowned. 'Kerry reckons she's psychic.

She… Well, she wouldn't say that if she didn't believe it was true.'

Finn rolled his eyes. 'Psychic? *Huh!* She seemed nice enough until she came out with *that* nonsense.'

'What's stranger still is that her predictions often come true. The first time she met Jake she told me I'd marry him. It seemed highly unlikely at the time.'

'Coincidence—a lucky guess,' Finn said dismissively.

'Superstitious nonsense?' Eliza said.

Finn agreed. The trouble was, he came from three cultures where superstitions were taken seriously. By the older generation, that was. Not by him. He was a facts and numbers man.

'But it was disconcerting,' he admitted.

'In this case she's got it wrong,' Eliza said. 'I'll say it again—back off from Natalie.'

'You're seriously warning me, Eliza?'

'As a friend. Yes.'

'And as a friend, I appreciate your concern—although I don't know where it's coming from. But I'd rather you wished me luck than tossed a bucket of cold water over me. Because I like Natalie and I'm going to continue to enjoy her company for the rest of the evening.' He kissed her on the cheek. 'Thank you for the dance. Again, congratulations to you and Jake. Now I'm going to march over there to your husband and claim my dance partner back.'

Natalia couldn't remember when she'd so enjoyed a man's company. Dancing with Finn, their steps perfectly matched, was magic. Chatting with him, laughing with him, deepened the spell.

But the enchanted evening was winding down. The bride and groom had left to a chorus of good wishes for their honeymoon and a long life together. Other guests were starting to disperse and the band had announced the last number for the evening.

Soon the big room would echo with emptiness. Her bodyguards would be discreetly waiting to escort her back to the harbour-side hotel where she was booked in under her Natalie Gerard name. She would never see Finn again. She felt plunged into gloom at the thought.

The last dance was a slow one and they danced it close together. She breathed in the scent of him, felt his warm breath ruffling her hair. All sorts of potential conversations were running through her head. But all she managed was to look up at him and stutter. 'I…I don't want the night to end.'

His green eyes met hers. 'Neither do I.'

Too many hopes and possibilities were trembling on her lips for her actually to articulate the words *I want to be with you.* But finally she managed to choke out an invitation of sorts—although not the one she really wanted to communicate.

'I'm staying at a lovely hotel. It has a very smart bar, open all hours. Would you like to come back for a drink? Or a coffee? Or…?' Her voice trailed away. She was articulate in five languages, yet she was stumbling on a simple offer to extend the evening with a drink in a bar.

He tilted her chin, so his gaze met hers. 'Yes—to whatever you're offering.'

'I have a car and driver booked,' she said. And there would be another car with the second bodyguard following.

'Cancel it. Let me drive you in my car,' he said.

For a moment she was tempted. There was nothing she would have liked better than to be alone with Finn in his car. But 'living dangerously' had its limitations. The helicopter accident that had claimed the lives of her brother, his wife and their toddler son had been an accident, not an assassination. But after such a tragedy, security for the remaining heirs had become an obsession with the royal family. She could not dismiss her bodyguards.

'I can't do that, I'm afraid,' she said. She held her breath. Would that be a deal-breaker for Finn? 'You would have to come in my car. Or we could go to the hotel separately and meet there.'

'I'll ride with you.' Did he, like her, not want to waste a moment of the limited time they had together?

She sighed her relief. 'Good. My driver is outside. I'll call him and tell him we'll have an extra passenger.'

Would Finn wonder why she should do that? Most hire car drivers wouldn't have to be notified of an extra passenger.

'I'll have to go back to the table and retrieve my handbag. My phone's in it,' she said.

'As long as you come straight back to me,' he said, in that deep husky voice.

'Count on it,' she said, thrilled by the look in his eyes.

She called her bodyguards and provided Finn's name. She knew they would immediately run a security check on him. Perhaps she was being foolish, but she felt sure nothing untoward would come up on the check. She scarcely knew him, but she felt she could trust him to be who he said he was. It was she who was twisting the truth about herself right out of shape.

'Ready to go?' Finn said when she returned to his side.

'The car will come around to the front to pick us up,' she said.

He put a possessive arm around her as they headed outside. She leaned into him, loving the closeness to his strength and warmth. Then felt bereft when she moved away from him for the sake of appearances as they reached the main doors.

The street level entrance to the grand old house was bracketed by tall palm trees and large old-fashioned carriage lamps. Cars and taxis inched forward on the circular driveway to pick up the departing wedding guests. Natalia spotted the unobtrusive dark sedan driven by her bodyguard in the line-up. The other bodyguard wouldn't be far away. Their orders were to be close by always.

She could not fault her parents for taking such good care of her, even if it did seem irksome at times. The terrible loss of her brother and his family—not just Carl, but precious two-year-old Rudolph, whom they'd all adored, and his mother Sylvie—had thrown them into despair.

Tristan had been forced to step up into a role he'd felt ill-prepared for. Natalia had been thrust into being second in line to the throne and her freedom had been severely curtailed.

Becoming second in line to a throne after a sudden death was a different matter altogether from being fourth in line behind three male heirs. She'd gone from being relatively independent to being cosseted. And the campaign to get her married to someone suitable and bearing further heirs had been stepped up. She'd begun to feel trapped—albeit in a golden cage—stifled, and more than a touch rebellious. She'd been determined to get permission to leave Montovia and attend this wedding.

Much as she railed against the stepped-up security, she could see the reasons why. But nothing was going to stop her enjoying every minute available to her with Finn.

She followed him to take their places near the cluster of guests waiting for their cars. Thankfully, Tristan and Gemma were not among them to see her looking so cosy with Finn. Her brother and his wife had left early because

Gemma hadn't been feeling well. On the dance floor, Natalia had done nothing to earn her brother's disapproval. That might not be the case by the time the evening was through.

It soon became obvious that they were going to have to wait a few minutes for her car. She didn't want to wait a second longer to be alone with Finn.

He seemed to feel the same. 'We don't have to get caught up in banal conversation about why the traffic is backed up,' he said. 'C'mon.'

Just a few steps took them away from the other guests until they stood shoulder to shoulder by the side of the portico, away from the lamps that lit the entrance, private in the shadow of a large camellia tree studded with luminous white blooms. Huge tubs of exotic flowering orchids hid them from general view—plants she would only see in a greenhouse back home. The air was rich with the scent of jasmine, romantic and intoxicating.

Everything about Australia was so different from her homeland of snow-capped mountains, vast lakes and the sharp scent of pine needles. And Finn was so different from any man she had ever met. Different in such an exciting way.

So far away from home she wasn't bound by the rules.

She shivered—not just because of a gust of cool, early spring air but because she felt a sudden nervousness about finally being alone with him and what she hoped that might lead to.

He turned to face her. 'Are you cold?'

'Just the breeze,' she said, wrapping her arms around herself, not wanting to betray how she was feeling about him.

Finn stepped closer, his gaze intent on her face. In the poorly lit gloom his eyes gleamed green. She forgot to shiver, almost forgot to breathe, seeing the expression in his eyes, the sensual set of his mouth. Her heart started thudding so erratically that surely he could hear it.

He gently disengaged her arms and held her hands by her side, his hands warm on her bare skin. For a long moment he looked into her eyes, and questions and answers were silently exchanged. Her lips parted in anticipation as he lowered his mouth to hers and she sighed with pleasure as he kissed her.

At last.

His mouth was warm and firm on hers in a kiss that was sure and demanding while gentle at the same time. Her eyes closed as she savoured the closeness of him and she kissed him back.

She was just getting into the rhythm of kisses given and returned when he broke the contact. She swallowed a whimper of dismay at the loss—she didn't want to sound needy.

'I've wanted to kiss you for hours,' he said, in that so-sexy deep voice.

'Me too,' she said. 'Kiss *you*, I mean. Please…please don't stop.'

He laughed, low and triumphant, and then kissed her again. His touch ignited the hunger for him that had been brewing since the moment she'd seen him. She'd been without a man in her life for a long time, but this wasn't just hunger for a man's touch—it was hunger for *him*, this man, Finn.

His tongue slid between her lips to meet hers. He let go of her hands to put his arms around her and draw her closer. She wound her arms around his neck and returned his kiss, loving the feel of his tongue, his lips, the taste of him. Starbursts of sensation seemed to ignite along every pleasure pathway.

He certainly knew how to kiss. And the fact that he was experienced was a point in his favour. She wanted a man who knew what he was doing.

Yes. Finn was the one. There was no doubt in her mind. Tonight, she wanted to lose her virginity to Finn.

CHAPTER FOUR

NATALIA COULD NOT get enough of Finn's kisses. *She could not get enough of Finn.* But did her kisses, so enthusiastically returned, betray her lack of experience? Could he guess at her untouched state?

The thoughts plagued her as the sound of her name being called—her fake name—made her reluctantly break away from his kiss to see that her car had reached the head of the line.

She had to take a moment to compose herself, and noticed with a secret thrill that Finn had to do the same. Then, with a gentlemanly hand on her elbow, he steered her to where the driver, cap firmly down to shield his face, held the door open for her.

She hoped the remaining guests waiting for their transport were too busy chatting among themselves to notice the signs of recent passionate kisses on an incognito princess slinking out from the shadows—her flushed face, her lack of lipstick, her tousled hair... Then she realised that because she was incognito no one would care. She was just another guest at a wedding.

The anonymity thrilled her.

Of course she'd been kissed before. Mostly by frogs, but also by a few genuine princes. But she'd never gone much further than kissing. Duty again. It was expected that a royal Montovian bride would be a virgin. Her marriage would be more about alliances and political strategy than passionate love. There had to be no doubt that any children born to the union were her husband's legitimate offspring.

The necessity for her to stay chaste until marriage had been drummed into her from the time she'd understood what it was all about. But she hadn't expected to still be a virgin at age twenty-seven. It was a situation she was beginning to find onerous. Most of her friends were married—mothers, even—while she was still wondering what it was like to make love with a man.

In the hours since she'd met Finn, she'd found herself even more curious.

She'd been expected to marry young to a suitable man of noble birth chosen for her by her parents. Her refusal to marry any of the palace-approved contenders had meant she had stayed single—and celibate—for far longer than might have been expected. She'd also had a full year in mourning for her brother, and had been uninterested in dating during those dark days.

In retrospect, it was fortunate that she hadn't allowed herself to be talked into marrying any of those 'suitable' men who'd proposed. Tristan had recently had the rules changed to allow Montovian royals to marry commoners, so he could marry Gemma, an Australian chef. The new rule hadn't really been tested, though, as Gemma had discovered a connection to British royalty. But Natalia was now, in theory, allowed to marry who she wanted.

However, the King and Queen were resisting that idea when it came to their daughter. The ace they held in their hand was that she had to get their permission to marry, whether the man was royal or not. So had Carl. As had Tristan. And Natalia knew they had a nerdy twenty-two-year-old duke lined up for her to meet when she got home. She'd promised to be nice to him, as the only other aristocrat on offer was his widowed uncle the Grand Duke, who'd just had a double hip replacement.

Now, she squirmed in her seat with the effort of keeping a discreet distance from Finn in the back seat of the car. She wanted more kisses. More caresses. *More Finn.* Her nipples tightened at the thought of it. And when he reached across the seat to take her hand in his she nearly jumped through the roof of the car at the sensual thrill that simple touch ignited.

There was another reason she was still a virgin at twenty-seven. She hadn't met anyone who had tempted her. If she had, she might have defied duty and lost her virginity before. But no man had aroused her desire.

Until now.

Finn prided himself on his ability to stay in control under any circumstance. He didn't permit himself to be distracted by emotion. His cool level-headedness in negotiation was one of the reasons he was so successful in business. Plus, he had an instinct to know when to take a strategic risk—perhaps honed by all those childhood games of mah-jong with his grandfather.

But the feelings that surged through him now, just holding hands with Natalie, had him stymied. He wanted her so badly he ached. As a rule, he was cautious about trusting strangers. He'd learned that in both his business and personal life. But in Natalie's case caution simply didn't come into it. He didn't know her, and yet he felt he knew all he needed to know.

However Eliza wouldn't have warned him off her without reason. Every instinct shouted that Natalie might not be telling him everything about herself. But he didn't care.

He just wanted her.

In the back seat of the limo it was all he could do to stay a respectable distance from her. Her fingers entwined with his was their only contact. Her dress had ridden up over her knees, despite her efforts to keep it modestly tugged down, treating him to an enticing glimpse of bare, slender thighs. When the driver took a corner sharply she slid closer, so her thigh nudged his. He had to invoke every ounce of restraint not to reach out and put his hand on her bare skin, push the skirt higher.

Lustful thoughts fogged his brain, but another insistent thought wound its way through the want and the need. *This woman was special.* It wasn't just about sex. She fascinated him. He hadn't believed the so-called psychic when she'd predicted a future for him and Natalie. Yet one crazy, unrestrained part of him wanted to.

It was all he could do not to pull her into his arms and take advantage of the privacy the back seat allowed. But he'd noticed Natalie's quick, nervous glances at their driver. The back seat was not private enough for her and he respected that. This had happened unexpectedly. He would let her lead the way. Whatever she was willing to give, he was willing to take.

He was surprised when the car pulled up in front of a five-star hotel in one of the best locations in the city—right on the edge of the harbour, situated between the icons of the Sydney Harbour Bridge and the Opera House. Somehow he had expected more modest accommodation—but then this limousine was hardly a budget ride ordered from an app.

It seemed the world of fashion was treating Natalie well. Which, to his relief, put paid to any lingering thought that she might be interested in what he had rather than who he was. As far as he knew, they were total strangers who had met by chance at a wedding. How could she know the extent of his wealth?

She thanked the driver graciously as the man held the door open for her. Then turned to wait for Finn to follow her out of the car. He nodded his thanks to the driver, but in truth he hardly noticed the guy. And he scarcely took in the elegant hotel entrance, the glass walls that looked directly through to the water, the uniformed doormen…

Natalie. She was the only sight that interested him and he could not keep his eyes off her.

She was flushed high on her cheekbones and her mouth, swollen from his kisses, was parted in an enigmatic half-smile. Her gaze was as focused on him as his was on her. Her eyes were the most extraordinary shade of iris-blue—he had only seen eyes like them before on one other person, although he couldn't for the life of him remember who it was.

Not that it mattered. Natalie's eyes were the only eyes that interested him. Ditto Natalie's face. Natalie's body. Natalie's soul. He wanted to discover more about her, to know what made her tick, nail down what it was about her that he found so extraordinarily appealing. He was tense, coiled—impatient to be alone with her. And not just for this evening. For the remainder of her stay in Sydney.

He could not let himself think beyond that, much as his thoughts strained to go there.

Gritting his teeth against his impatience, he followed her through the foyer of the hotel, all marble and glass and luxury appointments. 'So, what's it to be?' he asked, forcing himself to sound laid-back. 'The bar? Coffee?'

Her flush deepened and she looked down before she looked up. Natalie was a hot, sexy woman, and he suspected she would give as good as she got in bed. Yet there was a reticence in her that made her even more appealing.

He would enjoy peeling back the layers of her personality as much as he would enjoy peeling that pink dress from her body. It closed with a long zipper at the back— he'd done a recce on it when she had been kissing him so sensationally behind those pots of orchids.

'I thought, perhaps, my room,' she said. 'We could order room service. Whatever you want.'

He pulled her close enough to whisper in her ear. 'I don't want coffee. I only want you. Your room sounds like a great idea.'

Finn felt a shiver go through her. It wasn't the cold this time. With a rising sense of elation he realised her shiver was one of anticipation.

He was exalted by a feeling that had nothing to do with reason, rationality, common sense. Tonight might be the start of something that switched him to a different track. Despite the odds—and her living in another country—Natalie could become someone so much more than a time-stamped encounter at a wedding.

'Let's go, then,' she murmured as she slipped her hand into his.

They had the elevator to themselves. He only let her go long enough for her to tap the key card for her room number before he pulled her to him in a hungry, urgent kiss. With a murmur of need and pleasure that made his heart thud she kissed him back with equal urgency, looping her arms around his neck and drawing him closer.

Three walls and the ceiling of the elevator were mirrored, and he could see her reflection in all of them—sexy, vibrant Natalie, in her clinging pink dress, all curves and blonde hair tumbling untamed down her back.

He felt his life had been lived in black and white until she had flashed into it in a glorious kaleidoscope of glittering blue eyes and shiny red lips and the flash of diamonds from her earrings. He was enveloped by her as she pressed her curves against him, as he breathed in her heady scent—all his senses were invaded and overwhelmed by the urgency of his need for her.

When the elevator doors glided open they were both

momentarily stunned by the interruption. She broke the kiss, looked up at him from the circle of his arms, and started to laugh—a delightful sound that prompted a smile from him in response. He didn't let her go, rather walked her out of the elevator, mumbled a question about the direction of her room, and then kissed her again.

He joined in her laughter as they kissed and stumbled their way up the corridor. Alternating laughter with kisses, they staggered to her room—a spacious suite with glass doors to a balcony framing a view of the harbour and the night-lit Opera House. An enormous bed dominated the room.

They were finally alone, and their laughter faded, vanquished by kisses of increasing intensity, their breath coming in gasps and sighs.

'I…I haven't done this before,' Natalia murmured, somewhere between him caressing her through her dress and locating the pull of her zipper.

Hadn't taken a man back to her hotel room on such short acquaintance? Something about the edge of nervousness to her voice led him to believe her.

'You don't have to do anything you don't want to,' he said.

'Er… I—I haven't lived this dangerously, I mean,' she said, stuttering a little.

'Let me help you enjoy life on the edge,' he said, tugging on her zipper.

'You're still my tutor?'

'Always,' he said.

He pulled down the zipper, the sound of it echoing in the empty room, and started to push her dress off her shoulders, making each movement a caress. He kissed along the delicate hollows of her throat, across her shoulders, down towards the swell of her breasts.

She gasped with surprised pleasure. Then shrugged her shoulders to help him free her of her dress. It slid to the floor, where it pooled around her feet before she stepped out of it, leaving her in a lacy pink bra and panties. He drew in a breath of admiration and excitement. Her body was perfection—creamy skin, curves in the right places, long slender legs.

She went to kick off her stilettoes. 'Leave them,' he said, scarcely able to choke out the words. He had never seen a sexier, more beautiful sight than Natalie clad in just her underwear and her high-heeled shoes.

For Natalia, being stripped down to her underwear in front of a man was something new, but she found she wasn't nervous. Instinctively, she trusted Finn to guide her through this momentous journey. Besides, she was too caught up in the moment to worry about what might come next. Kissing Finn, she was overwhelmed by sensation, by the promise of his hard, muscular body intimately close to hers, the pleasure his clever hands and mouth were giving her.

Even his most fleeting touch ignited starbursts of sensation, made her throb in places she hadn't known could throb. She wanted more. So much more. *Finn.*

'We need to even the score here,' she murmured, impatient with the feel of his jacket against her exposed skin. She ached for skin on skin.

With hands that weren't quite steady she pushed aside his jacket. He took over, sliding his arms out of the sleeves, tossing the jacket without aim so that it fell discarded on the carpet. She went to unfasten his dress shirt and found not buttons but fiddly studs that presented a momentary setback. She fumbled through with a semblance of confidence—she didn't want him to guess this was the first time she'd undressed a man—then got the bow tie unfurled and discarded.

Silently Finn held up his hands and she saw that his sleeves fastened with cufflinks in the shape of tiny compasses—white gold with black stones she realised were black diamonds. No tossing *those* on the floor. She hastily placed them and the bow tie on the narrow table set along the wall, impatient to strip him of his shirt.

As she pushed his shirt off his shoulders and to the floor Natalia gasped. She had to quickly disguise her sudden intake of breath as a cough. Finn bare-chested was even more impressive than Finn fully clothed. Broad shoulders, sculpted arms, chest firmly defined, his belly flat and taut, with just a dusting of dark body hair. His olive skin was smooth and warm beneath her touch.

She took a step back to feast her eyes on him. 'You are the most beautiful man,' she murmured, scarcely able to get the words out with the quickening of her breath. She felt almost faint with desire.

'Beautiful?' he said, with a quirk of his dark brows. 'That's a word I'd apply to you, the most beautiful woman at the wedding. Now I have you all to myself.'

'A man can be beautiful, can't he? But I'll say handsome if you prefer. Though even handsome isn't enough to describe your…your perfection.'

'I'm blushing,' he said.

But he wasn't. He was smiling. And his eyes narrowed further with a look of intensity that let her know she was about to be kissed again. Eager for his touch, she parted her lips to welcome him, pressed herself closer to him, her softness against his strength.

When he cupped her breast in his hand she almost screamed with the pleasure of it. In turn, she explored him, his skin smooth and warm over hard muscles, his reaction letting her know he enjoyed what she was doing. She kissed a trail down his throat and he moaned his appreciation. His reaction excited her, taking her to heights she hadn't known existed.

There wasn't much clothing left between them, and as she felt Finn grasp the fastening of her bra she realised there soon wouldn't be even that. She plucked up the courage to find the fastening of his belt, with the aim of undoing it, but it wasn't as straightforward as she'd thought. It was impossible to concentrate on anything other than the sensations Finn was arousing in her.

Her legs were beginning to buckle beneath her from the intensity of her pleasure, the ache of anticipation. That big bed was beckoning.

She broke away from the kiss. Finn followed the direction of her gaze. 'Yes,' he said.

Effortlessly, he swept her up in his arms.

'You...you're going to carry me to the bed?'

She'd thought this kind of thing only happened in movies. The thrill was immeasurable. She couldn't wait to be initiated by Finn into the mysteries of making love.

'That's my intention,' he said. He paused. 'But first, protection.'

Protection? For a moment she didn't realise what he meant. Protection in case he dropped her? Then it dawned on her. She hadn't ever been in need of the kind of protection he meant.

She couldn't meet his gaze, rather looked out over his shoulder at the view of Sydney Harbour. 'I...er... I'm not protected.'

He groaned. 'I wasn't expecting... I don't have anything.'

'Then we can't—?'

'No. But no doubt the hotel stocks—'

'You…you mean order them from room service?' she said faintly.

'Or visit the concierge,' he said.

Natalia stilled in his arms as the full impact of what they were discussing hit her. *She couldn't do this.* What had seemed romantic, rebellious and rather racy suddenly seemed very, very foolish. There would be consequences if she flaunted the rules. Protection was called protection for a reason. Protection against pregnancy being one of them.

She was a royal princess. What if she got pregnant from a vacation fling—for that was all it could be with Finn. What if she were recognised? What if someone saw Finn go down to the concierge to buy protection and then go up to her room?

She wanted Finn. Wanted him so badly that for a moment there she'd almost been prepared to take the risk of saying yes to no protection. *But she couldn't have him.* Not like this.

Duty. Honour. Responsibility. *Doing the right thing.* They were values ingrained in her very being. How could she ever have thought she could evade them? She was the Princess of Montovia and as such she did not have flings. She might be pretending to be just an ordinary girl but she wasn't.

The rules and restrictions were there for a reason—and she had to live by them. Not play risky games. It might seem terribly old-fashioned, but that was the way it was in Montovia. She and Tristan and Gemma were working together to stretch the boundaries when it came to contemporary life—but they weren't there yet.

A sob rose up in her throat and she swallowed it. To make love with Finn was too much of a risk for her to take—no matter how much she wanted him. No matter how much she liked him. This wasn't the way to lose her virginity.

She remembered the security guards in the adjoining room. They would be aware she had invited a stranger to her room. They might very well be listening via some device to ensure she was safe. Nausea struck her at the thought of them hearing what she and Finn had been murmuring to each other. But even if they were not, a full report of her behaviour would go back to the King and Queen.

What if she didn't care? What if she decided to make love with Finn completely on her own terms? *And then never saw him again?* The answer—emotional agony. She wanted to lose her virginity with a man who would be part of her life for more than one night.

Finn still held her aloft in his arms. But she couldn't stay there. Not now.

She wiggled to be let down. Finn immediately released her and held her until she was steady on her feet.

'You okay?' he asked with a puzzled frown.

How could she have this kind of conversation while standing in only her bra and panties and a pair of high heels?

She took a deep breath in an effort to steady her racing pulse. 'Not really. No. I…er… About the protection… I… I…don't think we'll need it. We need to stop. You see, I—'

'This is moving too quickly for you?' His voice was gruff, but not unkind.

She nearly collapsed with gratitude at his understanding. For just plain Natalie, it had been going just fine. She ached for more, to discover what making love to Finn would be like—utterly, mind-blowingly wonderful, she suspected. But for Princess Natalia, this had gone too far already. She had stepped right out of bounds.

Mutely, she nodded. 'Er…yes,' she finally managed to choke out, wary of his reaction and unable to look at him, focusing on the toes of her stilettos instead.

She'd heard what men called women who led men on

and then said no and it wasn't pleasant. She was still throbbing with desire for him, and he must feel at least as frustrated as she was.

'It's not that I'm not enjoying this—I am, very much—but—'

He reached out to her, placed his fingers under her chin and tilted her face up so she was forced to look at him. 'It's too soon. I get that. I want you, but only if you're ready.'

No calling her a tease. No frustrated anger.

'I… I…' How could she explain when to do so would mean having to untangle the web of lies she'd woven since the moment she'd met him? 'As I said earlier, I haven't done this before.'

She hadn't done *any* of this before. She could only imagine how surprised he would be if she admitted to her virginity.

Finn stood there, unbearably handsome in just his trousers, the belt looped where she had attempted to tug it loose.

'No need to explain,' he said. 'You're worth the wait, Natalie.'

'Th…thank you. But you…you should probably go,' she said.

'If that's what you want,' he said.

He looked around for his clothes, so joyously removed by her in anticipation of what she now would never experience with him.

Mutely, she nodded. Suddenly self-conscious, she reached for the luxurious velour robe provided by the hotel and shrugged into it. She went to wrap it around her waist.

Finn watched her, his eyes half hooded in sensual awareness. 'No need to do that robe up. I like the view with it open so much better.'

'Oh…' she said, blushing. 'I'm glad. That…that you like the view, I mean.'

She took a step towards him. He took a step back.

'Don't tempt me, Natalie. I might not be as strong-minded if I have you too close.'

'Of course,' she said.

She really didn't know how to behave. This was all new territory for her.

'Have you been sailing on the harbour?' he asked as he put on his shirt.

She was taken aback by the sudden change of subject. Then she realised the effort it was taking for him to turn the conversation to something other than their thwarted sexual escapade.

'I've ridden the ferries,' she said. 'I took the Manly ferry all the way to Manly.'

He laughed. 'Not quite the same. How about I swing around here tomorrow and pick you up? I'll take you out on my yacht—we can have lunch on the water.'

'You have a yacht?' she asked, stalling.

She couldn't in all honesty accept his invitation. Yet to outright decline it would entwine her in a more knotted tangle of lies. She realised she was twisting her hands together, something she did when agitated, and forced herself to stop it.

'A very beautiful yacht.'

He shrugged on his jacket, swept up his bow tie and cufflinks and shoved them carelessly into his pocket. Such a shame to cover that expanse of splendid male body, she thought with fleeting sadness.

'The best place to see Sydney is from the water. You'd love it.'

She couldn't call herself a sailor, but there was nothing

she would like more than to be on a boat with Finn. If it were in any way possible she would jump at the chance.

'I'm sure I would,' she murmured.

'I'll see you at ten tomorrow morning,' he said. 'I'll call to confirm.'

'That would be nice,' she said.

It *would* be nice. But she would not be here at ten o'clock tomorrow morning.

She looked up at him. At his open shirt collar, his thick straight black hair dishevelled by her caresses, his handsome, handsome face, his intelligent, kind eyes…

'Finn, I'm sorry about tonight. How things ended. Or… or didn't end. I—'

'No apologies. No explanations. It moved too fast for you. We have tomorrow.'

'Er…yes.'

Tomorrow would come, but not for them.

He took her in his arms, kissed her swift and hard on the mouth. 'I wasn't keen on going to the wedding— I expected it to be insufferably boring. But it turned out to be anything but boring. Because of you.'

'The wedding was…magical. Because of *you*.'

She reached up to trace her fingers down his cheek to the corner of his mouth, frantic to store his face in her memory.

He caught her hand and kissed the centre of her palm. It was almost unbearably pleasurable.

'Tomorrow can be magical too. There's something very special about being out on the harbour. You'll see.'

'Yes…' she said, the word trailing away.

'I have to go, or I might be tempted to talk you out of your decision. Goodnight, Natalie,' he said, and turned towards the door.

'Wait.' She reached up, cradled his face in her hands. 'Thank you, Finn. Thank you for your patience with me.

Thank you for…for everything. The best thing I ever did was switch those place cards. I had the most wonderful time with you. More wonderful than you can imagine.'

She kissed him on his mouth, slow and lingering, for the last time.

'I…I don't know how to say goodbye,' she said, choking up.

'Then don't,' he said. '*Alla prossima*, as we say in Italian.'

'Until we meet again,' she translated.

'You speak Italian?' he said.

She nodded.

'There's so much I don't know about you,' he said slowly.

If only he knew just how much.

She would cry if he stayed any longer. Sob and beg him to stay, spill the truth about her deception, beg him to forgive her for her lies.

But she had sworn to her family to tell no one in Australia the truth of her identity. And the habits of duty and obedience were impossible to break. Especially with the fragile state her parents had been in since Carl's death.

'And me about you,' she murmured.

'We'll have to remedy that,' he said, looking down into her face, a slight frown creasing his brow as if he guessed that all might not be as it seemed.

She put up her hand in farewell. '*Ciao, bello,*' she murmured. *Farewell, beautiful man.*

'*Ciao, bella,*' he said. 'The most beautiful girl at the wedding.'

She smiled shakily. 'I don't know that the groom would agree.'

'It's what *I* think that counts,' he said. 'See you in the morning.'

He turned, opened the door and walked away, turning back once for a final smile.

Natalie watched him go until he disappeared around the corner of the corridor. Then she let the door slam loudly behind him in frustration and anger at herself— and to make it clear to her security guards that her visitor was not staying. Scandal averted.

Immediately she regretted letting him go. Realised she might have made the biggest mistake of her life.

She would never see Finn again.

When he got here tomorrow morning he would be informed at the desk that Ms Gerard had checked out. What the hotel wouldn't know—what Finn would never know—was that Princess Natalia of Montovia, along with her brother the Crown Prince and his wife the Crown Princess, had flown out of Sydney early in the morning on the royal family's private jet and headed home to their ancestral palace.

She dragged one foot in front of the other back into the room, now achingly empty of Finn's presence—but stopped when she noticed something glinting on the carpet. A cufflink. One white gold cufflink in the shape of a compass, its face picked out in tiny black diamonds. It must have slipped from his pocket.

She picked it up. Was it fanciful to think that it still felt warm from his body?

She held it to her heart and let the tears of regret and lost opportunity flow.

CHAPTER FIVE

Three months later. Royal palace of Montovia.

NATALIA DRESSED FOR dinner with her family almost automatically. She had her own private apartment within the palace, as did Tristan and Gemma. But she was expected to attend the regular receptions, rich with the trappings of royalty, in the state dining area, where the King and Queen entertained dignitaries both from Montovia and other countries.

Increasingly, Tristan, in his role as Crown Prince, invited people of strategic importance to their country, and also to the business interests he oversaw. Natalia hadn't requested an invitation for anyone since she'd got back from Australia. It seemed too much effort.

She slipped into a full-length gown in midnight-blue silk, embellished with embroidery and crystals, beautiful in its simplicity and perfect cut. She teamed it with elegant stilettos covered in silk dyed the same shade of blue and scattered with crystals. She fastened earrings glittering with sapphires and diamonds and a matching bracelet. But she took little joy in her outfit.

Since her return from Australia she'd had to invest in a new wardrobe as she'd dropped two dress sizes. To someone with her interest in fashion, and the almost unlimited budget of a princess, shopping should have been a delight. Not so.

She was too down in the dumps to appreciate how lucky she was to be replenishing her wardrobe in the fashion capitals of Paris, Milan and London. Too un-motivated to appreciate what a boost her now too-large wardrobe would give to her next auction. Too darn ex-hausted to put 100 per cent into working alongside Tristan in promoting Montovia's export business—something she'd wanted to do for ages. Too heartsore to engage in anything much but endless agonising about 'what might have been' with Finn.

To her friends who asked about her weight loss secret, what diet she'd followed to get so skinny so fast, she had no reply. Not an honest one anyway. She had sworn to keep her incognito visit to Sydney a secret. That meant she couldn't confide in anyone the exhilaration of being Natalie Gerard, or the consequent deep dip in her spirits since she'd returned home.

Gemma knew about the trip, of course, but she couldn't talk to her either, because that would mean confiding in her sister-in-law the emotional rollercoaster of her time with Finn. The high of her powerful attraction to him, the shared laughter and the fun. The soaring excitement of his kisses and caresses. The plunge into misery as she'd watched Finn walk away.

No, the regret, self-recrimination and guilt were all hers to suffer on her own, often in the restless, sleepless hours after midnight. She had not wanted to lose weight, but her 'diet secret' could be put down to loss of appetite, trouble sleeping and the thoughts of Finn that plagued her like a repeat cycle she couldn't switch off, making her feel on the edge of anxiety.

She had run away from the only man she had ever wanted. Over and over she had relived that scene in her hotel bedroom. Wondered again and again what it would have been like if she had let Finn carry her to that bed. Regretted more times than she could count that she hadn't gone all the way with him. Only to realise that if she had, how much worse leaving him would have been.

Or what if she hadn't left? Why hadn't she even entertained a plan of simply informing Tristan she would not be flying back in the royal jet but rather staying to enjoy a day's sailing on the harbour before going home on a commercial flight when she was ready.

Because she would have had to tell the truth about her identity.

She sighed as she gave a final smoothing to the back of her hair. Her day-to-day life was fulfilling, what with her charity duties and her work with Tristan. Although somehow, caught up in her grief over Carl and her parents' obsession with the line of succession, she had gone backwards in terms of personal freedom as she got older rather than moving forward. But that was her life right now, and she wasn't sure what she could do to break out of it.

Other than run away to Sydney and find Finn...

Now, she headed down in the elevator to the state rooms, weary at the thought of having to divide her time equally between the person on her right and the one on her left, making polite, diplomatic small talk that would advance the interests of her country.

When had the thrill gone out of such occasions? Had they ever been more than endless duty and obligation?

Mentally she chastised herself for such ungrateful thoughts—she led a life of unimaginable privilege and should be unquestioningly thankful that she had won the lottery of noble birth. But a nagging thought kept intruding—the happiest days of her life had been those when she'd roamed incognito around Sydney, her only real obligation being to hide her identity. The happiest hours of all were when she'd been with Finn.

It always came back to Finn.

Natalia pasted on her most regal smile. As both Princess and dutiful daughter, her role was to be gracious and charming to the guests while cocktails and canapés were served before a formal dinner. She chatted to both people she knew and people she didn't, switching from one language to another as required. She felt her parents' approving glances upon her. This was what she'd been trained for, but since her time in laidback Australia she sometimes felt like an outsider, looking in on the rituals that she had been part of since birth.

Her smile was beginning to feel forced by the time she caught sight of Tristan walking into the room, deep in conversation with another man in black tie. Good, her brother could take over some of the work they were meant to share. But as they moved closer she froze. His companion was tall, broad-shouldered, with thick black hair. Something about the way the man held himself caught her attention, and for a crazy, breath-stealing moment she thought it was Finn.

She gave herself a mental shake. *Don't be so ridiculous.*

Was her heart going to jolt every time she saw someone even vaguely resembling the Australian man she was unable to forget? She thought she saw Finn everywhere: getting out of a car on Bond Street in London, striding along the Rue du Faubourg Saint-Honoré in Paris, even on the streets of the Montovian business capital, St Pierre.

Of course it was never him—never the man she wanted. When they turned around they didn't resemble him at all and she felt deflated and embarrassed.

Finn had become an obsession.

And now her feverish imaginings had conjured up a phantom Finn, right here in the palace.

She headed towards Tristan, just to be sure. Tristan's companion, as if he'd sensed her gaze on him, turned around to face her.

Him!

Natalia had to grab on to the plinth of a nearby piece of priceless sculpture—irreplaceable if it wobbled and fell. She didn't care. She had to anchor herself or she might slide into a faint. She felt light-headed, dizzy, overwhelmed by a wave of sheer joy and exultation.

Finn. It was really him. There could be no mistaking his dark good looks.

Finn. Here in Montovia.

It was as if all her hopes and dreams of the last three months had materialised into six foot two of solid, handsome Australian male. Had he discovered who she was? Come after her? Had he longed for her as she'd longed for him?

Panic tore through her like a whirlwind. What could she possibly say that would make sense after the way they had parted? She had treated him with unforgivable rudeness, leading him on, standing him up and then disappearing. She wanted to throw herself into his arms and thank him for seeking her out. Apologise. Beg his forgiveness. *Grovel.*

He looked over and caught her eye. She attempted a smile, but it was as if her mouth had had enough of smiling that evening and she could only manage something that was more grimace than grin. His expression in return was polite, restrained—the kind of look she often saw on the faces of strangers in such a social situation, when commoners encountered royalty.

Her mouth went dry. All this angst for nothing.

He didn't recognise her.

* * *

Finn guessed the elegant dark-haired woman in the glamorous gown must be Tristan's sister, Princess Natalia. He was predisposed not to like her. Irrational, he knew, but the name was too uncomfortably close to the name of the girl who had so cruelly played him in Sydney and left him high and dry.

Tristan confirmed his guess as to the woman's identity. 'Come and meet my sister,' he said now, with an amused sideways glance that Finn did not understand.

'With pleasure,' Finn said, letting Tristan guide him across the room.

When he'd made fun of Eliza having a real-life prince at her wedding, he'd never imagined he would end up doing business with him. Or that he'd *like* the guy. He'd been briefly introduced to Tristan at the wedding, and then had been surprised to be contacted by him when Tristan was renegotiating the contract for the distribution of Montovia's renowned chocolate and cheeses into Australia, New Zealand and the Pacific region.

Finn had won the lucrative contract. He had also proposed to Tristan that he work with one of his other clients to develop a prestige Montovian chocolate liqueur. Tristan had been very taken with the idea and had invited Finn to visit his kingdom.

He'd flown in that morning via London, to the small town of Montovia, which took its name from the country. Stepping off the plane had been like stepping through a portal to a totally different world. The place was like something from a movie, where witches and wizards might suddenly appear. A fortified medieval castle was perched high on a mountainside above a lake, looking down on cobbled streets, gingerbread-style houses and the spire of an ancient cathedral. And now here he was, inside the grand stateroom of the glittering palace that Tristan and his family called home.

The Princess waited regally for them to approach—as, Finn supposed, a princess would. She was lovely—very slender, with dark hair twisted off her face in a severe up-do, as befitted the formality of the evening. She didn't smile, rather she looked serious, perhaps somewhat snotty. Again, he supposed that might be typical princess behaviour. But she did manage a tentative hint of a smile.

He frowned, chasing a memory. There was something familiar about her smile… But then the smile was gone, and so was his moment of fleeting recognition.

As he approached she held out her hand—pale, slender, with perfectly manicured nails. He hesitated. Was he meant to kiss it? Bow down before her? No. It appeared that a formal handshake was all that was required.

'My sister, the Princess Natalia,' Tristan said.

'Finn O'Neill,' Finn said in turn.

He took the Princess's hand in a firm grip and was surprised to find it trembled. How could she possibly be nervous? She must shake many strangers' hands on occasions like this.

Tristan briefly explained his business connection with Finn. 'You two might have already met,' he said, looking from one to the other.

Huh? No way would he have forgotten meeting a beautiful young princess. 'I don't believe so,' he said.

The Princess's long pause began to seem awkward. Did she speak English? Because he sure as hell didn't know a word of Montovian.

She cleared her throat, gave a little cough before finally she spoke. 'Hello, Finn,' she said. 'I…I'm as shocked to see you here as you must be to see me.'

Her English-accented voice was immediately familiar,

and plunged him back into a million memories of the enchantress back in Sydney who had made an utter fool of him. The woman who had bailed on him without a good-bye or any word of explanation.

He seethed at the mere thought of her. Maybe he really had fallen into a place populated by witches and warlocks, because *this* woman was claiming to be *that* woman and it could not possibly be true.

He decided to test her. 'Natalie Gerard?'

The Princess bit her bottom lip, avoided his gaze. 'There's actually no such person. But I called myself that when I was in Sydney. When…when we met at Eliza and Jake's wedding. I was incognito and in disguise.'

Finn stared at the woman who stood before him in the glittering dark dress. *This was not the person he had known in Sydney.* Natalie had long, thick blonde hair. Princess Natalia's hair was dark, almost black, and put up in that severe style. Natalie was curvaceous; Natalia was very slender. She wore an elegant, modest gown; the last time he'd seen Natalie she'd been wearing only her pink lace underwear.

Hell, Natalia was an uptight Montovian princess, who lived a life of immense privilege in a lavishly appointed palace. Natalie was a sexy, uninhibited English girl on vacation in Sydney, who had made him laugh and been out-and-out naughty. *This was crazy.*

And yet there was something hauntingly familiar about the expressions that flitted across her face.

'I don't believe you're Natalie. Are you her sister? Her cousin?'

This must be some kind of scam. Or real witchy stuff.

'No.' Princess Natalia's dark eyelashes fluttered and her lips curved in a tremulous smile, as if that was the most ridiculous of suggestions.

Natalie's smile.

The same curving of lush, beautifully shaped lips… the same perfect white teeth. Yet the smile seemed subdued, of lower wattage, not lit by the vivacity of Natalie. Finn looked closer, not caring that the intensity of his examination might breach some royal protocol. The eyes. Those beautiful iris-blue eyes.

He glanced back to Tristan. Not that he was in the habit of staring into another guy's eyes but, yes, they were the same blue, just a shade darker than his sister's. That was where he'd seen that colour before—when he'd been briefly introduced to Tristan at the wedding. Before the beautiful stranger across the aisle had captivated his attention.

'I really am Natalie,' the Princess said. 'We sat at the same table. We…we swapped the place cards.'

'You danced with my sister,' said Tristan. 'More than once.'

He'd done a whole lot more than dance with Natalie Gerard. But this woman? *He didn't know her.*

An older man in military uniform passing by caught Tristan's eye and he turned to acknowledge him. In the moment when Tristan was distracted, the Princess stepped closer.

'Don't you remember? You were my tutor in living dangerously,' she whispered.

Only Natalie could know that.

Finn reeled, shocked not just by the intimacy of her words but by her closeness, her floral scent—so achingly familiar that it jolted him with memories he had battled to suppress.

Tristan turned his attention back to them. The Princess rolled her eyes so only Finn could see and in a flash she was the mischievous Natalie he'd known.

What the hell...?

Natalie and Princess Natalia were like light and shade. Yet the more he looked at the Princess, the more he could see Natalie. Until they morphed into one and the same person. Was she a natural blonde or a natural brunette? Her deception sickened him.

He clenched his fists by his sides. 'I can't get my head around this. Why the disguise? Why the deception?'

'It was the only way I was allowed to go to Eliza and Jake's wedding and get a chance to see Sydney. If the media had known I was there, it might have deflected attention from the bride and groom.'

'Why would the media be so interested in *you*?'

She flushed. 'Because I—'

Tristan interjected. 'Because she is a beautiful European princess who isn't yet married. That's reason enough for their interest.'

'Did Eliza know who you were?' he asked. Then he answered his own question. 'Of course she does. She warned me off Natalie Gerard. Now I see why.'

Princess Natalia's eyebrows rose—they were black, Natalie's had been light brown. 'What did she say about me? Eliza and the other Party Queens were sworn to secrecy.'

'Eliza did not betray your trust,' he said, tight-lipped.

How right Eliza had been to try and steer him away from Natalie out of concern for him. That beautiful girl in the pink lace dress had been a liar and a fraud. And he'd been fool enough to have been taken in by her.

He cringed when he remembered how fascinated he had been by her. How genuine she had seemed. How achingly he'd wanted her. How he'd started to wonder if she could be more than a fling.

'My sister's escapade in Sydney must be kept a secret,'

Tristan said. 'No one must know about her time pretending to be a commoner.'

A commoner? Who used such terms in this day and age? A hereditary prince like Tristan, Finn thought grimly. And a hereditary princess like his sister. A woman who had made a game out of slumming it with the commoners in Sydney.

He was her dirty little secret.

'I would appreciate it if you kept that confidence now we are doing business together.'

Finn didn't miss the warning in the Crown Prince's words, or the appeal in the Princess's eyes. The Montovian deal was both lucrative and prestigious. He didn't want to jeopardise it.

'I won't spill any beans,' he said through gritted teeth.

This situation was utterly unreal. As if he was trapped in a dark spider's web.

'I appreciate your discretion,' said Tristan. 'I didn't make the connection with the man Natalia was dancing with and the owner of one of the biggest food import and export companies in Australia until I actually met you face to face.'

'Your sister looked very different then. I really didn't recognise her.'

He wanted to tell Tristan's duplicitous sister exactly what he thought of her. Which would hardly be appropriate, considering their surroundings. He took a breath to steady himself. Inhaled that exciting Natalie scent. Wanted to spit it out.

'My sister did a good job in keeping under the radar,' Tristan said.

'I was under strict orders not to let anyone know who I really was,' she said, with an undertone of pleading in her voice. 'There are three important rules a Montovian princess must follow: she must never attract attention for the wrong reason, never be the focus of critical press and never be seen to reflect badly on the throne.' She paused. 'Of course there are a whole lot of other rules too.'

'And by following those rules she enjoyed her vacation and avoided any scandal,' said Tristan, looking approvingly at his sister.

Tristan obviously had no clue that he and Natalie had done much more than chat and dance. Finn suspected that in Tristan's eyes her behaviour on the evening of the wedding would have been considered highly scandalous for a princess.

He remembered how passionate she had been. How intrigued he'd been by her. How gutted he'd been when he'd gone to the hotel the next morning to find she'd checked out and left no forwarding address. How furious.

She'd made a total fool of him. He wanted nothing to do with Natalie/Natalia. Yet his glance kept returning to her, and he was fascinated that this woman was the same one who had enchanted him in Sydney. She was, without a doubt, a mistress of disguise, totally without scruples— and a very good liar.

She looked up at him with those beautiful blue eyes that could lie and lie and lie. 'Finn, I'm sorry I wasn't honest with you. I had no choice.'

Everyone *always* had a choice whether to tell the truth or lie. He wanted to explain that to her. But in the interests of diplomacy and doing business with her family he could only nod tersely. Her behaviour had been unforgivable. The sooner he could turn on his heel and walk away from her, the better. That was if he was allowed to turn his back on her. He was a 'commoner' and she was royalty. Perhaps she expected him to walk backwards from her presence, bowing and scraping all the way.

No matter how lucrative the Montovian contract, he would never, ever agree to do that.

Tristan didn't seem aware of the tension between him and his sister. 'It is good that you two have reconnected,' he said. 'Because unfortunately an emergency calls me away from here tomorrow. Natalia, can I ask you, please, to stand in for me in my meetings with Finn?'

The Princess looked as disconcerted as Finn felt. 'What meetings?' she said.

'Tomorrow morning I have organised a meeting for Finn with our master chocolatier at the chocolate factory.'

'That's always a pleasure,' she said.

'And then a meeting with the Chocolate Makers' Association over lunch.'

She nodded. 'You will need to brief me on the agenda.'

Tristan turned to Finn. 'Natalia has her own interests, with her auctions and other charity work, but she also keeps her finger on the bigger picture of Montovia's trade interests, and works with me when required.'

What choice did Finn have but to agree? 'Fine by me,' he said.

'Natalia is also an expert on the castle and the old town. Natalia, could you please give Finn a tour of the castle in the morning and the points of interest in the town in the afternoon?'

'Of course,' she said.

Tristan gave a slight bow. 'I must attend to my other guests. I shall leave you to carry on your conversation. Finn will be our guest for three days. There will be other opportunities for us to introduce him to our beautiful country during that time.'

CHAPTER SIX

NATALIA HAD TO keep shooting glances at Finn to make sure he was real—actually here in Montovia, working with her brother, and now with her, to further her country's interests.

She wanted to reach up and touch him, to check he was indeed solid flesh and blood and not some hallucination she had conjured up out of her hopeless longing for him. But she didn't dare risk it—not a hand on his arm, not a finger trailed down the smooth olive skin of his cheek. She had seen Finn's eyes frost with cold disdain when he'd realised the truth of who she was, how she'd deceived him. Her touch would no longer be welcomed.

After Tristan had headed off towards another guest and left her alone with Finn, his expression didn't warm into anything less forbidding. Yet for all the shock of encountering him so unexpectedly, and his open hostility—for which she couldn't blame him—she felt an effervescent joy bubble through her. She'd thought she would never see him again anywhere but in her dreams. It was like some kind of magic that he was here, just touching distance away.

Finn. The strong attraction that had made every other man in the room—in the world—disappear from her awareness had not been dispersed by three months of absence. And now Tristan had delivered Finn back to her.

Soon they would be called to dinner. It was unlikely she would be seated near him. And there could be no mischievous swapping of place cards at a palace soirée.

She felt an urgent need to apologise, to explain, to try and salvage something of that memorable time with him in Sydney. But she did not want to be overheard.

'Finn,' she said in a low voice. 'I don't think we need an audience. Shall we move over to that corner of the room?'

He nodded and followed her away from the main body of guests towards the windows that looked over the lake, closed to the chilly November evening. It was only a few steps away but it gave them some breathing space without being so private that her tête-à-tête with a handsome man would give rise to gossip.

The heavy gold brocade curtains had been pulled back to give a dramatic view across the lake, with the full moon reflected in the dark water, gleaming on the permanent snow high on the jagged peaks of the mountains. Finn admired the view with what seemed like genuine appreciation. In other circumstances it would have been romantic.

But romance was, sadly, not on the agenda. This was more akin to a confrontation.

An uncomfortable silence fell between them. Finn was the first to break it. 'I keep telling myself there must be a rational explanation for your deception,' he said.

'Rational?' She took a deep intake of breath. 'There was nothing rational about how I felt about you,' she said in a voice that wasn't quite steady.

He frowned. 'What do you mean?'

'Meeting you in Sydney was so unexpected and…and wonderful. I had never felt like that about a man. I told you—you made the wedding magic for me. Logically, I should have said goodnight when the wedding wound up. But I simply couldn't bear to shake your hand and thank you for your company as I should have. I was desperate to cling on to every possible minute with you. But I had given my word not to reveal my identity to anyone.' She hesitated. 'Also, I wondered if you would treat me the same way if you knew who I really was.'

'That was my decision to make,' he said. 'You didn't give me the opportunity to make it. Yet you trusted others with the truth.'

'I didn't know you. I had to be cautious. You could have been a reporter for all I knew.'

But she had trusted him enough to want to make love with him. And had spent the last three months regretting that caution had kicked in.

'I trusted you to be who you said you were. But it was just a game to you.'

'No. It wasn't a game. I…I really liked you.'

But she hadn't been honest with him. *'Alla prossima,'* he had murmured, and she had translated, knowing it was a lie, that they would not meet again. Since then she had had plenty of opportunity to reflect on how he must have felt when he'd discovered she had gone without any explanation or goodbye.

She looked up at him, registered the shock he must have felt on seeing *her*, not the Natalie he had known. Maybe she had done too good a job on that disguise if he was having such difficulty reconciling the two aspects of her.

She tried to make all the regret she felt for treating him so thoughtlessly show in her eyes. 'Finn. I'm sorry for—'

His dark brows drew together. 'Sorry for what? Choose an option for your apology—you have several.'

He held up his left hand and ticked off her options finger by finger with his right hand. *Beautiful hands that had felt so good on her body.*

'Option one—lying so thoroughly about your identity. Option two—standing me up by disappearing off the face of the earth with no explanation. Option three—

making me go through that charade just now of guessing your identity.'

She swallowed hard against a lump of anguish. He thought so badly of her. 'I…I plead guilty to options one and two, but I'm innocent of option three,' she said. 'I expect you must be angry, but you can't pin that one on me.'

'Did you really not know I'd be here tonight? Or was that another game for the amusement of you and your brother?'

'I had absolutely no idea you would be here. Tristan had not informed me. I was so shocked I thought I was going to faint.'

His mouth twisted into a cynical line she hadn't seen before. 'You understand I might find it difficult to believe a word you say ever again?'

His words hit their target and she flushed. 'I get that,' she said. 'But I really didn't have a clue you would be here tonight—or indeed that Tristan was doing business with you. I don't know why he didn't tell me. Especially as he wants me to attend some of his meetings with our Montovian business people. I can only think he wanted to surprise me because he realised we'd met at the wedding.'

'He certainly surprised *me*,' he said, with a wry twist to his mouth.

'Me too—and I wish he'd told me. Although for me it was a pleasant surprise. I…I'm happy to see you again, Finn, in spite of the way it's happened.' She looked up at him, but his only response was a grudging nod. 'Possibly Tristan thought springing us on each other might be simpler than having to explain who I really was. Remember, he doesn't know about…about what happened after the wedding?'

'Perhaps,' he said—with, she thought, a slight thawing of his frosty demeanour.

'As Crown Prince and heir to the throne, Tristan is working hard to modernise the royal family and some of their really stuffy old ways of doing things. It's a big job and he's getting both Gemma and me involved in it. He's also become an active advocate for our country's exports. I wasn't trained in business, but I'm doing my best to help with the trade side of things.'

Finn frowned. '*He* was trained for it but not you, even as second in line to the throne?'

'It sounds very old fashioned, I know, but I was brought up to make a strategic marriage to a man of noble birth. Tristan studied law. My older brother studied economics. I was sent to a strict Swiss finishing school. However, once I'd graduated, with straight As in deportment and how to manage servants, I insisted I be allowed to follow my own interest and study architecture in London.'

'So there's no career in fashion?'

Again, there was that cynical edge to his voice. Again, she couldn't blame him.

'Well, not in the retail sense. However, I do work very hard on my fashion auctions, so that isn't a total fib.'

'Fashion auctions?'

She was pleased to see genuine interest. 'You haven't heard of them? I don't suppose you would have. As Princess of Montovia, I'm the patron of several charities—including my own favourite, which works with an international foundation to support the education of girls in developing countries. Long story short: a lot of designer clothes and accessories are only worn once or twice by people like me and my privileged friends. As a fundraiser, I organised an online auction of donated items which was so successful it's become a regular thing and it's getting bigger and bigger. We get both donations and bids from all around the world. The charity has really benefitted, way beyond the scope of regular donations.'

'That sounds admirable,' he said.

'I'm proud of it,' she said.

'It seems you should be.' He paused, searched her face. 'I'm still struggling to make sense of you being a princess. For instance, what do I call you? Natalia? Princess? Your Highness? Is bended knee required?'

'Natalia is fine. Or Natalie would work too. I *am* Natalie, Finn. Or I was in Sydney, where I was *allowed* to be her.'

She couldn't keep the wistfulness from her voice. It had been a taste of a different life. A bright, flaming light interspersed between various shades of grey, with Finn being the most brilliant of flames.

'Natalie Gerard told me she was single. What about Princess Natalia?'

'Notorious for being single. In spite of a lifetime of grooming for wifedom.'

'Notorious?'

She sighed. 'Now that you know who I am, I'll save you the trouble of looking up media reports about the "Heartbreaker Princess", or the "Bachelor Princess". I make great copy for the European gossip magazines because I've rejected the proposals of six palace-approved men. Actually, seven now. I've knocked back another one since I got home from Australia.'

'Wait. You can't choose your own husband? He has to be approved?'

Put like that, no wonder he sounded incredulous.

'Until recently Montovian royalty could only marry spouses with noble blood.'

'No "commoners" allowed?' he said, using his fingers

to make quote marks and his voice to let her know just what he thought of the term.

She realised how insulting the word was. Another anachronism for her and Tristan to work on.

'That's right. But then Tristan used his considerable legal research skills to search the royal archives and discovered that any reigning King could amend that rule. My father was persuaded to change it—the restriction has not made for happy marriages in our family, including that of my parents—so Tristan could marry for love. As it turned out, Gemma discovered she was distantly related to both the English and the Danish royal families, so the change in rule was not needed. I remain somewhat of a test case.'

'So you're allowed to marry who you want to?'

'In theory, yes. In practice, my parents still want me to marry a well-born European aristocrat. In fact, they have to give their permission, whoever I might want to marry. I am, after all, second in line to the throne. You may not know that my older brother Carl was…was killed in a helicopter crash, along with his wife and two-year-old son.'

Her voice hitched. It was still so difficult to talk about the accident, even to acknowledge that it had happened. She didn't think she would ever get over the loss of the brother she'd adored, his precious little son Rudi, or poor Sylvie, too young to die. One day Carl had been there, acting the bossy big brother, and the next he'd been gone. She didn't think she'd ever be able to come to terms with it.

'I'm sorry. I did read about the tragedy in my research on Montovia.'

Natalia took a moment to collect herself. 'Everything changed. Losing Carl meant I moved up to second in line to the throne. And Tristan had been quite the party boy until then. He had to step up to the responsibility of being Crown Prince and the future King. My parents threw a cordon of protection around me. Suddenly it seemed as though I'd been thrown back to the nursery.'

'If that was the case, how were you allowed to swan around Sydney by yourself?'

She shrugged. 'I wasn't. I could pretend I had absolute freedom, but my bodyguards were always close to hand.'

His dark brows rose. 'Your bodyguards?'

She nodded. 'That waiter at the wedding who was hovering solicitously nearby?'

'I thought he fancied you.'

She shook her head. 'Just doing his job. As was the chauffeur of the hire car. Both Montovian bodyguards.'

Finn ran his ran through his hair. Natalia ached to smooth it down for him but didn't dare. She wasn't sure what kind of reception she'd get.

'And at your hotel?'

'They shared the adjoining room.'

Finn's disbelief and horror was to be expected. 'You mean they could hear what was going on in your room?'

'Probably.'

She couldn't meet his eyes. She had asked her bodyguards not to mention that she'd had a visitor to her hotel room. They liked her. She sometimes thought they felt sorry for her, for the restricted life she had to live in spite of her wealth and privilege. There had been no adverse reports back to her parents. As far as they had observed it had been entirely innocent.

He swore under his breath. 'It just gets worse.'

'What do you mean?'

'My recollection of that day is vastly different from yours. It's like we were operating on two different levels of reality.'

'I'm still *me*, Finn.'

He shook his head. 'I don't know you, Princess Natalia.' He made a credible attempt at a bow. 'I knew Natalie. I liked Natalie a lot. She was gorgeous and she was fun. Things moved fast with me and Natalie—until she put on the brakes. That was frustrating, but it was her prerogative. We arranged to meet the next day and I went away a happy man. Then I turned up at her hotel, to take her sailing as arranged. Only to find she had checked out very early that morning. She didn't leave me a message at the desk to explain. No. She just disappeared. Standing there in that lobby, when I realised I'd been stood up in a spectacular manner, wasn't my finest moment.'

She cringed at the pain on his face. 'I really am sorry, but I can explain—'

'Can you?' He shrugged. 'After I got over my annoyance—and I admit my intense disappointment—I figured Natalie was a tourist, looking for some no-strings fun. She ran out of time and ran out of town. I'd been played. I should have known better.'

She gasped. 'It really wasn't like that.'

But that was how it must have appeared…

'So, what's *your* version of events?'

She shifted from one stilettoed foot to the other. 'I…I couldn't bear to say goodbye for real. I was scared I would break down and spill the truth about myself. Which would have got me into big trouble. I know I'm twenty-seven years old, but my parents aren't just my parents. They're the King and Queen of my country and their word is law. Our private jet was there to take me home with Tristan and Gemma. I was obligated to go with them. I wanted to part on good terms with you. So I didn't tell you I was leaving. It…made it easier.'

She closed her eyes at the image of Finn asking at the hotel reception desk for her, only to be told she'd gone. How must he have felt?

'Your definition of parting on "good terms" seems to translate as leaving after lie had been piled upon lie.'

'Guilty as charged,' she said, feeling inexpressibly sad.

She couldn't tell him about all that had motivated her without giving away her entire story. She was still a virgin. Her situation hadn't changed. To make love with him would have come with risks and consequences that hadn't changed in the three months since she'd kissed him good-bye at the door of her hotel room. Maybe now she might take those risks on board if she got the chance, but maybe duty would still win out.

She realised she could apologise all she wanted for the Natalie Gerard deception, but he would never forget what she'd done.

He would never again believe a word she said.

He looked down into her face, as if searching it for the answers he might sense she wasn't giving.

'Loss of face is important to me. You made me look foolish. Not to mention gutted at losing Natalie, who had made quite an impact on me.' He paused, took a step back from her. His expression hardened. 'But what happened in Sydney wasn't really that significant. It wasn't even a day of my life—or yours, for that matter. You've apologised. I've put it behind me.'

'I see,' she said, feeling as though she had lost for ever something of immeasurable value.

She saw from the set of his jaw that Finn the business-man had taken over.

'That's as far as it goes,' he said. 'There's nothing in the contract I've signed with your brother that necessitates me spending extended time with you. The business meetings are necessary, but there's no need for the guided tour. I just want to finalise my business with Tristan and get the hell out of here.'

Mutely, she nodded. 'Of course,' she finally managed to choke out.

She looked up at him and recognised the marvellous man she had connected with in Sydney. *Finn*. Every moment she had spent with him was seared on her memory. But he looked at her and didn't see Natalie. He saw a stranger who had lied to him, who had made a fool of him. She had hurt him. And he didn't want anything further to do with her.

She was in a room filled with other people, and the murmur of conversation was rising and falling around her, yet she had never felt so alone.

Finn felt bad at the Princess's shocked expression. There was hurt there, too, in those beautiful blue eyes. But he could only get his head around this very odd situation he found himself plunged into by thinking of Natalia as someone he didn't know.

She wasn't the woman he had fallen for in Sydney. Not fallen *in love* with. Of course not. For one thing, he was not a believer in love at first sight—he'd confused infatuation with love with Chiara. But his meeting with the woman he'd known as Natalie Gerard had been something bigger than just a casual hook-up at a wedding.

The fact she lived in another country had been cause enough for him to put the brakes on. However, his time with her had come skidding to an abrupt halt before he'd even had a chance to think about the wisdom of taking things further. This woman—Princess Natalia—was absolutely out of bounds in too many ways to count.

It wasn't just that she lived on the other side of the world from him, hers was a world where he was considered a 'commoner', lacking in status or authority. How could trying to rekindle those Sydney feelings go anywhere? For him a serious relationship—one day perhaps marriage—was all about a partnership of equals, working together to enjoy life together and then, when the time was right, raising a family. Like his parents, his grandparents, his friends like Eliza and Jake.

The sooner he put Natalie/Natalia behind him, the better.

He followed her to the football-stadium-sized dining room, noting the sexy swing of her hips. The sway was not quite the same as the one he'd seen before from her alter ego, as the Princess was wearing a restrictive long gown, but it was every bit as enticing.

He was still having difficulty getting his head around the fact she was 100 per cent Natalie, but the sway when she walked was undeniably hers. The way she'd looked so different in Sydney was a kind of witchery, a modern sleight of hand, magic performed by hairdressers and make-up artists and a princess who was a mistress of the art of dissembling.

The grand Montovian royal dining room, with its soaring moulded ceilings, was decorated like a museum, with priceless antiques, masterpieces on the walls, crystal chandeliers and gleaming gold place settings. Very formal…very European. Wealth beyond the bounds of imagination.

He was not seated next to Natalia, for which he was thankful. He had no desire to revive memories of the last time they had shared a table. It hurt too much to remember how happy he'd been in her company.

Man, had that Kerry woman got her predictions wrong. Her so-called psychic powers hadn't picked up on a false identity.

Princess Natalia was seated on the opposite side of the table. Close enough so he could observe her, not close enough to talk to her. She was so elegant, so poised, her smile so charming. The lights picked up the diamonds glittering at her ears and her wrists. A real princess. Yet she seemed subdued—as if someone had dimmed the lights on Natalie to result in Natalia.

He noticed she pushed the food around on her plate with her fork, scarcely a bite reaching her mouth. It wasn't the fault of the food, which was superb. No wonder she was so slender. Natalie had had a hearty appetite.

He would go crazy if he kept comparing them.

His mind finally grasped the fact that Natalia was indeed Natalie, but she seemed like a diminished version of the woman he'd met in Sydney.

He was seated near Tristan, alongside his cousin Marco and his wife Amelie. Over dinner, they talked about their time in the Montovian military, where service was compulsory for all young people.

Tristan had served, despite his royal status, and Marco—a count and high-ranking officer—had met his doctor wife Amelie—a Montovian commoner—while deployed on a peace-keeping force in an African country. They had only been able to marry because of the change in law Tristan had brought about.

It was such a different world to the one Finn had experienced growing up. Again he had the sense that he had fallen into a movie set. Perhaps even a different century.

Just before dessert was to be served, Finn found himself in private conversation with Tristan.

'Natalia tells me you have politely turned down her services as tour guide,' Tristan said.

'Yes, I have to catch up on some work between meetings.' It was as polite an excuse as he'd been able to come up with on the spot.

'Would you consider changing your mind?' Tristan asked.

The guy was a prince and Finn was a guest in his palace. Was this a lightly veiled order?

'I suppose I could...' he said slowly, not certain where this would take him.

'I would appreciate it if you'd spend that extra time with her,' Tristan said. 'You see, we're worried about Natalia. All the family have expressed their concern.'

'Concern?'

Tristan sighed. 'She is not herself since she returned from Australia. Almost as if she has disengaged from her life in the palace. She does her duty—Natalia is nothing if not dutiful—but she's lacking in zest, showing no real enthusiasm for anything, except perhaps her auctions. That's not like her at all. You must have noticed how thin she has become? That is in spite of Gemma organising special meals to tempt her appetite.'

An unexpected terror struck Finn's heart. 'You think she's unwell?' He choked out the words.

Her lies, the deception, his loss of face—all seemed suddenly insignificant now he was faced with the possible loss of this woman who had moved him to the edge of both love and hate.

'Perhaps... I don't know. I can't ask her doctor. Even the Crown Prince can't do that. My sister is an independent person.'

'But how do you think spending more time with me would help?'

'It has struck me that the last time I saw my sister laugh was when she was dancing with you at Eliza's wedding in Sydney. Perhaps you can make her laugh again?'

CHAPTER SEVEN

FINN HAD ARRANGED to meet Natalia, via an exchange of stilted phone conversations, early the next morning at the high, locked wooden gate that opened on to some stone steps leading up to the external walkways and corridors of the castle. As he approached he could see she was already there, her back to him, looking out to the lake below.

She was dressed in sombre colours: dark grey trousers, black boots, a thick wool light-grey jacket, a silver-coloured scarf. Her dark hair swung straight and loose to skim her shoulders, gleaming in the mid-morning sunlight.

Against the backdrop of the towering walls of the castle, the vastness of the lake, she seemed fragile and alone, and Finn remembered Tristan's concern. He thought about his own realisation that she might be suffering from depression, and felt a surge of remorse at how harshly he'd spoken to her the previous day, when she had tried so hard to be honest with him.

She needed kindness and understanding, not condemnation. He needed to tell her that. Explain his perhaps over-the-top reaction to the startling news about her identity. Make his own apologies.

As he walked towards her his shoes crunched on the crushed stone pathway. 'Natalia!' he called.

Startled, she turned to face him.

Her first expression on catching sight of him was, to his immense surprise, delight—quickly covered by a schooled indifference. She was aloof, but not in the manner of a princess—rather in the manner of a woman who had been told that the passion she'd shared was of no importance, easily forgotten.

Inwardly, Finn cursed himself for his thoughtlessness. And his dishonesty. He hadn't meant a word of it. He'd used those words to hide his battered pride and hurt that she had walked out on him without notice.

'You called me Natalia,' she said, after he'd reached her and stood hand-shaking distance apart.

'Yes,' he said. 'There's no point in arguing over semantics. Natalia is your given name. Natalie is the anglicised version of your name. I have a Chinese name—Ming-tun—which only my grandfather uses. What I'm trying to say is the name doesn't matter. It's the person.'

'Thank you,' she said. 'I like Ming-tun. What does it mean?'

Her cheeks were flushed pink with the cold and her eyes shone blue. She was every bit as lovely as a brunette as she had been as a blonde.

'It means intelligent. My grandfather had high hopes.'

'Seems to me you've lived up to your name. He must be proud.'

'I've done my best,' he said.

But how intelligently had he dealt with the revelation of her real identity?

He had studied hard at school and at university because it had been expected of him. His immigrant grandparents and father set great store on a good education. But all he'd ever wanted to do was to dive head-first into the family business. Although without his degree perhaps he would not have been able to drive the business forward so successfully, so quickly.

She looked up at him, her head tilted to one side, blue eyes narrowed. 'What made you change your mind?'

'About your name? I decided it was pointless thinking

of you as two different people when Natalia and Natalie are one and the same.'

'I didn't mean that. I meant you being here this morning. Last night, you seemed so sure you didn't want me to show you around. You said that we would meet at the chocolate factory.'

It's because your family are concerned you're depressed and it shocked me.

Tristan hadn't exactly said that, but his concerns about Natalia had immediately raised flags for Finn. One of his mates in high school had had an undiagnosed depression that had ended in a funeral after he had taken his own life. Finn had beaten himself up for not having been there for his friend.

His school had insisted that the boy's classmates attend extensive counselling, and ever since he'd been alert for symptoms of depression in the people close to him. He'd been able to get help for them when he'd seen the signs. He'd recognised them in Tristan's description of Natalia.

'Why did I change my mind? Perhaps the fact I don't speak a word of Montovian?' It wasn't the world's best excuse but he decided to run with it. 'Your cousin Marco warned me that many of the townsfolk don't feel comfortable speaking English, even though they study it in school, and that Montovian is a language almost impossible for a foreigner to learn.'

'It *is* a difficult language,' she said. 'However, Gemma is becoming fluent in it so it can be mastered. But that doesn't really answer my question.'

He squirmed just a little under the gaze of those perceptive blue eyes. 'I guess it doesn't,' he said. 'Truth is, I realised I'd be crazy to knock back the services of a guide who's a member of the royal family, who must know so much about Montovia.'

'It's true we've been around for centuries,' she said drily.

'That's exactly my point,' he said.

'I appreciate your worthy explanation, Finn. But I suspect the real truth is that Tristan coerced you into it.'

'Not true.'

She raised her dark eyebrows. 'Really?'

'Well, possibly true. Not coerced. He asked me to reconsider. He's concerned about you. Thinks you're unhappy. He thought I might be able to cheer you up. That I seemed to have the touch.'

She smiled—a slow, curving smile that was a ghost of her usual dazzling smile but still very appealing, with a hint of sensuality. He realised that she was remembering, as he was, just how he had kept her entertained back in Sydney.

'Tristan has no idea about you and me at the wedding, does he?' she said.

'Not a clue,' he said. 'He and Gemma left before the end, I believe.'

'So he didn't see us kissing behind the orchids and no one reported it to him, either. Gemma has certainly never mentioned it.'

Memories of the incident flooded his mind. How wonderful she'd felt in his arms. Her scent. Her taste. How sensual and exciting her kisses had been.

How much he'd wanted her.

'We were discreet,' he said, his voice suddenly husky as he looked down into her face.

'Fortunately for us they were very big planters of orchids.'

As they shared the moment of complicity her lips parted without her seeming to realise they were doing it, or that it looked like an invitation to kiss her again.

'How could I forget?' he said, wrenching his gaze away from her lips. He knew she knew he wasn't talking about the orchids.

'If Tristan knew—if my father knew—that you had come back to my hotel room, you would be languishing in the dungeons right now.'

He wasn't sure if she was joking or not. Not in this movie set of a home of hers. 'You have dungeons?'

'They're not part of my guided tour, but, yes. Genuine dungeons—damp, dreary and complete with medieval instruments of torture.'

'Don't tell me—some of them are specifically designed for men who compromise the virtue of Montovian princesses?'

'Indeed,' she said, with a hint of that mischief he'd liked so much. 'Custom-made to fit the crime.'

'*Ouch*. Dancing with a princess in those days really meant living dangerously.'

He grimaced and she laughed.

He'd made her laugh.

It made him feel good to see her laugh.

'Don't worry too much,' she said. 'The torture chambers are intact but they haven't been used for a long, long time.'

'Still, it might be wise to keep Tristan in ignorance about the extent of our time together in Sydney,' he said.

'Yes. He obviously likes you and trusts you. I don't believe he'd want to torture you just to defend the honour of his sister.'

'I sincerely hope not, if we're to do business together. He saw that you enjoyed dancing with me—that's all he needs to know.' He paused, not sure how far he should go in case she clammed up. 'He tells me he hasn't noticed you enjoying yourself much since.'

All traces of laughter vanished. Her mouth set in a

tight, unapproachable, distinctly unkissable line. 'That's probably true.'

She went to turn away, and he sensed her closing up on him. 'Natalia…' He put a hand on her shoulder to turn her back to face him, then dropped it immediately when she complied.

There could be no more touching—even through the thickness of a coat. Not now he truly understood the situation. He was careful. They were not completely alone on these battlements. There was a party of gardeners in sight, and no doubt they'd encounter other people.

'Is Tristan right? *Are* you unhappy? I've noticed how different you are from your time in Sydney. It's not just the hair colour—which I like, by the way. But it's as if… as if your light has dimmed.'

'That could be because it's winter.' She didn't quite carry off the light-hearted retort.

'Perhaps…' he said. 'You've lost a lot of weight, too.'

'Isn't there an old saying that you can never be too rich or too thin?'

'If you want to be thin, that's okay. But you do seem different. Not as vivacious.'

She closed her eyes tight for a moment, as if to give herself time to think. Or to look back into her past.

'I wasn't happy before I went to Australia. My personal life didn't seem to be my own any more. Not since Carl died and everything changed. That's why I wanted so desperately to go there. To be anonymous. To maybe find what was missing.'

She sighed—a sad sound that struck at Finn's heart. He wanted to take her in his arms to comfort her, but thought better of it.

'You saw me at my best. I was riding a high. I loved the

independence and the freedom to be myself. Of course it all came crashing down around me when I got back home.'

'Did you seek any help to deal with that crash? Because—'

She put up her hand in an imperious gesture to stop him from going any further. 'I don't want you feeling sorry for me, Finn. Because there's nothing to be sorry about. And I don't need help.'

'I don't feel sorry for you at all. I'm just concerned.'

She took a deep breath. 'That's very sweet of you. But I can deal with my…my unhappiness.'

'In other words—"butt out, Finn"?'

'Exactly.'

Finn detected the wobble of her lower lip and realised she might not be as composed as she wanted him to believe.

'I know I'm the girl who has everything. And I'm not ungrateful. But I'm nearly twenty-eight and I don't have my own life. No career—though the auctions have become a real interest. No husband. No children. Everything is about duty and doing the right thing by others. Marrying for the sake of the succession—not for my own happiness.'

'Would your family honestly force you into marrying someone you didn't like?'

He'd been presented to her parents the night before— King Gerard and Queen Truda. They'd seemed more modern and approachable than he'd imagined.

'*Like* being the operative word. *Love* doesn't come into it—and I won't settle for less than love. Tristan and Gemma have set the standard. My own parents have a miserable marriage. My father wasn't allowed to marry his girlfriend—a girl from a good Montovian family but not good enough for a future king. He put off marriage for as long as he could so he could be with her. Then he had to marry my much younger mother. She thought she was marrying for love—until she was sadly disillusioned by finding out that my father had kept his real love as his mistress and still does to this day. After my mother bore my father a male "heir and a spare", and then me, she was free to do what she wanted so long as she fulfilled her ceremonial duties as Queen when required. She was discreet about the lovers she took. And I think my grandmother actually *hated* my grandfather. Theirs was another marriage of convenience. She subjugated her misery into worthy causes.'

'And you were expected to do the same?'

'Until Tristan had the law changed. Before that I just kept saying no.'

'That was brave of you.'

'It wasn't difficult as none of the men appealed in the slightest. I wouldn't even have answered their posts on a dating site, we had so little in common—not to mention a total lack of chemistry. There was only one man who tempted me. He was good-looking, fun, my own age… I thought we might be able to make a go of an arranged marriage. Until I realised the love of his life was his very handsome private secretary—a charming guy.'

'I'm sorry,' he said, not sure what else to say.

'I needed an escape. Australia seemed to offer it. The whole Natalie thing was an adventure and the freedom was exhilarating.' She dropped both her gaze and her voice, scuffed the pathway with the toe of her boot. 'And then there was you. I…I wasn't expecting you.'

'I wasn't expecting you either,' he said. 'But there you were.'

He remembered standing respectfully, watching the wedding ceremony, and then feeling compelled to turn towards the beautiful woman on the other side of the aisle. After that he'd been unable to think of anything but her.

'I…I'd never been so attracted to someone. I didn't know how to handle it,' she said.

'It *was* powerful. The attraction came from out of the blue for me too. And then we hit it off. You were such fun. It wasn't just about how beautiful you were—*are*—it was the way we seemed to click.'

She looked up at him again. 'It was a first for me.' Her eyes were clouded with bewilderment and loss. 'I'm truly sorry for the way it ended. No wonder you're angry with me.'

He hated to see her hurting. 'Natalia, please… You don't need to say sorry again. Last night I should have made it clear that I accepted your apology for the way you left. Now, even in the short time I've been here in your country, I've got a grasp on the restrictions of your royal life.'

'Thank you. It's difficult to understand if you don't see all this.' She waved her hand to encompass the palace, the castle, the lake and the town below.

'I can also see you were telling the truth when you said you had little control over the situation in Sydney—why you acted the way you did.'

'I had to do the right thing. It was agony, watching you walk away, knowing I would never see you again. I can't imagine you believed that at the time, but it's true. I pretended I was ill all the way home on the plane so I didn't have to talk to Gemma and Tristan.'

'I searched for you. But I—'

Just then a buzzer went off on her watch. Startled, Natalia looked down at it. 'Where did the time go? Our window of opportunity for sightseeing is rapidly shrinking. Soon we need to head out to the chocolate factory.'

He wanted to say that the only sight he wanted to see was her, but knew that would be both cheesy and inappropriate—although true. Despite all his resolve, he found himself falling under her spell again. Only this time he knew who she really was—and that the impediments to any kind of relationship between them were insurmountable.

The girl he'd known as Natalie had said she'd lived in England, and his first thought had been that long-distance couldn't work. But distance seemed nothing compared to the chains of obligation tying Natalia to her life as a royal. At least this time around he knew what he was dealing with.

'Right,' he said. 'Lead on.'

'We won't get much more done this morning than an introduction to the castle. Considering our limited time, I'll take you straight to the walkway on the battlement walls. It has an interesting history and an amazing view.'

'I like the sound of that,' he said.

She paused and eyeballed him. 'It can be cold up there on the battlements. I hope you're dressed warmly enough?'

'These are my northern hemisphere winter clothes,' he said.

He was dressed in the warm cashmere coat, hat and gloves that he only ever wore on his frequent trips to Europe. It never got cold enough in Sydney for them to be taken out of his wardrobe. He didn't think he could bear to live in a cold climate such as this.

The large wrought-iron bolt on the gate slid open easily. Finn could only imagine the army of staff it took to keep an ancient monument like this in such good order.

As if reading his mind, Natalia paused as she pushed open the gate. 'There's a full-time architect, an engineer, and an army of stonemasons and tradespeople responsible for keeping the castle standing and in such good order. Fact number one—some of these walls that seem so solid are actually stone shells on both sides, filled with rubble. They were designed to withstand contraction and expansion in extreme weather. Imagine—they knew to do that all those years ago.'

'Clever,' he said. 'And getting the stone up the sides of the mountain must have been quite a feat.'

'A system of levers and pulleys, we believe,' she said.

He followed her up several sets of steep, narrow steps, cut into the side of the mountain, until they emerged onto an external corridor that hugged the solid walls of the castle on one side and a high wall on the other.

'Fact number two—'

'You're a really experienced tour guide.'

She laughed. *Laugh number two.*

'Let's just say it's not the first time I've given a visitor a private tour. But this part of the castle is actually open to the public at certain times in the summer.'

'Okay, so hit me with the next fact.'

'The castle was built as a fortress in the eleventh century.'

He whistled. 'That old?'

'Even older. Fact number three—it was built on the ruins of a Roman *castellum*, which was like a watchtower. This was a strategic place for a fortress. The mountains behind form a formidable natural barrier. They were virtually unscalable—especially in winter. Standing on the battlements above us on the lake side they had a clear view of any approaching enemies.'

'You know a lot about it.' He was surprised by her passion for her subject.

'Is it surprising that growing up here I've developed an interest in architecture and a passion for history? Over the centuries the original fortress building was extended to give us the castle we see now.'

'You sound like you've memorised the guidebook,' he said.

'I actually wrote the guidebook,' she said. 'In four different languages.'

'I'm seriously impressed,' he said. 'So tell me more.'

'You're not bored?'

'I'm fascinated.' *As if he could be bored by anything she said.*

'If you're sure?'

He looked down into her face. 'I'm sure,' he said. He didn't intend to say anything further but could not resist adding, 'Sure I've never met a more fascinating woman.'

She blushed high on her cheekbones. 'Thank you.'

'I thought it when we first met and I think it now. I like the way you're so passionate about your heritage.'

'I always have been—ever since I was a child. And as I got older I spent quite a lot of time in the palace archives.'

He could imagine her as a studious little girl and the image was endearing.

'Tell me more about the castle.'

'Fact number four—the south wing, where the palace is, was built not so much as a show of strength but to display the wealth of the royal family.'

'Where wealth equals power of a different kind of strength?'

'Exactly.'

For a moment he might kid himself that she was just a guide, parroting facts from a preset script. But there was no escaping the fact that she was a high-ranking member of the royal family, and that its wealth and power still existed today. Her role brought with it privileges, but also restrictions.

He was beginning to realise what being second in line to the throne actually meant. What it might mean to *him*. If he wanted to see more of her he couldn't just call her and ask her to the movies.

He looked around him with awe. 'The castle is indeed ancient and imposing. To think what these walls must have witnessed over the years…'

'It's mind-boggling, isn't it? This is actually the oldest part of the castle. Let me show you something rather special.'

'The entire place is special,' he said.

'I never take it for granted,' she said. 'I love my home and I love my country. It's just that when I was in Sydney I began to wonder if that was enough.'

For a long moment they didn't speak. He looked into her face, trying to read her expression of thoughtful sadness. 'Is that part of your unhappiness?' he asked.

She flushed pinker. 'Yes. No. I really don't know.' She looked down at her watch again. 'But what I *do* know is that we're running out of time. Follow me.'

She stopped just before the path started to widen and put her hand reverently on the thick wall. 'This is what remains of the most heavily barricaded area of the fortress. Fact number five: those slits were where arrows were fired from.'

'No boiling oil dropped down from above?' One of the computer games he'd enjoyed as a teenager had used that particular device to destroy the enemy. He'd always thought it particularly gruesome.

'That too,' she said, very seriously.

Not just for computer games, then.

'And cannonballs came later.'

'Your ancestors must have been fierce and formidable. And there were the dungeons with the torture chambers too.'

'Exactly.'

They kept walking as the pathway followed the contour of the mountain. It opened up to a lookout comprising several high-arched windows set in a stone wall facing the lake.

'Those arched lookouts came much later than the barricades we just saw. It's always been a popular place.'

Finn stared in wonder at the magnificence of the view framed by the windows. It looked out on not just the vast lake but further, to the system of smaller lakes it adjoined and then the jagged snow-capped mountains reflected in their stillness. Down below, the town, with its cobbled streets, looked like a toy town. The slightest of breezes chased wisps of white cloud across the brilliant blue sky. He found it mind-blowing to think this was her home... her heritage.

'This view is famous,' she said. 'And it's a favourite for postcards. Now it's famous in the family too, for being the place where Tristan proposed to Gemma. You mustn't repeat that, of course,' she said, putting a warning finger to her lips.

'Another secret for me to keep?' he said.

He realised that the castle and the palace were not just ancient monuments to power and tenacity, the seat of a ruling family dating back centuries, but Natalia's home. And that there would be no place there for a boy from Sydney, no matter how wealthy he might be.

If only Natalia was who she had first appeared to be— an ordinary English girl who could choose what she wanted to do with her life. Someone with whom he could—if he so desired—contemplate a relationship of equals.

Instead he'd met a princess. A woman with loyalties and obligations to the monarchy of which she was part. And that, he suspected, would come before any personal relationship.

It would probably be wise of him to cut his ties with Montovia. Forget the contract with Tristan. Cancel his remaining meetings with the good burghers of the kingdom. Fly home and forget Princess Natalia.

Trouble was, he couldn't forget her. He hadn't forgotten her in the three months between meetings. Possibly he was under some kind of enchantment—he would believe anything in these mythical, medieval surroundings.

The buzzer on Natalia's watch sounded again—a twenty-first century intrusion. She was organised and efficient—something he appreciated.

'Does that mean the tour is over?' he asked.

'Just this part of it,' she said. 'Next on your schedule is our meeting with Franz Schmid, master chocolatier. Montovian chocolate is, as I'm sure you know, a luxury product.'

'The platinum standard of chocolate—that's how I hear it described. The world's best. And that is what interests me about it as a product for import...not just for Australia, but for new markets in Asia.'

'There are a number of chocolate producers in Montovia with whom you'll be dealing, but Franz's business is the largest. It is also very dear to our hearts, as when we were children and started to make official appearances with our parents the chocolate factory was our favourite. Be warned: the scent of chocolate is intoxicating—from the large pods that hold the beans to the pralines and the truffles made from the chocolate butter. And then, of course, there is the taste...'

The chocolate factory was set on the shores of the lake, some miles outside the old town. Behind the façade of a centuries-old stone farmhouse was a small modern factory devoted to the creation of superb chocolate. It was spotless, with the production team—mainly women—wearing white overalls, head-coverings and surgical masks. Although he didn't understand Montovian, Finn could sense the buzz of excitement from the factory floor because the Royal Princess was on the premises.

The chocolatier, Franz, was as jovial as Finn would have expected from someone whose passion was something as delicious as his chocolate. Finn asked lots of questions, as the more he knew about the product the better he could sell it. He wasn't disappointed in the chocolatier's replies about fair trade single-origin cocoa beans, and the use of cream from cows grazing on local pastures. All were part of the story.

Finn was impressed with Natalia's knowledge and business acumen. Had Tristan asked her to lead this meeting because he saw her as his future liaison? If so, he wasn't sure how he felt about it. He could never see her as just a business contact.

When they reached the end of the tour Natalia asked if she could show Finn a project she had developed with Franz. 'I'm hoping you can help expand the market for it,' she explained.

Curious, he agreed.

She took him to a display of chocolate bars in distinctive pink wrapping. 'It's a premium milk chocolate, studded with freeze-dried Montovian raspberries,' she said. 'Quite irresistible.'

'Princess Natalia designed the packaging—it's the Princess Bar,' said Franz.

'All profits go towards the promotion of girls' education,' she said. 'So, you see, the more we can sell around the world, the better for girls.'

Finn spoke to her in an undertone. 'You say you haven't got a career? I think the entrepreneurial talents you've applied to your fundraising proves otherwise.'

She beamed, and again he realised how happy it made him feel to see her smile.

CHAPTER EIGHT

NATALIA WASN'T SURE which she dreaded the most—the summons to her mother's office for a queenly reprimand, or the summons to her mother's private rooms in the Queen's apartment for a mother-daughter chat.

Not long after she'd returned from her lunch meeting with Finn and the Chocolate Makers' Association, she had been invited by her mother to what she'd hoped would be the second kind of meeting. As soon as she saw her mother she suspected it might evolve into one of the queenly reprimand kind.

Her Majesty, Queen Truda, patted the place next to her on a gilded and upholstered love seat. The valuable antique was placed in front of French doors that opened to a balcony and looked down to the rose garden below. The roses had finished their autumnal flush of flowers, and now just a few frostbitten blooms were hanging on to their stems.

Her mother kissed her on both cheeks. She was elegant, blonde and had had a considerable amount of subtle surgery to keep her looking ageless.

On Natalia's twenty-fifth birthday she had suggested that Natalia was at the right age to start some preventative cosmetic work, with injectables and fillers. She had hinted that her daughter might have already left it too late to arrest wrinkles.

Natalia had politely declined. Her mother had warned her that she might regret not getting started with work on her face as soon as possible, and Natalia had gritted her teeth in an effort not to give a caustic reply.

The Queen's eyes were the same colour blue as the eyes Natalia saw when she looked in the mirror. But no amount of cosmetic surgery could erase from them the underlying sadness of being married to a man who did not love her and of having lost her firstborn son and grandson.

Right now they were narrowed—as much as her mother was able to narrow her eyes because of her frequent muscle-freezing injections. Natalia had been expecting an interrogation since the reception the night before. She was not to be disappointed.

'The Australian. Finn O'Neill. Tristan's new business associate. I saw you spent quite some time alone with him last night.'

'Yes, Mother.'

'Any longer and it would have been inappropriate.'

'Yes, Mother.' She'd learned young to agree with her mother whenever possible.

'I saw the way you looked at him.'

'What do you mean?'

'He's a very good-looking young man.'

'Yes, he is.'

'Is he the man you danced with at the wedding in Sydney?'

There was no use fibbing, or even prevaricating. Her mother would have read the bodyguard's reports. 'Yes.'

'Do you want him? In your bed, I mean?'

'*What?* Mother!'

'Well?'

Again she couldn't lie. Her mother knew her too well. 'Yes.' She couldn't lie to herself any longer, either.

'You know you can't have him?'

'Why not?'

'Because he's not suitable as a husband and you're not allowed to take a lover until after you're safely married.'

Natalia gritted her teeth. '*Why* is he not suitable for a husband? Under the new law I'm not bound to marry a royal. Finn is educated, successful, wealthy,' she said. Not to mention great company and a sensational kisser.

'*Very* wealthy. And he's squeaky clean when it comes to his finances. No criminal record either. Not so much as a parking fine.'

'So where is your objection?'

'I can't see that your marriage to someone like Finn O'Neill could work. You—*we*—live a rarefied kind of life that people not born to it might find difficult to adapt to.'

'Gemma and Tristan are perfectly happy.'

'They're the exception—and Gemma has had some teething problems. Not the least of which is giving up her life in Australia. But, without being sexist or elitist about it, it's a rare man who is going to be happy having a wife who is far superior to him in social status.'

'Of course that's being sexist and elitist, Mother,' Natalia said, unable to let the comment go. 'Surely it would depend on the individual's attitude?'

'Or a princess could renounce her title and all that goes with it.'

Natalia gasped. 'What are you saying?'

'It's an option—although not a desirable one.' Her mother took both her hands in hers. 'We *are* talking theoretically here, aren't we, my darling?'

Natalia couldn't help a heartfelt sigh. 'Yes. Purely theoretically. There's nothing between me and Finn.'

Her mother attempted to raise her perfectly arched eyebrows. 'Nothing at all?'

Natalia sighed again. 'Okay, so I kissed him at the wedding. But that's as far as it went.'

'You're sure about that?'

'Very sure.'

'You know there are good reasons for a Montovian princess remaining chaste before her marriage? I rather like the way that British Princess put it: she "kept herself tidy".'

'I know,' Natalia said.

The words had been quoted at her before. But that British Princess had been nineteen at the time. She was twenty-seven, for heaven's sake.

'The cute young Duke… You're sure you don't want to see him again?'

'"Young" being the operative word, Mother. He's sweet, but he's only just started shaving. Besides, I suspect he's in love with his seventeen-year-old sister's best friend and is waiting for her to come of age. And, before you suggest it, I have absolutely *no* interest in meeting his uncle—the hip replacement High Duke.'

'Don't call him that. He's a very charming and cultivated man. Handsome too. He thinks you're way too young for him. Besides, he's a widower and not looking for a new wife. A discreet relationship with a mature woman closer to his age would be more appropriate.'

'Mother! *You* like him!'

'And he likes me. Who knows what might happen?'

Her mother deserved some happiness—although she was bound to her father until one of them died.

'I'm happy for you,' Natalia said.

The Queen's face softened. 'Above all, Natalia, I want you to be happy in your marriage.'

'Happy with a palace-approved man, you mean,' said Natalia. 'That's never going to work for me.'

'I want to give you the best chance to make it work,' said her mother. 'There's no divorce for the royal family, as you know.'

'I know,' Natalia said.

She could recite all the rules and regulations that governed their lives. So could her mother—who was trapped in a miserable marriage. Sometimes Natalia felt she should hate her father for what he had done to her lovely mother. But he and his mistress truly loved each other, and had done since they were teenagers. They should have been allowed to marry. It was one of the reasons her father had agreed to change the law.

'I see Tristan has included you in his business meetings with the Australian. Not his wisest move. Be careful. Try not to be alone with him. Don't encourage him.'

'Mother!'

'I mean it, my darling. Even if the law says you can marry him, I don't see how it could possibly work. Your differences are too great. And you can't have him as a lover. I don't want to see you heartbroken.'

'I don't know where this talk of marriage comes from. Certainly not from me. There is nothing between me and Finn. I hardly know him.'

Her mother's grip on her hands tightened. 'You might *say* that, my darling, but I saw the way you were looking at him last night. And the way he looked at you. Nip it in the bud. That's my advice to you as your mother and your Queen.'

An hour later Natalia sat with Finn in her favourite chocolate shop and tea room in the heart of the old town. It was ornate and old-fashioned and hadn't changed at all in her lifetime.

'The three of us loved coming here as kids,' she explained to Finn, who was opposite her at a small round table.

He looked around him at the array of premium Montovian chocolates, the displays of cakes and pastries, the splendid samovar. 'My sister and I would have thought we were in heaven.'

'We did too. Our parents were strict. And our nannies followed their rules to the letter. But a visit to this place was our special treat—a reward for good behaviour.' She paused. 'I miss my brother Carl most of all when I'm here. Carl was a chocoholic before we'd ever heard the word. He was always negotiating increases in our chocolate allowance. Never just for himself, though. Always for all three of us. He was a born leader.'

'Tristan had big shoes to fill?'

'Yes. And he's filling them remarkably well. Having Gemma as support has really helped him, I think. It was such a dark time for us when we lost Carl.'

'Did you have grief counselling to help you come to terms with his loss?'

'You sound like a counsellor yourself when you say that.'

'I just wondered. Sudden change... Unresolved grief... All could contribute to your unhappiness.' His gaze on her face was intense. 'I don't like seeing you unhappy.'

Just sitting here with him, close enough so she could reach over and touch him, was making her feel happier than she'd felt for a long time—three months, to be precise. 'I'm not as unhappy as I was.'

'Why is that?'

'Who could be unhappy sipping the best hot chocolate in the world?' *With you.*

On her trip to Australia she'd found what was missing in her life. A relationship with a man who excited her. *Finn.*

'Good point,' he said.

'Nip it in the bud,' her mother had commanded.

Natalia had no intention of doing any such thing. She had never met a man like Finn and she intended to spend as much time as she could with him. If there was a chance to be alone with him, she would grab it. If there was a chance for her to go through with her original plan to lose her virginity to him, she would. She had a plan.

Of course it remained to be seen if Finn wanted to be any part of it.

She looked down at her watch. 'I've got my tour guide hat on again. The sun sets by five, and I would like to show you around the old town and through the cathedral while it is still light. I don't want to rush you, though. The town is beautiful, and you'll want to be able to divert down a cobbled lane or into a market square if something interests you. Our clock tower dates back to the sixteenth century. When the clock strikes the hour, medieval figures appear in rotation to strike the bell. It's quite a tourist attraction.'

'Another one of your favourite things about your home?'

'It never fails to fascinate me.'

'I look forward to seeing it. We Australians are interested in old buildings because we don't have many of our own.'

'So that timing suits you?'

'Yes.'

'Then this evening you will dine in Tristan and Gemma's private apartment at the palace. It will be much less formal than the soirée last night. And it goes without saying that any food Gemma serves will be superlative.'

'Will you be there too?'

'Of course.'

Finn leaned over the table to be closer to her, so their heads nearly touched. He lowered his voice to barely above a whisper as there were curious onlookers at other tables in the tea room. 'Will there be a chance for us to spend time alone together?'

'Is that what you want?' She also kept her voice to a whisper.

'You bet I do.' Her heart leapt. 'What about you?'

'Oh, yes,' she said, perhaps too fervently. 'But I will have to work around a directive from the Queen that I must avoid being alone with you.'

He frowned. 'Why is that? Does she think I can't be trusted with you?'

'I believe she thinks it is me who can't be trusted with you.'

'What the hell—?' he said, forgetting to keep his voice down. 'I mean, what the hell…?' he whispered.

She laughed.

'Laugh number three,' he said.

'What do you mean by that?' she asked, puzzled.

'I'll explain later,' he said.

She drew back from the intimacy of their heads nearly touching, made a show of pulling out her phone and scrolling through it, then spoke in a normal tone of voice.

'Tomorrow, according to your timetable, Tristan has you scheduled for morning meetings in our administrative capital of St Pierre. Tristan will accompany you for those. On your return to the palace you will be placed once more in my hands.'

Finn gave a discreet, suggestive waggling of his eyebrows, with just a hint of a leer that made her smile. 'I like that idea very much,' he said.

'Me too,' she murmured, trying not to think about what she would like to do to him with her hands. 'There's a visit to an artisan cheese producer. Then I'd like to take you out of town to visit our family's mountain chalet. It's our ski chalet in winter, but we often don't get good falls until January. A visit at this time of year will give you a taste of traditional Montovian rural life and an opportunity to hike. If we're lucky, there might be a dusting of snow.'

'I like that idea very much,' he said. 'But how—?'

She leaned over the table again. 'I'm working on how we can spend time alone. Trust me.'

'Can I really trust you?' he whispered with a wicked grin.

'Oh, yes,' she said.

At that moment the middle-aged woman Natalia had been expecting arrived and headed towards their table. Finn immediately got up from his chair.

She greeted her guest briefly in Montovian and then switched to English for introductions. 'Finn O'Neill—Anneke Blair.'

They shook hands.

'Anneke, Finn is here from Australia on a brief business trip and I've been charged with showing him around.'

Finn gestured around the tea room. 'Natalia has brought me here to chocolate heaven. What an excellent idea.'

'It is indeed,' Anneke said with a big smile.

'Anneke is married to Henry, who is originally from Surrey in the UK. He has been my English tutor since I started to speak. Anneke also speaks excellent English, and she knows more about the old town, its stories and secrets than even I do. So she will be joining us for our tour.'

'Thank you, Anneke,' Finn said. 'I appreciate you taking the time to do so.'

Her mother could have no complaints about her inclusion of Anneke. It would divert the Queen's focus from her and Finn, and it would send her the message that Natalia was, once again, being the dutiful royal daughter.

But not for long. She had plans for the chalet. *Plans for Finn.*

CHAPTER NINE

SEATED AT TRISTAN'S very hospitable dining table that evening, Finn was able to relax for the first time since he'd arrived in Montovia. The reason? He and Natalia were the only guests. And, as Gemma and Tristan were in the know about Natalia's visit to Sydney for Eliza's wedding, that meant he didn't have to hide the fact that he had met her before his visit to the palace.

Of course the extent of the time he and Natalia had spent together was still a secret shared only between them. As far as the others were concerned Natalia had danced with Finn and some of the other guests before waving the bride and groom off on their honeymoon when the wedding had wound up. Then Natalia and Finn had gone their separate ways.

That they had done nothing of the sort was a deliciously private secret between them that bubbled under their conversation and heightened the awareness between them with every glance.

Natalia sat across the table from him. She looked regally beautiful in a deep ruby-coloured velvet dress with long, tight sleeves. Adorning the creamy skin revealed by the V-neckline was an antique pendant of pearls, diamonds and rubies—no doubt a priceless family heirloom. Her hair swung loose, one side fastened over her ear with a pearl-covered hairpin.

She looked every inch the Princess, but warm and approachable too. Was it his imagination or did she look a little happier since he'd been able to make her laugh? He'd now lost count of the number of times he'd enjoyed the sound of her laughter.

To call the Crown Prince's private quarters an 'apartment' was clearly an understatement. Over two levels, it was more like a mansion. However, in contrast to the other parts of the palace Finn had seen, the design was sleek and contemporary. Natalia had whispered to him that Tristan had had the apartment gutted and redesigned after he'd inherited the Crown Prince title from Carl, to eliminate sad memories of his beloved older brother's tenure.

Wherever Finn was in the palace he was aware of the immense wealth of this royal family. Even the guest suite where he was staying was luxurious. But tonight's dinner reminded him of an evening with friends at home. Gemma had even cooked most of the meal, although there was a maid to serve and clear up.

And Gemma was obviously delighting in having a fellow Australian to chat to. 'Did you really not recognise Natalia at the soirée last night?' she asked, looking from him to her sister-in-law.

'I honestly didn't,' said Finn. 'It came as a complete surprise to me that the girl who sat next to me at the wedding was a princess in disguise.'

It was good to be able to discuss, even superficially, what he'd bottled up for three months. The way Natalia had stood him up in Sydney had been too devastating for him to share with anyone.

'I thought she looked gorgeous as a blonde,' Gemma said. 'I reckon long blonde hair is your look, Nat.'

'Thank you, Gemma,' said Natalia, smiling. She and Gemma were clearly good friends. 'But it was way too much upkeep. I'm happy to be back to my natural colouring.'

'I like it too,' said Finn, careful to keep the compliment

discreet and respectful. She would look beautiful whichever way she did her hair.

'What would you have done if you'd *known* she was a secret princess?' Gemma asked.

'Probably not have dared to speak to her, let alone asked her to dance,' he said.

'And that would have been a shame,' Natalia said lightly.

'Natalia tells me your business meetings have gone well?' Tristan said.

'Very well,' said Finn. 'And I enjoyed my tours of the castle and the old town.'

'Thank you, Finn,' Natalia said, doing a good job of appearing not to show any personal interest in him. 'Tristan, that brings us to our schedule for tomorrow. After Finn's visit to St Pierre with you, we have a visit to our favourite artisan cheese producer scheduled. As it's on the way to the chalet, I plan to take Finn up to the chalet afterwards. That area is a great showcase for rural Montovia without us having to go further afield.'

'You might be cutting it fine in terms of daylight,' Tristan warned.

'You're right. And if it snows those roads could be dangerous at night… I wonder if we should plan to stay there overnight? I've invited Marco and Amelie for dinner and they're keen to stay over. Would you and Gemma like to come too?'

'I'm afraid I can't,' said Gemma. 'Shame… I love the chalet. However, I have other plans for tomorrow.'

'So do I,' said Tristan. 'But it sounds like a good idea. It's like the land that time forgot up there.'

The whole place had that air about it, Finn thought. Though he was discovering that—palaces, medieval castles and quaint towns aside—Montovia was a forward, prosperous country, and highly successful as a financial centre.

'I'll inform the housekeeper at the chalet you'll be having guests for dinner and breakfast,' said Gemma.

'That's settled, then,' said Natalia, in a very businesslike tone.

Finn didn't dare catch her eye. Clever princess. He had no doubt she'd concocted the visit to the chalet to give them some time alone together, without flagging up the fact that there might have been more to the way they'd met in Sydney.

'Well planned,' he whispered to her when he got the chance.

'Even better than swapping place cards,' she whispered back, straight faced.

The dinner had started early and ended early, as Gemma was tired. Natalia, taking her place as hostess, escorted Finn back to his room on the floor below. She didn't have to—he knew the way—but he welcomed the extra few minutes with her.

Perhaps there were security cameras about, or simply observant eyes, but she acted purely within the boundaries of her role. Until she leaned forward for just a second as she shook his hand goodnight and whispered, 'I can't wait until tomorrow.'

Finn didn't know where this thing between them could possibly go. But he was only in Montovia for another two days and he was going to grab any time he could with her without worrying about what might come next.

CHAPTER TEN

NATALIA'S ACQUAINTANCESHIP WITH full-blown insomnia had been well and truly renewed. Last night she'd hardly slept. Thoughts of Finn had relentlessly churned around and around in her mind, keeping her eyes wide open until way into the early hours.

Her obsession with Finn was almost adolescent—what was a twenty-seven-year-old woman doing, getting in such a tizz about a man she'd only known in total for a few days? For all that wedding guest psychic's predictions, and for all her mother the Queen's warnings, not a word about anything serious had passed between her and Finn.

But to her it was a very big deal.

She had never felt like this about any man. She doubted she would ever feel it again.

The disaster of their parting in Sydney had been forgiven, if not forgotten. She needed to see if Finn saw the possibility of any kind of relationship blooming between them. This sneakily planned visit to the chalet might be the only chance she got.

He returned from his meetings in St Pierre at the agreed time. Natalia had been counting the moments until she saw him again—conscious of how limited they were. They met at the top of the circular palace driveway, which led to the road that twisted its way from the castle down the mountain to the town.

Finn had changed from his business suit and was appropriately rugged up in black jeans, a grey cashmere sweater and a smart charcoal quilted coat. He was as so-phisticated and stylish as any prince or duke, and a heck of a lot more handsome. Just looking at him sent shivers of want through her. But she forced herself to be profes-sional and impartial—as if she were simply dealing with a business contact.

'A four-by-four and a uniformed chauffeur,' he said. 'Interesting choice of transport.'

'The roads can be rough around the chalet. Ice and pos-sible snow can make them dangerous,' she said.

'Not quite what I expected for a princess-mobile.'

'The glass carriage and white horses won't cut it for today, I'm afraid,' she said, with a regretful shake of her head.

'I'm disappointed,' he said, with the grin that had the magic power to lift her spirits.

'But a princess doesn't drive herself around town,' she said. And then added as a murmured aside, 'And this way I get to sit in the back seat with you.'

Her heart was racing—not only at the thought of being alone with Finn but also at the audacity of her plan.

Being accompanied at the chalet by her cousin and his wife—both close friends who wanted to see her happy—might not be quite what her mother had in mind. But she'd had a lifetime of obedience. Her time in Sydney had made her see life with different eyes. Made her realise you had to grab opportunities when they were offered to you. You weren't always given a second chance. She fully intended to seize this one.

'Tell me about the chalet,' said Finn as he slid in next to her in the back seat. Close, but not too close.

He knew what was expected of him in public. But in private…? She shivered in anticipation.

'The chalet has nothing but happy memories for me.

It's high up on the mountain, above the snow line. The building started life as a farmhouse about three hundred and fifty years ago. It must have been a long way from civilisation then. In the old days the farmers were cut off from the town for most of the winter. Those remaining still live a traditional life.'

'I was beginning to think everything was ancient in your country until I saw St Pierre today. That's a very modern city.'

'Our country has one foot planted in the past and the other striding towards the future. I'm very proud of it.'

'And the chalet now?'

'My grandfather had it converted to make a private residence. It's rustic, traditional, built from stone and timber, with sloping roofs because of the snow. Humble in its own way. But the bathrooms are new and the heating has just been updated.'

'I wouldn't expect anything less from one of *your* family residences,' he said.

'Be warned—it's no palace. My grandfather used it as a hunting lodge and it still has that kind of décor.'

'I don't hunt,' he said.

'Neither do we. We only shoot animals with a camera. The land around the chalet is a conservation area now. Some of the animals that were hunted to the point of extinction are coming back. My brothers and I were able to run wild there like we were never able to at the palace— well, our version of running wild.'

'Do you use it for skiing?'

'The chalet is not near any commercial skiing areas. But we use it as a base for cross-country skiing. The trails are wonderful. Do you ski?'

'I like skiing. But I prefer sailing.'

'Er…of course,' she said.

Natalie hoped he wasn't remembering how she'd stood him up for their sailing date in Sydney. Then she wondered if he was a mind reader.

'Just a reminder—you don't need to say sorry again,' he said.

Compassionate. That was the word for the expression in his eyes. He now seemed to understand the challenges that came with the expectations of her privileged way of life, not just dismiss her as a 'poor little rich girl'.

She ached to reach over and take his hand. She knew it would not be wise, and yet some new rebelliousness wanted to draw his head down to hers for a kiss and do what any ordinary girl had every right to do but a princess of Montovia did not.

Instead, she shifted just a little farther away from him and forced herself to stick to the more sensible plan she had already put in place. Though his nearness, his scent, his warmth meant she was in a constant state of yearning for him.

What if he didn't feel anywhere near the same for her?

They had left behind the old town and the newer suburbs on its edge, flown through the cobblestoned villages, and were now steadily climbing the twisting roads up the mountain.

'Everywhere I look is a postcard,' said Finn. 'The land's still so green, with the colour from the trees holding the last of the autumn leaves, the black and white cows. Then there are the rustic houses and the stacks of chopped wood underneath, ready for the winter, the pumpkins piled in baskets. It's like it's all been posed for the camera.'

'Even the three tractors trundling down the middle of the road that we've had to overtake?'

'Even those,' he said with a smile. 'They were actually very smart tractors. Everything is so different from Australia—like a different world.'

'You must have seen a lot of the world for your business?'

'Yes—although I travelled first with my parents and grandparents, to visit family. Hong Kong, then Italy, Ireland later. I had a stake in all those countries—I belonged by blood. But even with our diverse background and urge to travel, we're an Australian family, through and through. Australia was good to my family. It will always be my country.'

'You're as patriotic as I am.' Somehow she hadn't thought of that. Hadn't factored in his own love of his country in her wild dreams about what might be.

'In my own way—as a citizen. As a ruler, you have a quite different relationship with your country. One I'm trying to get my head around. But I understand your connection to your family, because family is very important to me too.'

'Could you see yourself living anywhere other than Australia?' She held her breath for his answer.

'It's where I need to be. My business is based there… the Asian markets are the future for trade. I want to be part of that future.'

Natalia let out her breath on a slow sigh. 'I see.'

He turned to her. 'I had to give all that some thought when I was still at university.'

'What do you mean?'

'In my second year I spent my winter vacation in Italy.'

'Where it must have been summer?'

'Yes. I stayed in the town near Naples where my grandmother's family came from. I worked in a pizzeria, practised my Italian and met a girl. Her name was Chiara. I fell head over heels for her and she for me. I quit the pizzeria so I could spend all my time with her. Then I had to go back to Australia for uni.'

Natalia hated to think of him with another woman. It actually made her feel nauseous. She had to force her voice to sound light and neutral. 'A holiday romance?'

'It was more than that. We were engaged to be married. I thought it was for ever. I really tried to make that long-distance romance work. Once I even flew to Italy for a long weekend, so I could be with Chiara for her birthday.'

'I don't see a happy-ever-after ending to this story...' With a great effort of will, Natalia had managed to keep her voice at an even, conversational tone.

By contrast, Finn's tone darkened. 'Of course it ended. Now I can see it was inevitable. Then I was gutted. She didn't want to leave her family and friends. I had to finish my degree in Sydney. We were too young. Long story short: she met an Italian guy. She ended it with me quite brutally.'

'I'm sorry, Finn,' Natalia said—not sorry at all that he didn't get the girl, but sorry that the experience might have made him wary of long-distance relationships. 'What happened next?'

'From then on I've only dated women who live in Sydney,' he said, looking out of the window instead of at her. 'And I hold a very cynical view of love at first sight. I don't trust that it can work.'

So a girlfriend in Montovia was out of the question. Was that what he was trying to tell her? As for the 'love at first sight' comment—she wasn't sure what he meant by that either.

She decided not to try and second-guess him. Thankfully she could change the subject, as they had reached the small artisan cheesemaker who made some of the most prized cheeses in Montovia.

* * *

The cheesemaker's premises looked like yet another post-card view, Finn thought. The old stone buildings, the incredible green pastures, the mountains in the back-ground—all were breathtakingly picturesque. Natalia brought a flash of colour in a red coat and a soft pink beret and scarf that suited her brilliantly. He liked see-ing her in pink and red again rather than tones of grey.

'Before we go in, tell me again why we're here?' he asked Natalia.

'Matteo, the cheesemaker, prides himself on the qual-ity of his handmade, cave-aged product,' she said. 'His family had always made cheeses here, but on a very small scale for local consumption. The cheese became some-thing of a legend in Montovia and highly prized. There's a saying that good cheese makes milk immortal, and that truly applies here. Since Matteo took over he has grown the business, but still kept it on a small scale. His cheese commands top prices. He maintains exclusivity and that is one reason he doesn't want to export.'

'If he doesn't want to export, why am I seeing him?'

'For your interest,' she said. 'And so that if he ever changes his mind, he will remember you.'

'I follow your way of thinking,' he said, once again appreciating her and Tristan's business acumen.

He also appreciated the fact that the work Tristan did with the export of his country's products was not for per-sonal gain, but rather the promotion of Montovia.

'Although we do get a return in the form of taxes from successful businesses,' Natalia had shrewdly pointed out when he'd mentioned it.

Finn clicked immediately with Matteo—especially after they realised that while Finn's Montovian was non-existent, and Matteo's English basic, they both spoke fluent Italian, as did Natalia. He appreciated yet another side of Natalia as she spoke fluently in the language of his grandmother, complete with requisite hand gestures.

She would fit in with his family.

He shook his head to clear the thought. It was such an unlikely scenario.

Matteo took them through the process of making his cheeses. It started with milk from happy, stress-free cows, feeding on rich alpine pastures that included regional wildflowers, and ended in cool subterranean cellars, their walls lined with ancient wooden shelving stacked with wheels of prized cheese in various stages of ageing.

Finn was fascinated by it. The cheesemaking he'd seen before had been on a much larger commercial scale. Here, tradition dictated every step. What was it Tristan had said about the land that time forgot? And Natalia was a part of that tradition, bound by customs that hardly seemed relevant to modern life. Yet like this cheese, prized for its tradition, her traditions had shaped the woman she was.

After farewells had been made, Finn headed with Natalia back to the four-by-four, carrying a wheel of Matteo's finest cheese to take to the chalet.

'I actually understand why Matteo doesn't want to lose the essence of his cheese by over-expanding, even though I would very much like to have his business,' he said.

'I liked seeing your passion for the cheese,' she said. 'I understand now why you're so successful in your business—you care.'

Finn saw immediately why Natalia loved the Montovian royal family's chalet. It might have started off as a humble, rustic farmhouse, but it was now every bit the luxurious mountain retreat, in a traditional style of carved timber and stone, leather and wool.

Finn was wealthy, and he came from a comfortably off family, but the extent of privilege enjoyed by the royal family was staggering. The chalet kept a year-round staff, whose brief was to have the place ready at any time for the family to use—which seemed wildly extravagant. Although at the same time, it kept practically a cavalry of staff in employment.

He needed to keep his mind open—not view Natalia's life burdened with his preconceived ideas of what a princess should be.

Natalia introduced Finn to the middle-aged grey-haired housekeeper Hanna, and her husband the caretaker, Bernard. Finn was surprised when she greeted them with warm hugs and rapid chattering in Montovian. The caretakers did not speak English.

'Hanna was one of our nannies when I was young,' Natalia explained when they were on their own, coats off, enjoying a hot drink.

She looked elegant again, in slim trousers and a cream cashmere turtle neck. The room was heated by a blazing log fire in the most enormous carved stone fireplace Finn had ever seen.

'Hanna was loyal to us, and we are loyal to her. She is considered to be—what's the English phrase?—a family retainer.'

Natalia's English was so fluent Finn was surprised at the occasional reminder that it was not her native tongue.

'Hanna seems a nice person,' he said.

'She's warm and kind. Often we were left here with just Hanna and Bernard to look after us. We trust them both implicitly.'

'I've been meaning to ask… No bodyguards for you in Montovia? Or have I just not noticed them?'

'The royal family is loved here. We feel safe in our own

homes, our own country. Common-sense precautions are taken, of course—particularly in crowds.' She looked up at him, a smile dancing on her lips. 'By the way, there are no security cameras here.'

Finn liked the emphasis she'd put on the absence of surveillance. He could hardly wait to have her to himself, even if only for a few minutes, with no thought of anyone observing them together. If things went his way, they would need their privacy...

Natalia had placed him in a comfortable guest room at the other end of the chalet from her room. Her cousin and his wife would stay in the room adjoining hers. Finn wished his room was closer to Natalia's. However, no doubt room placement had to follow protocols like everything else.

'I'm near my cousin and Amelie,' she'd explained. 'But you'll find them sympathetic to our need to spend some time together while never appearing to be on our own.'

'Why is that?' He had met Marco and Amelie at the soirée on his first evening, and had enjoyed their company.

'Until the law was changed they were unable to marry because Amelie was a commoner. They had to keep their relationship secret. I sometimes manoeuvred things so they could be together.'

'So they want to return the favour?' he said approvingly.

Much as he liked the Count and his doctor wife, the Countess, he still wished he had Natalia all to himself. His imagination played with the idea of kissing her, of peeling off her clothes on that densely fluffy rug in front of the log fire, seeing the flickering shadows from the flames playing on her creamy skin.

But then it seemed the staff would always be present, so that was a scenario that was unlikely ever to be played out.

Marco and Amelie arrived, greetings were exchanged, and it was decided that the four of them would go for a hike on the trails through the forest surrounding the house.

'The light is already starting to fade,' Natalia said. 'So we won't go too far from the chalet.'

Finn was eager to get outside after their time cooped up in the car, luxurious as it was. He also wanted to snatch any opportunity to be alone with Natalia. He was only too conscious of the hours ticking away towards the time for his departure from Montovia the following afternoon. There were things to be said, decisions to be made. Non-verbal communication too, of the more intimate kind.

The chalet was not far behind them when Marco said he thought he'd spotted red deer and wanted to peel off from the pathway. Amelie followed him. Not a word was spoken but the message was clear. They were getting away to give them space.

He was alone with Natalia. At last.

CHAPTER ELEVEN

AT LAST. FOR three long months Natalia had dreamed of being in Finn's arms again. Now they were alone. She was trembling with awareness and anticipation. There was every chance it might happen.

It *had* to happen. She would die if it didn't. Not literally—she had never had suicidal thoughts. But her soul had shrivelled that morning she had left Finn behind in Sydney. And in the following months she knew her family had been worried about her mental health.

She'd been worried about her mental health. So much so that she'd sought medical advice. She'd been unable to be completely honest, though—rather she had explained that she'd broken up with an unsuitable man and was unable to come to terms with it.

The doctor had diagnosed situational depression, caused by a traumatic event in her life, and Natalia had done her best to follow the advice given on how to alleviate her symptoms. But it hadn't been until she'd seen Finn again that the cloud had started to lift.

Her life was fulfilling in so many ways. It wasn't that she needed a man to take it to another level. She needed *Finn*. She hadn't known what was missing until she'd met him, lost him and then been fortunate enough to have him fall back into her life. Now she'd been given a second chance to be with him, to get to know him, to discover if what she thought she felt about him was real.

Worth breaking the rules real.

Now she stood facing him under the canopy of a thicket

of spruce trees against a chilly blue sky. The forest seemed still and silent with expectation.

'Have they gone?' Finn asked.

Natalia nodded, too choked to utter a word. She looked up at him, thrilled by the intensity of his expression, his green eyes focused solely on her.

'Good,' he said.

He pulled her into his arms.

At last. Her heart sang.

She was wearing gloves, and so was he, but even through the layers of both their padded jackets she could feel his strength, his warmth.

Finn. She sighed her joy and relief. This was where she wanted to be. It had been three very long months since their last kiss. She couldn't wait a second longer for another.

She wound her arms around his neck and pressed her mouth to his, closed her eyes at the bliss of it, the tenderness, the way he tasted of coffee with a hint of toothpaste. He'd been expecting to kiss her. Maybe wanting it as much as she did.

'Finn...' she murmured urgently against his lips.

He kissed her back, his mouth firm and warm on hers, and there were no further words.

The kiss grew deeper, more demanding, more *thrilling*. Their breathing became more ragged, loud in the still of the forest. Her knees threatened to sag beneath her. Holding her tight, he nudged her towards a tree so her back rested against it. That made it easier for him to unbutton her jacket, to pull off his gloves and drop them on the forest floor, to slide his hands, bare and warm, under her jacket.

She gasped as he tugged her sweater from the waistband of her trousers, slid his hands around her waist. His hands felt so good on her bare skin. Three months of banked-up desire ignited and flared until she burned for him—more touch, more kisses, *more Finn*.

'You're wearing rather more clothes than when I last kissed you,' he said, his voice deep and husky.

Last time she'd been wearing just a pink lacy bra and tiny lacy panties. She flushed at the memory of it. She was wearing the same now—though in a smaller size.

'You're more encumbered too,' she murmured, as she stripped off her gloves and fumbled with the belt of his jacket, annoyed with herself that she wasn't more adept.

He pulled back from the kiss, panting. 'Any chance we can continue where we left off in Sydney?'

'Yes, please,' she said, scarcely able to get the words out. 'Though it's a tad chilly to get naked out here.'

But if he wanted to make love to her in the forest, if he wanted to lay her down on a bed of pine needles, she'd still say yes. Which was all kinds of crazy. And exciting. And likely to lead to frostbite in uncomfortable places.

'Are there bears and wolves?' he asked.

'Maybe,' she said. 'More likely foxes. And rabbits. Hares, too.'

'Hmm…' he said, nuzzling her neck. 'The rabbits don't scare me.'

'The hares can get a bit scary when they fight.'

'Maybe out here isn't the best place,' he said, releasing her with obvious reluctance. 'And not just because of the dangerous hares.'

'Wise decision,' she said, though her words were tinged with regret.

What if they didn't get another chance?

Her hair had got tousled and he smoothed an errant lock away from her forehead in a gesture that sent pleasure shimmying through her.

'Getting together isn't so easy this time, is it?' he said hoarsely. 'Back then we were two regular people, struck by an instant attraction, and possibilities were opening up ahead of us. We could choose what we wanted to do about them. It seemed so uncomplicated. Now we know how very complicated our situation is.'

'I know only too well,' she said.

'Try not to be alone with him.' Her mother's words hadn't been in the slightest bit ambiguous. *Sorry, Mother.*

He cupped her face in his large warm hands, looked deep into her eyes with an intensity that thrilled her as much as a caress.

'I still want you, Natalia. More than anything, I want you.'

'I want you too, Finn. I never stopped wanting you.'

'Back then I knew nothing about you except that I wanted you. Now I know everything I need to know.'

She stilled. 'Not quite everything,' she said, in a very small voice.

'What do you mean?' His face tightened and his hands dropped from around her to his sides. 'More secrets? More lies?'

She could see the disappointment in the twist of his mouth, hear it in in his voice.

'Nothing like that,' she said.

'No more big surprises—please, Natalia. Finding out you were a completely different person was surprise enough for me. I don't know that I can deal with any more.'

'It's not that. I have no more identities. No more lies. It's just…'

'What?' he said.

'Do you remember that night? In my hotel room?'

He grinned—a slow, sexy grin that sent a shudder of want spiralling through her.

'As if I'd ever forget.'

'Back then I told you I hadn't done that kind of thing before…'

'I remember. I guessed you weren't in the habit of taking a man you didn't know very well back to your hotel room. But it felt like we'd known each other for a long time, didn't it? That we knew each other well enough to—'

'You're right. I had never taken a man back to my room. But you have to understand I—'

'Hell, Nat, you don't think I'd pass judgement on you for that? I'm not in the habit of hopping into bed with someone I scarcely know, either. It was special that night. We both wanted each other too much to wait. We both knew the score.'

She bent down to pick up her gloves from where she'd tossed them on the ground. Pulled them slowly back on, first her right hand, then her left. *Delaying tactics.*

'That's just it. I didn't know the score. I didn't know *anything*.'

He frowned. 'I'm not sure what you're getting at.'

She looked down at the ground. Noticed his gloves were there too. She should pick them up for him. They were good ones. Leather lined with cashmere.

'When I said I hadn't done it before, I meant *any* of it. I…I hadn't done more than kissing.' Finally she looked up at him. 'I…I'm a virgin, Finn. A twenty-seven-year-old virgin.'

He stared at her, incredulous. If it hadn't been so serious she would have laughed out loud at the expression on his face.

'You're not serious? You seemed…experienced.'

She screwed up her face. 'I was learning as I went along. I'd never undone a man's shirt before in my life. You were a brilliant tutor.'

'I wouldn't have known. I couldn't tell. There was no need for tutoring. But why?'

'A Montovian princess is meant to go to her marriage a virgin. It's tradition. Certainty that the husband's heirs are his own is the theory. I should have been married by the time I was twenty. But, as you know, I resisted that idea and I got older and older. I've been waiting longer than was anticipated.'

'Whoa… This is taking some getting used to.' He ran his hand through his hair so it stood up in spikes.

'You don't mind?'

'Of course I don't mind. Why would I mind?'

'It's odd, I know.'

'There's nothing odd about it. It's just unbelievable. Although quite precious in a way. You've really never made love with a man?'

'Not even come close.'

'Surely you've fooled around?'

'No. You've got to understand, I've never met anyone I wanted to fool around with. There was a boy at uni I liked. But as soon as my parents got wind that I was seeing him they paid him off and I never saw him again. Remember, I've always been destined for a marriage with someone of suitable rank. Fooling around just wouldn't do. Besides, me being a princess was a barrier. Before you, there was someone who interested me—but it never went anywhere because he didn't want the spotlight that he knew would be on him if we dated. All I met were those suitable suitors.'

'Who were entirely *un*suitable?'

'You were the first man to see me in my underwear.'

He groaned. She was fascinated by the depth of agony in his groan.

'Don't remind me of how sensational you looked. Pink

lace against creamy skin…your beautiful long legs. How have you endured going without sex?'

'It's never seemed a hardship until now. I didn't feel I was missing out. I'd never met a man I wanted. Until… until you.'

She looked up at him. Her heart jolted at how utterly handsome he was. She still could hardly believe her hot guy from the wedding was here.

'You seemed so willing.'

'I *was* willing. Believe me, I was willing. I intended to lose my virginity to you.'

'You *what*? That night? It was to be your first time?'

'It might sound cheesy, but you woke me up.' She felt suddenly shy, but this needed to be said. 'The first time you kissed me you turned on a switch that flooded me with wants and needs I'd never felt before. It was time.'

'You chose *me*?'

'I chose you.'

He turned away from her, as if to gather his thoughts. Then he swung back to face her. 'I wish you'd told me. It's quite a responsibility for a man to be a woman's first lover. To make sure she enjoys herself.'

'Oh, I knew I was going to enjoy myself. The way you touched me, the way you made me feel…' Her heart raced at the memory of it.

He groaned again. 'Natalia, no. Don't remind me. Not out here, where we can do nothing about it.'

'Sorry,' she said, not feeling sorry at all, and loving the power she had to arouse him as he aroused her.

'But you stopped me. I thought that you'd suddenly realised how impetuous you were being. We were moving too fast.'

She sighed. How many times since had she regretted stopping him?

'The protection thing pulled me back to reality. All that stuff I'd blocked because I wanted more than anything for you to carry me to that bed and make love to me. It brought home to me the seriousness of what I intended to do—the risks I would be taking. But most of all I knew I was going back home in the morning. It was so new to me—to want a man the way I wanted you. To make love with you just the once and never again would have been devastating. It wasn't just about the rules. I was protecting my emotions too.'

He frowned. 'Why didn't you tell me at the time that you're a virgin?'

She took a deep breath. This topic took her sailing back into the troubled waters of her deception. 'Because then I would have had to tell you the truth about who I really was. And I just couldn't. Not then, and not afterwards.'

'And now?'

'Nothing has changed as far as my royal obligations go. But you've come back into my life and I want you just as much. More so.'

'What does that mean for us?' he said.

'You...you're saying there's an "us"?'

He turned. 'Come on, let's walk further into the forest. I need to think.'

'Good idea.'

She stooped, picked up his gloves, caught up with him, handed them to him. He stared at them for a moment, as if he didn't know what they were, before shoving them in his jacket pocket. She realised how difficult, how inconceivable, this—her life, the only life she had known—must seem to him.

He held out his hand to her and she took it. She walked alongside him, steering him in a different direction from the one she knew her cousin and his wife had taken.

He spoke again. 'At the wedding I started to wonder about an *us*—an impossible "us". Because you—so I thought—lived in England, and I'd tried long-distance before and it had been a disaster.'

'I can see that,' she murmured. She thrilled to his words. So he'd felt it too, back at the wedding—not just physical attraction, something more, something real, something life-changing.

'But still I started to think of ways I could perhaps *make* it work. Then… You know what happened next. You disappeared. An *us* was never going to happen because there wasn't a *you*. Then, at the soirée, the impossible, the amazing, the unbelievable happened and you came into my life again—a *you* who both was and wasn't *you*—and I couldn't see that there could ever be an *us*.'

It was a long speech, but Natalia had listened, enthralled. 'And now?'

'All I can think of is how much I want there to be an us. How much I want *you*. When we were admiring those vats of chocolate at the Montovian chocolate factory I was thinking about you, and how wonderful it was to be sharing the experience with you. When I was sampling Matteo's cheeses I was thinking about how much I wanted to have my arm around you.'

'And you are in my thoughts constantly. That you're actually here in Montovia makes me want to dance down the street.'

'The entire way up here in the car, admiring the scenery, all I wanted to do was pull you into my arms and kiss you senseless.'

'Why didn't you?' she asked, breathless.

'Because this is so much more complicated than us simply living in different countries on other sides of the world. You're the Princess of Montovia and I'm an Aussie guy from Sydney. The obstacles are onerous. Not just because you're a princess. Not just because you live on the other side of the world from me. But because when it comes to my personal life, I'm a cautious kind of guy. I don't let myself get involved too easily. Dip my toe in the water before I dive right in. I've steered clear of serious relationships while I've been building the business so rapidly. I don't need the distraction of anyone making demands on me.'

'Oh,' she said. The hot guy she remembered from the wedding had seemed anything but cautious.

'But when I met you at the wedding caution didn't get a look-in. I wanted to jump straight in without hesitation. And was so glad I did because you were amazing. Then I thought I'd never see you again. Now here you are. What a rollercoaster. Man, am I distracted. I *want* to be distracted. But all we had was a few hours in Sydney with no time to develop anything more than initial sparks. Is that enough to be an *us*?'

'It's a start. And what's wrong with a strong start?'

He stopped. Turned to her. Put his hands on her shoulders. Urgently searched her face.

'We need to talk. Because if there is a way ahead for us, now is the time for us to set our feet on the path. If there isn't, then we have to walk away before we really hurt each other and—'

The sound of stamping feet and muffled laughter, of loud rustlings in the undergrowth made them jump apart.

'Marco and Amelie—warning us of their approach,' she said.

She brushed her hair away from her face. 'Quickly. Do I look okay? Will they be able to tell we've been kissing?'

He kissed her again—swiftly, fiercely. 'You look adorable, beautiful…your cheeks flushed, your eyes sparkling.

I want the world to know you've just been thoroughly kissed by me. I don't want us to be skulking around bushes and hiding. We need to talk about our options.'

'We have options?' Could she allow herself to hope?

'Everyone has options. Even the impossible *us*. We need to analyse and weigh them up if we're to find our path.'

'That sounds so businesslike.'

'That's the way I am. I don't trust infatuation as a basis for life-long relationships.'

'Do you think this—between us—is just infatuation?' She didn't doubt what she felt for him went way beyond infatuation.

'I don't know. But it feels like something much deeper. It did from the get-go, if I'm to be honest. But it came from nowhere. Lasting relationships to me are partnerships based on a long getting to know each other process. We haven't been given that. It's like we're in a crucible. Your family doesn't talk dating—it talks *marriage*. Advance to "Go" before I've even got a counter on the board. I always expected there to be time for me to get to know a woman before the word marriage entered into it.'

'You make it sound impossible.' She put her hands to her face in despair.

Gently he took them away, looked into her face. 'Not impossible. Possibilities are what we have to talk about. In the meantime, I suggest you smooth down your hair, wipe that smear of lipstick from the corner of your mouth—here, I'll do it—then straighten your scarf, and by the time we get back to the chalet you'll look like all you did on this walk in the forest was explain to me about the regeneration of the wildlife and point out the eagle soaring above us in the sky.'

'What eagle?' she asked, looking above her.

When the others appeared, with Marco calling out an alert, that was what they found—her talking to an attentive Finn in her best tour guide voice.

'And that very eagle, represented with a sword in its beak, is on the crest of the royal family of Montovia.'

Clever Finn for thinking on his feet. For making her laugh. For making her think about possibilities.

But was what they had enough? Was it just infatuation? The thrill of the forbidden? Could she trust whatever had ignited so quickly between them?

When there was a ticking clock on the amount of time they had together how did she know he could give her what she wanted? True love. The kind princesses got in fairy tales, with happy-ever-afters, but the kind that had always seemed elusive to her as a real-life princess.

CHAPTER TWELVE

USUALLY THERE WAS nothing Finn enjoyed more in cold weather than a hearty meal and a good red wine enjoyed in a room lit by a roaring fire. It was the stuff of fantasy for an Australian boy from subtropical Sydney.

Hell, this whole situation he found himself in was the stuff of fantasy.

He was falling for a princess.

But he didn't know if it was real. He didn't have anything to compare it to except that long-ago romance with Chiara, which had seemed real enough at the time, but certainly hadn't felt anything like this.

This intensity, this overwhelming longing to be with Natalia, was something powerful and compelling. He recognised it as the most important emotion he had ever felt. But it was a recognition tinged with caution. He didn't trust sudden flames that could die out as quickly as they'd flared. Those flames had not been enough to sustain a relationship with Chiara.

The strong marriages in his family were based on partnerships. Didn't that require a slow burn, a getting-to-know-each-other before any commitment was considered? He wanted certainty. Could he get that with Natalia? He had no idea where such powerful feelings could drive him. But he knew he could not dismiss them.

He was seated next to Natalia at a long wooden table designed for way more than four, but cosy enough just the same. She wore a long purple velvet skirt and a long-sleeved scoop-neck silk knit top in silver—her version of informal dress. His black jeans and black cashmere turtleneck seemed more than appropriate.

At the table, he was being careful to keep a respectable distance apart from her, but she occasionally slipped her hand into his under cover of the tablecloth. Amazing how the simple act of holding hands could be so thrilling when it was with the woman he wanted almost beyond reason.

He didn't want to let her go.

'Did you enjoy our menu based on traditional home-style favourites?' she asked in her best hostess voice. But her eyes showed more than a hostess should to a single male guest. Did anyone else notice?

'The cabbage pie was delicious—something new for me. And the roast was superb—I really liked the warm potato salad.'

They were talking about potatoes!

He smiled and surreptitiously squeezed her hand. This single male guest probably wasn't doing a great job of masking his feelings, either. He suspected Marco and Amelie were aware of what was brewing between him and Natalia, and were complicit without actually coming out in the open with their approval.

The housekeeper was a different matter altogether.

'Hanna keeps glaring at me,' he murmured to Natalia. 'Do you think she's on to us?'

'No doubt she suspects something—she's fond of me and she wouldn't want to see me hurt. Her generation is fearful of any transgressions of the rules.'

'And you?'

'I need to know which rules I'm prepared to break,' she whispered. 'And the repercussions I'm prepared to suffer.'

His grip on her hand tightened.

They had to talk.

The evening passed very pleasantly, although all Finn

wanted to do was speak to Natalia on her own. He was scheduled to leave Montovia after a mid-morning business meeting the next day, which she was chairing on behalf of Tristan. The clock was ticking down on the time they had together.

It turned out that Marco and Amelie were just as good companions at dinner as they had been at the soirée. Finn learned a lot about living in contemporary Montovia, where young people were testing the old, traditional ways. And they, in turn, were curious about Australia.

'I would love to visit Sydney,' Amelie said.

'You and Marco would be most welcome as my guests if you do so,' said Finn. 'I have a large house on the harbour with several guest rooms.'

'And you, Natalia—you have always wanted to see Sydney, especially after Tristan found his beloved wife there,' said Marco.

Natalia choked on her chocolate pudding but quickly recovered herself. 'Yes, it is a dream of mine. I might even find myself a husband there.'

It was Finn's turn to choke on his pudding. He quickly downed a glass of Montovian spring water, drawn from a well on the property.

Amelie frowned. 'Is there something allergenic in this pudding? Please tell me before I try it…'

'Not to my knowledge,' Natalia said in a faint voice, fanning her face with her hand. 'Just…just the sauce is a little hot.'

Finn wished he could be open and honest about how he'd met Natalia. He wasn't accustomed to lying. Sooner or later he would blunder and make some indiscreet comment that might let the cat out of the bag.

Not long after dessert Marco asked permission for himself and Amelie to leave the table and retire to their room.

'He has to ask because I'm higher in rank than he is,' Natalia explained, after they'd said goodnight to the Count and his wife.

She led Finn to the adjoining room. Three large, comfortable brown leather sofas were arranged in front of another toasty fire. Stacked firewood was shelved on both sides of the fireplace and large metal fire tools hung from a rack. The fire gave a warm, inviting glow to the room, and the only other lighting was from table lamps.

'You have to give him *permission*? Even though he's your cousin…your friend?'

'We're so used to how things work, we don't question it,' she explained. 'I'm not sure that is something Tristan would be able to convince our father to change— not quickly anyway.'

Natalia sat on the sofa facing the fireplace and patted the seat next to her.

'I don't have to ask your permission to be seated?' he said.

She laughed. 'Of course not. You're a foreigner.'

He sighed, and knew it sounded heavy with the weight of his concerns. 'No wonder I find it difficult to get a handle on how it all works.'

'I understand how difficult it is for one not born to it. Gemma found it a steep learning curve. She says she still has much to learn. Not just about being royal, but also about being Montovian. But she's very happy with Tristan and has become a remarkable Crown Princess.'

Finn took his place next to Natalia on the sofa, sitting a polite distance away from her. If someone were to come into the room unexpectedly they would see nothing untoward.

Hell, Natalia's experience with men seemed so limited he wondered if the King and Queen posted surveillance on her dates. He shifted a few inches farther away from her, just to be sure, then angled his body towards her in an entirely acceptable conversational manner.

'Talking of Gemma—what is it about her and Amelie both wanting to go to bed so early?' he said. 'Don't they ever want to party? Is that a Montovian thing?'

'I suspect it's a woman in the early stages of pregnancy thing. Didn't you see Amelie's horror at the prospect of something harmful in the pudding?'

'A mere male wouldn't notice such a thing.'

'Women are attuned to notice such things in their friends. But we also respect the fact that women usually don't want to make any announcement until the pregnancy is safely established.'

'You think Gemma might be pregnant?'

'I suspect so—though we're such good friends I'm surprised she hasn't shared the news with me. I can't help but be concerned that something might be wrong, but I suspect she's simply being cautious.'

'If she and Tristan had a baby wouldn't it kick you down the line of succession? Perhaps she's worried that might upset you?'

'Upset me? I would be glad to be demoted in such a way. It would make my life so much easier.'

Hanna entered the room and Natalie had a quick exchange in Montovian with her. Then she turned to him. 'Hanna wants to know if you would like anything further. A camomile tea, perhaps?'

Finn shook his head. 'Nothing for me, thanks.' He looked up at Hanna and thanked her in Montovian. The older woman beamed at him before she turned to leave the room.

'Finn! You spoke in Montovian. When did you learn that?'

'Don't get too excited. I asked Tristan to teach me how to say "please" and "thank you" before we went into our meetings in St Pierre. Just to be polite. I think I've mastered it.'

'Your accent was perfect. Well done.'

He was glad she was pleased. Montovian would not be an easy language to master. But, as his mother often said, the first new language was the most difficult. The more languages you learned, the easier it became.

He watched as Hanna's back view faded from sight. As if by mutual agreement, he and Natalia both stayed very still and listened for sounds from the next room.

'When Hanna finishes in the kitchen will she go to bed too?' Finn asked.

'House servants in the royal households are obligated to be on call until the family and their guests have retired.'

'So if we stayed up all night, until sunrise, she and Bernard would have to stay up all night too?'

'That's how it works,' she said.

He frowned.

'You're aching to say something, aren't you?' she said.

'No. These are your ways and I'm not one to criticise. Where do they live?'

'Their home is a large, comfortable apartment beyond the kitchen.'

'What if we want to contact them for camomile tea?'

'There's a buzzer connected to their apartment. But I can't remember how long since it has been used. It might even need a new battery.'

'What do they do while they're waiting for the battery-less buzzer?'

'I have no idea. Perhaps watch television in bed?'

He smiled. 'And that's how you work around "how it works".'

'Tristan and I have our methods of getting around the old ways.'

'Which brings us back to us.' He looked around. 'Can we talk privately here?'

'As long as we keep our voices down.'

'I have no intention of shouting. But I *would* like to kiss you.' He kissed her on the cheek—a sweet, simple kiss. 'That's for being kind to your old nanny.'

She kissed him on the mouth. Just as quick, just as sweet. 'That's for you being you.'

He caught her hand, clasped it with his. 'Why do we have to skulk around? If I was here longer, couldn't we date? Your family want you to marry someone they consider suitable, but now there's no law against you choosing who you want to have in your life. This is such an artificial, pressure cooker situation.'

'As I told you, you're the first man I've been seriously attracted to. I guess I'm not sure how to handle it. I could scream and yell and defy my family—insist I want to be with you. Then you'd go back to Sydney, I'd never see you again and I'd have a lot of bridge-building to face with my family.'

'I want you. I like you. And I'd like to get to know you—not as a princess, with all the complications that comes with, but as a woman. Like we did at the wedding. I asked you on a date in Sydney. Have you ever wondered what might have happened if you'd spent that day with me on my yacht?'

'Many times…over three miserable months.'

'I searched for you for weeks, you know?'

'You must have been furious with me. Yet you searched for me?'

'Furious, yes—but worried, too, that you might have come to some harm. My male ego wouldn't let me accept that you could just walk away from the magic we'd shared simply because you didn't like me.'

She gasped. 'You *know* it wasn't that.'

'I know now. Back then I wanted an explanation for how you could just disappear. I thought you might have been kidnapped. Bundled into a boat. Thrown overboard from a ferry. I had all sorts of insane ideas. Anything but face up to the fact you'd played me. That for some reason you'd got me enchanted with you—got me believing you might be just a bit enchanted with me—and then callously dumped me.'

'I was actually very taken with you. That's the thing with enchantments. They entice and snare both ways.'

He kissed her again. So what if they were seen? He almost wanted them to be seen so they could be open about what was happening between them. But he suspected Natalia would suffer the consequences. Would she always be under the thumb of her parents because they were also her King and Queen?

'My next thought was it had to have been a scam. I checked my credit cards—perhaps when I'd gone to the bathroom you could have scanned them—but, no. My bank balance remained intact. My identity hadn't been stolen.'

She smiled. 'I don't exactly need the money.'

He smiled back. He'd appreciated her sense of humour from the get-go. 'Finally, when my desire to know more about you overcame my reluctance to admit my humiliation, I asked Eliza. The first person on her doorstep after she returned from her honeymoon was me, begging for details about Natalie Gerard.'

'Eliza? But she—'

'She kept your secret. She's loyal.'

'Good,' she said, with visible relief.

'I can still see my friend, standing there with her hands on her hips. *"I told you Natalie might not be who she said she was."* Her pity, and her righteous indignation that I hadn't listened to her, rubbed salt into my already stinging humiliation.'

'Poor Finn,' said Natalia.

'Poor Finn?' He snorted. 'I didn't get any information or sympathy from Eliza. *"I tried to warn you"*—that was all she said. Not one more word could I get out of her. Except yet another offer to fix me up with the world's most boring woman—Prue, whose place card we switched at the wedding.'

'Eliza called me at about that time,' Natalia said thoughtfully. 'Asked me if I remembered you. Of course I stuck to the script and said I'd danced with you at the wedding and we'd had coffee afterwards, but that was as far as it had gone. Mind you, while you were trying to find *me* I was frantically looking *you* up on the internet. Of course I found everything you'd told me about yourself was the truth. While all I had done was lie. I was a mess—couldn't eat, couldn't sleep…just torn apart by regret.'

'I had some crazy ideas about what had happened to you. But none nearly as crazy as what turned out to be the truth.'

'And yet you've forgiven me?'

'Because I've never met a woman who attracts me like you do—first as Natalie, now as Natalia. The more I know you the more attracted I am, and the more I find to admire in you.'

He was rewarded by her lovely smile, which lit up her eyes. 'I feel the same about you. I've really enjoyed our time working together.'

He leaned over to kiss her.

Natalia put up her hand to stop him. 'You know we really can't be caught kissing in here… We can't risk Bernard coming in to check if the fire needs another log, or to stoke it, or whatever one does with fires. Or Hanna coming in just wanting to keep an eye on me.'

He pulled back from her. 'Why? These constrictions seem unnecessary. We're both single. We're not hurting anyone by getting to know each other. Or kissing each other. And this fire is kinda romantic. Guy-type romantic, I mean. Forget the flowers and the girly frills. This is what does it for me. A warm rug, the flickering flames, cosy dark corners…and you and I snuggled on that rug needing nothing more than each other to warm us—'

'Stop it,' she said. 'That scenario does it for me, too. I want you Finn. It's torture sitting next to you on this sofa not being able to kiss you, touch you, explore you.'

He shifted in his seat, groaned. 'I can't believe you don't know what that kind of talk does to me.'

'I might have an idea, because I'm feeling the same way.'

She took a deep breath, which only succeeded in focusing his gaze on the swell of her curves in her snug-fitting top.

'Best then, I guess, that we're not distracted,' she said. 'No kissing…no touching.'

'But only because we've decided we don't want the distraction. Not because someone else has put strictures on us.'

'Agreed,' she said.

She turned to face him, their knees nudged and she didn't move back. Again he had the feeling that he'd fallen into a fantasy. It was as if she had conjured up this room—the blaze of the fire, the fresh smell of pine, and his beautiful dark-haired virgin Princess wrapped in her flowing long skirt like a woman in a medieval manuscript…or a movie…or a game.

He wanted the fantasy to be real.

He shifted away from the distracting contact, determined to move things along before Bernard appeared to tend to the fire, or the ancient metallic clock on the wall struck midnight and he was left on his own with only smouldering ashes, longing for one of the most unattainable women in the world.

'In my world, where we could date and get to know each other, and see if what we feel is infatuation or something deeper, I wouldn't be mentioning marriage so soon. But it seems your family want you on a fast track to marriage. No time for feelings to develop. No time for compatibility to be established. No time to be sure it's going to work.'

Her mouth turned down and her eyes clouded. 'We are a family who lost our heir—a beloved son, brother, husband, father—and his son.'

Finn wondered, not for the first time, why both heirs had been travelling together in one helicopter.

'Perhaps, as a result, my parents have become a little obsessive about ensuring the line of succession. Their great fear is the throne going to my uncle's branch of the family—who are dissolute, to say the least. That's not Marco's father, by the way, it's a different uncle. They want my children to be in line as back-up, I suppose.'

'Even though they would come after Tristan, and after his children and then after you? It's not likely they'd ever inherit the throne.'

'Not likely—but possible.'

'But even before your brother's death, you resisted an arranged marriage?'

'I believe in love and only love as a basis for marriage. Don't you?'

'Of course I do. A love that grows based on compatibility and shared interests and proves to be real. A partnership. After a long engagement. That's how it works in my family. My grandparents and my parents are happily married. Each anniversary is a big deal to be celebrated.'

'It's the total opposite in my family. I've told you about my parents and my grandparents. But it was my brother's marriage that really made me wary. Carl was introduced to Sylvie as a potential bride. She was beautiful and vivacious and he fell for her as she seemed to fall for him. But she didn't love Carl. She loved the idea of being Crown Princess, with all the wealth and status that came with it. She was demanding and capricious and she made his life hell. Once she'd had Rudi I don't think they even shared a bed. Poor Carl was so unhappy. Seeing that, I decided I'd rather stay single than marry a nobleman I didn't love. And then Carl died.'

He had to ask. 'Why were they all travelling in the same helicopter?'

'Because Sylvie insisted she didn't want to fly with Rudi behind Carl, in what she saw as a lesser helicopter not befitting her status. And, as he did so many times, he gave in to her to avoid a tantrum.'

'I'm so sorry,' he said. 'Such a tragedy.'

He pulled her to him in a hug and she did not resist. He wanted to protect her, this woman who was usually protected by two bodyguards, to wrap her in warmth and security and take away her pain. To make her laugh every day.

'When Tristan changed the rules more choices opened to me. But my parents can still withhold permission for me to marry someone of whom they disapprove.'

He considered her statement. 'They could make your life uncomfortable if they withheld their permission?'

'*Very* uncomfortable,' she said.

'Would dungeons be involved?'

'Who knows?' She laughed. 'Seriously? Not likely at all. And, apart from needing palace-sanctioned permission, I love my parents and want them to approve of my choice of husband and father for my children. And there can be no other option for me than marriage. Living with a man would never be sanctioned.'

'No doubt I'm not high on the approved list?'

'They believe a royal marriage has a better chance of working if both husband and wife come from the same social strata.'

'Yet that didn't work for Carl,' he said. 'And Tristan chose his own wife—breaking more than one tradition in the way he did it.'

'I could, as a citizen of Montovia, marry without the King and Queen's permission. It's me as a princess who needs it.'

He groaned. 'There's another obstacle around every corner. But I don't want to walk away from you, Natalia. I felt lost without you in St Pierre today.'

'And the palace seemed empty without you while you were away. I was counting the minutes until you returned. I'll really miss you when you leave tomorrow. I wish I could stow away in your luggage.'

'I like that idea. But you live in Montovia, with all the responsibilities entailed in your position as Princess and second in line to the throne.'

'And you live in far-away Australia, where your family is and your successful business.'

The logs in the fire shifted and moved in a shower of sparks. The huge, old-fashioned pendulum on the metallic clock on the wall tick-tocked the seconds away. Finn was conscious of their time together dwindling away.

He slowly shook his head. 'It's never going to be a simple boy-meets-girl scenario for us.'

'No. The stakes are so much higher when it's a princess and a millionaire tycoon.'

'But so are the potential gains,' he said, tracing his finger down her cheek and across the outline of her mouth so she trembled. He didn't care if someone barged into the room and saw them.

'I'm beginning to understand that,' she said, her voice unsteady.

'So we have to think about ways we can make long-distance dating viable.'

'We could just run away—be together somewhere we can just be ourselves, away from expectations,' she said.

'You *know* that's not an option.'

'I so want there to be a chance for *us*,' she said. 'To see if this is more than infatuation.'

'Me too,' he said.

Every minute he spent with her moved him further away from infatuation into something he couldn't yet put a name to.

'So what do you think are the possible options for us?'

Finn put up his hand to count off the options available to them finger by finger. It was a thing he did. 'Option one—we have a secret no-strings affair. I see you whenever I come to Europe. You sneak down to Sydney when you can.'

'I don't like the idea of sneaky and secretive,' she said. 'And I doubt it would make either of us happy.'

'I would rather be open about our intentions,' he said.

'So let's forget that option,' she said.

'So, option two, we date each other openly as best we

can, considering we live on the other side of the world from each other.'

'Which would give you the getting-to-know-each-other period you believe is so important,' she said.

'But it would mean we spend a lot of time apart and we lose our privacy.'

'The media would have a field-day once they got on to it,' she said glumly.

He shuddered 'Horrible. But it would be you they'd be after. I'd get off lightly.'

She shook her head. 'Uh-uh. Once they realise how incredibly handsome you are you'd become a target of the long-distance lens. You've already featured in an *Australian Bachelor Millionaires* article.'

'How did—?'

'I pretty much stalked you for a month after I got back from Sydney. After that... I...it became too heartbreaking.'

'I would have stalked *you* if I'd known who you were,' he said.

She looked so woebegone he could not resist kissing her. Then she snuggled close. He breathed in her scent, already so familiar.

'Still, I like that option,' she said. 'Although the loss of privacy might become an issue.'

'It would become an issue anyway,' he said. 'Because if it worked out between us the next step would be making things more permanent between us.' He put up his hand. 'That doesn't mean I'm proposing. This is a hypothetical discussion, based on the way things work in your family.'

If the day ever came that he asked Natalia to marry him he had strong, traditionally male ideas of how it would happen.

'Of course it's hypothetical,' she said. 'But then—again

speaking hypothetically—we would have to face the biggest of the questions. Who lives where?'

'Which means either you live with me in Sydney or I sell my business and live here?'

'That about sums it up,' she said.

He folded his arms across his chest. 'That would be a really big deal for me. To walk away from the company that was my grandparents' would be very hard in terms of family dynamics. I'm very close to my family. It would be difficult for all concerned if I become only an infrequent visitor.'

She crossed her legs, uncrossed them. 'And then there's my side of the story. I'd still remain second in line to the throne. To leave my country would be very difficult. I would almost certainly have to give up my title and all it entails. I was born to be a princess. I know nothing else. I can't earn my own living. The thought is terrifying.'

'It's *all* a bit terrifying,' he said.

She laughed, but there was an edge to her laughter. 'Can you imagine if anyone could overhear us? What a bizarre conversation. To be thinking so far ahead when, as you point out, we hardly know each other.'

'But the unique position we find ourselves in means we have to be aware of all the options.' He paused. 'Which brings us to option three.'

Natalia mock-cringed away from him into the back of the sofa. 'I don't think I'm going to like this one.'

'I sure as hell don't,' he said. 'Option three—total wipe-out, scorched earth, ground zero. We decide that "us" isn't going to work out.' He almost choked on the words. 'We say goodbye—for good this time—and I go back to Australia and wipe you from my life and, in time, from my memory.'

There was a long silence between them. He could hear

the old timbers in the chalet shift and settle, the sigh of the wind outside.

'And I stay here and make myself forget I ever met you,' she said finally, her voice wobbling. 'Easier said than done, you realise? I've tried and failed at that already.'

He took a deep steadying breath against the pain that surged through him at the thought of not having her in his life in any way. 'I would have to pull out of my contract with Tristan. Have no communication with Montovia ever again. It would be the only way I could deal with it.'

'Me too. It would be too painful otherwise,' she said slowly, wringing her hands in front of her. 'We…we have to be realistic.'

Realistic? Where did being realistic come in to his hopes for a new life in this fairy tale place full of castles and dungeons and magic, with the most beautiful Princess in the whole wide world?

CHAPTER THIRTEEN

NATALIA WAS REELING from the conversation she'd had with Finn. Yet it was a conversation that had needed to occur. So much for dreams and fantasies and longings…

But there was only so far this common-sense type of discussion could go. She felt propelled by an impulse far more visceral, urgent, intensely personal. Finn was in Montovia for only a little more than twenty-four hours— some of that sleeping time. She intended to claim that sleeping time for herself. To claim *him*.

From where she sat oh-so-safely apart from him on the sofa she faced him. They had been speaking in hushed tones. Now she spoke in a normal, conversational tone, using words that wouldn't matter if anyone overheard.

'Thank you, Finn. That's been a most interesting conversation. You've given me food for thought.' For all Finn had urged her to take the reins, she still felt she needed to work within the rules.

He sat up straighter, frowned at her sudden change of direction. 'Huh…?'

She got up from the sofa. Finn immediately did so too. She was wearing flats and he towered above her. Again she was struck by how handsome he was, dressed all in black, with his black hair and the vibrant green of his eyes, those sharp cheekbones, his fabulous body… He was the most gorgeous man she had ever met. No other man could ever match him.

And not just in looks. Enjoying a man's company as she enjoyed Finn's was a revelation. Business meetings became exciting when he took part. She had wanted him from the moment she had first seen him. She wanted him now. If he left tomorrow and it didn't work out she wanted no regrets.

She held out her hand for a formal handshake. 'Breakfast is in the same room as dinner, starting at seven. We have an eleven o'clock meeting. An early start would be a good idea.'

He took her hand in his firm, warm grip for the politely requisite time before releasing it. 'Yes...' he said, sounding puzzled.

She leaned forward momentarily, to whisper in his ear. 'Don't lock your bedroom door. I'll see you in ten minutes.' Then, in her normal voice, 'Goodnight.'

He grinned and winked at her. He *winked*. The Princess of Montovia wasn't used to being winked at and she loved it.

'Thank you again for your hospitality,' he said, very formally. 'Goodnight.'

She was conscious of his gaze upon her as she left the room. Her first impulse was to race to her bedroom. The faster she showered and changed, the faster she could be back with Finn. But she needed to act normally—not to draw attention to herself if anyone were to see her. All her life she had had to be aware of the staff who shared the royal family's personal space. For most of her waking hours she was observed, one way or another.

She forced herself to walk sedately to her bedroom.

Ten minutes later she emerged, enveloped in the luxurious Italian designer dressing gown she kept at the chalet and toasty Australian wool slippers that had been a gift from Gemma.

Cautiously she crept down the corridor towards Finn's room in the guest wing. She wasn't worried about Marco and Amelie. During dinner Amelie had taken her aside and told her how much she and Marco liked Finn and approved of him.

'Go for it, Natalia,' Amelie had said. 'We had to fight to be together. You might have to as well. Finn is wonderful—he's worth it.'

Encountering Hanna or Bernard would be a different story. They would consider themselves duty-bound to report to the Queen what they would see as a breach of royal morality. She was twenty-seven, for heaven's sake, not seventeen. It was about time she took charge of her own future—the first step having been her trip to Sydney.

She reached Finn's room without mishap, to find the door slightly ajar. She tapped so lightly she thought he might not hear it. But he was there within seconds. She gasped at the sight of him in black silk pyjamas with a fine grey stripe. They showcased his broad shoulders, his lean, muscular body. He was as covered up as if he were in trousers and a long-sleeved shirt, but somehow the pyjamas seemed so much more intimate. He was beautiful in an intensely masculine way.

Without a word, he took her by the hand and drew her into the room, then locked the door behind her. With a deep murmur of pleasure, he drew her into his arms and kissed her.

'This is nice,' he said, his voice deep and husky, when they came up for breath. 'I missed you. Even for ten minutes I missed you.'

'I missed you too.' Her voice hitched. 'I…I don't know how I'll bear it when you leave tomorrow.'

'Me neither. As you know, tomorrow I fly to Dublin with Franz, your master chocolatier, to meet my contact from the distillery and discuss the potential for a Montovian chocolate liqueur. Then I'm scheduled for meetings in London for three days before flying back to Sydney. Perhaps you could meet me in London?'

She shook her head. 'I can't. That would be such a red flag to my parents, and I'd rather keep them out of it until we know how it works out for us. Trust me—they will know your schedule and they'll put two and two together very quickly. To my knowledge, they're not aware there is anything between us…although my mother is suspicious.'

'Why is she suspicious? We have given her no cause—'

'She saw the way we were looking at each other at the soirée and drew her own conclusions.'

'Like I'm looking at you now, wondering what you have on under that dressing gown?' His eyes narrowed, gleaming with sensual intent.

'If you'd looked at me like that my mother would have had you evicted from the soirée.'

'And you?'

'I would have gone with you and dragged you back to my apartment.' She reached up to kiss him. 'I'll tell you later what I would have done to you,' she said, her voice laden with promise.

He gave a sensuous growl that both made her smile and sent desire rippling through her.

'I'll look forward to that,' he said. He held her close. 'But in the meantime we continue to keep under the Queen's radar.'

'That's the plan. We need to keep it that way while we figure out how we…*if* we can be together. I don't want my every move to be scrutinised until we invite it. It breaks my heart to say it, because I would love to meet you there, but no London visit for me.'

'Or Dublin or Sydney?'

'Sadly, no.'

He sighed, and she sensed his despair was as deep as hers.

'I won't be able to get back here to see you for another two weeks.' He frowned. 'The dreaded long-distance.'

'I know. I'm dreading it too—which is why I want to make the most of the hours we have left. We don't have much time to take up where we left off in Sydney.' She looked into his eyes. 'And that starts with you helping me out of this dressing gown.'

'Happy to oblige,' he said, his voice husky.

She noticed his hands weren't quite steady as he undid the tie, but they were sure and strong as he pushed the dressing gown off her shoulders, and they felt so good on her bare skin. The dressing gown slid to the floor. She was so new to this. A novice at being naughty.

What next?

She stood proud, wearing only pink lace bra and panties—the same kind as she'd worn in Sydney—and waited for his reaction. Would he notice she wasn't as curvy as she'd been before?

She was not disappointed by his reaction.

'Natalia…' he breathed, his eyes raking over her, gleaming with hunger and admiration. 'I can't believe you wore pink lace. That has figured in my fantasies for three months. You're incredible.'

She was so sure that this was what she wanted—that *he* was what she wanted.

'Not as incredible as you,' she said.

From somewhere came the skill to unfasten his buttons, slide her hands greedily over his chest, revelling in the smoothness of his skin over hard muscle. Such a beautiful man.

'I won't stop you tonight,' she said.

He stilled. 'Are you sure it's what you want?'

'I'm sure. I've thought about it. It's what I want. Is that consent enough for you?'

His hands gripped her upper arms. 'I want you—more than you can imagine. It's just I'm not sure it's right for you just now. The risks and consequences are still the same. If your virginity is such a big deal you were right to be cautious before.' He groaned. 'I must be crazy, holding back. Because there is nothing—absolutely nothing—I want more than to make love with you right now.'

'To be my tutor in living dangerously?' she murmured.

He smiled. 'I'm not convinced you need a tutor in love-making. I suspect you'll have things to teach *me*. You're a sensual sensation just waiting to be unleashed.'

'Really?' she said, thrilled at the prospect.

'Oh, yes. The thing is, it's not about me being the tutor and you being the pupil. It's about learning what pleases both yourself and your partner.'

'Like a…like a two-way learning process?' she said breathlessly.

'Exactly.'

He kissed her again, sliding his tongue between her lips, demanding and getting her response before he kissed a trail down her throat to the edge of her bra until she was melting with want.

'The thing is—though it's killing me to say it—I'm going to have to be the responsible one here. There are other ways—exciting ways—for me to please you and you to please me. I'm sure you know about them.'

'I…I haven't done them,' she said, excited in spite of herself.

'Did you know Tristan wanted you to act as my guide because the last time he'd seen you laugh was dancing with me at the wedding?' he asked.

'I didn't know that.'

With two fingers he tilted her chin up so she would look directly into his face. 'In these last few days I've made you laugh many times.'

'Yes,' she said. 'The dark cloud has lifted from me.'

'I've made you laugh…but I can also make you whimper with want, moan with pleasure, cry out in ecstasy, and then beg me to do it all again.'

She caught her breath as her heart started to hammer

and she throbbed in those places she hadn't known could throb until she'd met Finn.

'Can you?' she choked out.

'Oh, yes,' he said, stroking down the side of her breast, and along her waist. 'And that's exactly what I intend to do—starting right now. But you will leave this room still a virgin. I will not have dishonoured you. I hope you will lose your virginity with me when we make a decision about where we're going. But in the meantime you will in all conscience have done your duty to maintain what seems so important in your world.'

'But I—'

He slid his hand towards the edge of her panties.

'*Oh!*'

So that was what a whimper of want felt like.

'Do you want to talk some more? Or shall we take up where we left off three months ago and I'll pick you up and carry you to the bed?'

'The bed. *Please.* The bed.'

Natalia didn't know how much later it was when she woke in Finn's bed. She was lying naked next to him, her head resting on his shoulder, his arm encircling her and holding her tight. *Heaven.* She breathed in the scent of him. The scent of *them.* She felt relaxed to bonelessness after her initiation into the pleasures a woman could both take and give without technically losing her virginity. Never had she dreamed she could be so uninhibited.

She lay next to him, savouring his nearness, thinking. Thinking about Finn, about how unfulfilling her life had been until he'd reappeared in it.

What was the time? How much longer did she have left with him? *Her man.* Privately, that was how she thought of him.

It was still dark. But the nights were getting long at

this time of year. She couldn't risk being caught in Finn's bedroom.

Not wanting to wake him, she gently raised herself up on her elbow, looked across at the clock on the nightstand. It glowed in the intense darkness that was night at the chalet, without street lighting or any other buildings. It was not yet three a.m. There was still time.

Still time for *more.*

Everything she'd done with Finn had been intensely exciting and satisfying. But it wasn't enough. She still wanted him.

Her movement must have woken him. He stirred. 'Natalia...' he murmured. 'You're here.'

The joy and pleasure in his voice both thrilled and moved her. He turned, reached out for her.

'You're not going yet?'

Her eyes were getting used to the dark and she could see his face. His handsome, handsome face that had become so dear—so *beloved*—so quickly.

He was the one.

'No, I'm not going.' She reached out with newly confident hands to caress him, revelling in the feel of his body. 'I want you to make love to me, Finn. All the way.'

'But we agreed not to—'

'You were doing the honourable thing, and I appreciate your thoughtfulness more than I can say.'

'Not quite so honourable,' he said 'More trying to be sensible. More trying to...to protect you.'

'I'm frightened, you see,' she said, with a little shiver that had nothing to do with the cold.

'Frightened? There's no need to be—'

She took his hand. 'Not about that. I'm not at *all* frightened about that.'

She dropped a kiss on his hand.

'It's the rest of it. Earlier, on the sofa, when we were

discussing our options, I felt so brave—so confident that with you by my side I could reach out and take what I wanted. But in the dark I don't feel so brave. It's difficult to be both a Montovian princess and a feminist, but I do my best. However, it seems to me that when there are decisions to be made it's most often the woman who has to uproot her life. It would most likely be me who'd have change countries. I'm torn. I'm aching to be with you, but I also want to do my duty to my country and to my parents. They have lost one child already and they'd think that me going to Australia would be losing another.'

'I understand,' he said. He picked up a lock of her hair and wound it around his finger, as if binding her to him.

'And, while option two beckons so enticingly, I have to prepare my heart for the fact that option three might be the forerunner. If that's our option, and we have to say goodbye, I want to have been with you in every sense.'

She shifted so she could look right into his face, amazed at how unselfconscious she was about being naked with him.

'You're the one, Finn. No matter how things work out with us, you're the only man I've ever wanted—the only man I have ever imagined I could care for. Please make love to me. Give me memories, if nothing else, that I can carry with me no matter where life might take me.'

'*Natalia...*' Her name seemed wrenched out of him in a harsh, heartrending sob as he gathered her into his arms.

CHAPTER FOURTEEN

BREAKFAST AT THE chalet early the next morning was a subdued event. Amelie wasn't present because she wasn't feeling well. Morning sickness, Natalia suspected. For the first time in her life, she had a flash of concern for herself—what if she was pregnant? She dismissed the thought—Finn had been meticulous about protection. But then she allowed herself the momentary indulgence of wondering what a child of theirs might be like—almost certainly dark-haired, smart, attractive…

She cast a quick, surreptitious look over to Finn. He seemed sombre, with dark circles under his eyes. Neither of them had got more than a few hours' sleep. They'd found better ways to use their time rather than waste it on sleeping.

The intimacy they'd shared had gone beyond the physical. They'd both been in tears when they'd had to say goodbye in the last private moments they would share until heaven knew when. She had never felt sadder than when she'd sneaked out of his room just before dawn.

She'd felt awkward when she'd got to the breakfast table, to find Finn already there making polite conversation with Marco. Had Marco guessed she'd spent the night with Finn? The only evidence was a slight beard rash, but she'd covered that with make-up.

She longed to seat herself next to Finn—her lover!—as close as she possibly could. But that was out of the question. Instead she acted the gracious hostess to both Finn and Marco.

She gagged at the thought of eating—not the delicious bread rolls Hanna had baked fresh, not Matteo's fabulous cheese or even the finely sliced ham and fresh fruit. Black coffee was all she could tolerate. She was too miserable at the prospect of Finn leaving in just a few hours.

She was about to ask Finn and Marco for the umpteenth time if there was anything else they needed, when she looked up to see big fat snowflakes drifting past the window. She alerted the others.

'The first snow!'

She'd never lost the excitement of the first fall, but she wasn't always at the chalet to see it. Was it an omen that perhaps—just perhaps—things might work out for her and Finn?

With Marco predicting the possibilities of skiable snow, and Finn saying snow was a novelty for a Sydney boy, any awkwardness was smoothed over. And the snowfall propelled her and Finn to start their journey back to the palace straight away, as their driver was worried that the roads might be affected.

They needed to be back in plenty of time for their meeting with the Chamber of Commerce.

She and Finn passed their journey back to the palace in much the way they had the journey to the chalet. The only difference was that Finn spent quite some time on his cell phone, for which he apologised.

'I have to check all is okay with my meetings in Dublin and London.' He leaned over to her. 'I'm glad we've got one more business meeting together.'

'Even if it's likely to be the stuffiest,' she said.

'It's a way to extend our time together for as long as possible. No meeting could possibly be stuffy with you chairing it.'

'Thank you,' she said, aching to touch him—even put

her hand on his arm—but knowing it would not be wise. She mustn't risk any hint of scandal—not when they had been so discreet.

Finn was proud of the way Natalia conducted herself at the meeting later that morning. The men and women of the Chamber of Commerce were delighted that their Princess was taking an active interest in local businesses, and Tristan and his savvy sister—Gemma was again absent—worked well together. She would be an asset to any business. To any country.

To him.

It was a kind of torture to play the polite visitor when Natalia was in the room and all he wanted to do was be by her side, claiming her as his own. But he was just a guy from Australia, whose interest lay in the gourmet foods he could import at a profit into his country on the other side of the world.

He was very aware of how deep the roots of this country went. How old the traditions of the people were. How conservative their customs. To uproot Natalia might not be the best option for her.

His grandparents were great gardeners. He knew from working with them that sometimes a plant uprooted from a particular type of soil did not transplant successfully, but rather withered and died. Natalia was the most beautiful flower, adapted to thrive in this fantasy land of castles and dungeons and family retainers. Sydney was an altogether brasher place, and tough in its own way.

Natalia smiled at him from across the room. To chat about chocolate and cheese with her, without acknowledging that she had been in his bed last night, was excruciating.

What he felt for her was so much more than infatuation. It had been from the get-go. He realised that now.

Everything about Natalia felt so right, and just her smile sent his heart soaring to heaven. It had nothing to do with her being a princess, and everything to do with her being the perfect woman for him. Yet there were very real obstacles to be overcome.

He *had* to make option two work. In the next two weeks away from her, he would come up with a plan.

At the end of the meeting he shook hands with her in a formal goodbye that tore him apart. He could tell from the almost imperceptible quiver of her lower lip that she was finding it equally torturous. How quickly he'd learned to read her.

As he made his way to the official car that was taking him and the master chocolatier to the airport, and thence to Dublin, he found every excuse to turn back and see ever-diminishing last glimpses of her.

He had a horrible fear that her family would try to make sure he never saw her again. But he would never let that happen.

That afternoon, alone in her apartment, Natalia missed Finn so desperately it physically hurt. She literally could not think of anything else but him.

She had been premature in believing the dark cloud of gloom that had hung over her for so long had dissipated. It had eased. But it was still like a grey fog that strangled the vitality from her, misted her vision of any hope for the future.

He had gone.

The meeting with the Chamber of Commerce that morning had concluded only too quickly After she'd waved Finn goodbye, with the perfectly calibrated royal wave she had been trained to do from a little girl, she'd had a quick chat with Tristan to review the other meetings she'd had with Finn. Her brother seemed to have a high opinion of Finn, and she had sensed Tristan could become an ally if she ever had to fight for her right to be with a man her parents considered unsuitable.

She had to gather her allies. And Tristan had already fought and won his own battle with Montovian tradition.

After her exchange with Tristan she had pleaded a headache and headed for her apartment in the palace. The perfectly decorated apartment that felt suddenly as lonely as if she were in exile.

Despite thoughts of Finn and their options churning through her brain, she decided to try and sleep, fully clothed on her bed. After all, she had had virtually no sleep the night before. But before she was overwhelmed by drowsiness she phoned through to her mother's private secretary and booked an appointment with the Queen for the following morning.

She was pretty sure she knew what she had to do.

At some stage she awoke and reached out for Finn—only to find cold, empty sheets. Even after one night of sleeping in his arms she knew she wanted him always there—in her bed, by her side, sharing her life. Being with Finn had become more important than anything. This was—at last—love. That elusive emotion she'd feared she might never find. She just hoped—prayed—that Finn felt it too. Because she could never settle for less than his wholehearted love in return.

Holding that thought, she got up and showered, changed and climbed back into bed.

But sleep didn't come easily, and it was late by the time she drifted off again.

She was woken by the sound of her phone, saw it was still early, reached out to her nightstand, fumbled for the phone and looked for the caller ID.

Finn!

She was immediately awake. Then she burst into tears at the sound of his voice.

'Hey, what's going on?' he said. 'Are those tears I hear?'

She sniffed. 'No. Yes. I was just…overwhelmed to hear your voice. I…I think I had a deep fear I might never talk to you again.'

'That's not going to happen. We're talking now, aren't we? And we need to talk some more.'

'Where are you? In Dublin? London?'

'I'm here. In Montovia.'

She thought she was hearing things. 'At the palace?'

'I didn't think I should storm the walls and come and find you,' he said, in that laconic manner she liked so much. 'I'm at the tea room with the chocolate in the old town. Can you meet me here?'

'Now?'

'If a princess is *allowed* to do such an ordinary thing as meet a man for coffee.'

'This isn't a dream?'

'No.'

'Then the answer is yes!'

Fired with sudden energy, she quickly fixed her hair and applied make-up with hands that trembled with excitement. No matter how desperate she was to see Finn, the Princess of Montovia did *not* go outside the palace looking less than her best.

She threw on skinny black trousers, a tight black cashmere turtleneck, black boots with a heel that could handle cobblestones, and a gorgeous loose-weave wool short coat in different shades of pink that she'd been too depressed to wear after she'd bought it. Contemporary pink ruby earrings and a bracelet completed the look.

She booked a palace car to take her down to the old town and then ran from her apartment—something that really wasn't done in the corridors of the royal palace of Montovia.

CHAPTER FIFTEEN

NATALIA STILL WASN'T quite sure that Finn's call hadn't been a dream—a manifestation of her longing for him. But there he was, sitting at the most private table available at the tea room. He rose to greet her, darkly handsome in a superbly tailored business suit. Joy bubbled up inside her.

She forced herself to walk to him at a suitably sedate pace, when really she wanted to run and fling herself into his arms. She greeted him with a businesslike handshake, then sat down opposite him. This was one place where she would be observed and her behaviour noted by the townsfolk.

He'd ordered her the hot chocolate she'd been enjoying here since she was a child. He had a coffee in front of him—short and black. He offered her a chocolate croissant, but she declined.

'It's so good to see you,' he said, his voice hushed.

Hopefully there was enough clatter from the other tables to mask their conversation.

'Oh, Finn, I can't tell you how amazing it is to see you. I…I think my heart is literally jumping for joy. But what are you doing here? How…? Why…?'

'I cancelled my meetings in London, postponed my flight back to Sydney and flew back here from Dublin after the meeting. I stayed last night in a small hotel near the clock tower. Not that I slept.'

'Why didn't you tell me?'

'It was late when I got in. Besides, I needed some time to plan my strategy.' He leaned across the table towards her, his eyes intense. 'You see, beautiful, wonderful, perfect Natalia, I realised nothing was more important in my life than you. *Nothing.*'

'Oh, Finn, I feel the same.'

Her heart soared with the knowledge that he cared for her too. She ached to kiss him, but she knew they had an audience. A discreet, quiet audience, but an audience just the same.

'I wanted a plan for how to put option two into action. But option two without the separation, the long-distance angst. I decided I would come here to live. Not permanently. I thought three months…on a tourist visa. I could find an apartment here in the old town, so I would be near to you in the castle. As long as it had good Wi-Fi, I could work remotely. Then, as we discussed, we could start dating. Three months should give us time to get to know each other better.'

He looked very pleased with himself.

Her heart soared. 'But, Finn, I—'

He put up his hand to stop her. 'Hear me out. I can afford to ease off the pedal on my business for a few months. I've thought about what you said about being frightened. I realised I was scared too—of leaving behind my country and people I love to be a foreigner in a strange land.'

'It *is* scary,' she said.

'But that's exactly what my family did. My father left Ireland for a better life than on the small farm where he grew up. When my great-grandparents emigrated to Australia they left everything—everyone—for the chance of a better life. My Chinese great-grandparents were fleeing persecution…my Italian great-grandparents were fleeing poverty. In their day, there were only letters that took weeks to be delivered to communicate with the loved ones they'd left behind. My Chinese great-grandparents never saw their parents again. My grandparents had to fight prejudice and racism to be together and become the Romeo and Juliet of their suburb. *That's* the background I come from. Why shouldn't I be prepared to emigrate to build a life with you? I want to give it a trial for three months. That is if it's what you want too.'

Natalia laughed a laugh that she knew was tinged with hysteria. 'But I had the same idea. I decided we should try option two without all the long-distance to-ing and fro-ing by me living in Sydney for a while.'

'What?'

'Yes!' She lowered her voice. 'The plan I came up with was that I would come and live in Sydney for six months, so we could spend time together and get to know each other better. But perhaps three months might be more feasible. I would take a sabbatical from some of my charity commitments and work online for the auctions. I have good people to help here while I'm away. I thought of leasing an apartment near where Eliza and Jake live. You wouldn't be far. Perhaps I could meet your family, too? But the idea is to be *near* you, Finn. After our time in the chalet I cannot bear the thought of being parted from you again.'

'I hated being apart from you just that one night.'

He laughed, and she loved the edge of incredulous delight in his laughter.

'I can't believe we independently came up with two versions of the same solution at the same time.'

'Perhaps we can do both,' she said.

'Why not? I'll live in Montovia near you for three months…' he said.

'Then I'll move to Sydney for three months to be with you. I would *love* that. I was going to call you this morning to see what you thought of my idea.'

'And now I'm here to talk to you in person, because I couldn't stay away from you.'

'I've booked a meeting with my mother this morning, to tell her of my plans. But I'll go with you to Sydney anyway—even if she doesn't approve.' She paused. 'Your approval is all I need, Finn.'

'You have it wholeheartedly. We will make the decisions that affect our lives. And, while I'm certain I'll enjoy my three months living here near you, I will love having you in Sydney. I know my family will welcome you with open arms.'

'Oh, Finn, this is just wonderful!'

He leaned across the table and kissed her, his lips firm and possessive on hers. The kiss was short and sweet and utterly heartfelt.

And greeted by a chorus of applause and bravos.

Natalia broke away from the kiss and saw the smiling face of the tea room proprietor—a jovial, elderly man who had known her since she was a child. Everyone else in the shop would know who she was too, and about her history of turning down proposal after proposal, but all she saw were kind faces and goodwill.

She smiled back, unable to contain her joy that Finn was in her life and they could be open about what they meant to each other.

The alarm on her watch went off. '*Ack!* I'm meeting with my mother in twenty minutes. I've got to go—try and head her off before the news breaks that the Princess was seen kissing a handsome foreigner in the chocolate shop.'

'I'm coming too. We'll face her together. Let's start as we mean to continue—as a couple.'

They left the tea room to further applause, and headed for Natalia's car and driver.

'Wait,' Finn said. 'I have a suggestion. Rather than confronting the Queen with a *fait accompli*, why don't we ask her advice on how we can make it work?'

'Good idea,' Natalia said. '*Excellent* idea. You might end up a Montovian diplomat yet.'

Natalia was glad they'd agreed on Finn's strategy. When they entered the Queen's office she could tell by her mother's frosty expression that the news from the tea room had already reached her.

Her mother sat behind her ornate antique desk. She did not offer Natalia and Finn a chair, but rather let them stand. Finn gave a deep bow to the Queen, as Natalia had coached him. He did an excellent job. It was as if he were born to it.

'Your Majesty, Natalia and I beg your forgiveness for our indiscreet behaviour in the tea room.'

'We're in a relationship, Mother,' Natalie said. 'We couldn't help it. By the time you told me to "nip it in the bud" it was too late. This morning I was so happy I forgot I shouldn't be kissing Finn in public. Please take me off the royal matchmaking list. From now on I'm only dating Finn.'

'Where do you think this will take you?' said the Queen.

'To a future together, I hope,' she said.

She cast a sideways glance at Finn, who nodded.

Finn took Natalia's hand. 'We need to spend more time together, Your Majesty,' he said. 'However, that is complicated by the fact that we live in different countries on different sides of the world.'

'So I'm going to spend three months in Sydney with Finn,' Natalia blurted out.

So much for diplomacy. But she had lived by the royal rules for so long—she needed to make a strong statement about how now she wanted to live her life her own way.

With Finn.

'But first I plan to spend three months in Montovia, Your Majesty,' he said. 'We are seeking your advice on how we can best accomplish this. And of course Natalia will want to discuss with you the logistics of her taking some time to spend in Sydney.'

Natalia marvelled at how Finn had got the tone of his speech just right.

'Do you intend to live together?' asked the Queen.

'We intend to maintain separate residences,' he said. 'In both Montovia and Sydney. For three months in each country.'

'The King and I have given this matter considerable thought over the last few days.'

'What matter?' asked Natalia. 'Me and Finn? Mother, what do you mean, you and Father have been discussing it for the last few days? We have only just realised ourselves that we want to be together.'

The Queen quoted a Montovian saying that pretty much translated as telling them that she hadn't come down in the last shower. 'I saw how miserable you were when you got back from Sydney. How that misery lifted once this young man appeared at the palace.'

'Oh…' Natalia said, exchanging a glance with Finn.

'And if you make your living arrangements more permanent, where do you plan to live?'

'I would live wherever is best for Natalia,' Finn said.

'I realise that as second in line to the throne I am obliged to live here,' Natalia said.

She looked around her mother's ornate and exquisitely decorated office and thought about how much she loved the palace and the castle and being Princess of Montovia.

'Or I can make the choice to renounce my title.'

It hurt even to say the words. Renouncing her title would mean alienation from the family she loved. But she wanted to be with Finn—whatever the cost.

The Queen smiled the stiff smile that came from her regular wrinkle-fighting injections. 'Recent events have taken the pressure off you in that regard. Gemma is pregnant—'

Natalia clapped her hands together. 'I *knew* it. How wonderful! I'm so thrilled—'

Her mother raised her hand imperiously. 'Please let me continue, Natalia.'

'Yes, Mother.'

'Gemma is pregnant with twins. A boy and a girl. She has held off from sharing the news because there is a greater risk of complication with twins. However, her consultant has given her the all-clear to make the announcement. What this means for you is that once the twins are born you will go from being second in line to the throne to fourth. I know that will make you happy.'

'Yes, Mother it does.' She felt as though the enormous weight that had been crushing her since Carl's death had been lifted. 'I am delighted for Gemma and Tristan about the twins. And for you and Father. Not just because there will be new heirs, but new grandchildren.'

'It is happy news,' the Queen said.

Still there was the sadness of loss in her eyes, but there was also joyful anticipation of new life. The new babies would do much to heal the wounds in her family that had made Natalia's life so constricted.

'The best kind of happy news,' Natalia said.

The Queen continued. 'You should know that if you and Finn decide to marry you have our permission.'

Was she hearing things?

'Really?'

'I told you—I want you to be happy. It is not just the news about the twins that has prompted our decision. However, there is a condition. If you decide to make your home in Australia we would require you to make regular return trips home to Montovia.'

'To fulfil my royal duties?'

'To see your mother and father. We would miss you, my darling.'

* * *

After they'd left the Queen's office Finn asked Natalia to take him up to the arched lookouts, with their magnificent view across the lake.

'We need some privacy and a place to think,' he explained.

As they walked up the steps and along the battlements, holding hands, he marvelled to himself at how the castle, the town, the country that had seemed like a movie set, populated by witches and wizards, was now beginning to seem like home. Because it was Natalia's home.

Perhaps one day she would feel the same about the view from the veranda of his house across to the Sydney Harbour Bridge and the Opera House.

When they reached the middle archway he put his arm around her and pulled her close. In silence, they both looked out at the view. He wondered if Natalia, as he was, was taking some quiet time to process that astonishing pronouncement by the Queen—that she and the King gave their permission for him to marry her daughter.

She wasn't wearing a hat, and a teasing chilly breeze was lifting her hair and blowing it across her face. He turned her to him and gently pushed her hair back into place. Then he cradled her chin in his hands and tilted her face upwards, so he could look into her eyes.

'I love you, Natalia,' he said, his voice hoarse with emotion. 'I already know all I need to know about you and I know I could not imagine a life without you in it.'

His beautiful princess closed her eyes and then opened them again, as if scarcely able to believe she was here with him. Her mouth curved in the most joyous of smiles. 'Oh, Finn, I love you too. I think I fell in love with you that first day in Sydney. Only because I've never been in love before I didn't recognise it.'

'The whole time we've been discussing our three-month plan for option two I've been thinking we don't really need to spend time dating. I don't want to live apart from you. I love you. I adore you. I want to marry you, and have children with you, and wake up every morning to your face on my pillow.'

'Oh, Finn…' She sighed. 'That sounds like heaven.'

He reached into the inner pocket of his jacket and pulled out a small velvet covered box. 'Natalia, will you do me the honour of becoming my wife? I love you and I want to honour and cherish you for the rest of our lives— not because you're a princess, but because you're the most wonderful woman ever put on this earth.'

She put her hand to her heart, seeming almost too overcome to speak. But she managed to choke out some words. 'Yes, Finn—yes. I love you and I want to honour and cherish you too. More than anything I want to be your wife.'

His wife. Two such wonderful words.

He took her left hand and slid onto the third finger an engagement ring magnificent in its simplicity—a large, oval cut white diamond on a narrow platinum band. He'd guessed the size just right.

She held out her hand and splayed her fingers to admire the ring as its facets caught the light and glistened with tiny rainbows. 'It's beautiful. I love it. But how—?'

'My cousin in Dublin directed me to the best jeweller in town. I didn't think I'd get a chance to give it to you quite so soon.'

He kissed her long and sweet and tenderly.

Natalia pulled away from his kiss and leaned back against the circle of his arms. 'You realise this is where Tristan proposed to Gemma?'

'I do. I know how important tradition is to the older Montovians. Why not start some traditions for our generation?'

'When we marry you'll be a Montovian too. You become a citizen on marriage.'

'I'd like us to marry as soon as we can. But I'd still like to do the three months in each country. What do you think?'

'Me too. Only, because we're engaged, we might actually be able to live together. And, in light of your proposal, maybe I should come to Australia first, so we can be here in Montovia for the three months before the wedding.'

'I thought something simple, private…'

She gave a snort of most un-princess-like laughter.

'*Simple?* I am Princess of Montovia and my parents' only daughter. I'm afraid we can't have "simple". Don't even try to fight for it. We'll have a spectacular royal wedding in our beautiful cathedral with all the ceremonial bling. Nothing less.'

Finn realised that his private life out of the spotlight was about to come to a screeching halt. But with Natalia by his side he didn't care nearly as much as he'd thought he might.

'My family will love a big cathedral wedding,' he said. 'What about that glass carriage drawn by white horses?'

He was joking. Natalia was not.

'The horses—yes; the glass carriage—not possible. But there *is* a royal landau. It's an open carriage, so that means a spring wedding.'

'Six months away? Perfect timing. At the end of our time getting to know each other better.'

'I'm going to enjoy every second of it,' she said.

'We have a lifetime together ahead for us, my beautiful wife-to-be,' said Finn, drawing her into his arms.

He couldn't imagine ever feeling happier than he did at this moment, but he suspected that being married to Natalia would mean happiness compounding upon happiness.

EPILOGUE

Six months later

NATALIA COULD FEEL the goodwill emanating from the Montovian citizens who crowded the cathedral square, hoping to catch a glimpse of their Princess in her wedding dress as she alighted from the sleek black limousine with her father King Gerard. There was a media contingent too, with cameras at the ready, so sizeable it had to be kept in check by members of the royal family's personal guard.

There was intense interest in her love story with Finn all around the world. A beautiful European princess marrying a handsome Australian commoner was story enough. But the 'Secret Princess' angle was what had sent their love story viral.

Not long after they had made the formal announcement of their engagement some sharp-eyed person in Eliza's circle had noticed the resemblance blonde wedding guest Natalie Gerard bore to dark-haired Natalia, Princess of Montovia. And when photos of her dancing with Finn at Eliza's wedding were published, Natalia's cover was completely blown.

Now the whole world knew how they had met. But, despite media digging, no scandal had been unearthed. Rather, their story was being celebrated for its heady level of romance.

Natalia alighted from the car, waved to the crowd, then climbed the stairs to the cathedral on her father's arm, her long train trailing behind her.

At the top of the steps her bridesmaids were there to greet her, dressed in exquisite long gowns in gradating tones of pink—Gemma, new mother to the world's most adorable twins, Amelie, heavily pregnant, Finn's beautiful sister Bella, already a dear friend, and three of her close Montovian friends.

They clustered around her to pat her hair into place and adjust the filmy veil that covered her face, anchored by the diamond tiara her great-great-grandmother had worn, before it fell to the hem of her white lace gown. They fussed with her bouquet of indigenous Australian blooms—flannel flowers, white waratah and orchids, air-freighted from Sydney. Then they kissed her for good luck.

Her bridesmaids left her to walk in procession, one by one, down the long, long aisle to the high altar of the cathedral. The same altar where her ancestors, stretching back generation after generation, had wed.

Natalia stood with her father as the organ music swelled and she started her own stately march down the aisle to where Finn waited for her—her husband-to-be. There were gasps of admiration from the congregation as she made her way down the carpet.

She was pleased. She wanted Finn to gasp too. His reaction to how she looked was the only one she cared about. Her dress was made in a similar style to the pink dress she'd worn in Sydney when she'd first met him, only by the original Paris designer, and the silk lace was heavy and luxurious, the design simple in its construction.

Every pew in the cathedral was packed with people who had come to witness her wedding and wish her well. All she could see was a mass of smiling faces.

As she got to the first few rows she recognised her family and friends. The Queen in the ornately carved monarch's pew. Her new family, Finn's parents and his grandparents, whom she already adored. The other Party Queens and their husbands—Eliza holding her baby girl.

And next to Eliza sat her neighbour Kerry, she of the uncannily accurate prediction, who had been high on the invitation list. Her new prediction was for a long and happy life for the bride and groom and their three children yet to be born.

And then there was Finn—her beloved Finn—standing by Tristan, his best man. Her husband-to-be, tall and handsome, in an immaculately tailored morning suit. When she finally reached him, he was obviously too overcome to say anything, but his eyes told her everything she needed to know about how he felt about his bride.

Her father handed her over to the new man in her life and slid back to his pew.

'You are the most beautiful bride I've ever seen,' Finn whispered when he found his words. 'I'm a lucky, lucky man.'

'I'm the lucky one—to have found you,' she whispered back. 'Want to see my "something borrowed"?'

Her 'something old' was the diamond tiara. The 'something new' her gown. The 'something blue' was the sapphire and diamond necklace and earrings gifted to her by her parents.

She held up her right wrist. 'This is my "something borrowed".'

Finn stared at the fine platinum bangle from which dangled the cufflink he had left behind in her hotel room back in Sydney, where it had all started.

'So that's where it went,' he said. 'I was too busy searching for you to look for it.'

'I kept it close to my heart, always hoping I'd see you again,' she whispered.

Every day she fell more and more in love with him.

'We'll never be parted again, I promise you,' he said, taking her hand, drawing her close and facing the archbishop as the ceremony that would make them husband and wife commenced.

After the service had ended—having been conducted in both Montovian and English—Finn sat back in the antique open landau drawn by four perfectly matched white horses that was taking him and his brand-new wife on a ceremonial tour through the ancient cobbled streets of the old town of Montovia. It was a perfect May day.

The narrow thoroughfares were lined with well-wishers waving the Montovian flag, with its emblem of an eagle with a sword in its beak, and the occasional Australian flag. Along with Natalia he waved back, soon losing his self-consciousness at doing such an unaccustomed thing.

Again, he felt as though he'd been plunged into the set of a fantasy movie as the carriage wound its way through the shadow of the ancient castle that stood guard over the town, past the famous medieval clock and the rows of quaint houses that were multiple centuries older than anything in Australia—all to the accompaniment of the glorious chiming of bells from one of the oldest cathedrals in Europe and the cheers of the crowd in a language he was only just beginning to master.

He turned to his bride. 'I love you, Natalia, my wife, for ever and for always,' he said as he kissed her.

The crowd erupted with joyous cheering.

His heart was full of love and gratitude that, as in the best of fantasies, he and his real-life Princess Natalia were being given their very own fairy tale happy-ever-after and beginning their new life together.

* * * * *

CONFESSIONS OF A GIRL-NEXT-DOOR

JACKIE BRAUN

To little princesses everywhere…

CHAPTER ONE

HOLLYN Elise Phillipa Saldani always did what was expected of her. As next in line for the throne of the tiny Mediterranean principality of Morenci, she'd known from an early age what her duties entailed and she'd followed them to the letter. Which was why her driver looked at her as if she were speaking a language other than the four in which she was fluent when she said, "Take me to the airport, please."

"The airport, Your Highness?" Henry asked.

She settled back in the plush leather seat of the limousine and fussed with the folds of her full skirt. Even though her heart was hammering, Hollyn said with characteristic calm, "Yes. The airport."

Henry wasn't mollified. He lifted one bushy eyebrow and inquired, "Are we picking up a passenger, then, on our way to the annual garden party? The queen didn't mention it."

No, indeed. Her mother hadn't mentioned it, because Olivia Saldani wasn't privy to Hollyn's last-minute change in plans.

"We are not picking up a passenger." Hollyn moistened her lips. This was it. There would be no turning back once she said the words. Once she gave the edict, her will would be done. "You are dropping one off. Me."

Henry cleared his throat. "I beg your pardon. I must not have heard you correctly."

"Yes, you did." Despite her nerves, she smiled. "Your hearing is as good now as it was when you caught me trying to take out the Bentley with cousin Amelia when I was sixteen."

"Your giggles gave you away, Your Highness."

She sighed. "It's just Hollyn."

But she hadn't been "just Hollyn" in too many years to count. Not to Henry or the other people who staffed the royal palace. Or the citizens of the small kingdom that she would one day rule. To them she was Princess Hollyn, daughter of King Franco and Queen Olivia, next in line to the Morenci throne and rumored to be soon engaged to the son of one of the country's most celebrated and dashing young businessmen.

Duty. She understood it and accepted it. But that didn't mean she liked it. Or that she didn't wish, sometimes, that she could be an ordinary young woman, living a simpler life.

Holly.

The nickname whispered from her past, beckoning from across the Atlantic. She allowed herself the luxury of recalling the boy who'd called her that. In her memory, a pair of wide-set brown eyes crinkled with a smile that also caused his cheeks to dent.

At fifteen, Nathaniel Matthews had been surprisingly self-assured and determined to break free of the small community the past two generations of his family had so eagerly embraced. She'd found the tiny island tucked between Canada and America in Lake Huron a paradise.

She'd spent five summers on Heart Island, so named because of its shape, living in anonymity and loving every minute of her unregimented life. No teas or cotillions to attend. No fussy state dinners. And no boring garden parties where more eyes would be focused on her than the blooms.

"The airport," she said again. "A plane is waiting for me."

Not the royal jet, but a private one she'd chartered for this trip. In the rearview mirror, she saw Henry's brows draw together. His perplexed expression was endearing and nostalgic. She remembered that look of concern from the days when he'd taught her to drive on the palace grounds. Afterward, she and Henry had laughed like a pair of loons at her exploits, which included an encounter with a bee-infested log. It was doubtful this day would end with much mirth.

"I'm leaving, Henry."

"Your mother never spoke of it."

Hollyn fussed with the folds of her skirt again. She couldn't wait to take it off and change into something less formal. "She doesn't know."

Those bushy brows drew together a second time. "But, Your Highness…"

She closed her eyes briefly, feeling swallowed up by a life that so many other young women in her kingdom considered a dream. For her, lately at least, it had become a nightmare.

"It's Hollyn. Please, Henry, just call me Hollyn."

When he stopped the car at a light, he turned with a tentative smile. "Hollyn."

Despite her best efforts to remain firm, her eyes filled with tears.

"I need a holiday, Henry. Just a few days, a week at the most, to be by myself. My life has been decided since before my birth, and now, with all of the pressure to accept Phillip's proposal...please." Her voice faltered.

Perhaps it was that more than her words that caused Henry to nod. After all, she was known for her stoicism.

"The airport," he said.

"Thank you."

"My pleasure." He sounded only marginally concerned when he asked, "And what am I to tell Her Majesty?"

Hollyn took a moment, drawing in a breath and working up the nerve to go against her mother's wishes. No one crossed Olivia without expecting retribution.

"You are to tell her that, at my command, you dropped me off at the airport. I have a letter for you to give to her that will explain my decision and my whereabouts. It also instructs her not to censure you in any way for carrying out my orders."

He smiled as he shook his head. "I'd do it anyway, you know."

She did.

Their gazes caught in the rearview mirror. "Thank you, Henry. I know this is an imposition."

He shrugged and pushed his trademark black cap back on his forehead. "I've never considered you an imposition, Hollyn."

Her eyes pooled with tears upon hearing her given

name, uttered this time without any prompting. But there was no time to give in to sentiment, even if Henry would have allowed it. They had arrived at the small country's only airport. Henry brought the limo around to a private entrance reserved for VIPs and royalty. They were shielded from prying eyes, although an industrious paparazzo or two had managed to breach security in the past. She held her breath, silently chanting, "Not today. Please, not today," as Henry unloaded the luggage she'd stowed, unbeknownst to him, in the limousine's trunk. He added to the trolley the three sleek designer bags whose contents she could barely remember packing, she'd done it so quickly. But then, where she was going, she wouldn't need much. No ball gowns, no ostentatious jewels or tiaras. As she recalled, shoes had been optional.

"I hope you find what it is you seek," he said softly once they were inside. Then he wrapped her in the kind of hug a father might, though her own wasn't one for displays of affection, whether in public or private.

"At the moment, Henry, all I seek is peace."

"Then that, my dear, is what I wish for you." He kissed her cheek and stepped away. "Write?"

The corners of her mouth turned up in a smile. "I won't be gone *that* long. As I said, a week at most."

He remained serious. "Be in touch when you can."

"Of course."

An hour later, as she settled into one of the plush seats of the private jet she'd chartered, she thought of her request.

Peace.

She might as well have been asking for the moon. But

with most of the paparazzi tied up at the annual garden party, and no one but Henry privy to her travel plans at this point, perhaps she would be able to make a clean getaway. She'd worry about a "clean arrival" once she got to where she was going.

Nate was seated on the deck of his home. He was finishing up a burger that he'd picked up from a local pub before heading home, and enjoying a cold beer when he spied the Cessna riding low on the horizon over Lake Huron.

Hell of an evening to land a seaplane, given the wind.

Even on the relatively protected waters of Heart Island's Pettibone Bay, whitecaps sent waves crashing on the beach with unrelenting precision. Forecasters were calling for a doozy of a storm, likely to hit sometime before midnight. The islanders, especially those along the coastline, were battened down, ready. Storms such as these weren't uncommon in summer, which was why people with any sense were already in for the night, their planes and boats secured to wait out the worst of the weather.

What in the hell was Hank Whitey thinking?

Sure, the pilot had a penchant for taking risks. Last week, he'd bluffed his way through their weekly poker game with a pathetic hand of cards. But Hank generally wasn't one to take risks with his plane; the aircraft was his livelihood.

Nate went inside, set his unfinished beer on the counter and headed out. Not only was he curious about Hank's explanation, but the man was also going to need a hand.

By the time Nate jogged down to the sand, Hank had already bypassed the dock at the Haven Marina, which was part of the resort Nate owned. On a really calm day, Hank might have moored there. Today, not a chance. The waves tossed the small plane around as if it weighed no more than a fishing bobber.

Nate would give Hank this. The guy was a capable pilot, even if his judgment was a bit questionable. Just beyond the plane, a jagged outcropping of rocks lined a slim finger of land that jutted to where a lighthouse stood. With the wind pushing toward those rocks, it took experience and skill to guide the Cessna toward the sandy beach instead.

Nate waited until the single engine was cut and the plane's propeller finally stopped chopping the air before he kicked off his shoes and waded out into the thigh-deep water. The waves made keeping his balance difficult and the cuffs of his shorts were wet in no time. Hank's door opened and the man let out a whoop of joy, which was entirely appropriate given the circumstances.

"You're damned lucky to be in one piece!" Nate shouted to be heard over the wind.

"Hey, Nate. Can't tell you how glad I am to see you."

"Glad to see you, too, Hank. Alive. What in the hell were you thinking?"

The passenger door opened then. A woman, beautiful and amazingly composed under the circumstances, smiled at Nate. "I'm to blame, I'm afraid. I was so eager to get here that I offered Mr. Whitey triple his normal fee."

Her crisp accent had Nate's brows tugging together. He knew that voice. He blinked. He knew…that face.

Despite all of the years that had passed, he knew it in an instant. Heart-shaped, with a delicate nose, a pair of perfect lips and eyes as blue as Huron's deepest waters.

His gut clenched as time reeled backward. He was a teenager again, carefree, happy, experiencing his first love…before having his heart brutally ripped from his chest.

"Holly?"

"It's been a long time."

She had the nerve to smile, which caused his teeth to clench. After all these years, he still felt betrayed, even if he also understood why she'd misled him. She hadn't owed him the truth.

That didn't stop him from wanting an explanation now. "Why are you here?"

Her smile disappeared. Her composure slipped. "I needed to get away. I needed…a holiday."

He could read between both the lines in her words and the one now denting the flesh between her eyes. She wanted normalcy. Anonymity.

That's what her American grandmother had been after, too, when she'd insisted Holly spend her summers on the island when she was a girl. From ages ten through fifteen, Holly and the older woman had shown up faithfully the second week in June and then stayed through the second week in August, renting the largest and most secluded of the resort's cottages.

He and Holly had become fast friends when she was ten and he was twelve. When she'd been fifteen to his seventeen, they'd had more on their minds than seeing who could swim the fastest to the floating dock out in front of his parents' house.

"So, you nearly killed Hank here? Well, I guess your wish is his command."

"I coulda said no, Nate," Hank argued, no doubt perplexed by the irritation in Nate's tone.

Nate was a little perplexed, too. This anger, these emotions, they belonged to the past. Yet he couldn't stop himself from adding, "No one says no to a princess, Hank"

The other man looked confused. Holly looked desperate. "I'm just an ordinary woman, Nate."

The wind gusted, and the waves slapped higher on his thighs. He decided to allow the distinction for now, even though he knew firsthand that nothing about her was ordinary. Hell, he'd known that to be the case even when he hadn't been privy to her true identity and royal lineage.

He waded the rest of the way to the plane's float. "Put your arms around my neck."

"Excuse me?"

Perversely, he enjoyed the fact that her eyes widened. *Nervous, Princess?* he wanted to ask. It would make him feel better to know that she was as shaken by this unexpected reunion as he was. Instead, Nate nodded in the direction of the shore. "Unless you'd rather walk to the beach, I'll carry you. I'm guessing those pretty shoes of yours probably aren't meant to get wet."

They were red leather flats with fat bows stretched across the toes. He could only guess what they cost. In her world, they would be considered casual. As would the understated linen suit she'd paired with them. In his, they would pass for Sunday best. If this was the kind of clothing she'd brought to blend in with the locals and

the majority of tourists, she was going to stick out like
a sore thumb.

"Right." She gave a quick dip of her chin before tilting it up. He remembered that defiant gesture from their
childhood. She'd used it whenever he'd issued a dare.

"We don't have all day," he prodded when she hesitated. "I have to help Hank secure his plane for the
night."

"I'm not staying," Hank called from the other side
of the Cessna. "Got a card game waiting for me back
on the mainland. Gerald's cousin is in town. Guy is
damned unlucky at poker, but he bets like a Vegas high
roller."

"You're staying," Nate disagreed. "One suicide mission an evening is enough. You can bunk at my place."

Hank cocked his head to one side as if considering.
"Got any cold beer?"

"Yeah."

The other man shrugged. "I guess I can be persuaded. 'Sides, the guy's here through the weekend.
I'll settle for picking *your* pocket at cards tonight."

Nate turned his attention back to Holly and held out
his arms. She offered a tentative smile as she reached
for him, and then she was in his embrace. She felt a little
too good there, a little too perfect, with the side of her
body pressed against his chest. Nate recalled the girl
she'd been: long-limbed and lithe, verging on skinny.
This was no girl he held. While she was still slender,
during the intervening years she'd filled out nicely in
all of the right places.

He started toward the shore, eager for the safety of
the sand so that he could release her. Be free of her? Not

likely. Until today, he'd thought he had been. Now? He was cursing his arrogance. She'd always been there, in the back of his mind.

His stride was purposeful, but perhaps a little too fast given the conditions and the added distraction of a beautiful woman in his arms. She had his hormones starting to lurch as powerfully as the surf. He stubbed his toe on a rock and managed to right his balance only to lose it again entirely when his other foot connected with another one.

"Nate!"

Holly's grip on his neck tightened to a choke hold as he veered from one side to the other. He tried to right himself, but it was too late. Momentum and waves were working against him. He knew a moment of utter defeat just before he toppled over, sending them both into the chilly, knee-deep water. It was too shallow for her to be submerged completely, but between the waves and the splash their bodies made going down, they were both good and soaked. The hair on one side of her head was slicked to her face. So much for the shoes he'd so chivalrously offered to help save from harm. They likely were as ruined as her oatmeal-colored pantsuit.

He expected outrage from her, perhaps even a good dressing down. She was a princess, after all. And he was but the owner of a small, albeit well-tended, resort.

But what he heard over the wind as Holly pushed to her feet was laughter. Unrestrained, boisterous laughter.

"That was smooth, Nathaniel. Yes, indeed. Very smooth." Grinning, she put out a hand, offering to help him up. She looked just then very much like the impish young girl who used to take such delight in playing pranks on him.

Nate felt like an idiot, and he knew he looked ridiculous. That didn't stop him from clasping her palm. Nor did it prevent him from joining in her mirth as he rose and shoved the hair back from his face. The situation *was* funny, even if it came at his expense.

Behind them, Hank was chortling away, too. Nate groaned. His reputation was toast. Unless he got lucky and the storm took out the phone lines and closed the locals' favorite tavern, news of this mishap would be the talk of the island before another sunset.

"Sorry about that. I lost my footing." As they reached the shore, he couldn't resist adding, "I might have maintained my balance, but you've put on a few pounds since we were kids."

Holly turned. Her mouth formed an indignant *O* as she thumped his chest with one small fist. "A gentleman isn't supposed to say such things to a lady."

Her words, even though they were said in jest, caused him to sober. She was more than a lady, she was a princess. Just that quickly, the gulf between their worlds gaped wide once more.

Hooking a thumb over his shoulder, he said, "I'd better go and give Hank a hand."

It took no more than fifteen minutes for Nate and the pilot to pull the plane ashore and beach it. Just to be on the safe side, they used the trunk of a big cedar tree that leaned toward the lake as a mooring. The Cessna wouldn't be going anywhere, despite the coming storm. Nate hoped the same could be said for all of the boats and the several large yachts moored at the resort's marina. Time would tell.

All the while, Holly waited patiently out of the way, soaked to the skin and shivering, but no complaints passed her lips. And he'd been expecting them. When her luggage was unloaded, her expression was one of chagrin.

"Just how long are you here for?" Nate asked, eyeing the trio of designer bags.

A pair of delicate shoulders rose in a shrug. "Perhaps as much as a week."

He ran his tongue over his teeth. "A week, hmm?" He could pack for a week in one small duffel, especially this time of year.

"I wasn't sure what I would need," she said.

For a moment he forgot that he was speaking to royalty. She was simply Holly. "Tank tops, shorts, a pair of comfortable walking shoes, maybe a hoodie for cool nights and a swimsuit would do."

"I packed those…. And a little bit more."

"So I see."

The contents of his closet could fit in those bags, but Nate decided to give her a break. After all, he'd been around enough women to know they had a whole different definition for the word *essentials*.

She reached for the smallest bag. It had wheels, not that they would do much good on the sand. "Sorry to be an imposition."

An interesting choice of words, to be sure.

"Where are you staying?" he asked.

Her expression brightened. "I'd hoped to rent the

cottage Gran and I always stayed in at your parents' resort."

"My parents are gone."

"Gone?" She looked alarmed.

"Retired," he clarified. "They moved to Florida four years ago." Just after he'd returned to the island from a job at one of the swankiest hotels in Chicago.

"The resort?"

Normally, it would give Nate great satisfaction to claim ownership and to admit that he'd expanded the place considerably since taking over. But this was *Princess* Hollyn Saldani. He doubted she would be impressed.

"I'm the owner now."

"Oh." One syllable that told him how enthused she was, but he'd give her this, she rallied fast. "I was hoping to find a place available."

"Sorry." He shook his head slowly, not sure whether he was relieved or disappointed. "We're all booked up at the moment. In fact, I don't know that there's a vacancy anywhere on the island until after the Fourth of July."

Usually, given how far north the island was, its resorts weren't full with patrons until after Independence Day. But this year, warm weather had come early and people from downstate were willing to make the drive and then the short ferry trip from Michigan's upper peninsula to the island.

"I wasn't thinking. I should have made arrangements ahead of time," she murmured. "Do you suppose there are any homes for rent on the island? I'd love to be on the water, of course, but I'll take what I can get at this point. Beggars can't be choosers."

It was an interesting statement coming from a woman who was next in line to the throne of her own kingdom.

"I don't know of anything offhand. You can check, but given the time of day and the storm, my guess is that most places are closed for the night." He snorted. "You know the island. Sidewalks pretty much roll up after eight o'clock."

He imagined she'd grown accustomed to glitzy, late-night parties with exclusive guest lists and the finest gourmet cuisine. Yet she didn't seem bothered by the prospect of no real nightlife here.

Her smile was nostalgic, damned near fond, when she replied, "Yes, I remember."

Was that *really* why she'd come?

Sure, she'd told him she needed to get away, but weren't there all sorts of fancy spas in Europe—and America, for that matter—more likely to fit the bill for a royal retreat than an out-of-the-way island that catered to the needs of middle-class tourists seeking good fishing, great scenery and a slower pace?

Hank reached them then, toting the last of her bags.

"Don't worry, miss. Nate's house has plenty of room. You can stay there at least for tonight." He glanced at Nate for corroboration.

What else could Nate do but nod? The quiet evening at home he'd envisioned just an hour ago now included two overnight guests. He knew from previous experience that Hank snored like a drunken sailor. Nate also knew that it was Holly who would keep him awake this night.

CHAPTER TWO

HOLLY wasn't sure what to do since Nate's invitation was begrudging at best.

That hurt. Not that she'd expected him to greet her with arms wide open. In fact, she hadn't been expecting to see him at all. She remembered how determined he'd been to leave the island for big-city living. But his displeasure right now was palpable, even if, for just a moment when they'd wound up sitting in the lake, he'd reminded her of the handsome young man who'd made her teenage pulse race with a simple smile.

As tempting as it was to turn down his offer, she had to be pragmatic. As she recalled, the island had a finite number of accommodations available. She would be lucky to find anything else on such short notice, so she followed him and the pilot up the beach.

Tomorrow, she could return to the mainland if need be. Tonight, she needed a place to stay. Jet lag was catching up with her. And that short flight over from the mainland had left her with white knuckles and a queasy stomach. In hindsight, she shouldn't have chanced it, especially this late in the day, with no firm reservation and a storm blowing in. She'd not only risked her life, but also the life of the pilot. A fact Nate had been only too happy to point out. Despite what he must think, it wasn't like Holly to be so thoughtless. But as with everything the past several days, desperation had her acting out of character.

Her hasty plan's imperfections were glaringly obvious now. She should have been more thorough in her arrangements before packing her bags and jetting across the Atlantic. That much was clear now. What had been as transparent as glass less than forty-eight hours ago was that she had to get away.

She caught up to Nate and glanced sideways at his stern profile. He wasn't exactly glad to see her. But it was her own emotions that gave her pause. She wasn't sure how she felt about seeing him again.

Once upon a time, she'd thought… Mentally, she shook her head. It was foolish to recall those dreams. They'd been unrealistic then. Now, they were unfathomable. Once again, she felt the grip of destiny tighten around her like a vise. There was no escaping it. Not completely, anyway, even if she hoped to find respite for a few days or a week. Holly groaned.

She didn't expect it to be heard over the wind, but Nate turned and asked, "Something wrong?"

"No."

"No?" His brows rose.

His wry expression and disbelieving tone came as a bit of a surprise. Back home no one would have dared to question her—well, except for her mother, who browbeat Holly regularly over the most minute of things. Holly needed to be perfect. Or at least give the illusion of perfection at all times. Interestingly, coming from

Nate, she rather enjoyed it. She'd much rather he treated her as an equal, even one with whom he was angry.

They reached the house, a cedar-sided bungalow that she remembered from her visits to the island as a girl. Back then, he'd lived in it with his parents, and she'd always been welcome inside for a bite to eat or to watch the telly on a rainy afternoon. His mother, she recalled, had been amazingly tolerant of such things as sandy feet and soggy swimsuits.

From the outside, the place looked much the same except for a newer and larger deck that wrapped around to the side entrance. Hank beat them up the steps and shucked off his shoes before opening the squeaky-hinged screen door and going in. That left Holly and Nate standing on either side of the welcome mat.

Nothing about Nate's demeanor at the moment was very welcoming.

"This is too much of an imposition," she began. It definitely was too much of something.

"It's fine," Nate insisted. "No big deal." He toed off his soggy shoes and pushed them against the side of the house next to Hank's battered sneakers.

"I'll pay—"

"It's only one night, Holly...Hollyn...Princess...." He shoved his damp hair back from his forehead in agitation. "What am I supposed to call you?"

From his tone, she imagined he already had a pet name or two in mind. "Holly is fine."

She *wanted* to be just Holly again. That was, after all, why she'd made this rash trip in the first place.

He looked doubtful, but nodded. "I insist you stay, all right? As my guest."

His words might have been more reassuring had they not been issued through clenched teeth. But any retort she might have offered was lost when he reached for the back of his damp T-shirt and pulled it over his head.

Holly swallowed hard, but that didn't keep her mouth from watering. As a teenage girl, she'd admired Nate's form. He'd been wiry then, lean and several inches shorter than the six foot three she judged him to be now. He'd shot up, filled out. Quite obviously, he worked out. A sculpted abdomen such as his was no happy accident of genetics.

"Your turn."

His words startled her. She felt her cheeks grow warm, though it wasn't only embarrassment that caused the building heat.

"I beg your pardon?"

"Your shoes. If you wouldn't mind, take them off out here."

Half of his mouth crooked into a wry smile as he draped his shirt over the banister. He was enjoying her discomfort, enjoying that she was as off balance now as he'd been while wading through the surf earlier.

Holly glanced down at her feet. The shoes he'd tried to spare damage with his chivalrous offer to carry her ashore were not only wet, but also covered in sand and other natural debris from their trek over the beach.

"Your mother never minded the sand."

"She did, but she was too polite to say so. Regardless, since I clean the place now, I make the rules."

"Right." Envisioning him with a mop in one hand and a feather duster in the other helped take some of the sting out of his words.

She did as Nate asked and padded inside behind him.

Hank already had made himself at home on the couch in front of the television. His stocking feet were propped up on the coffee table, a long-necked brown bottle was in one hand and the remote control was in the other. A baseball game was on. Holly didn't know much about the American pastime, but she'd always enjoyed listening to the announcers explaining what was going on. Their voices were so soothing, spiking here and there as warranted by a key play. The sound made her nostalgic. As did the house, even though the furnishings now were more masculine and sparse than the fussy decor that had obviously been Mrs. Matthews's taste.

Gone were the knickknacks and kitschy collections that had filled two curios cabinets. Gone was the mauve-and-blue color scheme, the lace curtains and flowered camelback sofa. Now the main living area sported top-of-the-line electronics, a brown leather sectional and some surprisingly high-quality pieces of artwork, all of them seascapes.

Nate must have noticed the direction of her gaze. "Rupert Lengard," he said, supplying the name of the artist. "I wish I could say they're originals, but they're limited edition prints."

"They're stunning." She pointed to one. "That looks like that little island we used to take the canoe out to."

They'd pretended to be castaways and had even tried to erect a tree house à la the Swiss Family Robinson. But getting building supplies over in the canoe had proved too much of a hassle. They'd made do with a lean-to crafted from sticks and cedar boughs.

"Horn Island," Nate said. "Lengard spent a couple summers on Heart and the surrounding islands. All of the prints I bought are local scenes."

She admired the subject matter as much as the artist's obvious skill. "I'll have to see about getting some of them for home."

"His stuff is not exactly on par with Poussin or Renoir."

Apparently, Nate thought only work of old-world masters would suit her sensibilities. Holly decided to set him straight. "My tastes run a little more modern than that. Like you, I buy art, whether prints or originals, because I like it, not because of the value an insurance appraiser might put on it."

Nate nodded curtly. It sounded like he might have said, "Touché."

But he was already turning away and heading over to the couch.

"Anything else I can get you, Hank?" Nate asked dryly.

The other man either missed the sarcasm or chose to ignore it. "You got anything to munch on? Like nachos maybe?"

Holly hid her grin.

"You want nachos?"

Hank dragged his gaze from the television. His expression was hopeful. "Yeah."

"They sell them down at the Fishing Hole Tavern. Bring back an order for me, too, while you're at it," Nate replied before using his shin to knock the other man's feet off the table. To Holly, he said, "Follow me. I'll show you to your room."

He went back to grab her bags from their spot by the door and started for the stairs. At the top, he turned right and continued to the room at the end of the hall.

She stood uncertainly at the threshold after he entered. "But th-this is your room."

And it was just as she recalled it, though she hadn't spent much time in it as a girl. His parents wouldn't have allowed that, especially once she and Nate were teenagers.

Even though they were both adults now, she felt awkward and oddly aware. She blamed it on the fact that he was shirtless and she was…tired. Really, really tired.

"Not anymore. I have the master these days. After my folks moved out I did a little renovation work and added an en suite bathroom, so the one in the hall is all yours." His brows rose in humor. "Well, yours and Hank's. You'll have to share."

He set down her bags and crossed to open the window a few inches. He repeated the process for the one on the opposite wall. The wind rushed inside, ruffling the edges of the curtains and bringing with it the mingled scents of cedar trees and wood smoke. She recalled that earthy scent from those summers long past. Nostalgia had her smiling. A lot of fireplaces would be in use tonight if the temperature outside continued to drop. Her gaze veered to Nate and her smile disappeared. Holly wasn't feeling chilled. Quite the opposite. Even wearing wet clothes, all it took was an eyeful of the taut muscles that defined Nate's shoulders, and she had to fight the urge to fan herself.

He turned around to find her studying him. God only knew what her expression revealed. He was one of the few people around whom she had ever been herself, which was ironic, she realized now, since he hadn't known her actual identity.

She folded her hands at her waist, cleared her throat and said the first thing she could think of. "It's windy outside."

"The storm."

"Yes. The storm."

They eyed one another for a moment longer. "You can close the windows in a minute. Just give the place a chance to air out. It's a little stuffy in here. This room doesn't get much use."

A little stuffy? She could hardly breathe. But that had nothing do with stagnant air. It had everything to do with the way he was looking at her. She saw speculation in his gaze and, she thought, guarded interest. It dawned on Holly then that she must look a fright. Her soggy clothes were molded to her body, her makeup was nonexistent, and her hair... She reached up to run a hand through it only to have her fingers tangle in the snarls.

She pulled her hand free and managed to say, "It's fine."

He didn't appear convinced. In fact, he was shaking his head. "You know, the more I think of it, you belong in the master suite. You'd definitely be more comfortable in there."

He reached for her bags. She put out a hand to stop him. "Don't be silly. This is fine," she said again.

"It's not up to the standards you're used to," he said quietly.

"I'm not picky, Nathaniel." She went with his full name, hoping to get a rise out of him.

His gaze connected with hers. "You're a princess."

Holly folded her arms over her chest and the ache she felt building there. "You say it like it's some sort of disease."

"I'll apologize for that. But the fact remains, you're used to better than…this." He glanced around as if seeing the room for the first time. Clearly, he found it lacking. His gaze returned to her. "You're used to better than anything I have to offer, for that matter."

"Nate."

Before she could protest further, he was at the door, his hand on the knob. This time, his gaze didn't quite meet hers. "I'll leave you to freshen up. We can discuss your accommodations later."

The door closed. Holly stared at the scratched wood for a long time afterward. What had just happened? In the span of the past half hour, he'd gone from being smug and a little indignant to being uncomfortable and, unless she missed her guess, embarrassed. That wasn't the Nathaniel Matthews she remembered. He'd been fearless, formidable and a touch arrogant at times.

He'd been determined to take on the world. He'd seen no limit to the possibilities life had to offer him. She'd admired his conviction that he could be anything, do anything, go anywhere and answer to no one but himself. For a while, Holly had even begun to think like he did. Then she'd returned to Morenci, after what turned out to be her last summer on the island, and her mother had set her straight.

"You're no longer a child, Hollyn. You'll turn sixteen soon. It's time for you to fully embrace your royal responsibilities. You're a princess. You need to start acting like one at all times."

Her girlhood dreams had been dashed.

What, she wondered now, had made Nate change his plans? Or was it simply a case of growing up? After all, he'd been a boy when she'd known him.

Well, one thing was clear. The man who'd just closed the door was a stranger, even if so many things about him seemed familiar.

Nate changed into dry clothes and headed downstairs. In the kitchen, he pulled a fresh bottle of beer from the fridge, uncapped it and took a liberal swig.

God! What must she think of him? He probably came off as backward and irascible. He hadn't exactly rolled out the welcome mat upon learning she was Hank's passenger.

Welcome mat. He grunted now and took another gulp of beer. She was used to red carpets, state dinners and probably parades held in her honor. He'd even botched his attempt to carry her to shore. Still, she'd laughed. And in that moment he'd glimpsed the girl she'd been. The girl who at first had been his fishing buddy and who, later, when he was teenager, had kept him awake and confused on hot summer nights.

Now she was a woman. A beautiful woman. Staying under his roof. And, even though his parents were a couple thousand miles away enjoying their retirement and unable to act as chaperones, Holly was as off-limits as she'd been when his hormones had been raging as a teen. Hank sauntered into the kitchen then. They did have a chaperone after all. Nate couldn't make up his mind whether to be grateful or not.

"Where's Holly?" The other man's beer was empty. He helped himself to a fresh one from the fridge, shooting the cap in the direction of the trash can in the corner.

"Upstairs, probably getting out of her wet clothes." It was the wrong thing to say, Nate decided, when his imagination kicked into overdrive.

"I didn't realize you two knew one another. She didn't mention it on the flight over."

"We don't. Well, not really." Nate shrugged. Since Hank was waiting for more of an explanation, he added, "We spent several summers together when we were kids. It's been years since I last saw her."

That wasn't quite true since all he'd had to do in the interim was pick up a magazine or turn on the television and more times than not there was a feature on Morenci's future monarch. But then his Holly and Hollyn Saldani had always seemed like separate people to him. Until today. Today he was having a hard time keeping them straight.

"She looks familiar," Hank was saying.

Nate chose not to reveal Holly's secret. It was only because the pilot had the loosest lips in three counties, he told himself, and she'd already made it clear she'd come here to get away from the public eye. Besides, the last thing Nate wanted was for his peaceful little island to be overrun with journalists and paparazzi and royal gawkers. That would be bad for business.

Liar, a voice whispered. He ignored it. On a shrug, he replied, "I know. She has one of those faces."

Hank seemed satisfied with the answer, but he was still curious. "Where's she from? I know she's not American. She has an accent of some sort even though she speaks really good English."

Again, rather than lie outright, Nate chose to be vague. "Abroad somewhere. But some of her family vacationed in these parts."

He frowned after saying so. Had it really been her grandmother that she'd come to the island with? Or had the older woman been some sort of governess? He still had so many questions about the woman who had been his first love…and a total stranger.

The laid-back pilot appeared to accept the explanations Nate offered. Of course, Hank was easy to please. He had free, ice-cold beer, a place to sleep for the night and cable television, assuming the storm didn't knock it out.

Nate thought that was the end of their discussion of Holly, until the guy commented, "She sure is a pretty thing."

Nate swigged his beer and mumbled a response.

"And generous." Hank grinned. "You wouldn't believe what she paid me to fly her here."

"You were risking your life," Nate reminded him dryly.

The other man laughed loudly. "Maybe so, but neither of my ex-wives thought my life was worth that much."

The other man's attitude rubbed Nate the wrong way. "Well, it's easy to be generous when you've done nothing to earn the money in your wallet."

"She's loaded?"

Nate shrugged. "Her family's well-to-do. Old money." Really old money and a pedigree that could be traced back through the generations.

"Is she single?"

His gut clenched. "Far as I know." Though rumors were circulating in the media that an engagement was in her future. The first time Nate had heard them aired on a news program he'd not just been angry, he'd felt a little sick to his stomach. Neither reaction made sense. Nor did his reaction upon seeing her today.

"Imagine that. Pretty, single and rich." The other man pushed back his mop of unkempt salt-and-pepper hair. "Think I stand a chance?"

"Sorry, pal." Nate clinked the neck of his beer bottle against the one in Hank's hand in seeming commiseration. "I think she's out of your league."

Hank didn't appear overly troubled by the assessment. "What about yours?"

"Definitely."

Nate studied the bottle's label after he said it. He'd done all right for himself in life. In fact, he was quite pleased by how far he'd come.

After high school graduation, he'd gone on to college. Nothing Ivy League, but his grades had been good enough to get him into a Big Ten school. He'd made the dean's list all four years at the University of Michigan. After earning a bachelor's degree, he'd moved to Chicago and had taken a management position at one of the hotels on the Miracle Mile.

His parents had been proud of him, though their unspoken disappointment that he hadn't wanted to take over the family resort had been clear. But they'd given him space and offered him choices. And after four years in the Windy City, he realized how much he missed the slow pace of life on the island. He missed the quiet mornings and spectacular sunrises on Lake Huron. When he'd packed up his belongings and left the island, he'd been so sure he wanted big-city living—the decadent nightlife, the pricey condo overlooking Navy Pier, the designer-label clothes and gourmet restaurants.

Everything had been great for a while, even if he'd still felt more like a tourist than a resident. He'd enjoyed making a name for himself. He'd enjoyed hearing the praise from his boss, and the predictions from corporate that he would be another rung up the ladder soon, maybe even managing a hotel of his own.

Then his parents had announced their retirement and their plans to sell Haven Resort & Marina. They wanted to move south to warmer climes. Nate had been pole-axed. Oh, he'd expected them to retire at some point. It wasn't as if they hadn't talked about it over the years. And he'd long known they had their eye on a condo on Florida's Gulf Coast. The winters on the island could be brutal and long, especially on achy, aging joints. But talking and doing were two different things.

Confronted by reality, he'd come to a couple of conclusions. One, he didn't want to live in Chicago. It was a great city, full of energy and excitement, but it wasn't for him. Not long-term, anyway. And two, he didn't want anyone but him to own the resort that his grandparents had started from nothing during the 1950s.

So, he'd gone home, not with his tail tucked between his legs, but confident that he'd made the right decision. He'd never regretted coming back. In fact, he'd been

damned pleased with the changes he'd made, and those
he continued to implement to bring the property up-to-
date so that it would appeal to the needs of a new generation of tourists. The marina and outbuildings were
in good shape. And he was renovating the cottages as
money permitted. He'd completed half of them already,
doing much of the work himself in the off-season. Gone
were the mismatched furnishings and bedding, the ancient appliances and worn vinyl flooring. What he'd
replaced them with weren't high-end, but they were
durable, fresh, contemporary and comfortable. And the
cottages now sported neutral color schemes and even
some artwork from a local woman who specialized in
nature views. They weren't as good as the ones captured
by Lengard, but they complemented the decor and had
helped bring some commissions the young artist's way.

Last year he'd added Wi-Fi and cable television, and
he'd partnered with a local couple to offer guided hikes
through the huge swath of federally owned land on the
northern tip of the island that was home to all sorts of
wildlife, including a couple of endangered bird species.
In the spring, when the morel mushroom hunters came,
he'd joined forces with one of the island's restaurants
for cooking demonstrations. In addition to families and
fishermen, his resort now appealed to naturalists and
others embracing a greener lifestyle.

Winters were still pretty quiet. Only the heartiest
of tourists ventured north during that time of year. But
already he was making plans to attract more snowsho-
ers, cross-country skiers and snowmobilers, which was
why he had purchased another dozen acres of land just

beyond what he owned now with plans to add trails and maybe even a few more cabins down the road.

His parents were impressed with the changes he'd made, even though he'd suggested most of them while they still owned the place. But the status quo had been good enough for them. He'd understood and accepted that. But within days of the transfer in ownership, he'd rolled up his sleeves and begun the transformation.

Now, business was up. Not just for his resort, but for other establishments on the island, thanks to a joint marketing campaign that he'd spearheaded. The head of the local chamber of commerce hadn't been pleased, since Nate basically had gone around Victor Montague's back. But everyone else was happy with the results.

Yes, he was proud of what he'd accomplished. Proud of what he'd made not only of the resort, but also of his life. Which was why it galled him to find himself glancing around his kitchen, another of his renovation projects, and wondering what Holly thought of his quaint home and simple life.

"Nate?" Hank gazed at him quizzically.

After another swig of beer, he muttered, "Definitely, she's out of my league."

Holly stood at the base of the steps. She hadn't intended to eavesdrop on Nate's conversation with Hank, but it was hard not to hear the men. The house was small. Their voices carried.

Out of his league?

She supposed she could understand how Nate would think that. He wasn't the first person, man or woman, who had acted as if she were made of priceless spun glass. A number of her childhood friends had become overly deferential and awkward around her once they had finally grasped her status as their future monarch. She recalled how isolated it had made her feel. How utterly lonely.

"That's just the way it is," her mother had told her matter-of-factly when she complained. "They treat you differently because you are different. You're special, Hollyn."

Holly hadn't wanted to be "special." She'd wanted friends. True friends who wouldn't purposely lose at board games or let her pick the movie every time they got together. Friends who would confide their secrets. Friends in whom she could confide hers and not risk having her private thoughts written up in the tabloids. That had happened when she was fourteen. She'd complained about an argument with her mother, who'd felt Holly was too young to wear makeup. The headline in the *Morenci Daily* two days later read: "Queen and her teen nearly come to blows over mascara."

Her mother had been livid. Holly had been crushed, and, hence forward, very, very careful.

After that, the closest she'd had to actual girlfriends were her cousins, Amelia and Emily. As the second and third in line for the throne behind Holly, they understood what it was like to be in the spotlight, photographed, quoted—or misquoted as the case may be—and constantly judged on their appearance and breeding as if they were entries in the Royal Kennel Club's annual dog show.

Yet, even with Amelia and Emily, the older they grew, the more she sensed a distance and a separation between them. And, yes, she could admit now, she'd noticed a certain amount of envy and bitterness that while Holly would have a prime place in Morenci's history books, their lives would be mere footnotes and largely forgotten.

Their emotional defection had hurt. But not as badly as overhearing Nate's assessment of her. He made her sound shallow, spoiled.

Spending money she hadn't earned?

As far as Holly was concerned, she was always "earning" her keep. Long ago, her life had ceased to be her own, if indeed it ever had been. She was public property. Her photograph was sold to the highest tabloid bidder, in addition to being plastered on everything from teacups, decorative plates and biscuit tins to T-shirts and tote bags that were then gobbled up by tourists.

She told herself the disappointment she felt about Nate's assessment of her was because she had so hoped to feel "normal" here. She had hoped to be treated as she had been treated as a girl coming to the island with her grandmother: Accepted for who she was rather than the crown she would someday wear.

A small sigh escaped. She was being foolish.

At least Nate hadn't told Hank the truth about her identity. If it meant letting the other man and the rest of the folks on the island think she was some snobby socialite eager for a taste of the simple life, so be it. Anonymity in itself was a gift. One that she hadn't enjoyed in more than a decade.

The men came out of the kitchen, both of them stopping with almost comedic abruptness when they spied her. Nate looked guilty, his gaze cutting away a moment before returning to hers. No doubt, he was wondering how much she'd overheard.

Hank, however, was grinning broadly.

"Hey, there, miss. I see you're none the worse for wear after your unexpected dip in the lake." He elbowed Nate in the ribs.

Nate flushed. So did she. Holly hardly looked her best. She'd changed into dry clothes, but they were wrinkled from their time spent in her bag. And while she'd combed the tangles out of her hair, it was still wet. She'd remembered a blow dryer in her hasty packing job, but she hadn't thought to bring an adapter. And, of course, she smelled of lake water.

She fiddled with the ends of her hair.

"I wanted to take a shower, but I'm afraid I couldn't figure out how to work the faucet so that the spray would come out."

"It's finicky," Nate said. "I should have thought to show you before coming downstairs."

"That's all right."

"I can show you now."

"Thank you. Oh, and I wasn't sure what to do with my wet things." She'd hung them over the shower curtain in the bathroom.

"I can toss them in the dryer."

She nibbled the inside of her cheek. The pants and jacket were both made of linen. The blouse was silk. "I don't suppose the island has a dry cleaners?"

Nate shook his head.

"The town on the mainland does," Hank supplied. "It's right next to the grocery store. I can take them with me when I fly back tomorrow and drop them off for you."

"Oh, that's all right. I don't want to be a bother." She added an appreciative smile.

"It's no trouble. None at all," he insisted.

This was exactly the sort of deferential treatment she was used to…and did not want. "I'll think about it," she answered diplomatically.

"Come on. I'll show you how to work the shower," Nate said, as if sensing her unease.

She followed him back up the stairs to the bathroom, hurriedly snatching a pair of white silk panties and a delicate lace-edged bra from the curtain rod and hiding them behind her back.

Nate coughed. They both smiled uncomfortably.

"Um, about the shower. You, uh, turn this knob." He demonstrated as he instructed. "The farther right you turn it, the hotter it becomes." She was thinking something on the cool side. "You'll probably want it somewhere in the middle. Then you flip this little lever on the side."

Again, he demonstrated. The water sprayed out from the showerhead. Small beads of it ricocheted off the tiled surround and landed on his forearm. The hair there was bleached as light as some of the streaks on his head, alluding to his time spent in the sun. Indeed, he had a good tan going. In comparison, Holly was ridiculously pale. It had been that way when they were kids, too, although by the end of her visit, she'd always managed to look like a regular beachcomber—or a commoner, as her mother complained.

No doubt Olivia had worked herself into a good fit

by now, despite the note of explanation that Henry had delivered on Holly's behalf. She felt a little guilty, a little queasy. And a lot rebellious, because she wasn't going to return for at least a week. Maybe longer. And even though her mother considered her engagement to Phillip a done deal, Holly was far from convinced.

Nate turned off the shower and stepped back. She glanced away.

"Everything okay?"

She pushed away all thoughts of her mother, Phillip and the responsibilities waiting for her upon her return. She was free now.

"I didn't see the lever," she said quietly.

"No one does. It's old-fashioned, which is why I had them all replaced in the cottages when I took over. Saved me or whoever else was manning the front desk at the marina office a lot of phone calls." He tucked his hands into his pockets. "I haven't gotten around to this one yet."

"I'm sure it hasn't been a priority."

"Not exactly," he agreed. "I've put most of my time and resources into the cottages."

"Walking up from the beach, it looked like there were more of those than there used to be."

He nodded. "I was always after Dad to expand, but he said he and Mom had enough to keep them busy with what they had."

"I liked your parents." She smiled, enveloped in simple and homey memories so unlike the majority of those from her childhood. That, too, she realized now, was part of the reason she'd come here. Simplicity. Her complicated, overrun life yearned for it. "They always made feel at home when I stopped over from my grandmother's cottage, even when they had work to do and guests to attend to."

"They liked you, too. They were always after me to be as polite as you were."

They both laughed. Then sobered. Silence stretched. For a moment, given the way he was watching her, she thought he might stroke her cheek. He'd raised his hand. But it fell away and he blurted out, "Fresh towels."

Holly blinked.

"Um, for your shower. They're in the cabinet next to the sink. Washcloths, too."

"Right."

"One more thing, Holly."

She nodded, feeling ridiculously expectant as she waited for him to continue.

"Don't flush the toilet right before you get in the shower or you'll wind up scalded." He cleared his throat. His cheeks grew pink. "Another of those things I haven't gotten around to updating."

CHAPTER THREE

THE storm was in full swing by the time Holly came downstairs an hour later. Rain pelted the windows and lightning illuminated the inky sky, followed by loud crashes of thunder that shook the home's foundation.

It was a spectacle to behold, by turns frightening and thrilling. Even so, Hank was sprawled out on the couch, his snores competing with the storm. She envied the man's ability to fall asleep so easily. Even on perfectly quiet nights, Holly seldom slept soundly. She usually had too much going through her mind to relax and simply drift off. She'd tried the old remedies, such as counting sheep and listening to soothing music. Neither had much effect. Meditation sometimes worked. As did reading really, really boring accounts of her country's gross domestic product.

The royal physician blamed her insomnia on anxiety and had prescribed pills that she rarely took. They made her too groggy the next day, as if she were walking through a fog. She preferred to have her wits about her, even if it meant slumbering off sometimes during a dinner party. A picture of her with her eyes closed and her chin resting on her chest had graced the front page of a newspaper not long ago.

"This is exactly the kind of publicity you need to avoid," her mother had warned. "Royal or not, the press can turn public sentiment against you in a heartbeat."

Even so, Holly had been reluctant to take the pills. Still, she wondered if she would come to regret not bringing them with her for this trip.

Nate stood at the glass door that opened to the deck, one hand in the front pocket of a pair of wrinkled cargo shorts, the other holding a beer. He'd taken a shower. She'd heard the water in his bathroom running not long after she'd shut off the water in the guest bath. His hair was still wet. He wore it on the long side, though not as long as he had as a boy. Back then, it had nearly brushed his shoulders. Now, it just grazed his collar. The color had gotten darker over the years. It bordered on brown, but the sun had left its mark with the kind of highlights that women—and some men—spent vast sums of money at salons hoping to achieve. She couldn't imagine him sitting still long enough to let a stylist work her magic.

"It's impolite to stare, you know."

Too late she realized that he'd been watching her reflection in the glass.

"Yes. It is. I apologize."

She crossed to where he stood. Just as she reached his side, a bolt of lightning zigzagged across the sky, followed closely by a deafening boom. She jumped. Nate's arm shot out, encircling her waist. Then Hank snorted and they broke apart, both of them turning to watch the pilot as he stirred, but only enough to roll over on the couch. He didn't wake.

"He sleeps like the dead," Nate remarked, taking a pull of his beer. He seemed to remember his manners then. "Can I get you something to drink?"

A cup of freshly brewed tea would have been lovely. And way too much trouble. She nodded toward the beverage in his hand. "A beer, please."

His brows arched in doubt. "A beer?"

"That is what you're drinking."

"Uh-huh. It's a beer." He stated the obvious, clearly expecting her to change her mind.

"Then that's what I'll have. Please."

"Okay," he said, sounding none too convinced. But he went to the kitchen. He returned a moment later with a second long-necked bottle. Before handing it to her, he paused. "I'll get you a glass."

"No need. I can drink out of a bottle." Before he could protest, she took a sip.

This American beer was less robust than the ales favored in her country, but she liked the taste. Even more, she liked the seeming normalcy of drinking a beer from a bottle and watching a storm roll over the big lake.

"I'd forgotten how fierce the thunderstorms here can be."

"They pack a lot of punch," he agreed. "It has to do with the water. They tend to pick up steam moving over the Great Lakes. The good news is they usually pass as quickly as they come."

"I remember. Tomorrow, when we wake up, it will be like it never happened," she murmured.

But Nate was shaking his head. "There will be plenty of fallout. And I'll be out there cleaning up the debris. Everything has consequences, Holly."

"Are we still talking about the storm?"

He shrugged.

"You're angry with me." She said it as a statement rather than a question.

"Angry?" The corners of his mouth turned down in denial. "Why would I be angry? I mean, who am I to be angry?"

"Don't." She plucked at the edges of the label on the beer bottle. "I wanted to tell you who I was, Nate."

"But you didn't." Despite his claim that he wasn't angry, it was obvious in his tone.

"No. I didn't."

"Why?"

She sucked in a breath, memories of those carefree summers making her want to sigh. At last, she said, "I didn't want things to change. I wanted to be just Holly."

"You were never just Holly." His tone was as low and ominous as the storm.

"I was," she insisted. "Here, on this island, for all of those blissful summers, I was just Holly. I can't tell you how much I looked forward to coming to Heart each year. I started counting down the days just after the New Year. I didn't have any obligations when I was here. This was every bit the haven your resort's name proclaims it to be."

But Nate was shaking his head. "It was a fantasy," he insisted.

"All right." She wouldn't parse words. "It was a fantasy. But I needed it, Nate. Desperately."

She still did. He didn't know what it was like. How utterly on display she'd always felt back in her country. So little had been private, especially since her mother had insisted on granting the media unprecedented access.

Holly's first birthday? The cameras had been rolling, the entire party nationally televised so that everyone in Morenci could ooh and aah as the little princess messily gobbled up cake, opened her presents and then toddled on shaky legs around the palace garden. Sure, it had served as a fundraiser for a leading birth-defects charity, but still, it had set the tone. Every birthday, every milestone after that, had been open to the public via the media.

It was tiring to be smiling for the cameras at all times. It left very little room for one to be oneself. Sometimes, Holly felt like a fraud. She wasn't always happy or poised or eager to share her attention with whomever was demanding it.

Heaven help her, but sometimes she wanted to be selfish and irritable, maybe stamp her feet in protest or outrage or just because she was having a bad day. Perhaps even raise her voice or slam a door or break a dish. As if… She nearly laughed, just thinking of how outrageous such things would be. She hadn't been allowed the luxury of a tantrum.

But then, a couple of weeks ago, the idea of packing her bags and taking off unannounced had seemed outrageous and undoable. Perhaps there was hope for her after all.

Holly glanced at Nate. Given his rigid posture, she half expected him to disagree. Instead, he nodded slowly.

"I guess I can understand that."

"You can?"

He turned to face her. "After college, I worked in a very upscale hotel in Chicago. We catered to a lot of celebrity clientele. I know actors and rock stars aren't quite the same as royalty."

"Close enough," she murmured.

"Yeah. Well, I realized pretty quickly that their lifestyle wasn't always as glamorous as it seemed to much of their adoring public."

"It's not," she agreed softly. She scratched at the bottle's label again with one of her nails and frowned. "Everyone thinks they know you."

He turned. "I didn't know you at all."

"Nate—"

He was already facing the window again as he added, "Anyway, with all those pushy managers, obsessed fans and paparazzi trying to get to them twenty-four seven, I figured out pretty quickly that it's got to be annoying."

"There's very little privacy." Thinking again of her mother's open-palace-door policy, she added, "Very little."

"Yet you managed it for five summers."

Her lips curved at the memories.

"You know, running around in shorts and bathing suits, with my hair pulled into crooked pigtails, I didn't look very much like a princess. I think that's why I got away with it." She laughed ruefully. "Now, had I been wearing my royal tiara…"

As jokes went, it fell abominably flat. Nate wasn't amused. Far from it, if his tone were any indication.

"I felt like an idiot for not figuring it out. Holly… Hollyn." A snort escaped as he glanced her way. He raised his beer, took a sip. His gaze still on her, he said, "You must have thought I was pretty dense, especially those last couple of summers."

"No, Nate. Never. Honestly. I thought you were…" *Perfect. Gorgeous. My one true love.* She felt herself blush.

He apparently thought he had his answer. "You did."

"No. You were…my best friend."

Even before the words were out, Holly was calling herself a liar. He'd been so much more than that. Of course, she'd been fifteen years old at the time, flush with hormones and full of girlish fantasies about the future she and Nate would have together. A future that could never be.

"I missed you, Nate."

Her whispered words surprised them both.

It was a moment before he said, "That first summer you didn't show up on Heart, I all but haunted the cabin where you used to stay with your grandmother. I was sure you were just late. But guest after guest arrived and none of them was you. My parents finally started telling me in advance who had rented the place. It was getting embarrassing, I guess."

Beyond wryness, was that pain she heard in his

voice? It was selfish of her to hope so. Nonetheless, she did, recalling how she'd begged her mother to let her go and, then, begged her grandmother to intervene again.

"I can't, my girl," the older woman had told her. "It's time for you to accept your destiny. But I hope you'll never forget who you really are."

How ironic that all these years later, Holly still wasn't sure.

"So, was she really your grandmother? For a while, after I found out the truth, I thought maybe she was just another part of your cover."

"No." Her smile was fond. "She was really my gran."

"Your mother's mom," he guessed. "Now that I think of it, she had a bit of a Texas accent."

"As does my own mother, when she allows it to slip. Which is rare." Holly frowned. "She put her past behind her." Feeling disloyal, Holly added, "She wasn't exactly accepted in Morenci at first, despite her position." Every misstep and gaffe had been fodder for the gossip mill. The old guard was appalled that a Texas beauty queen had snagged their bachelor king.

"That must have been difficult for her."

"It was." It also was the reason Holly had given her mother as much free rein with her life as she had. She knew how hard Olivia had tried to fit in. How much she had sacrificed to belong. She was finally getting the respect she deserved. But it had come after years of scrutiny and criticism.

"So, your mother wanted you to come here."

Holly's laughter erupted. "Good heavens, no." She

took another sip of beer and composed herself. "It was Gran's idea. She was determined that I should know and appreciate my American roots. A friend of hers came to the island one summer, told her how wonderfully secluded it was. She rented the cottage under an alias and set the plans in motion. Her objective was that I would have as normal a childhood as could be had under the circumstances."

"Hard to fault her for that."

"My mother did," Holly replied dryly. "Believe me, it was a regular argument between the two of them."

"A battle royale?"

She sent him a black look.

"Sorry." He sipped his own beer. "So, what about your father? What did he think of your summers abroad?"

Her father? King Franco was a busy man. Sometimes she wondered if he remembered he had a daughter. She'd long felt like a disappointment.

"My father didn't think them necessary. After all, being royal is all he's ever known. But he didn't really care one way or another." She swallowed, determined to keep her tone nonchalant. "My being born female was a bit of a letdown, especially since he and my mother had no other children."

"But you're still the heir to the throne, right?"

"Yes."

"So?"

Holly shrugged. "He wanted a son." A fact that had caused Olivia no small amount of anxiety and dismay.

Her mother had already felt her new country found her lacking. When she failed to produce a male heir, well…

"I'm glad he didn't get his way."

Her cheeks grew warm. Even the storm's fury faded into the background as they eyed one another. Nate lifted a hand, stroked her cheek with his knuckles. The touch was light and brief. Her body's response was neither. And that was before his head tipped down and his lips brushed hers.

They'd kissed before. Her last summer on the island. A lifetime ago. The moment remained enshrined in her memory. It had been her first real kiss. Afterward, her heart had hammered and her breath had hitched.

"I love you."

The words had slipped out, soft and almost inaudible. But Nate had gathered her close and kissed her again, this time with more urgency. Even so, that long-ago kiss was nothing like this one, even if it held much of the same desperate yearning.

She'd never known this kind of need. It was every bit as brash and demanding as the storm battering the island. As such, it refused to be denied. She wound her arms tighter around Nate's neck, pulling their bodies together and giving in to the kind of passion that she'd only glimpsed in the past, and never with anyone but this man.

"Holly." Nate murmured her name.

His use of her nickname was enough to snap her back to the present. As much as she might wish things could be different, she was no longer an idealistic girl. She understood the futility of "if only," and so she ended things before they could progress too far.

Afterward, Nate pressed the cold base of his beer bottle against his forehead and closed his eyes.

"Some things get better with age," it sounded like he murmured.

She touched her lips. Indeed, they did.

"I wrote you a letter the first summer I didn't come. I wanted to explain why I wouldn't be here."

He lowered his hand, opened his eyes. "I never got a letter."

"That's because I didn't send it." It was folded up and tucked in her bureau drawer along with the other mementos of their summers together. Seashells, a picture of the first fish she'd caught, an old-fashioned glass cola bottle they'd found during a hike on the beach.

"Why?"

Because I was a coward. Because I was heartbroken. She sipped her beer, took her time swallowing.

"Because I didn't think you would understand."

"What I didn't understand was how you could just not return. Or write back. You never wrote back, Holly."

Guilt nipped hard as she recalled the letters Nate had written to her in care of the post office box her grandmother had set up. Gran had forwarded the letters faithfully, and Holly had read every one, her heart breaking anew when they'd finally stopped coming, although that was exactly what she'd expected to happen. What she told herself she wanted. Nate needed to move on with his life. Just as she was moving on with hers.

Hank snuffled loudly on the couch. Where the thunder hadn't roused him, the sound of his own snoring apparently did the trick. His eyelids flickered and he pulled himself to a sitting position, then scrubbed his face and offered a sheepish smile.

"Guess I drifted off." His gaze darted between the two of them. "Did I miss anything?"

"Just one hell of a storm," Nate said evenly before heading into the kitchen.

Holly waited until the weather settled down to call her parents. She had been gone nearly eighteen hours. Her father would be irritated by her disappearance. Her mother would be livid. A small part of her hoped they would also be worried. Instantly, she felt guilty. Of course, she didn't want them to worry. Besides, she was a grown woman. Wanting them to worry was childish, petty.

She sat on the edge of the bed and pulled out her cell phone. While she'd been in the shower, Nate must have been in her room. The window had been closed and the bed remade with fresh linens. A pale lavender coverlet was turned down, revealing floral sheets beneath. Leftovers from his parents, no doubt. The other ones would have been perfectly fine, but she appreciated his thoughtfulness. If only she could be sure it was thoughtfulness. Recalling the conversation she'd overheard earlier, she wondered if hospitality had been at the root of his actions, or embarrassment.

She's out of my league.

Long ago, Holly had come to terms with the fact that to some people—most people—she would always have a title before her name. Ultimately, that was why she hadn't been completely truthful with Nate when they were children.

When she'd started coming to the island at ten, her being a princess had been an afterthought in her mind. He was the son of northern Michigan resort owners. She was the daughter of European royalty. Later, she'd liked just a little too much that he saw her as a girl rather than, well, a goal. Even back then, the mothers of sons from around the kingdom had been busy trying to arrange meetings.

As if she hadn't felt conspicuous enough.

"Winning your favor would be quite a coup," Olivia had explained, when Holly had asked her mother about the fuss.

For the mothers or for the boys? she'd wondered. But Holly hadn't bothered to ask.

She frowned now. Not at the memories of awkward first dances and dinners, but at her phone. She wasn't getting a signal.

She was halfway down the stairs when Nate started up. They hadn't finished their earlier conversation; instead she'd taken the easy way out and retreated upstairs after Hank's untimely interruption.

They eyed one another warily now.

"Need something?" Nate asked.

"I was hoping to place a call to my parents, but my cell isn't receiving a signal."

"Only a couple of carriers work on the island and even then, service is spotty at best. You can use the phone in the kitchen," he offered.

It was on the tip of her tongue to remind him she would be phoning abroad and certain charges would apply. But since she'd already offended him once by offering to pay for her room, she remained mum. Somehow, she would find a way to compensate him.

"Thank you."

He nodded and started up. Two·steps past her he stopped. "Do your parents know where you are?"

"Not exactly." The note she'd had Henry give Olivia just said that Holly was safe and would be in touch with contact information.

"Does anyone?"

She offered a half smile. "You do."

He frowned. "This island is a good place to get away, Holly, but people here read newspapers and own televisions. We're not backward."

"I never said you were," she replied defensively.

"But you thought it."

She folded her arms. "You don't know what I think."

"You're right. Sorry." The apology turned empty when he said, "I don't know you well enough."

She swallowed, a little unnerved by how badly it hurt for him to say so. There was a time when she'd thought he was the only person on the planet who remotely got who she was.

Nate continued. "Look, all I'm saying is that even Hank thought you looked familiar and he's hardly the sort to pay attention to the news, much less the tabloids."

She lifted her chin a notch. "As you said earlier, I managed to hide in plain sight when I was a girl."

"Yeah, but as *you* said earlier, you were decked out in shorts and pigtails back then."

"I left my tiara home for this trip, too," she said dryly. "And I didn't pack a single ball gown. I think I can fit in. Before the flight over with Hank, a woman in town told me I looked like Princess Hollyn. We both laughed. After all, what would Princess Hollyn Saldani of Morenci be doing here?"

"It's not the French Riviera," he agreed on a drawl.

"No. It's far more appealing."

Her satisfaction at his surprise was short-lived.

"Never been there, so I wouldn't know." With a shrug, he continued up the steps.

CHAPTER FOUR

"WHERE in God's name are you?" Olivia boomed as soon as she came on the line, her tone far more threatening than the earlier thunder.

Just as Holly had suspected, it wasn't worry that had her mother's voice rising a couple of octaves, but outrage. Holly brought the receiver back to her ear and replied, "I'm safe."

"That's not an answer, Hollyn."

"And I'm not a child, Mother."

"Then stop acting like one and return home immediately. You have obligations. You have functions to attend, some of which we have already had to postpone or cancel."

"I'm sorry."

Her mother's tone moderated and lost the Texas twang it acquired whenever Olivia was good and upset. "When can we expect you?"

"As I said in my note, I won't be gone long. I'll be home in a week." Holly wasn't sure what made her add, "Or closer to ten days."

"Hollyn!"

She held the phone away from her ear again, missing part of what her mother was saying. What she caught when she brought it back was "People are depending on you."

Holly's shoulders sagged even as her chest grew tight. "I know they are, Mother."

"I might have expected a stunt like this when you were in your teens, but you're a grown woman. I know it's different, but when I was your age, I was already wearing the Miss Texas crown and had competed nationally. I was living up to my obligations."

Vastly different, and that was your choice. But Holly didn't say the words out loud. She had no desire to rehash what was a very old argument and one she apparently had no hope of ever winning. In addition to knowing best, her mother was always right.

"Where are you?" Olivia asked a second time. "I'm assuming that you are no longer in Morenci. We've already checked all of your usual haunts and hideouts. Discreetly, of course, since the photographers have been on the lookout for you as well."

"Actually, I'm no longer in Europe. I'm in America."

"Heart Island."

Holly was sure her mother issued the words through clenched teeth.

"Yes."

"Why in God's name would you go there?"

Olivia had never understood either Gran's or Holly's attachment to the island. There was nothing to do on that rugged patch of land, she claimed. No department stores to shop at, no fancy restaurants to dine in, no culture whatsoever to be had unless one went to what remained of a British fort, one of the last holdings from the War of 1812. The fort itself had burned to the ground, but some of its foundation remained, and a large, green historical marker rose in the center, explaining the place's significance.

Big whoop, to use Olivia's old vernacular.

"It's peaceful here," Holly said. Even as the storm rumbled in the distance, she knew that to be true.

"It's peaceful at that discreet little spa that's tucked up in the hillside just outside Cannes."

Another argument that Holly couldn't win. Her and Olivia's views on what constituted a relaxing sojourn were just too different, which explained why her mother had been bored to tears the couple of times during Olivia's childhood that Gran had taken her camping. Fishing, beachcombing, hiking trails—those things had amounted to torture in Olivia's book.

As Gran used to say, "I guess my love for the outdoors skipped a generation."

And Olivia's love for wearing fancy gowns and a crown had skipped a generation, too.

"Phillip has called several times already," her mother said now.

Holly wanted to feel elated at the news or at least suitably guilty that the man she'd been linked with for the past several months was anxious to reach her. What she felt was…nothing. There was a great black hole in her emotions where Phillip was concerned.

They'd met more than a year ago when his company had been awarded one of the kingdom's highest honors for its environmental record. Her mother had insisted Holly call him personally after the award ceremony to invite him to the special dinner for honorees held at the palace.

She'd done so, and she'd sat next to him in the palace's opulent dining hall. They'd talked, laughed. It had been enough to convince Olivia of their suitability, especially given his flush bank account and impeccable breeding.

After that, Phillip had turned up at all sorts of events at the queen's urging. Holly was used to her mother's machinations. She'd seen no harm at first, despite Olivia's claim that it was time Holly settle down and marry.

"You'll be thirty before you know it." That warning first came not long after Holly turned twenty. These days it was her mother's stock phrase.

Phillip was handsome, thoughtful and accomplished. He treated Holly like the queen she would someday become. Both in public and in private he said all of the right things. He did all of the right things, too, deferring to her position, all while making it clear he was in no way without authority.

Yet, if he never called her again, Holly would easily forget he existed. That wasn't right, but it was a fact. One that only she seemed to think mattered. Even Phillip had changed the subject the few times she'd tried to broach it with him.

"You had plans to attend the opera for the opening night of *Madame Butterfly* last evening," her mother was reminding her. "His family box remained dark. We issued a press release saying you'd fallen ill, which also helped to explain your earlier absence from the annual garden show, but you know how easily rumors get started and then spread, Hollyn. I'm sure they are already swirling."

"Yes." And her mother was only too happy to help them along when it suited her agenda. Hence the widespread notion that an engagement to Phillip was imminent, even though Holly had been dragging her feet in accepting his proposal of marriage. "I'll call him later. Apologize."

Holly would, too. Phillip was a decent man. He deserved that much.

"He's worried about you. And a little hurt."

Holly felt a twinge of guilt. No matter her feelings—or lack of them—where Phillip was concerned, she hadn't intended to make him worry or hurt his feelings. "Phillip said that?"

"Well, not in so many words," her mother replied. "But I could hear it in his voice. You took off without a word to anyone, including him."

"Did you tell him the truth? Or does he also think I'm unwell."

"I thought it best to tell him the truth, just in case your image winds up in the tabloids, completely refuting our claims of illness. After all, the two of you are betrothed."

Holly's guilt evaporated. Annoyance took its place. "Phillip and I aren't betrothed. Yes, he's asked, but I haven't said yes, Mother."

A moot point, apparently. This was yet another decision being made by forces beyond Holly's control. Olivia's next words made that much clear.

"But you will. He's perfect for you, Hollyn. So much more pragmatic than you are, my dear," she said on a sigh. "That's exactly what you need. He'll help keep your feet planted firmly on the ground. Together, the two of you make an excellent team."

A team?

How lovely. And how romantic. But to her mother's way of thinking, when it came to the marriage of her only daughter, true love wasn't as important as blood-lines and tradition.

Olivia had her reasons, and Holly understood them even if she wasn't quite willing to bow to them any longer. Her parents' romance had been scandalous and deemed unacceptable by the older guard, including Holly's father's parents. Even though both of them were deceased now, Olivia was still desperate to toe the line and make her daughter do the same.

It had taken Olivia years to be taken seriously. For that reason, she was determined that her only child be above reproach.

Her mother continued. "Just as importantly, Phillip is the ideal husband for Morenci's future queen." Olivia ticked off his attributes, all of which Holly had heard before. "He comes from a prominent and well-regarded family. He has his own fortune, which grows daily thanks to his business acumen. If there are skeletons in the man's closet, none have been found. And believe me, your father and I have hired the most tenacious people to look."

"Mother—"

"I want to spare you the scrutiny your father faced for marrying me."

"You're a wonderful queen and a caring mother." It was true. Even as Holly chafed against Olivia's sometimes overbearing actions, she understood it was love that guided them.

"A spring wedding would be lovely," Olivia was saying. "It would give Morencians something to look forward to. And, God knows, with the current economic conditions and that nasty flood that damaged so much of the business district last fall, they need something to buoy their spirits. Your nuptials, my dear, are just what the doctor ordered for our country."

Forget the weight on her shoulders. Now, Holly felt queasy, and her legs turned to rubber. Before they gave out completely, she managed to slip onto one of the chairs at the kitchen table. Outside, the rain that an hour ago had been torrential was merely insistent as it tapped at the window.

She rubbed her left temple, feeling the beginnings of a headache start to take hold. So much responsibility, Holly thought, as the heavy yoke began to settle firmly into place once again.

"Mother, please."

"Fine. I'll leave talk of weddings to a later date. When can we expect you?"

"I already told you—"

"When?" Olivia interrupted.

A cartoon stuck to Nate's refrigerator door caught Holly's attention. It showed a sloe-eyed man lounging on a dock with a pole in one hand, a beverage in the other. Gone Fishing, it read. So simple. So utterly ideal. "A week at the earliest. I'll call if I decide to be longer."

"H-H-Hollyn!" Olivia sputtered.

Holly talked over her protest. "Sorry. I have to go.

There's a storm here and the reception isn't very good. I'll call again soon. I promise. Give my love to Father." And with that, she hung up.

Nate spied Holly when he reached the bottom of the stairs. She was seated on the couch with her arms wrapped around her knees, which she'd pulled to her chest. Her gaze was on the window, but he doubted she was seeing anything, both because of the darkness and the vacancy of her expression. Even a far-off flash of lightning failed to make her blink.

He almost turned back around. He didn't want to disturb her. But she looked so lost, and, given her pose and the way she'd pulled back her hair, a lot like the girl she'd been.

"I'm thinking that phone call didn't go very well."

She started at the sound of his voice and uncoiled. It was almost comical the way she smoothed down her shorts once her feet were settled on the ground, as if she were wearing a silk ball gown rather than simple cotton.

"Not very well, no."

"Parents worry," he said, thinking of his own. "I talk to my folks regularly and without fail my mother still asks if I've been taking my vitamins."

He'd hoped to get a laugh out of her, or at least a smile. Her frown deepened. "My relationship with my parents, my mother in particular, is a little more complicated."

"I know." He took a seat on the couch, leaving a full cushion between them.

"Sometimes I feel like she's more worried about how

I'll fare in the history books a few generations from now than, well, about me. I know she has her reasons, but..." Her frown deepened. "Let's talk about something else."

"Okay. What?"

She turned, the beginnings of a smile turning up the corners of her mouth. "How about you? From what you said earlier, I know you attended university and after graduation lived in Chicago for a time. What else?"

That was broad enough to keep him talking for hours. Nate would much rather rehash her life. God knew, he wanted some of the blanks filled in, blanks that the tabloids couldn't possibly know or get right. Had she really been in love with him all those years ago? Had she hoped, as much as he had, that they could find a way to be together? Did she love this guy she was supposedly going to marry?

Instead of asking any of those questions, he nodded.

He wasn't completely comfortable talking about himself, especially since his life, even what he considered the highlights, might not be all that exciting from her point of view. But she smiled, nodded encouragingly, as he told her about the summer internship he'd had between his junior and senior years of college at a hotel in New York's Times Square.

"New York is something," Holly said. "So much energy and so much to do. It's my mother's favorite city, though she wouldn't admit to that publicly for obvious reasons."

"It's something," he agreed. Though he had a feeling she'd enjoyed a bird's-eye view from some penthouse apartment, where he'd shared a tiny walk-up with four other interns in a section of the city that wouldn't make it on any tourist maps.

"Anyway, after graduation from the University of Michigan, I took a job in Chicago and attended Northwestern in the evenings to earn my MBA."

"I'm impressed."

He shrugged, but damn if he wasn't warmed by her compliment.

"And now I'm here."

"Doing what you love."

She'd summed it up perfectly. All he could do was nod.

"I envy you that," she said softly.

"You envy me." He realized as soon as he said it that he'd insulted her.

"My apologies. I forgot. I have the world by its tail. I have no cares, no concerns, no worries whatsoever beyond which silver spoon to select to eat my next meal. I'm not allowed to envy anyone anything."

She started to rise to her feet. Nate put a hand on her arm to stop her. "I didn't mean—"

She closed her eyes and exhaled slowly, as if reaching deep inside herself for patience. Apparently, she found it. When she opened her eyes, she looked calm and only the slightest bit weary. She straightened her shoulders, tilted her chin up. She was the polar opposite of the woman he'd come across mere minutes ago, legs pulled to her chest and lost in thought.

If Nate had to pick one word to describe her it would be *regal*. And he meant it as a compliment, even if he also knew what it was costing her. *I'm always on dis-*

play, she'd said earlier. Which meant she knew how to play the part of princess.

"Of course you didn't. It's all right. I'm tired and being insufferably rude, especially after all you've done for me."

He'd offered her a place to stay for the night—a little begrudgingly at first—showed her how to operate the ancient shower in the guest bath, shared a beer and allowed her the use of his phone. He'd hardly been put out. He said as much.

"But I do appreciate it, especially since my visit was so unexpected."

Nate rose to his feet. He felt like a champion heel. Holly was apologizing, but he was the one who was sorry. Not only for the thoughtless comment he'd made, but also for the effect his words had had on her mood. It was as if a light had been doused. He didn't like knowing he'd done the dousing.

"It's no problem, you being here. If I've seemed, well, a little brusque, it's just that I'm not good with surprises," he said. "I like to know what's coming next."

"I'd rather enjoy a few surprises now and again. Part of the problem for me is I know exactly what to expect. The script has been written. I'm just acting out the scenes."

He'd never thought of it that way.

"I think I'll retire now."

"It's been a long day," he agreed.

"Yes. Very."

He waited until she was at the base of the steps to turn out the lamp. Enough light spilled from the open door of his bedroom at the top of the stairs to keep them from tripping.

It was odd, walking up to his bedroom with a beautiful woman at his side and knowing they would part ways at the top of the steps and nothing would happen but sleep. Or sleeplessness, as the case likely would be for him.

He'd entertained overnight guests of the opposite sex before. He was a grown man, after all. And he'd hardly lived as a monk.

But this was different. This was something…more. He might not like it, but that was a fact. He'd accepted that earlier when they'd kissed. The mere memory of it would haunt him, just as memories of a suntanned teenage girl had haunted him for the past decade, whether he'd wanted to admit it or not.

At the top of the steps, she turned, as he'd known she would, starting to the opposite end of the house after offering a polite smile and the appropriate good-night wish. Words stuck in Nate's throat, jumbled up on his tongue.

I'm glad you're here. He nearly said it. And he *was* glad. In spite of everything and all of the conflicting emotions seeing her again had prompted, he was.

But instead of telling her so, he stepped into his bedroom and closed the door. After stripping off his shirt and shorts, he stretched out on the cool cotton sheets, eyeing the shadows cast from the lamp on the nightstand, as his mind tried to make sense of his thoughts.

He'd gotten over Holly. A long time ago, in fact. It hadn't been easy those first couple of summers, but then he'd gone off to college, dated other girls both on the island and elsewhere. Even if none of those relationships had lasted long or held any deep meaning for him, it wasn't as if he'd been pining. He'd figured the feelings he'd had for Holly had only felt so intense because he'd been young and in love for the first time.

That had made sense.

Now, here she was again. Back on the island after all of these years. She'd been in his life for mere hours, already upsetting its careful balance in ways he couldn't begin to fathom. And while Nate wished he could say that he'd been right, that immaturity and imagination had been responsible for those inflated feelings of the past, he knew he would be lying.

She was special.

Nate the boy had loved Holly the girl. After the kiss of a couple hours ago, he knew that Nate the man could very well wind up in a similar predicament.

If he allowed it.

He didn't plan to allow it. After all, just like before, she would be leaving. In mere days, she would go back to a life that Nate wasn't part of and never could be.

No, he wouldn't make the mistake of falling in love with Holly twice.

CHAPTER FIVE

NATE awoke just before dawn, not that he'd slept much knowing that Holly was just down the hall, stretched out between the sheets he'd spread over his boyhood bed.

Oh, the irony, given the many fantasies he'd entertained of her there back when they both were teenagers, when his hormones had been churning on high.

Between her nearness and Hank's buzz-saw snoring, Nate barely had managed a few hours of shut-eye. Add to that his anxiety over the extent of the storm's damage to the resort, and it was no wonder he was suffering insomnia. At first light, he dressed and prepared to head out.

Hank was still sleeping. The noise coming from the other man's room confirmed as much. Nate glanced down the hall. Before he could stop himself, he was at Holly's door. He leaned in close and listened. The only sound he could hear was breathing and it was coming from him. She was probably dead to the world, a casualty of jet lag. He started to step away, then stopped. Even though it made absolutely no sense, and he knew he was being unforgivably rude, he slowly turned the knob, pushed the door open a crack and peeked inside.

Just as he'd suspected, Holly was asleep. She was

on her side, facing him. She looked lovely, if troubled. Even in sleep her brow appeared furrowed. She'd come to the island to get away. Even as he wanted to believe it wasn't his business or his concern, he couldn't help wondering, from what exactly? She'd mentioned how scripted her life was. But she was a princess, high enough up the royal food chain that surely she could call some of the shots. So what exactly was she running from?

Or whom?

That guy she was linked to? Nate's hands fisted at the thought.

She sighed then, turned. Honey-colored hair spilled over the pillow. His pillow.

Lucky pillow.

A sound rose in his throat—part moan, part curse. Nate closed the door with a smart click and hurried downstairs. Mere minutes later, armed with a Thermos full of black coffee and a clipboard, he hopped in his pickup truck.

He spent the first hour riding from one end of the resort to the other, jotting down notes and prioritizing the cleanup as he went. This was how he approached problems: head-on and with a plan. Doing so was not only practical, but in this instance it also helped keep his mind off of Holly.

As he drove, a calm settled over him, despite the obvious fallout from the storm. This was his kingdom. Last night, he'd experienced some doubts. They'd cleared off with the storm. He'd made the right choices in his life. This was where he wanted to be. The resort was a grand enough dream for him. He was happy here. The island was home.

He'd already called in the Burns twins to help. The boys were seventeen, with strong backs and a deep desire to earn enough cash to buy their first car. Their dream vehicle was a vintage restored Mustang the island's only doctor had put up for sale. So they were only too happy to hear Nate had extra hours for them to work.

As he drove, Nate stopped to chat with any guests who were out and about. Several of them were, especially those who had come to the island to fish.

"That was quite the storm last night," Ernie Smithe commented. "Reminded me of the one back in eighty-seven."

The older man haled from a suburb just outside of Detroit and had been coming north for two weeks in June for as long as Nate could remember. He was seated at the picnic table just outside his cabin, a steaming cup of coffee at his elbow as he went through his tackle box.

"Yes, it was." Nate nodded at the selection of lures. "What are you fishing for this morning?"

"Anything that will take the bait." The older man laughed then. "I haven't had too much luck trolling off the little islands just outside the bay."

"Perch are biting off the marina's dock. Your best bet is minnows." Nate sold them for a couple dollars per dozen in the shop. "Tell the kid working the counter that I said to give you a complimentary bucketful."

The way Nate saw it, it was a small price to pay for the fact the storm had taken out the resort's cable television. He made a note to himself to tell anyone who worked the desk that minnows were on the house for the rest of the day.

Ernie thanked him. Nate started on his way. As he passed his cottage, he thought he saw movement through the kitchen window. He pulled the truck to a stop and headed up the steps, bracing himself a moment before pulling open the door. He wasn't sure what to say. *Good morning* would be appropriate. But for some reason asking if she'd slept well seemed a little too personal.

Then again, that kiss had been nothing if not personal.

He scrubbed a hand over his face at the memory, felt the stubble. He hardly looked his best. He didn't want to care. But he did. God help him. He did.

It turned out there was no need for divine intervention. The person standing in his kitchen was Hank. The other man was hunched over the counter helping himself to a bowl of cold cereal.

"Mornin'," he mumbled around a mouthful of fortified flakes.

"Hey." Nate glanced past him. The television was on but the living room was empty.

"She's not up yet," Hank said, doing a lousy job of hiding his amusement.

Nate ignored him. "I checked on your plane."

That got his attention. "How'd she fare?"

"No worse for the wear. Good thing we beached and tethered her, though. A couple of the boats that were moored in the shallows got tossed about quite a bit. One is going to need a new prop."

"Good thing," Hank repeated, his complexion a little pale. He set the now-empty bowl in the sink. "And thanks for the place to stay last night. You're not a bad host, Matthews, even if we never did get around to that poker game."

Nate laughed. "No problem."

Hank hitched a thumb over his shoulder in the direction of the stairs. "So, what are you going to do about your other guest?"

"What do you mean?"

"The lady needs a place to stay," Hank reminded him. As if Nate needed reminding on that score.

"I'll find her something on the island."

"Sure about that?" Hank scratched his scruffy chin. He had a good decade on Nate. Right now, he was acting as if he were his father. "You said last night most places were full up. Kind of scolded the girl, as I recall, for coming without advance notice."

"I'm sure there's something she can rent." Especially given Holly's unlimited budget. With that kind of cash to flash around, even the exclusive private summer residences that dotted the bay's eastern shore would likely be open to renters. Since Hank seemed to be waiting for greater reassurance, Nate added, "I'll drive her around later, see what's available."

"As long as you're sure she won't wind up down at the campground."

"The campground." Nate snorted out a laugh. The Holly he'd known as a child would have been fine in a pup tent, roasting marshmallows over an open fire and swapping ghost stories. They'd done just that her second summer on the island. In separate tents pitched outside the cottage her grandmother rented. This Holly? She would be carried off by the mosquitoes that sometimes were mistaken for Michigan's state bird.

He laid a hand over his heart. "I promise, I won't allow her to wind up at the campground."

"Okay." Hank nodded. "I'll be heading out in a bit. I've got a couple fares scheduled for later this morning. You tell her she can call me if need be. I'll come back for her in a flash."

"I'm sure she won't be needing your services."

"Just see that you tell her." The other man was all business now. Nate would have found Hank's edict annoying if he didn't also appreciate that he was looking out for Holly.

That made two of them.

"I will."

Holly woke to the far-off squawk of seagulls, the sound of gently lapping waves and the smell of freshly brewed coffee. The storm was long gone, and from the sunshine peeking through the curtains, it was but a distant memory at this point.

She stretched on the mattress and smiled sleepily as she regarded the outdated, overhead light fixture. Overall, she'd slept well, deep and dreamless. It was peaceful here, and so quiet.

She amended her opinion a moment later when the jarring roar of a chainsaw had her lurching out of bed. A peek out one of the windows and she found its source. Nate was just down the beach from the cottage, holding the offending power tool in his hands and using it to slice through the thick trunk of a fallen cedar tree.

She noted other trees and branches strewn about

the beach and wondered what the full impact of the storm had been on the resort. She glanced around. Hank wasn't with him. Nor was the pilot's seaplane visible on the beach. But Nate did have a couple of helpers, teenage boys unless Holly missed her guess. And from the looks of it, they were as impressed with his skill with the chainsaw as she was.

She decided to get dressed after a glance at the clock on the nightstand revealed it was closing in on noon. Noon! By her calculations, she'd slept nearly a dozen hours. How on earth had she managed to sleep that long? Sure, she was jet-lagged. But back home she routinely ran on four to five hours of sleep a night, and even that, lately, had been punctuated with bouts of wakefulness.

Dressed in a pair of white capris, a crisp cotton blouse the color of raspberries and the burnished silver gladiator sandals that she'd picked up after attending a fashion show in Milan, she headed downstairs. As she'd already determined, Hank was nowhere to be found. He'd probably flown to the mainland hours ago, which meant she had no way back. At least not right now. Which meant she was at Nate's mercy. She wasn't sure how she felt about that.

In the kitchen, there was exactly one cup of coffee left in the maker. Though she preferred tea, she didn't feel like rooting around in Nate's cupboards to see if he had any. She poured the coffee for herself, shut off the pot and instantly felt guilty. Americans liked their coffee, or so her mother claimed. Nearly thirty years in Morenci and Olivia still eschewed tea in favor of a nice cup of Colombian. She could drink a pot by herself, all while complaining about the effects of caffeine on one's body and complexion.

Holly decided to make a second pot. She would bring a cup out to Nate. It would be a peace offering of sorts…. A thank-you, she amended. She eyed the maker dubiously. As enamoured as she was with prospect of cooking, she didn't have much skill in the kitchen. *Much* as in next to none. Anytime she attempted something remotely culinary her mother would remind her they had "staff" to deal with that.

Thus, Holly also had little experience when it came to small appliances, and this looked nothing like the ones she'd glimpsed in the palace kitchens. Still, it seemed simple enough. Besides, the brewing instructions were listed on the inside of the lid that opened where she had to add the water. How hard could it be? Only an idiot could screw it up.

It turned out Holly was an idiot.

One look at Nate's face after he took the first sip and she knew it for a fact.

God bless him, the man managed to swallow what he had in his mouth rather than spit it out in sprinkler fashion. But his grimace spoke volumes.

"That's…a little strong," he said after a moment.

"I followed the directions," she countered as the identical-looking young men standing on either side of Nate studied their sneakers.

"Let me guess. You used the scoop in the coffee jar as your measure."

"Of course I did."

"It's double the amount."

"How was I supposed…?" She let the question trail

off and crossed her arms over her chest instead. "Real men like it strong."

Nate blinked at that. The teens eyed one another, their expressions all but asking, "Did she really just say that?" From what Holly knew of the American teenage boy's vernacular, she added, "Dude."

"I like my coffee strong," Nate said in seeming agreement.

"Good."

"I just prefer to have my stomach lining left intact afterward."

Delivered as it was in that even pitch of his, with the beginnings of a smile turning up the corners of his lips, it was hard to take offense. Impossible, in fact. Holly dissolved into giggles. The boys joined in her laughter, too, but only once Nate had let out a snort of amusement. As one who appreciated loyalty, she instantly liked them.

"Sorry," she said at last. "Truly, I wasn't trying to poison you."

"It's okay." He tossed the rest of the coffee to the ground and handed back the cup. "I appreciate the effort."

Whether intended as a peace offering or as a thank-you, the coffee seemed to do the trick. Some of the old ease they'd had with one another returned.

Nate seemed to remember his manners. "Josh and Joey Burns, this is…Holly. She used to come to the island a lot as a kid. She's back now for a short visit."

She refused to acknowledge the way her heart sank at his description of her visit as being short. What else could it be? It wasn't as if she could stay on Heart indefinitely. She couldn't just quit being a princess and relocate to a foreign country. Could she?

"Holly?" Nate prompted.

"Sorry. My mind wandered." Wandered? It had taken a trip into uncharted territory. She pasted on a smile. "It's nice to meet you both."

"Hi," each of the boys said, looking a little shy and adorably awkward as they accepted her outstretched hand.

"You talk funny," Josh—or was it Joey?—said. His cheeks turned blotchy immediately·after saying so. "I don't mean funny, more like, you know, different. You have an accent of some sort."

"Smooth," his brother muttered half under his breath.

"I'm not from your country," Holly said. She couldn't help thinking they had a bit of an accent, too. American English definitely carried a different sound than British English, which she was far more used to.

The other brother spoke up then. "Has anyone ever told you that you look like someone famous?"

Holly and Nate traded glances.

"No. Whom do you mean?" she asked, keeping her expression carefully blank. This was exactly what Nate had warned her would happen, and what she wanted to avoid.

"Lady Gaga."

"What?" Holly let out a completely unladylike snort of laughter that would have earned her mother's censure. As it was, it had Nate's eyebrows rising. "I can honestly say that no one has ever told me I look like the pop star."

"Not when she's done all up for, like, a concert or an

awards show or anything," Josh was quick to correct. "She can be pretty out there. But you kind of have the same eyes."

"Really." More amused than incredulous now, Holly sent a grin in Nate's direction. "Lady Gaga. What do you think?"

He shook his head. "Sorry. I'm not seeing it."

She turned back to the twins. "Don't feel bad. Nate is more of a country-Western sort. Or at least he was back when we were children."

Garth Brooks, George Strait, Alan Jackson and a little Brooks & Dunn had been staples on his stereo. He'd known the songs by heart. He'd even taught Holly to two-step. The first time she'd gotten the movements right without his prompting, he'd swung her around in a circle and kissed her cheek before setting her down and quickly stepping away. They'd been on his parents' deck. She'd been fourteen. He'd been…her world.

"I've grown into a heavy metal fan since then," he informed her now.

Holly's mouth gaped open a moment before she could say, "You did not."

He merely shrugged. "My college roommate was a huge AC/DC fan. It was either learn to like screeching lyrics and wicked electric guitar riffs or sleep at the library. I chose the path of least resistance and the most shut-eye. Besides, it's not so bad once you get used to it."

"'Back in Black.'" One of the boys nodded and grinned. "Totally."

"Totally," the other one echoed.

"Righteous," Holly said, flipping what she thought

was the sign she'd seen rock stars use, but earning confused glances from all three of the males in her presence. She could only hope the sign she'd flashed hadn't been offensive.

"Start loading these logs into the pickup," Nate instructed.

The boys did as they were told. Holly asked in a lowered voice, "Did I get that wrong?"

"A finger or two. You gave us the Boy Scout salute." Nate started to chuckle.

"Oh." She picked a coffee ground out of the otherwise empty cup. "Heavy metal. I guess it makes sense that your tastes have changed since I was last here."

She tried to keep her tone light, but the way Nate was looking at her made it difficult.

"We were kids then."

"Children," she agreed.

His gaze skimmed down. Awareness simmered between them.

"Not all of my tastes have changed," he said.

"No?"

He glanced away. When his gaze returned to hers it was far more impassive. "I still like toasted marshmallows."

Nate told the Burns brothers to take a break for lunch and walked with Holly back to the house, intending to do the same. He was still a little surprised that she'd come out to find him, bringing with her a cup of coffee no less. The worst cup of coffee he'd ever had, but still. It was definitely the thought that counted.

"It looks like you have a lot of work to do," she

remarked, stepping over one of the many downed branches strewn over the resort grounds.

The beach had been cleared first and the sand freshly graded. Already, families were out, lounging in chairs and watching their children build sand castles or play in the water. This was exactly why it had been the priority. When people came to an island, they expected unfettered access to the water.

"Enough. But it's not as bad as I feared it would be." He gave her a quick summary of what his morning tour had turned up. "Besides, the twins will help. They're good kids. Strong backs and a burning desire to make a buck. They have their eye on a car. A real babe magnet."

Holly's brow crinkled.

"A stylish ride sure to turn all the young girls' heads," Nate translated.

"You drove a station wagon, as I recall," she said.

With the resort logo plastered on the doors. He grimaced. "That was the opposite of a babe magnet."

"And yet you managed to turn my head." She blushed after saying so and then changed the subject. "The twins seem nice."

Nate nodded. "Although maybe not all that bright." He gave her arm a poke. "They thought you looked like Lady Gaga."

"Yes." She shook her head. "I'm still trying to figure out if I should be flattered."

She batted the lashes on the eyes the boys claimed were like the pop star's. The gesture was silly, as silly as the boys' assertion. But Nate's mouth went dry as he stared at her. He'd always thought Holly's eyes were one of her best features.

"They're so damned blue," he murmured.

"Pardon me?"

Nate fiddled with the clipboard he'd snagged from the front seat of his truck. He'd brought it with him mostly to keep his hands occupied. Wouldn't it just figure that it was his mouth making him into a fool?

"Uh, Hank took off a couple hours ago."

"Yes. I noticed that his plane was gone when I left your house."

Of course she had.

"He had some fares, so he needed to return to the mainland."

It was a lie—little and white—since the pilot would have stuck around if Nate hadn't insisted that he would find Holly a place to stay.

"I guess this means I'm at your mercy." She blushed again.

Nate's heart did a funny little flip. Holly. At his mercy. He was guy enough that some serious fantasies could be attached to such a statement, benign though she'd intended it. He nearly pinched his thumb under the board's clip, and cleared his throat.

"After we eat lunch, I'll take you around to the other resorts as well as to the real estate office in town. Nadine Masterson runs it. She'll know if there is anything available to rent, even if it's not listed. Some of the more exclusive places aren't advertised."

"Thank you. I appreciate it."

Holly's smile was polite. And fake. It was the kind of smile she wore for public appearances. Since Nate was privy to the real thing, he spotted the imposter easily enough. Less than twenty-four hours in her presence and he'd already figured out that retreating behind good manners was a way for her to mask her true feelings. She'd never done that as a girl. Back then, she'd given as good as she'd gotten, arguing and opining like a champion debater. He'd been fascinated by her passion for life and adventure and, later, for him, as innocent as it had been.

Recalling that now, he asked, "Why do you do that?"

She blinked. "What do you mean?"

"You're saying one thing when it's clear you mean another."

"I'm afraid I still don't know what you mean."

"You're smiling, saying how appreciative you are, but I don't get the feeling you're very happy."

"Why wouldn't I be happy?" she argued. "As I said, I appreciate the trouble you're going to, helping me find a place to stay elsewhere on the island."

Nate thought he had his answer. She hadn't just come to Heart Island. She'd come to the Haven Resort. "If I had a cottage available, I'd rent it to you. I know I may not have been very gracious when you first arrived last night, but…"

She smiled—the real thing this time—and clasped her hands in front of her. "I believe you would. Thank you, Nate."

He hadn't done anything. Yet. But he would. He would see to it that Holly found a place to stay on Heart and that she enjoyed her time away from her royal duties.

Maybe along the way, she not only would remember

the girl she'd once been, she would find a little of that girl's spirit still within her.

They ate a simple lunch of grilled cheese sandwiches. Unfortunately, one look through his refrigerator and pantry and that was about all Nate could come up with.

He'd meant to get to the grocery store. He was even running low on staples such as milk, eggs and bread. Truth be told, Nate dined out more than he ate in. He liked the company to be found at the Fishing Hole, a pub on the other side of the bay that served the best deep-fried white fish on the island. Even if he came in alone, he never sat alone. Everyone knew everyone. The island was a community in the best sense of the word.

Holly didn't complain about the pedestrian fare. Not that Nate expected her to. He'd already figured out that she hadn't changed quite as much as he'd thought she had in terms of her tastes, and that, despite their earlier conversation, she would kill him with kindness rather than utter any intentionally rude comments.

He missed the young woman who had been full of opinions and dreams, which she'd shared without any prompting at all. One, he still remembered.

"I'm going to be an artist someday. So good, that you probably won't be able to afford my work."

The memory had him asking, "Do you still paint?"

She had a mouthful of grilled cheese. She stopped chewing, blinked a couple of times. It was a moment before she swallowed and could reply.

"I…no. Not much. There's really no time."

"I'm surprised." And he was. "I remember someone once telling me that a person makes time for the things that are important."

"I was never any good at it. It's not as if anything I painted was going to wind up hanging in a museum or for sale in a gallery."

"That doesn't mean it wasn't important."

"I…I…" Whatever she'd intended to say went unfinished. Instead, she stood, pushing back from the table so abruptly that her chair nearly tipped over. Her expression wasn't sad exactly. Nor did she appear angry. But it was clear she was upset.

"Hol—"

But she was already gone, her footsteps thudding on the carpeted steps.

Holly paced the length of her room, equal parts agitated and embarrassed. She'd acted like a fool, dashing out of the kitchen like that. But she couldn't stay, not when Nate saw her so clearly. She'd felt naked, exposed and ashamed. Ashamed of how she'd let her needs and desires be subjugated.

She'd loved painting, especially with watercolors. In each brushstroke she'd found respite from daily pressures. Yet she'd allowed herself to be steered away from being an artist and toward being a patron of the arts.

"I remember someone once telling me that a person makes time for the things that are important."

Yes, she'd said that. She'd believed it, too.

How had she allowed herself to forget?

CHAPTER SIX

As Nate suspected, pretty much every resort on the island was at capacity. Even a couple of the questionable places on the far side of the island were posting No Vacancy signs.

Holly had been awfully quiet throughout their drive. He'd made no mention of what had happened in the kitchen. It was clear she didn't want to talk about whatever it was that had prompted her hasty departure.

Beside him in the cab of his truck, he heard Holly sigh.

"It's not looking good, is it?" she said.

"No, but we'll swing by the real estate office. As I said, Nadine has resources that I don't."

"Maybe I should just call Hank to come get me."

"And what? Go home?"

She stared straight ahead. From the way her nose wrinkled, he was pretty sure she found the option distasteful, yet she said, "God knows, my mother would be relieved."

Would Nate be? Would he be relieved to have the status quo restored? It was a question he wasn't ready to answer. So, he reminded Holly, "You came here looking for something."

"Yes, I did." She plucked at the hem of her blouse. "Something that may no longer exist, and even if it does..."

"Yes?" he prodded.

"You not only have to make time for the things that are important, Nate, you have to have the courage to make that time."

It was an interesting answer. One that begged questions. But Nate didn't ask what she meant. She wasn't the only one lacking for nerve. "We'll go and talk to Nadine. There's plenty of time to call Hank later if nothing pans out."

"All right."

She leaned her head back on the rest. They were on one of the island's main roads. Every car that passed going in the opposite direction, the driver waved.

"People are so friendly here," she remarked.

"We all know one another, the locals, that is. And, even the tourists do it once they've been around for a while. When people wave, the natural reaction is to wave back."

"Like this?" She cupped her hand slightly and gave what he thought of as a royal wave. A smile turned up the corners of her mouth.

"That's a 'how do you do' sort of wave. Here on the island, we keep our fingers splayed a bit and use more wrist. It says, 'Hey. How's it going? Have a good one.'" Nate demonstrated.

"I see what you mean," Holly said in mock seriousness. They passed a pickup truck and she gave her best imitation.

"Now you're getting the hang of it."

They both laughed.

She turned and smiled. "Thank you, Nate."

"For teaching you how to give a proper Heart Island wave?"

"For making me laugh and, well, ferrying me about from place to place."

"It's nothing."

"It is," she disagreed. "I've taken you away from your work for a good portion of the day, and after a vicious storm no less. I'm sure you have better things to do with your time."

"Other things to do, maybe. But not better," he corrected on a smile.

He reached across the truck's bench seat and gave her hand a squeeze. He wanted to hold it, weave his fingers through hers and maybe stroke the soft skin he encountered with the pad of his thumb. Instead, he released her hand and gripped the steering wheel with both of his.

"To Heart Island Realty," he said.

The business in question was located near what the islanders referred to as the Four Corners. It was the main intersection just off the ferry landing on the island, and as such, the hub of commerce. Whether tourist or local, pretty much everyone converged on the Four Corners at one point or another during the week.

Stub's Grocery dominated one corner, a hardware and feed store another. The remaining two were taken up with Mary Sue's Mercantile, which sold men's, women's and children's clothing as well as home goods; and Dan's Laundromat, which both shared a parking lot with Phoebe's Frozen Treats. Just down from that, and in the same shared parking lot, was Heart Island Realty.

Nate pulled his truck into one of the available spots. Together, he and Holly entered the business.

Nadine Masterson glanced up when the cowbell over the door rang. She was a pretty woman, petite, with brown hair that she wore short these days. She was the same age as Nate. She and her younger sister had moved to the island when Nadine was a senior in high school. It had been quite an adjustment for both of the girls, even though they hadn't come from a large city. Even small cities had a broader social circle than the island did. Nate had asked Nadine to their senior prom. They'd dated on and off over the years, never seriously, but they enjoyed one another's company. Their nights out had become a little more frequent since his return to the island a few years earlier. Still, they were anything but exclusive and not in what he would consider a committed relationship.

He began to wonder if maybe she felt otherwise when her face split into a grin when she glanced up and saw him. The smile was a little more intimate than the one saved for a mere friend. The way Holly stiffened, Nate figured she'd picked up on that, too. He could have smacked himself upside the head for his lapse in judgment. Well, there was no help for it now.

"Nate Matthews," Nadine was saying as she came around the desk. "If you aren't a sight for sore eyes on a what has otherwise been a really lousy day."

"Hey, Nadine." He reached for Holly, who stood just behind him, and guided her forward. He immediately regretted the proprietary hand he'd rested on the small of Holly's back. Both women seemed to have a visceral reaction to the gesture.

Nadine's smile evaporated. Holly jumped.

"And who might this be?"

"This is—"

"I'm Holly. An old friend of Nate's family." She stepped to the side, just outside his reach, and extended a hand to the other woman.

"Nadine Masterson."

"It's nice to meet you, Ms. Masterson." Holly folded her hands in front of her. "I arrived on the island rather unexpectedly late yesterday. Unfortunately, Nate's resort is full, but he brought me to you in the hope that you might find something available for me elsewhere on the island."

How nonthreatening was that? Nate nearly felt insulted.

Nadine divided a gaze between the two of them. Nate could only imagine what she was thinking, and it was a good bet he would hear all about it the next time they ran into one another at the Fishing Hole.

He wouldn't have to wait that long, he decided, when Nadine said, "You arrived yesterday, Holly?"

"Yes, late. Hank Whitey flew me over from the mainland."

"Really. That was bold of him, considering the storm."

"It was before it hit."

"I see."

Two words that in Nate's experience were women-speak for anything but.

Holly didn't bat an eye. She remained the picture of

calm and contrition. "Hank and I wound up overnight guests at Nate's home."

"How convenient."

"Yes. They are both very kind men. But then, in Nate's case, given how far our families go back, I'm sure he felt obligated to look after me."

Nadine's brows rose at that. Her gaze cut to Nate for a moment before returning to Holly. "Just how far back do you go?"

"To childhood. In fact, I haven't seen Nate since we were mere children."

Okay, that was an exaggeration. It's not as if they'd been toddling about in diapers, but he decided not to correct her.

Holly said, "We lost touch over the years. I wasn't even aware that his parents had retired and were no longer in charge of the resort when I decided to come for a visit."

"Oh." Nadine's posture was no longer quite so rigid.

"Now, I'm hoping to get out of Nate's hair, I believe the saying is, and find a place to stay for the remainder of my trip."

"And how long might that be?"

"Ten days." In his peripheral vision, Nate saw Holly lick her lips before adding, "Or so."

Interesting. The duration of her visit kept lengthening. Equally interesting, he wasn't sure how he felt about that.

"Let me see what I can do." Nadine returned to her desk and booted up her computer. A few keystrokes later, she was frowning. "I hate to tell you this, but pretty much all of the private residences that rent out are booked at least through Sunday." It was Thursday. "After that, I can set you up in a nice chalet on the eastern tip of the bay."

"You'd be directly across the bay from the resort," Nate added.

"I thought that was all state or federally owned land?" Holly said.

At Nadine's questioning gaze, Nate said, "We used to hike it when we were kids." To Holly, he replied, "There are a few acres of private land along the coast."

"It's a little secluded as a result," Nadine added. "But it has a generous private beach and offers terrific views of Lake Huron. It also comes with the use of a couple of personal watercraft and a canoe. The owners live downstate. They're rarely here, so they rent it out. It's in high demand."

"I can see why. It sounds lovely."

Nadine sucked air in around her teeth. "Yes, well, its rental price reflects that."

She rattled off a sum that was three times more than the going rate of Nate's largest and most well-appointed cabin. He could only imagine what the inside of the chalet must look like as Nadine was telling Holly about a jetted tub in the master bath and granite countertops and a wine cooler in a gourmet kitchen. He'd gone by the outside in his fishing boat on several occasions. It certainly didn't lack for windows or outdoor living space with a deck that wrapped around the lower floor and a balcony off the upper one.

"The owners only rent by the week, so if you stay, say, ten days, you would still have to pay for the full two weeks."

"It will become available on Sunday?" Holly asked, clearly unaffected by the amount.

Nate saw Nadine's eyes widen slightly, as if she'd figured it would be too rich for Holly's blood. If only she knew. Still, she was all business.

Nadine folded her hands on the desk blotter. "Yes. That's when the current guests are scheduled to leave. Checkout is noon. You could check in by three o'clock, maybe even a little earlier depending on how much work housekeeping has to do."

"Thank you. I'll take it. For two weeks."

Nadine gaped and so did Nate, neither of them quite able to contain their surprise. One week had become ten days and now ten days had turned into two weeks. Two weeks that would start on Sunday.

"Don't you want to see it first?" Nadine asked.

"No. I'm sure it will be fine."

"All right." Nadine typed up the rental agreement. If she wondered at the Texas post office box Holly gave for an address, she never let it show. However, her eyes widened for a second time when Holly opened her handbag and paid the entire sum in traveler's checks.

Handing her the receipt, Nadine asked, "So, where will you be staying between now and Sunday?"

Though the question was tendered casually, there was nothing casual about it. And they all knew it.

"Somewhere on the mainland." Holly turned to Nate. "I'll need to call Hank when we get back to your house."

"Sure."

He turned and thanked Nadine.

"Will you be at the Fishing Hole tonight?" she asked.

"I, um…" His gaze cut to Holly. "Probably not. I've got a lot of work to catch up with at the resort."

Nadine nodded. Holly smiled politely. No one made direct eye contact. As they took their leave, Nate couldn't escape the feeling that he was in hot water with both women.

Holly was fuming, even though she told herself she had absolutely no right to her anger. Still, she felt like a fool, and that seemed reason enough to give it vent. She waited until they were in the truck, seat belts buckled, to say in as casual a tone as she could muster, "Your girlfriend is very pretty."

Nate cleared his throat as he stuck the key in the ignition. "Nadine is *not* my girlfriend."

"Oh?" Holly puckered her lips, unconvinced. "Does she feel the same way?"

The truck's engine revved to life, and he shifted into gear. He spared her a glance before he looked both ways for oncoming cars and then pulled out of the parking lot. The truck's tires squealed and spat gravel, and she figured she had her answer, even before Nate said, "Look, we date…sometimes. Okay?"

Why did hearing him say that make her heart hurt? And it did. There was a funny ache in the center of her chest. Which was ridiculous. She had no claim on Nate. Whatever had been between them had ended practically before it began, and that was a very, very long time ago.

Their kiss of the evening before flashed in her mind, every bit as impossible to ignore as the lightning that had flashed in the sky during it. With it, needs she hadn't known existed had filtered to the forefront.

"You might have mentioned it." The words slipped from her lips before she could stop them.

"I didn't see the need," he said. He shifted in his seat. Squirmed? "For that matter, I don't see why it should be a problem."

"Problem? I can assure you, it is *not* a problem." She shook her head and crossed her arms over her chest. Did she sound as pathetic and juvenile as she felt?

"You're acting as if it is," Nate replied.

Apparently so.

She dropped her arms. "All right, it's just that I felt very foolish back there."

Her revelation seemed to take him by surprise. "Why?"

"I felt like I was in the middle of a...a..." Holly gestured with her arms as she searched for the right word. "A lover's quarrel."

"Nadine and I are not...serious."

But apparently they were lovers. Or they had been. That ache was back, and so was the small voice in Holly's head that kept telling her to let the matter drop. It was none of her business. Besides, what right did she have to question Nate's personal relationships when there was a man waiting for her back in Morenci that everyone assumed she would agree to marry in the near future?

Since she couldn't ignore the ache, she ignored the voice and pressed on. "Serious or not, Ms. Masterson clearly was not pleased when she found out that I had spent the night in your home. Has she ever spent the night there?"

She studied his profile. A muscle ticked in his jaw,

telling Holly she'd struck a nerve. "I'm not going to answer that. What I will say is this—I can't help how Nadine feels or what she thinks."

"It doesn't bother you?"

"She and I aren't serious," he said again, this time through clenched teeth.

Holly let out an inelegant snort.

Nate swore and then swerved. The truck left the main road and pulled onto a narrow two-track that was mottled with mud puddles from the previous night's downpour.

Holly braced her hands on the dashboard as they rattled over the rutted road.

"Wh-where are we g-going?"

"To see the secluded beach house that you just rented for a two-week stay."

"Do you mean to tell me there is no proper road?" Apparently the word *secluded* should have been written in capital letters.

"Sure there is. This is what's called a shortcut." He winked, though nothing about his demeanor at the moment was particularly friendly or relaxed.

"Nate, please slow down." Her molars smacked together a couple of times after she said it.

"It's just a little off-roading," he defended. "I wanted to give you a bit of the local experience."

Just then, the truck's front right tire hit an especially deep rut. Mud splattered the windshield and the side of the vehicle. Unfortunately for Holly, she hadn't had either the foresight or the time to roll up her window. Great gobs of thick brown matter rained in on her.

She let out a squeal of outrage befitting both a woman and a princess.

Nate took one look at her—she could imagine what he saw given the condition of her blouse—and expelled an oath aimed at himself. He hastily stopped the vehicle and began handing her napkins that he pulled from the glove box.

"God. Oh, God. I'm really sorry. I…I was going too fast."

"Yes," she said drolly. She pulled down the sun visor and studied herself in the mirror attached to the back of it. She was as speckled as a leopard.

"I am sorry, Holly."

"We've established that." She swiped at the side of her face, succeeding only in making several small spots into one large smudge.

"Are you going to say anything?" Nate asked.

"I believe I have been speaking."

"But not talking. To me." He grabbed a napkin and dabbed at her shirt, stopping just short of her breast. "I'm making it worse."

"No. I don't think it can get worse."

He closed his eyes and sighed before leaning his head back against the rest. "This makes two outfits of yours that I've ruined."

He looked and sounded so miserable that she was left with no choice but to take some pity on him. "What is that saying? You're on a roll."

Nate turned his head and opened one eye. "Can you forgive me?"

"They're just clothes, Nate." She patted her gritty

face. "And I was due for a facial. A mud treatment such as this would set me back quite a bit in Paris."

He laughed. The sound held more relief than humor. "I was being an idiot."

"If you're expecting me to disagree with you…" She let the sentence trail off as a challenge, adding in a pair of arched brows for effect.

"I was mad, okay?"

Holly figured that much out for herself, but over what exactly remained unclear. "Why? Because it was none of my business?"

If he'd said yes, she could have lived with that. In fact, she probably would have apologized, too, because he would have been right.

But what he said instead floored her.

"Nadine and I have gone out on and off for years, even…even during high school."

As in, not long after Holly was out of the picture. She pretended to blot at the splotches on the front of her blouse, when in fact she was pressing against that persistent ache in her heart.

"So, you're high-school sweethearts? That's the term for it, right?"

"Yes." He grabbed her hand. "But no. Nadine and I aren't high-school sweethearts. We're just…just two lonely people waiting for the right person to come along." He squeezed Holly's hand. "I don't want you to get the wrong impression of me. I've broken no promises to Nadine, because I've never made her any. And I've always made it clear, or at least tried to, that we… we're not headed anywhere but where we are right now."

Not my business.

Not my business.
Not my business.

Despite the phrase she chanted over and over again in her head, Holly still heard herself ask Nate, "And where might that be?"

He let go of her hand and scrubbed his face. He took his time answering. When he did, she understood perfectly why he'd hesitated.

"In my case at least, it's waiting for someone I can never have."

CHAPTER SEVEN

NATE knew he'd just dropped one hell of a bomb. Holly's shell-shocked expression confirmed as much. He hadn't meant to say it. Part of him wanted to take it back. But it was a fact. One he couldn't deny while sitting across from the only woman who with whom he'd ever felt like he could conquer the world.

Except that he couldn't.

Even assuming she felt the same way, they couldn't have a future together. Morenci's future queen and an American resort owner? Yeah, right. That would never fly.

He glanced over at Holly, who was staring out the window in silence. He wasn't sure what he expected her to say. It certainly wasn't, "I'm seeing someone, too."

Which is what she told him a moment later.

"Ah. Oh. Right." He'd read the news stories, of course. He nodded, not sure what else to say. After all, it made sense. She was halfway through her twenties, the heiress to not just a vast fortune, but to an actual kingdom. She would be expected to marry. He swallowed thickly. And carry on the royal lineage.

On the seat beside him, Holly was saying softly, "He is a nice man. Kind. And very bright."

They were the right words, perfectly acceptable adjectives considering the subject matter, but Nate found the way Holly was studying her hands to be far more revealing.

"You don't love him."

"No." She glanced his way. Even though she smiled, he saw the sadness in her eyes.

"But?" he pressed, knowing the conjunction fit into the equation somewhere.

"My mother thinks Phillip is perfect."

Phillip. The guy would have to be named Phillip. It was a very, well…royal and no-nonsense-sounding name. Nate would bet the title to his resort that the guy never went by plain old Phil.

He was probably going to regret it, but he asked, "So, what does this Phillip do for a living?"

"He's a businessman like you," Holly told him. If only she'd left it at that. But, no, she continued with, "His family owns several oil refineries in my country. Since he's taken over from his father, he's put environmental concerns ahead of corporate profits, which earned him the Royal Medal a couple of years ago. That's how we met."

"Wow. The Royal Medal." Morenci's highest honor. Nate ran his tongue over his teeth. "And a green guy to boot, huh?"

"The environment is important."

"You don't have to tell me," he said. The great outdoors was his meal ticket. "So, um, what happens now?"

"I'm not sure." She shook her head slowly. Her gaze fixed on some point in the distance that he was sure she wasn't seeing, she repeated, "I'm not sure."

Had she not looked so miserable, Nate might have pressed.

Instead, he said, "The island is a great place to think."

Then, without another word, he started the truck. Slowly this time, he drove down the two-track, careful to avoid the worst of the ruts.

It took another twenty minutes before the truck emerged from the dappled green canopy of the woods to a small clearing just up from the lake. There was no sandy beach here, but plenty of reeds and water lilies in the bay's rocky shallows. Before that, the landscape was dotted with wildflowers and the occasional poison ivy plant.

"This is pretty," she remarked. The line between her brows softened as she scanned the scene before her. "It would make a lovely painting."

"A watercolor?" That had been her favorite medium.

She nodded, her gaze riveted on the lake. "The way the colors meld together, teals and blues. It's breathtaking."

It *was* breathtaking. This, Nate knew, was exactly why he'd given up skyscrapers and the madness of city living. As much as he'd thought he'd wanted an urban lifestyle after growing up on a speck of land in the middle of one of the Great Lakes, the truth was he was small-town at heart. He wouldn't make any apologies for that. He glanced over at Holly, noting the rapturous expression on her face, and he knew she wasn't expecting one.

* * *

She started toward the lake.

"Just watch where you walk." Once he had her attention, he pointed out the three-leafed plant that could cause a couple weeks of grief to those who came into contact with it. They both knew that from personal experience.

Once they were almost to the shore, he turned Holly to the right. The chalet was a couple hundred feet down the shore from them. A man and a woman sat on the lower deck. The current occupants were making good use of the gas grill. The scent of sizzling steaks wafted on the breeze along with their laughter.

"That's where you'll be staying."

"Oh, it is lovely."

"And a good hiding place."

His assessment made her frown. "I'm not running away," she insisted.

"Getting away."

She nodded and murmured what sounded like, "Thinking."

"I'm there." He pointed across the bay to where the green tin roof of his lakefront cottage glinted in the sunlight.

Holly turned to him. On a smile, she said, "We'll be next-door neighbors, of a fashion."

"I guess so." He reached out to scratch at a patch of dried mud on her nose.

"I'm a mess."

"A pretty mess," he clarified, resisting the urge to drop a kiss on the very nose he'd just tried to rid of dirt.

"I need to get cleaned up."

Nate nodded. She was right, of course. He should

take her back to his cottage where she could shower
while he swung by the marina. He'd been gone several
hours. In the meantime, a couple of yachts were due in
today, one of them making the Saint Lawrence loop that
took the big crafts from the open waters of the Atlantic
Ocean all the way inland to the Great Lakes system.
This one was out of Fort Myers, Florida, and was destined for Chicago.

Despite his responsibilities back at the marina, Nate
said, "Lake's right there."

"Excuse me?"

"The lake." He nodded in its direction a second time.
"It's still a bit chilly this time of year." In fact, this far
north, it rarely became anything other than what the
polite termed *refreshing*. With a grin, he added, "But I
never knew you to mind a cool dip."

"Are you daring me, Nathaniel Matthews?"

How was it he found her arched eyebrows and use
of his full name so damned sexy?

His first genuine smile in days unfurled. "Yes,
ma'am. I believe I am."

Her chin rose. "I don't like to swim alone. In fact,
that was my grandmother's rule."

"Swim with a buddy," he finished for her before his
throat closed.

"So…" Holly blinked guilelessly at him as she
backed toward the water, shedding her shoes as she
went. "Will you be my buddy, Nate?"

I'll be anything you damn well want me to be, he
nearly replied.

But that would be foolish, not to mention presump-
tuous. Holly wasn't asking him to be anything but a

friend. She had someone waiting for her back in her country. Someone she might not love, but who was far more suitable to her station in life.

He reminded himself of that fact again and again as he watched her wade backward into the water, her smile as tempting as a siren's song. He found it didn't matter. He loved seeing her like this: smiling, having fun and acting very much like the girl she'd once been.

Except she was all woman now.

Awareness pummeled Nate as the waves lapped gently at Holly's body, first wetting her calves and then her thighs. Soon enough, the capri pants she had on were soaked. They stuck to her body like a second skin, tugging a groan from deep in his chest. Need built inside him, even more fierce than the likes of which he'd experienced the evening before when he'd kissed her. Nate decided it was just as well that when the water reached her waist, Holly turned and dove under.

She bobbed to the surface a few feet away. Then she stood. It was all Nate could do to remain on his feet— his knees felt that weak.

The water was just below her breasts now. And the blouse she wore had turned all but translucent, molding to her curves. The water was *very* cold indeed.

He held his breath as she leaned over and used her cupped hand to splash some of it on her face and hair, removing the last traces of mud.

"Aren't you coming in?" she called to him as she straightened.

Any other woman and he would have been galloping through the surf at that invitation. But this was Holly. If Nate waded in to where she stood, he would want to touch her. He would *need* to touch her, he amended silently. Just as he had the other night. And if he touched her…

Well, it wouldn't be a good idea. For either of them. He decided to leave it at that, even though his imagination was, at that very moment, busy filling in all of the blanks.

"Nah. I'll sit this one out. I can be your buddy from here."

He lowered himself onto a stump, watching enviously as she played in the surf.

Lucky water. Lucky waves.

A moment later, she waded ashore, wringing out her hair and the ends of her blouse as she came.

"All better," she announced, gingerly picking her way through the rocks and vegetation.

Nate begged to differ, but he merely nodded.

When she reached him, her brows drew together. "Nate, didn't you warn me to watch out for poison ivy around here?"

"Sure did." He repeated the old saw: "Leaves of three, leave 'em be."

She pressed a finger to her lower lip. "I fear you may be surrounded by it."

He glanced about only a second before launching himself off the log. Damn, if she wasn't right. How could he have missed it, trained outdoorsman as he was? But, of course, he knew. He'd been distracted.

Very, very distracted.

To her credit, Holly didn't tease him for the faux pas he hadn't made in a dozen years. Nor did she laugh. She didn't even crack a smile. Though, from her expression, he could tell it was costing her. Nate did the only thing that he could under the circumstances. He forgot all about dignity and decorum. With a whoop suitable to the Native American warriors who had long ago occupied the island, he made a beeline for the water, stripping off his shirt and shedding his shoes as he ran. He could only hope that any of the plant's oil on his body would be washed away before an allergic reaction had time to get started.

He blasted through the shallows, despite the rocky bottom, and headed for the drop-off he remembered to the far right of where they'd come in. Just at the threshold of where the water changed from aquamarine to deep blue, he tucked himself into a ball, launched himself in the air and hollered, "Geronimo!"

Unfortunately, his launch turned out to be a bit premature. In his defense, it had been a long time since Nate had done a cannonball at this actual site. Years, in fact. He landed on his bottom end with a thud just shy of the deep water. Thank God he was still wearing his shorts or his butt would have endured a sandpapering the likes of which the old cabinets in some of the resort's cabins had endured prior to being refinished.

"I give you a six," Holly hollered from the shore. She was holding up the corresponding number of fingers and grinning madly.

She looked adorable and desirable, two adjectives Nate normally wouldn't put together. But this *was* Holly. Just that quickly, he was sucked back in time. Foolish though he knew it to be, he called, "Come on out, sunshine, and show me what a ten looks like."

She planted her hands on her hips, her smile just this

side of jaunty. "Do you really think you can handle the embarrassment, Matthews?"

Though he could reach the bottom, he flipped onto his back and floated as if he hadn't a care in the world. And, damn, if he didn't feel that way at the moment.

"Bring it on," he challenged.

She dashed through the surf, grinning like a kid the entire time. No one would mistake her for a princess just then, Nate thought. Idly, he wondered what old Phil would think. When she reached the drop-off, she executed a perfect tuck-and-launch before disappearing under the water.

Oh, yeah. A definite ten.

Then she rose up from the water like some damned mermaid, flipping back the honeyed locks of her long hair, and he doubled the score.

"So?" she asked.

He waded toward her and took the plunge. Literally. The lake bottom fell away and Nate found himself treading water, his arms reaching for and then reeling in the one woman who filled his fantasies, but who could never fulfill the dreams he'd almost forgotten existed.

"You're a ten," he said truthfully, as they treaded water together.

"Really? I haven't lost my touch?"

"Not in the least." Then, even though Nate called himself a dozen kinds of fool, he kissed her.

Holly forgot to kick her legs. Come to that, she forgot to breathe. They wound up submerged, mouths locked together. Desire like she'd only allowed herself to imagine washed over her, as insistent as the waves.

Nate kicked upward, taking them to the surface, where they both gasped for air. Even so, they remained locked in an embrace—an embrace suited to lovers, given the way their bodies were pressed tightly together. His warmth helped take away the lake water's chill.

The first word Holly managed was not *thanks* or even *sorry*. Rather, it was "Please."

It was a foolish plea. Please what? She wasn't sure she had an answer for herself, let alone one for Nate. Thus it came as a relief when he didn't ask her for clarification. Instead, he kicked sideways, one arm jutting out in powerful sidestrokes that moved them inland. Before she knew it, her feet were once again planted on the seabed. They rose together. She felt oddly vulnerable, naked in a way that went beyond her soaked clothes. And one glance down had her cringing. Good heavens, her shirt was nearly see-through and the bra she was wearing wasn't much better.

Embarrassment made sense right now. But another emotion lingered with it, oddly reminiscent of the feeling she'd gotten when she'd secretly chartered a jet to America and then asked Henry to drive her to the airport.

On the shore, they picked up their discarded shoes and headed for the truck in silence. All the while awareness taunted her. The man looked good in wet cargo shorts, better, in fact, than most men of her acquaintance managed to look outfitted in designer attire.

Nate pulled a folded blanket from the truck bed,

shaking leaves and debris from it before handing it to Holly.

"You're probably cold." He cleared his throat.

Holly felt her cheeks grow warm. Yes, that much *was* obvious. Gratefully, she pulled it around her body and slipped into the truck's cab. In addition to her breasts' embarrassing reaction to the chilly water, her teeth were chattering and her skin was prickled with gooseflesh, which was why she found it amazing that she still felt on fire.

The drive back to the main road was quiet. Nate drove slowly this time, glancing sideways with each rut they hit. Holly never said a word. She didn't complain. She didn't tease. She simply remained silent, her hands gripping the edges of the blanket around her. He could only imagine what she was thinking. God, he'd screwed up royally. No pun intended.

He hadn't meant to kiss her. Again. He knew better after that kiss the night before. But once she'd been in his arms, her body pressed against his… He swallowed thickly now.

I'm not a saint.

But it was more than his lack of restraint that was the issue here. It was the woman. Holly was his first love, and even though Nate had long tried to deny it, she was his *only* love. Which was why he would both treasure and regret kissing her today. This was a memory that would haunt him long after the woman was gone.

He had barely pulled the truck to a stop outside his cottage and she had already unbuckled her seat belt and was reaching for the door handle.

"If you could telephone Hank while I change my clothes, I would appreciate it," she called over her shoulder as she headed into the house.

The screen door squawked open before slamming closed behind her. Nate sighed heavily. So, she really did plan to return to the mainland for the time between now and when she could check in at the chalet. It made sense. Perfect sense. What didn't make sense was the fact that Nate sat on his deck, sipping a beer, rather than making the requested phone call.

Holly was only in America for a short time, he rationalized as he waited for her. That was long enough to disturb his peace, but not nearly long enough to satisfy his curiosity or his interest. He was being selfish perhaps, and definitely foolish, but he wanted as much of her as he could have, even if afterward her memory made him ache.

Besides, for a little while this afternoon, she'd looked so carefree and happy. Her laughter had echoed across the bay, every bit as enchanting as the loon's call first thing on quiet mornings. He liked knowing that he had a hand in that. Taking another sip of beer, he decided that perhaps his reasons weren't so selfish after all.

Half an hour later, he was still sitting in his favorite lounge chair, staring out at the view, when she opened the sliding glass door and joined him. She'd pulled her hair into a simple ponytail and had changed into a pair of crisp tan walking shorts. The blouse she wore was red, with rolled-up cuffs that buttoned just above her elbows.

"So, what time did Hank say he would be here?" she inquired.

Nate glanced past her. Just inside the house was the same stack of luggage with which she'd arrived the day before.

Had it really been a mere day since Nate's life had been turned upside down? In less than twenty-four hours he'd gone from wishing she'd never come to wishing she never had to leave. He'd never been much of a fan of roller coasters, but he'd ride this one to the end.

"He, uh, can't." Nate rose upon saying so. It felt wrong to remain seated when offering a lie.

Holly blinked. "He can't."

"Sorry. No. His plane is booked. For the next few days, in fact." Nate marveled at his talent for lying. If only he were this good when it came to playing poker with the guys. He would have been able to pay cash for the parcel of land just up the beach, rather than having had to jump through hoops to secure a bank loan.

"Another pilot, perhaps?"

"Hank said the pilots he would recommend are busy right now." He hunched his shoulders. "Apparently, the storm threw schedules off."

Holly's expression darkened as reality set in. "Oh. Oh, my."

"It's all right. You can stay here until Sunday." Nate felt the need to restrain his hands by putting them into the pockets of his still damp shorts when he added, "As my guest. In the, um, guest room."

Also known as his boyhood bedroom. Fantasy central.

"I don't know."

She nibbled her lower lip. God help him, Nate wanted

to do the same. Instead, he reminded her, "You slept in there last night."

"Yes, but…" She gestured with her hand. "Hank."

Ah, yes. Their snoring chaperone.

Guilt nipped at him only a little when he said, "Holly, come on. Despite what just went on at the lake, you can trust me."

She looked abashed. "Of course I can. I didn't mean to imply otherwise. It's just…"

"Just what?"

They eyed one another for a moment. Then she leveled him with her words.

"I don't know that I can trust myself."

Nate did the only thing a man could do after a beautiful woman offered up a declaration like that. He hightailed it to his pickup truck and sped away. In this case, only a short distance away. Specifically, to the resort's marina, even though it was close enough to walk.

Good God! What was he getting himself into? After slowly making its way to the top, that roller coaster he was riding was not only taking a steep plunge, but also threatening to go off the tracks.

Holly didn't trust herself around Nate?

He'd be lying if he claimed that wasn't music to his ears. His ego wasn't hurting at the moment, either, though other parts of him were damned uncomfortable, and not all of them could be found in his shorts. But he'd gone through this once before with her. He'd gotten involved, put his heart on the line. It had wound up good and busted.

The difference this time, Nate reminded himself,

was that he would be going in with his eyes wide open, well aware that the odds were stacked against anything long-term. Sure, Holly was eager for a simpler life and confused about her supposed engagement to a man her mother had all but handpicked for her. But none of that meant she and Nate had a future together.

How would that work anyway? Which one of them would move? She couldn't very well govern her country while living in his. And he couldn't imagine giving up his blissfully low-key lifestyle to live in Morenci's stylish capital city and run with the jet set.

The twins were at the marina when he entered the shop, which also served as the resort's front desk. So was Mick Langley, who'd worked the main cash register since Nate was a toddler.

The man's hair was solid gray now and his big hands gnarled with arthritis. He was past the age of retirement. Well past it. But he put in a full day's work five days a week and he never complained. Heck, even on his days off he could be found somewhere on the resort grounds. He loved the place as much as Nate did.

"Hey, Nate."

"Mick." He glanced out at the marina, where a couple of big cabin cruisers were moored in the outermost slips. "Those yachts get in without incident?"

"Yep. The Burns brothers might be young, but they've been taught well."

"Thanks to you."

The older man acknowledged the compliment with a shrug. "They're an asset to the resort. So are you. You've done your folks proud."

"Thanks."

Nate wondered what his parents would think if they knew Holly was back. They'd liked her. They'd also witnessed his heartache.

"They comin' for a visit anytime soon?" Mick asked.

"I spoke to my mom a couple days ago. They're thinking the end of July, but no firm plans have been made yet. Dad's playing in a local golf tournament."

It seemed his dad was always playing in a golf tournament these days, Nate thought fondly.

"Be good to seem 'em." Mick nodded.

"Yes."

Eager for something to occupy his mind, Nate went behind the counter and scanned the day's receipts. They'd rented out two fishing boats and a handful of canoes thanks to the calm waters after the storm. Bicycle rentals were up, too.

He tucked the receipts back in the drawer. "Anything else I need to know about?"

"Not really." Mick scratched one wiry sideburn then and snorted. "Gave out a lot of free bait today."

Nate nodded. "I figured our guests deserved a little perk after the storm knocked out the cable."

"I'd say that was a good call. Been a lot of fishing from the dock today. Adults, kids… In my book that sure beats sitting around watching the boob tube anyday."

Holly had liked fishing. She'd even baited her own hook back in the day.

"They catch anything?" Nate asked.

"Sure did. Saw a few of them haul in some serious keepers."

"Yeah?" Half his mouth crooked up in a smile, even as his mind wandered again to the "keeper" he'd pulled out of the bay a few hours earlier.

"A couple twelve-inch perch," the older man said.

"Hmm. Not bad."

"And a sixteen-inch rock bass."

Nate blinked at that. "Off the marina dock. Really?"

Mick was nodding. "A kid of about ten hauled that one up, and with a bamboo pole of all things. No proper reel even. Even the old-timers who camp out at the end of the dock were impressed."

"And a little envious, I bet."

"Yep. That kind of luck and the good memories of today will bring the family back next year."

Which gave Nate an idea.

The older man's expression soured, but Nate was only half listening as Mick launched into a lengthy complaint about the cormorants he'd seen earlier on a sandbar a hundred yards off the marina. The diving birds could ruin a good fishing spot.

Nate was busy putting together some supplies. The rod he selected offered good flex. The reel wasn't top-of-the-line, but it would do the job. He had bobbers, sinkers and hooks in the tackle box back at his house. As well as the other equipment necessary to do a little recreational fishing.

Meanwhile, Mick had wound himself up good. "Damned birds are pests!" Next he would be declaring that they should be shot on sight regardless of their protection under the federal law as migratory fowl.

Nate glanced over at him when Mick became silent. A frown wrinkled the older man's forehead.

"What are you doing there? Something happen to that fancy rod and reel of yours?"

"This is for someone else. A guest." Nostalgia had him smiling. "She used to be one hell of an angler."

"She forget to bring her stuff this trip?"

"Something like that," Nate replied.

Mick seemed to accept the explanation. Then he remarked. "I saw you out driving with a girl today. The Burns boys told me she was an old friend of the family."

Nate cleared his throat. "Old friend. Exactly."

Mick looked about as convinced as Nate felt in offering the description. He tried again. "Holly. You remember her." How could anyone forget her? "She, um, used to come here with her grandmother when she was a kid."

Mick's eyes narrowed. "That skinny little kid with the funny accent?"

Nate nearly choked on his laughter. He figured Holly would be as amused by the description as he was. "That's one way to describe her. She wasn't from around these parts." He coughed and added a vague "Europe."

"Europe?"

Let's not go there. So, Nate redirected. "Yes, but her grandmother was from Texas. Add those two locations together and it's no wonder you thought she talked a little funny."

The older man was nodding, "Sure, sure. I remember her now. The grandmother was a looker. I seem to remember some talk…" Mick's words trailed off and he glanced sharply at Nate.

"The island gets under people's skin. Once they've come here, experienced it, they always find their way back."

"I'd say so." Mick's expression was knowing.

CHAPTER EIGHT

SHE was the one seated on the deck enjoying a beer when he arrived home a couple of hours later. Any awkwardness she might have felt evaporated when she spied the fishing pole.

Her eyes lit up like a kid's at Christmas. "Is that for me?"

Nate nodded. "I didn't figure you had remembered to pack your fishing pole."

He'd attached the reel at the marina. It just needed tackle and some bait and she would be ready to cast the line into the bay.

"It's perfect."

"It's a fishing pole."

"Yes, but you're the only person I know who would think to give me one."

From her tone and glowing expression he knew she meant that as a compliment.

"Thank you."

"You're welcome."

"Can we go fishing?"

"Right now?"

Some of her excitement dimmed. "I'm sorry. You probably have other things to do."

He couldn't think of one. For that matter, even if he did, he would have cleared his schedule, just to see her eyes light up again.

"It's not that, Holly. It's the license. We used to sell them at the marina, but since the state Department of Natural Resources and Environment started leasing office space from us last summer, we decided to leave that to them."

"They're closed for the day," she ventured.

"Besides, the best fishing around here is in the morning off the marina dock."

"I guess I can wait." She leaned the pole against the cedar siding. "Patience is a virtue, or so I've been told."

Patience. Nate was feeling anything but at the moment. Need growled along with his stomach.

"Dinner," he blurted out. "We should eat."

Holly claimed not to be hungry, but she was a guest in his home, under his care, and he knew she hadn't eaten much all day. Now it was past seven o'clock.

Briefly, Nate considered making spaghetti. He was quite capable of boiling water, cooking pasta and heating up sauce from a jar. Chop up some lettuce for a salad, add in some garlic toast and it was a tasty and filling meal. One that had been a staple of his diet during college. It still was when he chose to eat in. But spaghetti—even paired with a salad and some garlic bread, neither of which he had on hand—wouldn't address the main issue.

If they stayed in, they would be alone. No chaperones. No excuses to heed. As much as Nate wanted to be with Holly, he didn't want to rush things. That roller coaster be damned. She wasn't the only one who didn't trust herself.

"How about we go out?" he asked.

"If that's what you want."

What he wanted? Nate bit back a groan. He wasn't going to go there.

"Out. Definitely." He hitched a thumb over his shoulder. "I'm just going to change my, uh…" He motioned to his clothing, wondering what he had in his closet besides T-shirts that didn't require an iron's attention.

Her brow crinkled. "Should I change as well?"

"No." She was perfect just as she was.

Upstairs, Nate decided on a quick shower and, after a glance at his reflection in the mirror, a shave. He took a little extra care with his hair, adding in some styling gel that the woman who regularly cut his hair had recommended. He was overdue for a cut, so he hoped it would tame the worst of his waves. While he was at it, he gargled with a mint-flavored mouthwash and slapped on some cologne whose cap was layered in dust from disuse.

In his bedroom closet, he found a pair of khaki shorts. No cargo pockets on the sides of these. He added a pale blue button-down shirt. He could have left it untucked, but he decided to go the more formal route, which required him to add a belt. Sandals and sneakers were out. Nate had a pair of deck shoes…somewhere. He found them under his bed surrounded by dust bunnies.

"You look very nice," Holly said when he came downstairs. "And do I smell cologne?"

Nate felt heat gather in his cheeks. "I showered," he said by way of explanation.

"Your hair looks different, too."

He shrugged. "Combed it."

"Very debonair." She tucked away a smile. She was teasing him.

"I may not be Prince Charming, but I don't always look like a beach bum."

It sounded like she said, "Who wants Prince Charming?" But she'd turned away to collect her purse from the couch.

In the truck she asked, "Are we going to the Fishing Hole? I wasn't old enough to get in there the last time I was on the island."

Nate shook his head. "I was thinking of something a little less rowdy. There's a place called Beside the Bay that has a great outside patio."

It catered to the yacht crowd and high-end tourists who rented out high-end homes, such as the one Holly would be staying in. It was by far the fanciest establishment on the island, with a Cordon Bleu-trained chef and a stellar wine selection.

"Is the restaurant new?"

"Pretty new." He nodded. "But it's been in business for half a dozen years."

Beside the Bay was done in what designers would call rustic chic. The building itself was Frank Lloyd Wright-inspired with an iron roof. Hanging baskets and pots that were overflowing with flowers welcomed diners to its entry at the end of a flagstone path that led from the parking lot.

They were shown to a table at the interior of the restaurant, away from the big windows that looked out onto the lake. That was a bit of a disappointment, since the view was five-star.

Even as Holly was resigning herself to a seat indoors, Nate was asking their hostess, whom he of course knew, "Would it be a problem, Danielle, if my friend and I were to dine outside this evening?"

"Not at all, Nate."

Only a couple of other tables were occupied on the deck, and the people sitting at those were sipping drinks rather than dining. But a smiling waiter brought them a couple of menus a few minutes later and took their drink order. Nate requested an imported beer. Holly went with white wine.

"This is a lovely spot for dinner, Nate. Thank you."

"The view is hard to compete with, but the food is pretty good, too." Curiosity had him asking, "What kind of places do you frequent back home? Are you still a fan of pepperoni pizza?"

"I am." She laughed. "Not that there are many places in Morenci that serve the kind found here in the States." Holly leaned closer and in a low voice confided, "For my sixteenth birthday, my grandmother had a pizzeria send me a dozen pies via airmail."

"I'm thinking they probably weren't still hot when they arrived."

"They were frozen. I ate one a week for three months, despite my mother's warnings that the grease would make my face break out."

"So, if you don't hang out at the local pizzeria, where do you go to eat?"

"I don't dine out very often," she admitted. "Not at

restaurants at least. Mostly, when I'm not eating in, I'm at some sort of official function, a charity ball or state dinner. The food is wonderful, of course, but…it's not the same."

"That's because it's work."

She glanced up. "Yes. Exactly."

"That must be hard."

"It's…expected."

"Doesn't make it less difficult."

"No."

The waiter arrived with their drinks and took their entrée orders. They'd decided to forgo an appetizer since their meals came with salads and a cup of the day's soup. They both went with blackened lake trout.

Once they were alone again, Nate asked, "So, where do you and Phillip go on an evening out?"

"Actually, Phillip and I rarely appear in public unless it's at official events."

Hence the swirl of rumors regarding the serious nature of their relationship, he guessed.

"So, you dine in?"

"Yes. At the palace. And…"

"His home?" he finished for her.

Holly nodded, her gaze riveted to the lake. The sun was just starting to lower over the bay, but he doubted that was what captivated her attention. "In addition to his family's estates in Morenci, he has a lovely villa in the south of France."

Despite her rather unimpressed tone, Nate's head felt as if it would explode. He wasn't going to try to compete with the guy. There was no reason to, but still…

A small voice reminded him that Holly didn't love

Phillip. As much as Nate wanted to latch onto that, he couldn't help wondering if she could be happy living a different lifestyle. One slower-paced and far more casual. And not just for a couple of weeks, but 24/7? Even as he was telling himself that some things just weren't meant to be, he was recalling her expression when he'd given her the fishing pole.

Before either of them could speak again, a woman appeared at their table. She was older, a little on the plump side, and carried in her hands a little dog that was outfitted with more bling than most Hollywood starlets wore on Oscar night.

There was a good bit of the South in her drawl when she said, "I hate to interrupt your dinner, young lady, but I just have to say what a striking resemblance you bear to Princess Hollyn of Morenci."

"That's very kind of you," Holly replied, neither acknowledging her true identity nor denying it.

"Oh, my gosh! And you talk like her, too!" the woman exclaimed with such excitement it caused her little dog to start yipping.

The other diners glanced their way. Nate's stomach pitched and rolled. This was it. She was exposed. Holly, on the other hand, appeared unaffected.

In a confidential tone, she said, "I'll let you in on a little secret."

"Yes?" The older woman leaned in eagerly.

"I'm a celebrity impersonator."

The woman's eyes widened. "You're kidding."

"No. I make a good living at it, too. I think it's my accent that clinches it for me. I've worked for years to perfect it."

"It's very good. You had me fooled."

"Not to brag, but my agent tells me I'm the best of the bunch."

"Oh, you are," the other woman gushed. "You absolutely are."

"Thank you for saying so. It's always good to hear from an objective person. My mother, of course, thinks I'm spot on." Holly shrugged. "But she's my mother. What else is she supposed to think?"

The woman nodded before casting a sheepish glance Nate's way. "I'm sorry to have interrupted your dinner." Her gaze back on Holly, she said, "I was going to ask for your autograph and to see if you wanted to take a picture with me."

"Really? I'm so flattered."

"But since you're not who I thought you were…" The woman's cheeks flamed scarlet. "I mean, I'd be happy to have my picture taken with you anyway."

"That's kind, but I think you should aim your camera lens at that incredible view." Holly pointed to the lake, where the sun was starting to set. "It's far more memorable than I am, believe me."

"I think I'll do just that," the woman agreed. "Thank you, by the way."

"For?"

"Being so gracious. I've approached real celebrities who weren't half as kind and patient as you are, and you're not anyone." She coughed delicately. "Well, you know what I mean."

"I do. And the pleasure was mine."

Holly was grinning from ear to ear when the woman left.

"I'd say you handled that encounter like a pro," Nate told her.

"I was feeling inspired." Holly shrugged then. "Besides, if I had been rude or standoffish, it only would have raised her suspicions."

"Is that the only reason you weren't rude or standoffish?" he asked.

"Of course not. People are curious. Most of them, such as that woman, mean no harm. They are what you would call starstruck."

Nate grinned. "You make a good celebrity impersonator, by the way. Do you do that often?"

"Actually, that was a first for me."

"Really?"

"I'm not often without a royal escort. Still, it seemed like a good idea in this instance," Holly explained. "After all, she had me pegged. Flat-out denial only would have made it worse. This way, she feels like she's part of the deception."

It was hard not to marvel at Holly's cleverness and composure. "She didn't even want to snap your photograph."

"Exactly."

He liked her all the more for the jaunty smile she beamed at him afterward. There was so much of that young girl he remembered still inside her.

Their drinks arrived along with a basket of freshly baked rolls and their salads.

Nate raised his beverage in a toast. "To a rising star."

Holly clinked her wineglass against his beer glass, but she set it back on the table without taking a sip. She seemed circumspect when she said, "I am hardly a star.

I was born into my position and the corresponding celebrity. I've done nothing to earn either."

"I don't know about that. I mean, the position part, I'll give you. You were born into the role of princess. Call it fate or luck or whatever. But how you choose to act in public and use celebrity is entirely up to you."

"It's a lot of responsibility." He saw her swallow and her shoulders sagged a little, as if bowing under the weight of that responsibility.

"It's a lot of power, too," he said quietly.

"I have no power, Nate. I can't even decide my own future." Her laughter was surprisingly sardonic. She must have realized it. She added in a tone more suited to a civics teacher, "The royal family's role in Morenci is purely ceremonial and has been for more than a century. We don't set policy or make laws."

"But you still wield a lot of influence, Holly. It's up to you how you choose to use it. I think you know that, which is why you've been a voice for orphans in some of the world's poorest countries and championed access to education for girls in cultures that traditionally reserve that right only for boys."

"You've been reading up on me, I see." She leveled the accusation playfully, but a hint of embarrassment stained her cheeks as she reached for one of the warm rolls.

"I've followed your life over the years," he admitted. Odd, but a day ago no one would have been able to force Nate to make such a confession. Now, he continued, "I wondered how you were and what your life was like when the public wasn't watching. I wondered, you know, if you were okay."

In the images of her that he'd seen on television or in print she'd seemed so reserved, so…lifeless.

"You were worried about me?" She broke off a piece of roll.

Dangerous territory, he decided, but he answered truthfully. "I was." As mad as he'd been, and as hurt, he'd also been concerned.

"I wondered if you were all right as well. And if… if you'd forgiven me."

He hadn't. Until she'd returned. Holding a grudge made even less sense than holding on to the tender feelings he had for her. But those tender feelings, he knew, would be much harder to set free.

"I'm not mad anymore. You did what you felt you had to do, maybe even what was for the best. But I wish you'd sent that letter you told me you'd written. I wish I would have heard it from you rather than seeing you in a televised special on European royalty not long after you'd turned sixteen."

She pinched her eyes closed. "I am sorry."

"It's the past, Holly." He reached across the table, found her hand and gave it a squeeze. "What do you say we just concentrate on the here and now."

"The here and now," she repeated. She reached for her wine, and this time after their glasses clinked together, she took a sip.

With both the past and the future put out of mind, they enjoyed the rest of their meal. The conversation centered mainly on small talk, but it veered into personal territory enough that it was impossible not to enjoy himself. She was fun and funny, smart and interesting. She was, in short, every bit as remarkable as he remembered her being.

Once they left the restaurant, his hand slipped to the small of her back. Nate had to remind himself this wasn't a date. Indeed, the very reason he'd taken Holly out was to avoid being alone with her. Of course, now, night had fallen and they were heading back to his quiet cottage. Together.

The easy conversation they'd enjoyed during dinner was long gone by the time he pulled the truck to a stop and came around to open Holly's door.

"Thank you again for dinner," she said once they were inside the cottage.

They both glanced uncertainly toward the stairs. "You're welcome."

"Maybe tomorrow you'll let me treat you."

She'd offered tonight. He'd refused. It wasn't pride, or even the fact that she was female that had caused him to do so. Rather, the old-fashioned belief drilled into him by his mother that when one had a guest under one's roof, one picked up the tab.

Just as his mother had drummed it into Nate's head that a man never pressed or pressured a woman.

"Maybe," he replied, to stave off an argument.

She nodded. "I…I'm rather tired. I think I'll turn in."

"It's been a long day," he agreed.

"Especially for you. I only woke up around noon." It was half past nine now. "You were up much earlier, I would imagine."

"That I was."

"Nate…" She took a step toward him.

He resisted doing the same. That foot and half of

space between them was the only thing keeping his hormones in check. "Good night, Holly."

Holly nodded in understanding. "Good night."

She wasn't halfway up the stairs before Nate knew he would be sleeping outside on the deck.

It was the only place he trusted himself to be with Holly under his roof.

And didn't it just figure, as miserable as he already felt, the first itchy welts from the poison ivy had started to appear on his calves.

Holly didn't know how she managed it, but she spent the following night within easy reach of Nate Matthews without, well, ever *reaching* for him.

To think her mother felt Holly needed to work on her self-control. Olivia would be amazed—and, no doubt, relieved.

Of course, it helped immensely that after that first night when she and Nate dined together, they barely saw one another. Friday morning, she awoke to find him gone, and a blanket and pillow taking up space on one of the deck's lounge chairs. He'd slept there, she knew. Because she'd heard his footsteps on the stairs not only coming up, but also going down a moment later as she'd lain awake holding her breath and foolishly wishing he would tap at her door.

That evening, he came home well after dark, although he thoughtfully had one of the island's delis deliver a meal for her to eat. She dined alone on the deck, trying to take delight in the view, but missing his company.

The public thought she had it made. She felt no bitterness over that fact. Now. Interestingly, nor did she feel the old sense of resignation.

She'd come to Heart Island for a last reprieve. Literally, for a final bit of time in the sun before taking on the latest yoke of royal responsibility: marriage and the whole business of begetting heirs.

Holly had thought that coming here would make it easier to accept her future. But if anything, seeing Nate again and stealing romantic moments that both of them likely would live to regret had only made it more difficult.

Given the way he was avoiding her, she figured he felt the same way.

It didn't help when Nadine arrived at the cottage on Saturday, Holly's final night. The other woman came, ostensibly, to deliver the keys to the place Holly had rented on the other side of the bay, even though Holly wouldn't be able to check in until the following afternoon. But the way she glanced around spoke volumes. She perceived Holly as a threat.

If only.

"Nate isn't here," Holly said. She folded her hands at her waist and smiled her most serene smile. Oh, what it cost her on the inside.

"Oh, I wasn't expecting to find him home. I saw his truck up at the marina."

"Then what were you hoping to find?" Holly's face began to ache beneath the smile.

"I don't know what you mean." The other woman blinked innocently.

Holly blinked back. "Oh. I'm sorry. I must have been mistaken."

Nadine expelled a breath then. "No. I'm the one who's sorry. I...I've been curious."

"About?" Holly asked, even though she was sure she knew.

"You and Nate and..." She swept her hand in an arc. "And your living arrangements."

"Sleeping arrangements, I believe, is what you really mean."

Nadine had the grace to grimace and then to apologize again. "I'm sorry. You seem like a very nice person and you've already told me that you and Nate have known each other since childhood. I must seem a little pathetic."

"Not at all." *Suspicious and territorial, certainly. But not pathetic.* Holly would feel the same way if she were in the other woman's shoes.

"Nate might have mentioned that we date."

"He did. Yes."

"It's not serious."

He'd told her that, too. "But you would like it to be," Holly said sympathetically.

"Yes." Nadine fiddled with the band of her wristwatch. "We get along very well, Nate and I. We like a lot of the same things—movies, food, you name it. But I've always sensed that he was holding back."

She glanced up at Holly then. Nadine no longer looked like the successful businesswoman she was, or the jealous, sometimes girlfriend who'd brashly come calling on a potential threat. Now, she just looked vulnerable...and uncertain.

She was saying, "I told myself it was just a typical case of commitment phobia and that eventually he would come around. But…"

Holly waited silently for the other woman to continue. What could she say? *Don't worry about me as competition. Even if Nate does have feelings for me, they can never come to anything.*

"I think he loves you," Nadine announced. "I think he's always loved you."

Holly's mouth dropped open, but the denial drumming in her head never made it to her lips. And, even though she knew it was foolish and hopeless, her heart thunked almost painfully in her chest.

He loves me.

The door opened then. At the threshold stood the man in question, his expression wary as he divided his gaze between the pair of them.

"Hi."

"Nate!" Nadine pasted a smile on her face that did nothing to camouflage her guilt. "Hi."

He nodded to Holly before saying, "I thought that was your car I saw drive past the marina."

"I…I came to give Holly the key to the place she rented for the next couple weeks."

It was completely plausible. Nate seemed to relax. For her part, Holly held up said key and smiled.

"It will be ready anytime after noon tomorrow. The current occupants have checked out early, but housekeeping hasn't finished up inside yet."

"I'm not in any hurry," Holly said. She flushed immediately. It wasn't exactly the right thing to say.

Nate pointed toward the kitchen. "I just came home

to grab a bite to eat. You're welcome to join me. Both of us."

Holly didn't bother to add that she'd already helped herself to some leftovers from the previous night's take-out.

"Thanks for the offer, but I can't stay. I...have a little work to finish up at the office before I can finally knock off for what remains of the weekend," Nadine explained.

"Okay. Well, good seeing you."

"Yes. You, too. And thanks again for bringing me some business." Nadine worked up what passed for a smile.

"No problem."

Holly turned to him the moment the other woman was out the door. "Are you oblivious or just insensitive?"

"What do you mean?" Nate toed off his shoes slowly, like a man who clearly knew that he'd stepped in something messy.

"Nadine is half in love with you!" Actually wholly in love with him, but Holly sought to leave the poor woman some dignity. After all, she knew how Nadine felt.

His brow furrowed. "Why are you so worked up?"

She didn't have an actual answer for him, at least not one that made sense, so she crossed her arms and remained stoic.

Nate continued. "The other day you were upset over that fact for a different reason, if I'm not mistaken."

He had her there. Holly tried again. "You need to be honest with her."

In an instant, Nate went from being cautiously baffled to angry. "I've been nothing but honest! With her. With you." He jabbed a finger in Holly's direction. "The one I've lied to all along has been myself! I've pretended that I'm over you. Well, guess what, Princess. That's never happened."

His outburst left Holly speechless for a moment. As he raked the hair back from his forehead, she found her voice.

"I just want you to be happy, Nate."

"So, what? You want me to marry Nadine?"

No! Her response was as visceral as his earlier one had been. But what Holly managed to say, and in a tone that was amazingly neutral under the circumstances, was, "If that's what it takes, then yes."

"So, because you're willing to make a lifetime commitment to someone you don't love, I should, too?"

She stepped back as if he'd struck her. Before she could respond, he was already apologizing.

"God, Holly. I'm sorry. That was uncalled for. Our situations are vastly different."

"Yes."

But as Holly laid awake long into the night, she found herself wondering if they had to be.

CHAPTER NINE

NATE was still asleep on the deck when Holly crept downstairs early the next morning and took the cordless telephone from its cradle in the kitchen. She'd reached some conclusions during the long, sleepless night. The first was that she needed to call Phillip.

After speaking to her mother that first night on the island, she'd left a brief comment on his office voice mail, well aware he wouldn't be at work to receive it. It was the act of a coward, she could readily admit. Well, an actual conversation couldn't be put off any longer. In fact, it was something that should have occurred a long time ago, not long after she and Phillip were first introduced. Certainly after he'd first broached the subject of marriage.

Nate was right. Holly wasn't without power. And, while her options might be limited, she wasn't without choices, either. She would not marry a man she didn't love, regardless of how "perfect" her mother and others in Morenci deemed him to be.

Phillip answered in French on the third ring. He'd been raised speaking French, which, along with Italian and English, were all spoken in Morenci. She answered in kind.

"Bonjour."

"Hollyn! God in heaven!" he declared. "I have been so eager for your call."

"Did you not receive my earlier message?" she asked.

"Yes. But it was so brief and you sounded, well, you sounded very unlike yourself. It only served to make me more concerned."

Holly wanted to be touched by his words. She wanted to feel even a glimmer of the warmth that she'd felt upon hearing Nate's confession that he'd been worried about her when she hadn't returned to Heart Island that first summer.

But that great void inside of her remained empty, just as she'd known it would. There was no love to fill it up. Respect and affection were insubstantial as substitutes.

"I must apologize for leaving so abruptly. I've been in touch with my mother and so I am well aware of what an inconvenience my absence has been for everyone."

"Yes, it has been a bit of a trial," he concurred. "But we've managed. The press, they are none the wiser, and I have enjoyed this bit of sport in tricking them."

"Wonderful." What else could she say?

"You will be home soon, yes?"

"Yes."

Too soon for her liking, Holly thought, her gaze on the horizon, where the first fingers of light had stretched over the bay. The scene was so peaceful, she closed her eyes and tried to capture it in her memory.

"Excellent. Excellent. I have an important dinner with some foreign investors on Wednesday. I was hoping that you would accompany me. They asked specifically if you would be there. You know how fascinated some people are with royalty."

Indeed, she did.

"Wednesday?" That was three days away. "I hadn't planned to return by then."

"But you will have been gone nearly a week, Hollyn." His voice took on an impatient edge. "Should your absence continue, well, it will become much more difficult to explain…to everyone. More engagements will have to be postponed or canceled. Your mother assured me—"

Holly was done letting her mother to speak for her, as well-intentioned as Olivia might be. "I am allowed a life of my own," she replied, amazed she'd said so, but in no hurry to take it back.

Her words as well as her tone must have surprised Phillip, too. "Is everything all right?"

"Never better. I am just making it clear that, royal or not, I am allowed to have a life."

"Of course."

But his tone was filled with more bafflement than agreement.

Holly pressed ahead. "I understand that I have obligations, but if I were ill or otherwise indisposed, well, other arrangements would be made."

"Are you ill, *ma chérie*?"

She held back a sigh. "Not how you mean."

"Ah. I think I understand," Phillip replied.

"You do?"

"You are a princess, yes. But a woman first. I have moved slowly with our romance out of deference for your royal position, but perhaps that is not what you've wanted. Perhaps I have been remiss in declaring my-self." His tone lowered to an intimate level and he added, "In declaring my feelings."

Alarm bells were going off in Holly's head. Dear God! Surely he didn't think she *wanted* him to declare them? Maybe at one time she'd hoped that hearing pretty words might soften her heart toward him, but they would only further complicate matters now.

She rushed to assure him, "Your feelings have been very clear, Phillip. Indeed, they have been clear from the beginning. I fear, however, I have not been clear in my feelings. I am quite fond of you, certainly. And I have been flattered, very flattered, by your interest and attention these past several months."

"Flattery is not what I was hoping to achieve," he remarked dryly.

"I wish I could tell you that I have…romantic feel-ings where you are concerned, but I think it is best for me to be honest. I enjoy your company and treasure your friendship, but—"

"Let us leave it at that, *ma chérie*. That way I will have my pride."

"I'm sorry, Phillip. Truly."

"As am I."

Nate shifted on the lounge chair and stifled a moan. His back was killing him. But he didn't care. The conversa-tion he'd just overheard trumped physical discomfort.

He'd averaged a B in French during the four years he'd taken it in high school, and he'd never become fluent. But from Holly's subdued tone and some of the key words he'd picked up on her side of the conversation, it was clear the news she'd delivered to Phillip was not good.

Nate resisted the urge to pump his fist in the air. Such a reaction would have been juvenile. But he didn't try to subdue his grin. As the sun broke over the water, even the wicked itching on his legs from the poison ivy couldn't dampen his good mood.

Holly's bags were once again downstairs and lined up at the side door when he popped in just before noon. While he'd been at the marina office helping Mick with the week's checkouts, both cabins and boat slips, she'd been busy. And not only was her luggage ready, but she'd also brought down her bedding. Now, she sat in his kitchen munching on toast that was closer to black than brown, and drinking a cup of the coffee he'd made before heading out.

"All ready to go, I see. And you even stripped the bed."

"It's what a good guest should do." But then she looked dubious. "Right?"

"Sure." Though Hank had shown no such compunction.

"Nadine called a bit ago and said housekeeping had finished up. I can check in whenever I want."

"Well, then, let's not waste time. It's going to be another gorgeous day. You're going to want to spend it on that fancy deck."

She smiled uncertainly. "Nate."

"Yes?" He wondered if she would bring up her earlier phone conversation. Just as Nate wondered if her breaking things off with Phillip had anything at all to do with him. Regardless, he was glad she was taking a stand and taking back some of the power she'd claimed not to have.

"I...I... If you wouldn't mind stopping at the grocery store in town I would be most grateful. The cottage is stocked with all of the basics such as spices and condiments, from what I've been told, but that I will need to bring my own meals."

He glanced at the burned toast, but resisted asking what she knew of making meals.

"What's that on your legs?" she asked as he toted her bags outside.

"Calamine lotion," he muttered.

"Cala—" She wasn't quite successful at swallowing her laughter.

"Go ahead," he offered. "Get it out of your system."

"I don't know what you mean," she replied innocently, even as amusement shimmered in her eyes.

"You're dying to tease me about catching poison ivy."

"I wouldn't dream of it." He gave her extra points for her serious expression. "Tell me, does it itch as horribly as I remember from my third summer here?"

"Worse," he grumbled, but mostly for effect. The fact was it was hard to remain irritable recalling how absolutely adorable Holly had looked that year dotted with the same pink lotion that now covered the better part of his calves.

Nate accompanied Holly inside the island's small market, leaving her to her shopping while he picked up a few staples of his own. Like most weeks, he'd probably dine out as much as he would dine in, so he didn't bother with much more than the basics: bread, more coffee, a bag of donuts, lunch meat and potato chips and two boxes of cereal. He'd stop to pick up milk on the way back.

"I see you've covered the basic food groups," Holly remarked when they ran into one another in one of the aisles. Where he'd grabbed a handcart, she was pushing one and had it filled with an assortment of fresh fruits and vegetables, homemade bread, cheese, wine and some tasty-looking cuts of meat.

"Do you know how to cook those?" he asked, nodding toward the T-bone steaks.

"I'm not helpless." She sighed and rolled her eyes. But her expression clouded a bit. Perhaps she was recalling burnt toast and bitter coffee.

"I'm just asking."

"And I've answered."

"Two steaks, I see. Are you planning for company?"

"Two steaks. Two meals."

"Ah." He rubbed an ankle against the opposite calf. Damned poison ivy.

"I'm ready to check out if you are."

"After you."

Nate intercepted a few curious glances from other customers as they headed to the checkout. The woman at the cash register was more obvious in her interest, but then Melinda Townsend was the island's biggest gossip. As she ran Holly's purchases over the scanner, she baldly asked, "Are you famous?"

Holly made a tsking noise. When she spoke, she somehow managed to flatten her vowels. Nate thought he even detected a bit of Texas twang when she said, "You know, I get that all the time. People are always thinking I look like some Hollywood starlet or reality TV star."

"You look like that girl from the tabloids." The woman pointed to the magazine rack next to the checkout counter. A picture of Holly taken at an event a few weeks earlier stared back at them. Unless Nate missed his guess that was Phillip in the background.

"She and I have a similar bone structure," Holly agreed. "Don't feel bad. You're not the first person to mistake me for her."

Melinda eyed her. Nate held his breath. Then the woman said, "You're way prettier."

"Well, thank you."

As compliments went, it was an interesting one. Holly had just been told she was more attractive than, well, herself.

"I bet you wish you had her bank account, though," Melinda said. "She's loaded."

"Money can't buy happiness, as the saying goes," Holly replied on a shrug.

"Maybe not, but I wouldn't mind trying to find out." The other woman's laugher boomed. She glanced past Holly to Nate. "What about you, Nate? Would you mind being as rich as a princess?"

He set his handcart down on the conveyor belt behind the last of Holly's purchases. He'd be happy with the princess, rich or not. But what he said was, "I'm content with what I have. It's more than enough."

"That's only because you're not greedy," Melinda said. She sent a wink in Holly's direction. "Nate's a local and his tastes are simple. He's beer and pretzels rather than champagne and caviar."

What Melinda said was true. He wouldn't—couldn't—feel ashamed. In fact, what shamed him now was that he'd felt ashamed when Holly first arrived. But he was proud of what he'd accomplished, just as he was proud to be building on what his parents and grandparents had started on Heart Island.

"Beer and pretzels," he agreed with a lift of his shoulders. "That's me."

"Oh, that reminds me," Holly said.

She dashed away only to return a moment later. To her purchases she added a six-pack of Nate's favorite beer. He was left to wonder if she'd acquired a taste for it or if she planned to invite him over at some point during her stay.

She'd already loaded her purchases into the bed of his pickup when he met her outside a moment later.

They didn't take the "shortcut" this time. Nate took the main roads out to the cabin. They had to stop along the way to let a lazy doe cross the road. Despite the late hour, the big deer was in no hurry. A moment later, a couple of speckled fawns loped after her.

"It's a wildlife sanctuary through most of here. The deer seem to know it. They're not nearly as skittish as they are on public land where hunters are allowed in the fall."

"I didn't mind waiting. She and her babies were worth a little inconvenience."

"They're something," Nate agreed, pressing the gas pedal. "As often as I see them, I still think so."

"They'd make good subject matter."

"For?"

"A painting. I've never done anything but still life

and landscapes. It would be a challenge to try to capture movement and energy."

Moments later, they arrived at her rental. He helped her carry her bags to the house and then stood at the door. He didn't want to leave.

"If you need anything…" he began.

"I know where you live. I'll send up a white flag on the pole off the deck if I find myself in a fix," she promised on a smile.

White flags symbolized surrender, but he didn't say so. "Well, then…"

"Well…"

He shifted his feet on the small rug just inside the doorway. "Maybe I'll see you around."

"I hope so. I won't be going much of anywhere since I haven't any transportation. Maybe you can stop by when you're not busy with work."

Nate nodded, already planning to clear some time in his schedule.

CHAPTER TEN

EARLY THE next morning, Holly tried her hand at fishing. Before leaving the resort the day before, she'd acquired the necessary license and had purchased a bucketful of bait from the marina. After two hours from her deck, she'd caught nothing but weeds and eventually lost her hook. She set the minnows free before calling it a day. Still, she'd had a good time.

But it only took twenty-four hours of solitude for Holly to start wishing for some company. Not just anyone's company. Nate's.

As much she was enjoying her time alone and as utterly beautiful as she found the bay, each time she looked across its sheltered waters, her gaze was drawn to Nate's cottage. The distance was too far to make out any details beyond the actual structure. But every now and again she thought she caught a flash of reflection from his sliding glass doors and imagined him coming out on the deck and maybe staring across the bay to where she was.

She'd come here seeking peace, thinking it was the place that she longed for. Now she knew differently.

It was the man that she wanted.

She went inside for another glass of iced tea. She'd

bought the powdered mix. All she had to do was add water, which took all the guesswork out of it. But she wasn't sure she liked the taste as much. Imitations rarely measured up to the real thing, she knew.

Looking in the refrigerator, she contemplated what to make for dinner. The evening before she'd gone with a turkey sandwich. Today, she'd made toast for breakfast, slightly burnt once again, and had assembled another sandwich for lunch. The sad fact was, despite her grand illusions when she'd gone to the grocery store, Holly didn't know what else to make or how to use the oven. The home had a gourmet kitchen. What it was missing was a gourmet.

A knock sounded at the door as she reached for the deli meat. She went to answer it with a smile blooming on her lips. Only one person knew where to find her. Sure enough, all six foot three of him was standing on the welcome mat, looking gorgeous.

"Hello, Nate."

He smiled. "I hope I'm not disturbing you."

"Not in the least. Come in. Please." She stepped back and he came inside. He was wearing his usual cargo shorts and a short-sleeved shirt that bore the name of the resort on the front. His hair was tousled from the breeze, the ends bleached blond from the sun. The bridge of his nose and cheeks were slightly pink beneath his tan.

"You need to put on more sunscreen," she said absently. "Your face is a little burned."

He touched one of his cheeks, wrinkled his nose. "I put some on this morning, but never got a chance to reapply it."

"Busy day?"

"Very." He shrugged. "That's the way I prefer it. It means business is good, which in turn means I'm doing something right."

Holly liked that about him. He was a hard worker and not one to take anything for granted. He'd gotten his work ethic from his parents, she knew. That's where she'd gotten her own. They might be royals, but her parents weren't ones to loaf around. They saw it as their job to promote the country and champion worthwhile causes.

"I saw a couple of the big boats leave the marina this morning."

"Yeah. They headed out first thing, eager to make the most of the calm water. It's going to get a little choppy later."

"Is another storm blowing in?"

"No. Just some wind and high waves. Big as those boats are, they wouldn't have any trouble weathering them, but it's best not to take chances."

A week ago, Holly might have agreed. Right now, she wasn't so sure. Sometimes a little risk-taking was worth it.

"So, what brings you by?" she asked.

She didn't realize she was holding her breath while she waited for him to respond until it escaped in a whoosh when he said, "Your mother."

"What?"

"She, um, called about an hour ago. She was a little perturbed that you haven't been in touch and that you are hard to reach." Half his mouth crooked up in a smile. "I got quite an earful."

Holly bet he had.

"I'm sorry for that."

"It's all right. I did my best to reassure her that you're fine. But she, um, wants you to call her as soon as possible. It's a matter of some urgency, according to her."

"Everything is a matter of urgency where my mother is concerned," Holly said dryly.

"But you'll call her, right?"

She sighed. "I've been avoiding doing that."

"Any particular reason?"

His expression was nonchalant, but she thought she detected a bit of challenge in Nate's tone.

She didn't know anything about poker, but she decided to lay out all of her cards. "I've ended my relationship with Phillip."

"Oh."

"Oh?" She folded her arms over her chest. "That's pretty monumental, especially where my mother is concerned. I'm sure she's gotten wind of my decision and is eager to try to talk me out of it."

He shrugged. "Ultimately, it's your choice."

"Yes, it is." Again she felt a surge of power. "My life. My future. My decision."

"Spoken like a true princess." He brushed his knuckles over her cheek.

She fought the urge to shiver. The yearning was back, along with the first hot licks of desire.

"Would you…would you like something cold to drink?" she asked.

"I can't stay."

"Oh."

"Another time?"

She nodded.

He turned to leave, then stopped. "Oh, I got this for you."

It was then she noticed the bag in his hand. Inside was a rudimentary set of watercolors, paintbrushes and a tablet of heavy-weight, cold press paper.

"It's not the best quality," Nate said as she pulled everything out and laid it on the counter. "But it was all I could find at the mercantile. I thought it would give you something to do."

Her heart swelled. Over the years she'd received all manner of pricey gifts, none as precious as this. Just as with the fishing pole, it told her he understood her. He knew her. The real Hollyn Saldani. That was a gift in and of itself.

"Thank you."

"No problem." He pointed toward the window. "That view begs to be painted."

"I don't know that I can do it justice."

"The enjoyment comes from trying," he reminded her, before leaving.

Holly called her mother an hour later and regretted it almost as soon as Olivia came on the line.

"You need to come home at once, Hollyn, and fix things with Phillip."

"There's nothing to fix, Mother," Holly said patiently. "We dated for a while, long enough for me to know that he's not the man I see myself marrying." Her gaze strayed to the countertop, where the painting supplies beckoned. No, indeed, Phillip wasn't the man she wanted to spend her life with.

"Nonsense—"

"No," Holly interrupted. "It's not nonsense. It's a fact. I do not love Phillip. I doubt he loves me. We might be well suited according to you, but my opinion is the one that matters here."

"Hollyn, what in the world has gotten into you?"

The same thing that got into her parents three decades ago when they'd decided to buck convention and get married even though doing so meant going against tradition and public opinion.

"I'm deciding my future."

She hung up on Olivia's sputtering protest.

Unlike the day before, Nate didn't have a reason to stop by Holly's place, but when he took out a small fishing boat late the next morning, he found himself trolling by the front of her cottage. She was on the deck, a makeshift easel set up in front of her as she painted.

"Morning, neighbor!" she called when she spotted him.

"Morning," he replied.

She shaded her eyes from the sun. "Are you coming ashore?"

He hadn't planned to. For that matter, he'd only planned to take the boat out to test its rebuilt motor.

"For a minute." He maneuvered the craft to the dock and secured it before hopping out and heading up to the house.

Holly was wearing a simple cotton dress. The ties of a pink bathing-suit top peeked out from the back of the neck. Her feet were bare, and her legs and arms had picked up a little color during her time on the island.

More than pretty, she looked content. Nate wished he could say he was feeling the same. He'd never been more keyed up. As much as he wanted her, he didn't want to complicate her life.

Keep it casual, he told himself. Keep it light. No strings. No binding ties of any sort.

"You're staring." She dabbed at the paper.

"Just enjoying the view."

"The lake is out there." She pointed with her paintbrush, managing to look prim despite the speckle of blue on her cheek.

Nate let his gaze wander south, taking a deliberate tour of her figure before returning to her face. A little flirting wouldn't hurt. "That's not the view I'm enjoying."

She made a show of rolling her eyes, but her shy smile and rose-tinted cheeks told him she wasn't immune.

"I see that you're making use of the paints I brought yesterday."

"This is my third attempt."

He stepped behind the easel she'd created using the seat of a kitchen stool. She'd begun to fill in the outline of the bay, with dreamy shades of blue and green. His house was across the way, a mere speck on the horizon, but there nonetheless.

"It looks good," he said.

She rinsed her brush and shrugged. "It's been a long time since I last dabbled."

"But you're enjoying yourself."

She beamed a smile at him. "Immensely."

That was all that mattered.

"Relaxation looks good on you." He meant only to squeeze her arm, but his fingers failed to release her and instead he found himself pulling her close.

"I am relaxed. I've slept like a baby the past couple nights," she had to go and tell him.

He settled his hands on her waist. "I haven't been sleeping at all."

She set the paintbrush aside. "I'm sorry to hear that."

"Probably just as well. I think I know what I'd be dreaming about."

"Those are called fantasies, Nathaniel." She slapped his chest and tried to look insulted.

He merely grinned. "Which explains why I've been having them while I'm awake."

Her breath hitched. They both grew serious.

"What are you doing for dinner tonight?" she asked just before he could lean down and kiss her.

"I hadn't thought that far ahead." In fact, he wasn't thinking at all at the moment.

"I have two steaks, as you may recall."

"And my favorite beer." Nate nuzzled her cheek.

"Uh-huh." That sexy hitch was back.

"So, is that an invitation?" he managed to ask.

"It's actually more like the solicitation of a favor."

His brow crinkled in confusion.

"I don't know how to work the grill." He opened his mouth to reply, but she put her hand over his lips. "If you're going to say I told you so or make some sort of comment about my being helpless, you can save your breath."

He pulled her hand from his mouth, kissed the palm.

"I wouldn't dream of it."

Indeed, Nate couldn't help thinking that if anyone were helpless here, it was he.

He was back that evening just after six o'clock. He didn't question his decision, though he did question his sanity. Phillip or no Phillip, he kept reminding himself there was only one way this could play out once Holly's time on the island came to an end. Long-distance love affairs were hard enough to manage without all the baggage theirs would come with, assuming that was even what she wanted.

But he decided he didn't care. Bottom line: he wanted Holly. And if he could only have her for a brief time, then he'd have to be content with that. So, he'd showered, shaved for the second time that day and then slapped on some cologne.

His parents called just as he was heading out, both of them on extensions so they could all talk at once. When he'd casually mentioned that Holly was on Heart, his father had sighed. His mother, meanwhile, had grown oddly quiet. He'd expected her to pepper him with questions. The only thing she said after regaining her voice was, "Be careful, son."

He'd laughed. "Be careful. Mom, she's a princess, not an ax murderer."

His mother hadn't laughed. "I know how you felt about her before."

"We both do," his father had added.

"Just…be careful."

"You don't have to worry about me," Nate had assured them. Now, as he followed Holly out onto the deck, he wasn't so sure.

She'd changed into a sleeveless, pale yellow dress whose ruffled front was set in perpetual motion thanks to the breeze. The wind had kicked up since the morning, as the weather forecasters had predicted. The bay was now dotted with whitecaps, and waves crashed at the shore rather than gently rolling onto the sand.

He felt a bit like those waves, set into motion by forces outside his control. Tugged and pulled by fate and the beautiful woman who was now handing him a cold beer that she'd pulled from the bucket of ice on the deck.

"I trust you don't need a glass."

"Nope. Straight from the bottle's fine." He unscrewed the top and helped himself to a long swallow.

She followed suit. "For me, too."

Because he wanted to kiss her, he took a step back instead. "Did you finish your painting?"

She shook her head. Her hair was clipped back at her nape, so the movement of a pair of drop earrings caught his attention.

"Some things take time," she said.

And patience, which had never been Nate's long suit, especially where Holly was concerned. He was a grown man, yet he felt just as he had all those summers ago, desperate to kiss her, wanting to make love to her.

"Are you hungry?"

"Starving." And steak was going to have to do. He set the beverage aside and eyed the huge, stainless steel gas grill. "That's some monster."

Holly looked alarmed. "Does that mean you don't know how to work it, either?"

He laughed, and the sexual frustration he was feeling ebbed to a tolerable level. "I'm a guy, Holly. Guys are born knowing how to grill. I think I read somewhere that it's hardwired into our genetic code."

A couple of minutes later, he had the thing fired up. He found Holly in the kitchen making a salad to go with the steaks.

"I'm afraid this won't be much of a meal. I didn't think to buy any rice or potatoes while I was at the market. And the truth is I wouldn't know how to prepare them either. Apparently the rudiments of meal preparation are not hardwired into my genetic code."

"The rolls you bought are fine."

She pulled a face. "You're just saying that to make me feel better."

He grinned. "Is it working?"

"Somewhat."

"The salad looks good."

"Yes, well, it doesn't require much skill to shred a head of lettuce."

"You had to dice up the tomatoes," he pointed out.

She smiled at that and her hands stilled. She leaned her hip against the counter after she turned to face him. "You know, I think I would enjoy cooking."

"So take it up."

Nate half expected her to shrug off the idea. The woman who had arrived on the island mere days ago would have. She'd seen herself as powerless, a prisoner of fate. The confident woman standing before him now replied, "You know, I think I will." Her expression turned thoughtful. "I could hire someone to teach me or even ask the head chef for some lessons. The palace has excellent kitchen facilities."

Nate's heart sank a little as he pictured her in a great, cavernous kitchen with a Cordon Bleu-trained chef offering instruction, so far away from him compared to the woman who now stood barefoot in this kitchen with a dishtowel wrapped around her waist and an open beer sitting within arm's reach.

"Nate?"

He realized he must have been frowning and shook off his sudden melancholy. "I'd better get those steaks on the grill."

They dined on the deck, taking care to keep track of their napkins, lest the breeze carry them away. As it was, it had made off with a couple pieces of lettuce from Holly's plate, pushing them across the glass tabletop before dumping them in Nate's lap. They'd both laughed.

Holly finished off the last of her steak and sat back on a satisfied sigh. Oh, how she wished she could bottle up this contentment.

"This is what I missed the most," she said quietly. "This...this normalcy."

"We're nothing if not normal around these parts," Nate teased. He grew serious then, set his knife and fork aside and gave her his undivided attention. "What constitutes normal back in Morenci?"

She exhaled slowly. "Well, I don't have an actual job, but I do have a full schedule most days. Awards to present, public appearances to make, ribbons to cut, that sort of thing. Three days a week I make time for my pet projects."

"The charities and causes you've chosen to champion."

"Exactly."

"It sounds like you're very busy."

"I don't mind. At least I feel useful, like I have a purpose. But I rarely get to be myself. To sit beside a lake with a handsome…friend and just relax." She shook her head. "It's ironic."

"What is?"

"My mother was a small-town girl who dreamed of wearing a crown. I'm a princess who dreams of being a small-town girl."

Olivia's dream had come true. She'd made it work despite the obstacles in the beginning that threatened to doom her relationship with Holly's father. Holly remembered her grandmother once saying that neither Morenci nor the king knew what hit them after Olivia arrived for a pageant there three decades earlier. *Indomitable*— that was the word the media often used in reference to the queen. Now, Holly was realizing the apple hadn't fallen very far from the tree.

"I can be myself here." She reached over to cover his hand with hers. "I can be myself with you. I think that is what brought me back here in the first place."

"I'm glad you're here."

She swallowed, felt the need to ask, "Will you still feel that way when Hank comes to collect me in a week?"

It was the great white elephant between them. Yet she was relieved when he chose to ignore it.

"Let's not talk about a week from now." His expression clouded, but the corners of his mouth rose in a wry smile. "As I said before, let's just deal with the here and now."

"I've never been much for living in the moment," she admitted.

"Neither have I. I've always set goals, made plans." She watched his Adam's apple bob just before he said, "But sometimes you just have to take what you can get when you can get it. So, I'm going to sit on this fabulous deck this evening, with an especially beautiful woman, drink another cold beer and enjoy the present."

Her heart rejoiced, even as it broke a little. The future was too much to consider. The here and now was within reach. Holly intended to grab it and hold on tight.

"So, you're going to sit in that chair and enjoy another beer, hmm?"

"I did mention that I would be doing so in the company of a beautiful woman."

"Especially beautiful is, I believe, how you phrased it."

"Glad to know you were paying attention."

"So, you're just going to sit?" she said again.

One of his brows rose. "Is there something else I should be doing?"

She couldn't resist teasing him. "Well, the plates need a scrub. Back home, I have people to do that for me."

"We've already established that you're not back home and that on my island, you're just plain old Holly." He pushed his dirty plate toward her on the tabletop. "I believe I saw a dishwasher in that fancy kitchen, so your manicure is safe. It will do the heavy lifting for you.

All you've got to do is load the thing, add a bit of detergent and push Start."

"Hmm. It sounds rather complicated. Maybe you could show me? I'm a visual learner. I can read or hear instructions a million times and not understand, but if I see something demonstrated just once, well, I'm a natural."

His eyes narrowed. "You don't say?"

"Truly."

"Then, by all means, let me demonstrate."

They both rose and went inside, carrying their plates and utensils with them. But the demonstration Nate had in mind had nothing to do with the pedestrian chore of loading a dishwasher. Thank God! As soon as they reached the kitchen and their plates were on the counter, he pulled Holly into his arms.

"I've been wanting to kiss you since I arrived," he confessed.

"I've been wanting you to kiss me since then."

"Then we're of a like mind."

"I would say so."

Gone was some of the awkwardness they'd experienced before. Holly had come into her own. She wound her arms around his neck and pressed her mouth to his before he could say another word.

Their mouths met, their bodies molded tightly together. Perfect, Holly thought. No one else could fit her so perfectly. His mouth was hot against her. His need and seeming desperation rivaled her own.

I love you, she thought. *I've always loved you. I always will.*

But she reminded herself to live in the moment. No

planning. No future dreams. Just right now. And right now she was feeling not just needy, but greedy.

She had his attention when her fingers began working the buttons on the front of his shirt. He pulled back enough to look down at her hands and then back at her in question. *Are you sure,* those gorgeous dark eyes asked.

"I want you, Nate."

With those simple words, everything changed, including their positions. Somehow she wound up underneath him on the living room's plush sectional. His mouth was hot against her throat, his hands tugging at the dress's sash belt.

"Let me," she said. But the strip of fabric was good and knotted. "I think I saw kitchen sheers in one of the drawers. Or a butcher knife," she panted. "A butcher knife could slice through this silk."

Nate's laughter rumbled low. Holly felt its vibration more than she heard it. "I take it you're not concerned about the outfit then?"

"Let's just say I have other things on my mind than fashion," she managed to reply.

"Good." A moment later she heard a rending of fabric. The belt gave way. "Problem solved," Nate said, helping her up so he could push the dress off her shoulders.

Holly became suddenly shy. She'd never been with a man. Not like this. She'd fooled around some. She was human, after all. But she'd learned early that boys could kiss and tell. And not just their friends and classmates, but any reporter eager for a story about Princess Hollyn. Even with Phillip, she'd held back, mostly because his touches and kisses had done little to ignite her passion. Indeed, for a while, she'd wondered if maybe she was just one of those women who didn't feel much passion. Not frigid exactly, but, well, indifferent.

Well, she wasn't feeling indifferent now. Desperate, needy, maybe even a little depraved given the direction of her thoughts, but definitely not indifferent.

"Something's wrong."

"Nothing's wrong," she disagreed.

"You're quiet."

"Am I supposed to be loud?" she asked.

Nate frowned. "Have…have you ever…"

Embarrassed, she pushed him away so she could sit. "I'm not completely inexperienced."

"Okay." He settled onto the cushion next to her and grabbed her hand. "But have you done…this?"

"I'm twenty-five, Nate."

"Answer the question, Holly."

"If I say no, is it going to change anything?" she asked.

His answer was an emphatic, "Hell, yes!"

Not exactly what she wanted to hear. She started to rise, but he pulled her back to the couch. He cupped her face, kissed her tenderly.

"You didn't let me finish. Yes, it's going to make a difference."

"Why?" she asked.

"Because I'll be sure to take my time."

CHAPTER ELEVEN

I SHOULD regret this, Nate thought as he watched Holly sleep. But he regretted nothing. Even the fact that in a week she would disappear from his life, likely forever.

At least this time he would know why and would know it was coming. Maybe that would make it easier to accept.

She stirred, mumbled something in her sleep. The evening before, she'd surprised him, and not only with her inexperience, but also with the passion she possessed despite that. She was his, he thought with an astounding amount of possessiveness. No matter where fate took them, she would always be his.

He glanced at the clock. Already, the sun was up and light was flooding through the French doors that led to the master suite's second-floor balcony. He didn't want the day to start. He wanted even less to leave her. But some things couldn't be wished away and his livelihood was one of them.

He eased his arm from beneath her. She stirred just as he swung his legs over the side of the mattress.

"Are you going?"

"I've got work to do."

"Will you be back?"

Today for sure. Tonight? Oh, yeah. It was only beyond this week that neither could offer any guarantees. "You mentioned something about chicken breasts."

"I bought a couple at the market, yes."

"I'll bring something to pair them with and we'll make them on the grill."

"You never did show me how to work the dishwasher," she reminded him. She stretched languidly and it was all Nate could do not to climb back into bed with her. The resort be damned.

But he mustered up some resolve. "It can wait until later." He leaned down and nuzzled her neck, feeling overly protective and oddly vulnerable. "I won't be too long."

"See that you aren't."

How was a man supposed to ignore a request like that? And coming from royalty no less? Nate rushed through his day, preoccupied and, okay, a little high on life. He'd had sex before, but he'd never made love. There was a definite difference.

Thank goodness for Mick. He kept Nate from making a monumental mistake on the bill for one of the yacht slips. Nate's misplaced decimal point could have cost Haven a bundle.

"Where's your head, boy?" the older man asked. His smile suggested he knew.

"Sorry."

"She's a pretty one. Are you heading over to see her again tonight?"

Not much got past the old man.

"As soon as I can."

"Why not be on your way now, then? I can finish up

here." Mick added, "And I'll probably be a darn sight more accurate with the receipts than you are anyway."

Far from offended, Nate smiled. The older man didn't need to offer twice. "Thanks. I think I will."

One day floated into the next. Holly tried to remember the last time she'd felt so happy and free, but she couldn't. Even her childhood memories on the island were unable to compete. The man made all the difference, she decided, as she rolled over and snuggled against Nate's side.

He opened one sleepy eye briefly and smiled. Just when she thought he'd returned to slumber, she felt a hand stroke her bare hip. It ended at the slope of her breast, his touch growing more insistent.

"You're awake," she accused.

"I'm up, if that's what you're asking." Male laughter followed.

It was dark yet, not quite four in the morning. "Let's go outside."

"Outside?"

"For a swim."

"That bay is cold," he objected.

"Without our suits."

It was all the enticement he needed. Half an hour later they stumbled back inside, shivering and laughing like a couple of loons before they sobered. Then they made love in front of the gas fireplace downstairs. She watched Nate's face in the flickering glow of the flames, determined to memorize his every expression as need overtook reason.

"I love you," she whispered, but far too low for him

to hear. Still, it seemed important to her to say the words aloud. And though she knew she had to let go, that they both needed to step away from the looming precipice, she was overcome with emotion when she thought she heard him whisper the same thing back.

Holly was leaving.

Actually, she'd extended her stay and had remained on Heart the full two weeks of her lease at the cottage. But that didn't matter to Nate. All that mattered now was that, in mere hours, she would be going away. And he knew from previous experience how it felt to lose her.

Oh, he'd told himself to live in the moment, but he knew he'd been a fool. He was in love with Holly. How could any man watch the woman he loved walk away and not grieve?

The sky was impossibly blue on this day. Nary a cloud breached its perfection. It might as well have been overcast or crowded with thunderclouds. That would have better suited Nate's dark mood as he sat on her deck and waited for Hank's Cessna to swoop out of the sky.

She was equally as quiet as she sat on a lounge chair beside him. He knew her thoughts as well as his own, which was why he didn't try to stop her or urge her to stay a little longer. They'd been on borrowed time as it was. They'd both known that going in.

The Cessna came into view. Hank dipped the wings in greeting as he passed and then circled back for a landing. The floats skimmed off the water's surface once before touching down for good.

"He's right on time," Nate remarked quietly.

"Yes. At least this trip should be less eventful," Holly noted.

Hank taxied the seaplane toward the dock. Nate went out to help him, grabbing the rope the other man threw to him.

"Hey, Nate. Gorgeous day, huh?"

A grumble served as his reply.

Hank turned to Holly and asked, "All set, pretty lady?"

"Not hardly," she surprised them all by saying. "I wish I could stay…indefinitely." Her gaze was on Nate.

"We both knew you would have to leave." It killed him to say so.

"I'll try to come back soon."

He nodded. They both knew it was a lie. This was it. The end of an otherwise perfect love affair.

Hank went to fetch Holly's bags from the deck, leaving the pair of them to say their goodbyes. Not that they hadn't done so already. Hell, the entire morning had been one long and painful farewell.

"I'll call when I get home."

"Do that," Nate said.

But he knew a moment of doubt. Would she? Once she'd settled into the routine of her other life, would Holly remember to call or even email Nate? Or would her time on Heart Island be filed away as a beautiful memory? Yes, as she'd said, she could be herself here. But the rest of the world expected her to be a princess.

"I've got all your bags stowed," Hank said as he loaded the last of them into the seaplane. "I'll be ready to take off when you are."

"Thank you, Hank."

"I guess this is it," Nate said.

"You make it sound very final," Holly objected.

He exhaled slowly. "It is what it is."

"You don't think I'll be back?"

"I hope you will, but our lives are going to pull us in two different directions," Nate said practically. He wasn't trying to hurt her. Quite the opposite. He wanted to be sure she knew he understood.

"That doesn't mean we have to go in those directions," Holly said. "You're the one who once told me I wasn't without choices and that I needed to make time for the things I felt were important."

Indeed, he had. Yet, he wasn't sure how to respond to her words now.

"Would you come to Morenci if I asked you to?" she said softly.

"I… Would I…?" She'd caught him off guard. "The resort…"

"For a visit, Nate."

He felt foolish. "Sure. I mean, I could swing a week or two, especially in the off-season."

"You love it here," Holly said quietly.

"I love you."

The words were out before he could stop them. He wondered if he would have tried to if given the chance.

Her eyes grew moist. A tear slipped down her cheek. "I love you, too, Nate."

The kiss they shared wasn't as passionate as some of the others had been. No desperate urgency now. But the emotions behind it would stay with Nate a lifetime.

He'd thought he knew what heartbreak felt like. This was total annihilation.

The pressure only grew worse as he helped her board the plane. The door slammed shut as his own eyes watered and her image grew blurry. He pushed the plane away from the dock. The prop revved to life, the sound intensifying long before the plane actually moved. He stepped back and waited where he was as it glided over the calm water of the bay, picking up speed as it left Nate and the shore behind.

He raised a hand and waved just as the floats left the water's smooth surface. Holly's plane had lifted off safely. Meanwhile, Nate's heart had crashed and burned.

"This weekend is the annual Royal Gala," her mother was saying. "You're cutting it close with your late arrival. Luckily, Anna is standing by," Olivia said of the royal seamstress. "You'll need a final fitting on your gown."

"Yes."

Olivia plucked at Holly's sun-bleached curls. "And you probably should have your hair treated. A good deep conditioning is in order. It looks dry."

"Yes."

Her agreement did little to assuage Olivia.

"Is something wrong?"

"What could be wrong? I'm back where I belong, doing what needs to be done," Holly reminded her.

"Yes, but you're…so unhappy."

"I've *been* unhappy, Mother."

"But not like this," Olivia replied. "I've never seen you like this."

Which made sense, since Holly had never felt like this. It had been all well and good to tell Nate that they would live in the moment while they were living in the moment. Now that the moment was over, the pain was almost too much to bear.

"Mother, did Gran ever try to talk you out of marrying my father?"

Olivia blinked in surprise at the question. "Talk me out of it? No. But she was clear on what it would entail. She made sure I went into it with my eyes wide open and then backed me all the way as I fought like a tiger cat to fit in and be accepted, especially once you were on the way."

"That must have been hard for you."

"At first." Olivia sucked in a breath. "It was one thing for them not to accept me. I wouldn't allow them to turn their backs on you. You're the throne's rightful heir, after all."

"And if I don't want it?"

Olivia's footsteps echoed to a halt in the long corridor. She snagged Holly's arm, forcing her to stop as well. "My God! You're in love with that boy."

"He's a man now. But yes. I love Nate Matthews. I loved him when I was a girl and I love him now."

"But…you can't mean you want to turn your back on everything I've worked so hard to ensure you had. You're accepted here, Hollyn. No one dares question your right to ascend the throne, not like they did with me."

"That was important to you."

"Very," Olivia replied. "That's why I've done all that I have."

She hugged her mother. "Thank you for that, Mother. Truly, thank you. But I'm happiest being…ordinary."

Olivia hugged her back fiercely before pulling away. Holding Holly at arm's length, she said, "But you're not ordinary."

Holly closed her eyes in defeat. As soon as she did, she felt her mother's lips press to her cheek. "When a woman is in love, she's…extraordinary," Olivia whispered.

CHAPTER TWELVE

"How are the day's receipts looking?" Nate asked Mick as he came in the marina.

"Better than you do," the older man remarked.

And wasn't that the truth.

Holly had been gone two days. It might as well have been ten years. God, Nate missed her. He ached with it. He'd slept with the phone by his side the first night, eager for her call. It hadn't come.

"One of the Burns boys took a phone message about an hour ago," Mick was saying. Nate's heart soared until the older man added, "I spilled my coffee on it, but it looks to be an invite to meet for drinks at the Fishing Hole when you get out of work."

Probably one of his poker buddies. They usually called him up when they were running low on funds and hoping for someone to buy a round. Well, he had no plans to indulge them.

He put in a couple more hours before calling it a day. And what a day it had been. Though it wasn't exactly in his job description, he'd helped change the prop on a slip owner's fishing boat. He'd also spent a couple of hours teaching some of the resort's youngest guests the finer points of baiting a hook. Despite a good scrubbing, he still smelled a little bit like diesel fuel and the water in the big filtered tank where they stored the minnows.

He started for home, but pointed the truck in the direction of town instead. The invitation from friends beckoned. There was nothing waiting for him at home. And no one. He'd wind up staring at the phone again, willing the damned thing to ring. The pub, on the other hand, would be full of friendly and familiar faces, cold beer and banal conversation. That's what he needed.

He got a whole lot more the moment he stepped through the pub's door. He spotted Holly.

She was impossible to miss. And not because she was the only woman in the place wearing a skirt and looking like she could grace the pages of a fashion magazine. No, she was standing atop the pool table and, from what he could gather, leading the crowd of locals in a line dance to an Alan Jackson song. It was a bit of the traditional boot-scooting he'd taught her way back when with what appeared to be some Celtic footwork thrown in.

Lord of the Dance at a hoedown?

Damned diesel fumes. They had him seeing things. He rubbed his eyes. But the image didn't go away, and he wasn't sure he wanted it to. He became mesmerized watching the hem of Holly's skirt as it flitted back and forth just above her knees with each shake of her hips and flick of her feet. Then her gaze found his and her footsteps faltered before she stumbled to a stop. Her already flushed cheeks turned all but crimson.

"That's all I know," she shouted apologetically when the crowd of mostly locals started to grumble.

Melinda from the grocery store was among them and the first to offer Holly a hand down from the table.

Since Holly had already seen him, it was only polite to go over and say hello. Under other circumstances, he might have offered to buy her a drink, but he had a feeling she'd already had one too many. Oddly enough, when he reached the table where she sat, Holly was sipping from a glass of plain old cola. The remnants of what appeared to be the pub's famous bacon and cheddar-loaded potato skins were on a platter in front of her.

"Hello, Nate." Holly pushed out the extra chair with her foot as an invitation for him to join them. "I was wondering if you got my message."

"I… Mick spilled coffee on it. I wasn't sure who it was from," Nate admitted.

"Hmm." She frowned. "But you came anyway."

"I wanted a beer."

She smiled around her straw. "And now? Is that all you want?"

"I…" *Hold on to some pride*, he ordered himself. "What are you doing here?"

"Well, I was dancing." Holly set her beverage aside. "For the record, I was dared."

As much as Nate wanted answers, he laughed. At the absurdity of the statement as much as the ridiculous amount of dignity she managed to muster in uttering it. "Gee, it makes perfect sense now why I should find you on a pool table in a pub doing a tush-push when I thought you were back in Morenci."

In a way, it did make sense. Holly never could turn down a dare. She reminded him of that now.

"You know I've come to hate being predictable. It's nice to shake things up a little every now and then. I believe that's the expression."

"Uh-huh." But Nate was sure of little else at the moment.

Holly went on. "The man standing next to the jukebox was a little surly with me at first." She pointed to the big hulking man most locals left alone. "He told me they don't play any opera in here. I think he was just having a little fun with me."

Nate glanced over to where she pointed. Actually, Zeb Barlow probably hadn't been teasing. The island's only mechanic had a bad attitude when it came to tourists, especially those who looked the part, which Holly definitely did wearing a skirt, sexy sandals and a pearl necklace. She might as well have had on a tiara. Jeans and sneakers were dress code here—or, in Zeb's case, stained brown coveralls and steel-toed boots.

"I told him I wasn't interested in a night at the opera. I was looking for some proper dance music," Holly said.

Despite the fact he was dying for an explanation, Nate's lips twitched at her *proper* tone. "I bet that went over well."

"He dared me to show him my best moves. So, I was. It was the bartender's idea that I get up on the pool table to do it. And then people just started joining in and asking me to show them more. I threw in a toe kick I learned in the Celtic step class Mother insisted I take, and the next thing I knew I was leading a line dance."

She sounded amazed. And a little proud.

"You're here," he said. He stroked her arm, just to

be sure she wasn't a figment of his imagination. Soft skin warmed his fingers.

"I'm here." Her smile wobbled.

He cleared his throat and pulled his hand back. "For, um, how long this time?"

"I'm not sure yet," she admitted.

His bruised heart took a tumble.

The waitress came by and cleared away the empty potato skins tray, as well as a couple of empty drink glasses.

"Can I get you anything, Nate?" she asked.

"Whatever you've got on tap is fine, and another drink for the lady."

"Nothing for me," Holly corrected.

"You still haven't told me why you're here."

"I should think that would be obvious."

Under normal circumstances and with another woman, perhaps, it might have been. Tonight, here, with Holly, Nate's brain felt fuzzy and too slow to comprehend. And his heart was just a little too battered to hope.

"Let's get out of here," he said. "It's too loud to talk."

But she shook her head. "In a minute. I have one more dance. Maybe you'll join me for this one."

She marched to the jukebox and inserted a dollar bill before pressing some buttons. God only knew what line dance she would be leading the pub patrons in next. He had no plans to join her.

Zeb strolled over and commented, "She's a pretty little thing."

"She's mine," Nate shot back. And dammit if he wasn't going to make sure she knew it. Whatever the obstacles, they'd figure them out. They'd make this work, because nothing in his life worked without her.

He pushed to his feet as the first strains of music filled the bar. No country twang or do-si-do beat. Rather, Van Halen's power ballad "When It's Love."

Nate grinned as he recognized the tune. That last morning, he'd been humming it in the shower while he'd washed her back…and then her front.

"I'll make a hard rock fan of you yet," he'd teased.

Apparently, he had.

The crowd around him melted into an indistinguishable kaleidoscope of colors and shapes as he made his way to Holly. She was smiling.

"It's kind of catchy," she said when he reached her. "Although not the easiest to dance to."

"Maybe I'll just stand here and hold you in my arms then."

"Suits me," she replied as he slipped his left arm around her waist and scooped up her right hand in his.

Holly settled her cheek against his and sighed.

"About the length of your visit this time," he began. He wasn't going to take a week or ten days or so for an answer. It turned out he didn't need to.

"I was thinking I'd stay…forever."

He stopped moving and pulled back so he could see her face. "Holly?"

"I love you, Nate."

"And I love you. But—"

She put her fingers over his mouth. "No buts. That's where it ends."

"You're wrong." He kissed the hand he planned to put a wedding ring on as soon as he could manage it. "This is where it begins."

EPILOGUE

HOLLYN Elise Phillipa Saldani had been born a princess. Three years after her return to Heart, she was a bona fide islander with a new name. The locals not only had accepted Holly Matthews as Nate's bride, but they also fiercely protected her from the prying eyes of outsiders, whether they be paparazzi, traditional journalists or merely nosy tourists.

For the most part, Holly found that while people— including guests at the resort—were often curious about her, they mostly left her alone. Especially now that the uproar over her decision to abdicate her claim on Morenci's throne had died down.

Her cousin Amelia had been only too happy to take Holly's place. As much as Holly had chafed under the public spotlight, Amelia seemed to enjoy it. And while Holly's parents weren't exactly thrilled with her decision, they respected it.

And they had accepted Nate.

Three years married to a man she loved so deeply had confirmed one thing: her mother was right. No woman in love was ordinary.

Nor was a woman expecting her first child. Holly

touched her stomach in wonder. She still couldn't believe it. She was nearly three months along.

Nate jogged out to where she stood on the marina dock. Worry creased his forehead. She hadn't been feeling well lately, which was why he'd insisted she go see the doctor.

"Mick said you needed to see me right away. Everything go okay at your appointment?"

"Better than okay." She handed him the grainy black-and-white ultrasound photo. "They said it's still too early to tell if it's a girl or a boy."

"A b-baby?" Nate eyed her blankly for a moment before his disbelief finally ebbed. Then he scooped her up in his arms on a whoop of joy. "We're going to have a baby!" he shouted to no one in particular.

He tripped on one of the mooring lines. Just as he had that day three years ago when he'd tried to carry her to shore, he lost his footing. They both wound up going off the side of the dock into the water.

They came up laughing, wrapped together.

"Looks like we're in over our heads," Nate said on a grin.

Holly grinned back. "I wouldn't have it any other way."

* * * * *

LET'S TALK
Romance

For exclusive extracts, competitions
and special offers, find us online:

MILLS & BOON

THE HEART OF ROMANCE

A ROMANCE FOR EVERY READER

MODERN

Prepare to be swept off your feet by sophisticated, sexy and seductive heroes, in some of the world's most glamourous and romantic locations, where power and passion collide.

HISTORICAL

Escape with historical heroes from time gone by. Whether your passion is for wicked Regency Rakes, muscled Vikings or rugged Highlanders, awaken the romance of the past.

MEDICAL

Set your pulse racing with dedicated, delectable doctors in the high-pressure world of medicine, where emotions run high and passion, comfort and love are the best medicine.

True Love

Celebrate true love with tender stories of heartfelt romance, from the rush of falling in love to the joy a new baby can bring, and a focus on the emotional heart of a relationship.

Desire

Indulge in secrets and scandal, intense drama and plenty of sizzling hot action with powerful and passionate heroes who have it all: wealth, status, good looks…everything but the right woman.

HEROES

Experience all the excitement of a gripping thriller, with an intense romance at its heart. Resourceful, true-to-life women and strong, fearless men face danger and desire - a killer combination!

To see which titles are coming soon, please visit

millsandboon.co.uk/nextmonth